THE
CONSULTANT

Also by Tj O'Connor

New Sins for Old Scores

The Gumshoe Ghost Mysteries

Dying to Know

Dying for the Past

Dying to Tell

THE CONSULTANT

A JONATHAN HUNTER
THRILLER

Tj O'Connor

OCEANVIEW PUBLISHING
SARASOTA, FLORIDA

ISBN 978-1-60809-283-3

Cover design by Christian Fuenfhausen

Published in the United States of America by Oceanview Publishing
Sarasota, Florida

www.oceanviewpub.com

10 9 8 7 6 5 4 3 2 1

PRINTED IN THE UNITED STATES OF AMERICA

For Wallace K. Fetterolf
The Real Oscar LaRue

June 24, 1924–August 16, 2015

It is foolish and wrong
To mourn the men who died.
Rather, we should
thank God that such men lived.

—GENERAL GEORGE S. PATTON

ACKNOWLEDGMENTS

THIS NOVEL WAS not my first rodeo—my fourth and ninth actually if you count the first draft several years ago and the rewrites I did this past year—but without question, it was the most difficult. Oh, not because I languished in the writing or struggled with characters and plot (I did, but that's normal). No, it was because I wrote the first draft while my friend and mentor Wally Fetterolf—to whom this book is dedicated—looked on and badgered me for perfection. Five years later, after having shelved it to write four mysteries, I was halfway through the rewrite when I lost Wally to age and a bad heart. For the next year this novel was a difficult slog. Memories and loss can be a painful companion. I almost didn't get it right, and if not for the guidance of my brilliant agent, Kimberley Cameron, and my new editor extraordinaire, Terri B, I never would have made it through. I did, and Wally would have loved this final work. Along the way, a very good friend and a real-deal ops-guy, Mike P., jumped in for a lot of laughs, advice, and critiques that kept the story close to home for both of us. Thank you all.

Of course there are the usual gang to thank, too, whose help was invaluable—my beta readers: Jean my magnificent daughter and critic; Gina; Natalia; and Nicole. Oh, yeah, also my wife, Laurie, and daughter Lindsay who loved to join us for the great evenings out with great food and spirits while critiquing the books they've never read. But who's keeping score? Not me . . .

Finally, and perhaps more importantly, a very special thanks to Bob and Pat G. for inviting me to Oceanview. Your confidence and encouragement has been wonderful, and I hope this is the beginning of a long dance.

THE
CONSULTANT

CHAPTER 1

Day 1: May 15, 2130 Hours, Daylight Saving Time
East Bank of the Shenandoah River, Clarke County, Virginia

THE GUNSHOTS TOOK me by surprise and, without luck, might
have killed me.

The first shot splayed a spiderweb across my windshield before
it whistled past my head, peppering glass needles into my face.
The second smashed my driver's-side mirror. An amateur might
have panic-braked and skidded to a stop—a fatal mistake. The
shooter hesitated, anticipating that decision, and readied for
my failure.

Training. Muscle memory. *Response.*

I gunned the engine, wrenched the car to the left to put more
steel between me and the shooter, and sped forward, looking
for cover.

My headlights exploded and flashed dark. Bullets breached
the windshield. The rearview mirror and rear window were gone.
Had I not flinched, one shot would have found my right eye but
shredded my headrest instead.

I careened to a stop at the bottom of the boat launch—
vulnerable. The shooter was ahead in the darkness, likely
maneuvering for another shot. A closer shot. The kill shot. He'd
be closing the distance and finding a new advantage.

Luck had its limits, so I dove from the car and rolled to cover behind it. I fought to control the adrenaline and bridle my thoughts.

Easy, Hunter, steady. Listen—watch—survive.

I stayed low and crept along the side of the car, looking for better cover. Spring rain made the darkness murky and dense. The Shenandoah River was to my left some fifty feet. A blind guess. Overhead, two dark spans of the Route 7 bridge blocked what little light there was but provided some cover from the rain. The six substructure supports in front of me might afford me cover. They also afforded the shooter cover. He was hidden and waiting. Still, Kevin Mallory was nowhere to be seen. Under normal conditions—and normal is relative with me—I might have judged the shots' origins. Driving headlong into an ambush on terrain I'd long ago forgotten, in darkness and rain, I was all but defeated.

Silence.

Easy, Hunter, easy. Count your breaths. One, two, three.

Out there, somewhere, someone wanted me dead.

Worse. I was unarmed and alone.

Jesus. Where was Kevin?

The boat launch was just a small gravel lot tucked beneath the expanse of the Route 7 Bridge across the Shenandoah. At night it should have been empty. It was nearing ten p.m. and I hadn't expected to find anyone but Kevin. Yet, while we'd been estranged for years, under bad circumstances, I doubted he was hunting me.

Although, I do tend to bring out the worst in people.

Ahead, perhaps seventy-five feet, a dark four-door SUV faced an old pickup. The vehicles were nose to nose like two dogs sniffing each other.

No movement. No sound.

One, two, three. I ran to the nearest bridge support, stopped, listened, and bolted to the rear of the SUV.

Silence. Safety. But something else—a dangerous odor. The pungent scent of gasoline. A *lot* of gasoline.

I got down on one knee and looked around. The dome light was on and the driver's door was ajar. Something lay on the ground near the left front fender. A large, bulky something that washed an angry tide of flashbacks over me.

I'd seen silhouettes like that before.

A body.

Bodies look the same in any country, under any dark sky. It didn't matter if it were the rocky Afghan terrain or along a quiet country river. Their lifeless, empty shells were all hopeless. All forsaken. All discards of violence. The silhouette three yards away was no different. Except this wasn't Afghanistan or Iraq. It was home.

I made ready.

No muzzle flash. No assassin's bullet. I crept to the SUV's rear tire, crouched low, and slithered to the front fender.

The body was a man. He lay three feet in front of the fender and precariously vulnerable beneath the spell of the SUV's dome light. He was tall and bulky. Not fat, but strong and muscled.

No. No. God, no!

After fifteen years of silence and thousands of miles, I knew the body—the man. His hair had grayed and his face was creased with age and strain. The years had been hard on him. Years he was here while I was forever there. Always elsewhere. He'd built a life from our loss while I'd escaped—run away. He once warned me that my life's choice would leave me as I found him now, alone and dead. The irony churned bile inside me.

Kevin Mallory.

"Kevin," I blurted without thinking. "Kevin, it's me. It's Jon."

My mouth was a desert and the familiar brew of adrenaline and danger coursed through me. In one quick move, I leaped from the

SUV's shadow, grabbed his shoulders, and tried to drag him back to safety.

No sooner had I reached him when a figure charged from the darkness toward us. His arm leveled—one, two, three shots on the run—all hitting earth nearby. I threw myself over Kevin. Another shot sent stone fragments into my cheeks and neck. The figure reached the rear of the pickup, tossed something in the bed, fired another wild shot, and retreated at a dead run.

Lightning. A brilliant flash of light, a violent percussion, then a *whoosh* of fire erupted from the pickup. The flames belched up and over the side panels. They spat light and heat. The truck swelled into an inferno.

The heat singed my face. I gripped Kevin's shoulders and dragged him the remaining feet behind the SUV. He was limp and heavy. The raging fire bathed us in light, and I finally saw him clearly. His eyes were dull and vacant. His face pale—a death mask. If life was inside, it was hidden well.

The truck was engulfed in flames, and the heat was tremendous. It reached us and felt oddly comforting amidst the spring dampness and dark.

"Kevin, hold on. Hold on." I looked for an escape.

I saw the next shot before I heard it—a flash of light where none should be—uphill near River Road. Seasoned instincts threw me atop Kevin again. Glass crackled overhead and rained down. I grabbed for the familiar weight behind my back, but my fingers closed on nothing.

Dammit.

I hastily searched him. No weapon. All I found was an empty holster where his handgun should have been. Where was it? In a desperate move, I rolled off and snaked forward beneath the truck's firelight and groped around where he'd been. It took several long, vulnerable seconds. I dared not breathe or even look for the shooter, fearing I'd see the shot that would end me. Finally, my fingers closed on a wet, gritty semiautomatic.

As I retreated to the SUV, something moved in the darkness. I pivoted and fired two rapid shots, spacing them three feet apart.

Response. A shot dug into the gravel inches away to my left.

Rule one of mortal combat—incoming fire has the right of way.

Retreat. The flash was a hundred feet away. The shooter had withdrawn and angled south down River Road.

Should I take him? Could I?

One, two, three. Reason, Hunter, reason.

The shooter had fired at least fifteen rounds. Fourteen at me and at least one into Kevin. Had Kevin returned fire? How many rounds did his semiautomatic have left? I was on turf all but forgotten, armed with a handgun that was perhaps near-empty. The shooter must have a high-capacity magazine with plenty of ammo to cut me to pieces. He'd already proven willing and capable of killing. He knew my location. I knew nothing.

Revenge would wait.

I sat back against the SUV's tire and pulled Kevin close, keeping one arm around him and the other holding the handgun ready. The truck fire raged but was easing. The gasoline that had been splashed over it was consumed and only the paint and rubber were burning. Soon, though, the fire might breach the gas tank.

I pulled Kevin close and braced myself.

"Kevin, wake up. It's me—Jon. I'm here."

"Jon?" His eyes fluttered and half-opened. "I . . . so sorry . . . Khalifah . . . he's . . . find G. Find G . . ." He gasped for breath. "Khalifah . . . G . . . Baltimore . . . it's not them. Khalifah . . . so sorry . . ."

"Sorry for what? Who's Khalifah? Did he shoot you?"

"Tomorrow . . . not them. G . . . Khalifah is . . ." His body went limp.

I shook him easily. "Kevin, I don't understand. Tell me again."

"Find G . . ." His eyes fluttered again, and he clutched my arm with limp, sleepy fingers. "Find . . . Hunter . . ."

"Tell me who did this."

"G . . . Jon . . . tell no one. Maya . . . *Maya* . . . Maya in Baltimore . . ." He fumbled with something from his pants pocket. He gasped for breath and pressed that something into my hand. "So sorry . . ."

I opened my hand. He'd given me a small, ripped piece of heavy folded paper with handwriting scrawled on it. I couldn't make out the writing and stuffed it into my pocket. "Kevin, what are you saying? Hold on. Dammit, hold on."

"Go . . . please . . . not them . . . it's not . . ." He tried to breathe but mustered only a raspy gag.

"Kevin!"

Silence.

His body shuddered. A long, shallow sigh.

No. No. No . . .

My fingers found warm, sticky ooze soaking his shirt. The rain had slowed to a faint mist and, except for the river's passing and the grumble of fire, there was only silence. Then, somewhere along the highway miles in the distance, sirens wailed.

"Hold on, Kevin. They're coming. My God, hold on."

I checked his pulse and wounds. Both were draining away life.

I pressed my hands into the ooze but couldn't force its retreat. For a few seconds, I was fourteen again. The dull sickness invaded me as my parents were lowered side by side into the earth. The ache started in my gut and swelled until I spat bile and rage.

It was happening again.

The man who raised me—the man I'd abandoned—slipped away. The emptiness and loss attacked. I had to fight or it would destroy me again. This time, there was nowhere to run.

I closed my eyes and willed the anger in, commanding it to take hold and fill me.

I remember, Kevin. I made you a promise. I'm late, but I'm here.

He was limp, and I clutched him. A rush of words filled me that I'd wanted to say for so many years. But before I could speak just one, my brother was gone.

CHAPTER 2

Day 2: May 16, 0245 Hours, Daylight Saving Time
West Bank of the Shenandoah River, Clarke County, Virginia

A FLASH OF car lights swept through Caine's night vision, momentarily washing the scene's clarity with a greenish tint inside the monocular lens. Across the Shenandoah, a police cruiser pulled into the boat launch, and its headlights passed directly across his night-vision scope. Because it was designed for extremely low light, the sudden brightness disrupted his view for the second it took the device to correct the light sensitivity.

Caine slipped the scope into a pocket and lifted the standard binoculars from around his neck. He refocused on the crime scene across the river. The enhanced night-vision images were clear and the line of police cars that poured light onto the scene made his job easier. He was only a few hundred yards away across the river, secreted behind a fallen tree and halfway up the wooded hillside. The darkness and spring foliage made his seclusion almost guaranteed. But in his line of work, guarantees were not to be relied on.

That mistake had already been made. Across the river, hours earlier, there had been guarantees. Those guarantees were supposed to be a riskless transfer with no problems. Money for product. Betrayal for money. Simple.

There had been too many surprises. Too many mistakes. Too many bodies.

Caine studied the figure talking with the detective whom he knew by name. Bond. While he had never met the detective face-to-face, he knew that should they, the encounter would get *complicated*. But it was the other man—the surprise arrival—that unnerved him. That man had materialized from nowhere. He drove into an ambush he shouldn't have. He had responded like a professional, someone accustomed to such violence, trained and skilled. He hadn't panicked. Hadn't retreated. He counterattacked.

He was a dangerous man. Was he part of this? A player not yet declared in the game? Had Khalifah failed to give him all the intelligence he'd needed? Or, perhaps more to the point, had Khalifah been caught unaware, too?

An icy warning surged through Caine's veins.

He tapped the earbud in his right ear and waited for the connection. The voice answered as it always did, in Farsi.

"*Salaam.*"

"*Salaam.*" Caine continued in Farsi. "There is a problem."

"What now, Caine? Have you gotten your arms around Saeed?"

"I'm working on that." Caine gritted his teeth. He didn't like being pressed on something so dangerous and difficult by someone who was not taking the risk. "It's something else. A witness."

The voice paused before returning with an intensity framed with worry and the late hour. "A witness?"

"Yes. He literally drove into the cleanup." Caine let it sink in. "He's a pro."

"A pro? Out here? This is rural Virginia, not Kandahar."

"I'm here."

"You were invited." The man paused too long. "I'll find out who this pro is."

"This could disrupt the plan." Caine took a moment to sweep the binoculars across the line of police cars and ambulances across the river. "If it does, we could lose the targets."

Silence.

"If . . ."

"I do not accept 'if.'" The voice was hard, flat, without inflection of concern. "You must deal with Saeed Mansouri and handle Khalifah's targets. No one must interfere. No one."

Caine already knew the answer, but he asked anyway. "The witness?"

"You may have to act."

"Again?"

Silence.

Caine didn't like that answer. "That isn't in the plan."

"None of this was the plan." The voice was gritty now. "Give me a day to take care of him."

"If you can't?"

"Then you'll have to."

CHAPTER 3

Day 2: May 16, 0245 Hours, Daylight Saving Time
East Bank of the Shenandoah River, Clarke County, Virginia

"YOU DIDN'T KNOW Kevin's married? About Sam?" The burly cop shook his head and didn't conceal his disgust. He dropped his notebook onto his unmarked cruiser and stared at me as though I'd just insulted mom and apple pie. "What kind of a brother are you?"

The kind who left two decades ago and never looked back. "Look, Officer . . ."

"Detective," he snapped for the tenth time. The ice in his voice showed he'd counted, too. Bond was a plainclothes version of the uniformed cops milling around the crime scene. His close-cropped sandy hair, brooding posture, and bulging sleeves were intimidating enough without the bulldog stare he locked onto me. "Detective David Bond. So, the only thing you understood him saying was Khalifah and 'it's not them'? Something about 'G'? "

"And Baltimore. Something about . . ."

"Baltimore. Yeah right."

Bond was just to the bad side of hostile with me. While I didn't like it one bit, I got it. Kevin was a cop—one of their own. When a cop goes down, they take it personally—they're no longer objective investigators or patrolmen. They feel it deep and hard. They don't want only justice. They want revenge.

I glanced over at Kevin. His body was partially shrouded while the coroner worked on him. Without having to see beneath the sheet, I still saw his face and felt his lifeless body in my arms. I'd be seeing his face over and over. It took years to forget my folks' burial. Kevin might haunt me forever.

"Hey, yo. Mallory? I asked what Kevin meant by—"

"I don't know." I shook off bad memories. "He was dying. I didn't take notes."

"Watch it, Mallory." Bond raised his chin. "I don't like your lip, even if you're Kevin's brother."

Mallory? Me? Yes, me. *Oh crap.* I used to be Jonathan Mallory. Was I still a *Mallory*?

The name stung deeper than the windshield shards in my face. I hadn't gone by Mallory for too many years to count. I'd almost forgotten its claim on me. Was there even a trace of Jonathan Hunter Mallory left? Now, the name was foreign and deceitful. I'd simply been Jonathan Hunter for eighteen years. Failing to explain that to Bond would cost me later. Now was not the time. Any revelations of my past would take too much explanation. Too many questions. Too much time. They just might land me in a jail cell. A jail cell would lead to computer checks, fingerprints, and telephone calls. If the dominos started falling toward me, each one would raise Bond's radar until it was on high alert. My long-lost name had no residences, no past employers, and no library card.

Jonathan H. Mallory was as dead as Kevin Mallory—and for much longer.

In the end, though, the problem wasn't whether I was Jonathan Hunter or Jonathan Mallory, or both. No. Jonathan Hunter was just one of me. I have a few *noms de guerre* on passports, driver's licenses, and credit cards. I have several sets of each. If Bond peeked behind the curtain, he would bring bigger trouble than anything I could imagine, and I needed none of that. Assuming, of course, he wasn't the stereotyped muscle-bound, crew-cut, angry copper stuffed into a golf shirt and khakis that he appeared to be. If he were a real detective—a thinking man—then my cell was just a police car away.

Let me explain.

Ten days ago, I, under the name of Jeremy Kelly, left the rocky Afghan mountains bound for Qatar. In Doha, I, as Martin Levinson, business development entrepreneur, skipped town on a transport for Germany. After another day of metamorphosis, I flew to Washington, DC, walked through US Customs, and became Christopher James. After a visit to my stash of stateside belongings, Mr. James became this "me," Jonathan Hunter, international security consultant and world traveler extraordinaire. Jeremy, Martin, Christopher, and Jon—damn, it sounds like a rock band, doesn't it?—are all me.

There are others, too.

Why the subterfuge? I'm a consultant. Sort of a handyman for very special clients. Well, *one* very special client. In my business, particularly when in faraway, dangerous lands, one needs a new identity from time to time. One also needs to shed them and slip another on fast. So, if I'm on a job in say, Islamabad, and things get unfriendly, it's harder to hunt me down when the guy who stirred up trouble never existed in the first place. You'd never find me on any visa list, passenger manifest, or hotel bill, either.

For now, though, I'm Jonathan Mallory—five-eleven, one-ninety, fit and toned, with dark hair, tanned complexion, and three days' scruffy beard. The name fit like an old suit made for a younger man thirty pounds ago. *Forgive me, Kevin.*

"Mallory?" Bond pulled me back to the here and now. "You listening?"

"Yeah, yeah." I rubbed my eyes. "I need to get some sleep. I've answered your questions. It's very simple, Detective. I don't know any more than I've said. We done?"

"No, we're not done." Bond leaned in close and drilled his pen into my chest. "Your brother? You know, the corpse in the mud? He's a BCI agent and that makes this a big deal. We're going over everything twice."

By twice, he meant fifty times. By BCI, he meant the Virginia Bureau of Criminal Investigation, the state's version of the FBI. Kevin was a state cop. A detective. I'd learned that from our last phone call. How many years ago? What I didn't know about him outweighed what I did. Like that he was a husband and father.

But what about G? Khalifah? Maya in Baltimore? What else?

Something tickled my brain, and I slipped the heavy, folded paper that Kevin had given me out of my pocket. It was torn from some kind of pre-printed paper, more like light cardboard, with a decorative double-red lined border partially remaining on one side. On the other was a barely legible, hand-scribed address—25783 Christ.

I handed the paper to Bond. "I just remembered. Kevin had this."

"You just remembered?" Bond read the paper and looked at me shrewdly. "Just now?"

I shrugged.

"What's it mean?"

"I don't know." I wasn't lying. "Listen, I'm tired. In shock. Give me a break, Bond."

"Detective Bond." He stuffed the paper into his pocket. "Let's start over."

"No." I walked a few feet away and leaned on another cop car. "There's nothing more for me to say." Shock gripped my brain as I struggled to make sense of the past few hours. "I doubt you'd listen anyway."

I looked over at the smoldering pickup truck as a fireman probed the truck bed with a long bar. I lost interest when Bond came close again.

"Look, lose the attitude and give me the truth."

"I already did. You just haven't written it down."

He pushed his pen deeper into my chest. This time, it threatened to puncture my lung. "Watch your mouth, Mallory. You're nothing like your brother. You're just a smart-mouth asshole who showed up too late for his murder."

He didn't even swing and he hit a home run.

"Or maybe you didn't." He eyed me. "What do you think, Mallory? Is that what this is about? Maybe there wasn't any shooter."

"Fuck you."

"Whoa." Bond's breath was hot on my face. "I don't know who you think you are, but that attitude isn't helping. Your brother's dead. You haven't helped tell us with who or why, but you're damn sure smack in the middle of it."

Yes, I was. Damn smack in the middle. The question was, in the middle of what?

Guilt stabbed my gut and twisted. He might be right. Well, maybe half right. If I'd met Kevin a day sooner—swallowed my pride and taken an earlier flight—he might be alive. Maybe I could have stopped this. Perhaps the body lying in the mud would be the killer instead.

Maybe. Perhaps. *Damn*.

Someone near the pickup yelled, and several deputies and plainclothes detectives ran over. A fireman reached into the truck bed with a gloved hand. He lifted something black and charred into the lights cast by the surrounding cop cars.

A human arm. It was dark and burned crisp and still smoldering.

"Wait here, Mallory." Bond hurried over to the truck.

The activity around the firemen escalated until two crime scene technicians took over and the cops moved back. They began photographing the truck bed from a tall folding ladder and recording notes on a notebook computer.

Bond returned to me and gestured toward the truck. "How is it you left that body out of your story?"

"My story?" I looked at the pickup. "I hate being redundant, but fuck you."

The body in the pickup truck was news to me. But it explained one thing. The shooter braved open ground to reach that truck and torch everything. He had no way of knowing I was unarmed at that point, but he took a desperate chance to destroy the truck and the body inside.

What was so important about him to brave a bullet? Kevin was dying. The attack was already over. The shooter could have escaped unseen but risked everything to burn the truck and body. Was it Khalifah?

"Look, try to keep up, Detective. It's simple." From my perspective, it was. "I rolled in here to find Kevin and someone started shooting. He took out my rental car, and at one point, he charged us—Kevin and me—tossed a flash-bang into that truck, and escaped."

Bond cocked his head. "A flash-bang?"

"Yeah, you know magnesium and ammonium." I cocked my head. "A couple million candles of flash and one hundred seventy-plus decibels of bang."

Bond's jaw tightened. "How is it you know about flash-bangs? What about the body?"

Give me a break. "Look, I was trying to save Kevin. It was dark and rainy and I stayed with him. I didn't run around investigating. There could have been ten bodies out here, and I wouldn't have seen them."

"Maybe." Bond backed off a couple steps and looked across the lot. "Agent Bacarro wants to speak with you."

"BCI?"

"Oh, no, it's your lucky day. She's FBI." Bond's smirk was sand ground into the cuts on my face. "She's the task force boss. So, watch your mouth. She's not as nice as me."

Terrific. I'd killed Taliban nicer than him.

The crime scene hushed when two medics placed Kevin onto a gurney and shrouded his body. When they rolled him over the gravel, they nodded to me before they slipped the gurney into the coroner's van. Bond said something, but I hadn't listened. The van's doors slammed closed, and, a moment later, Kevin left our favorite childhood fishing hole for the last time.

Something stole the air around me. Daggers stabbed my gut. Thoughts swirled, collided, and refused to land. I couldn't catch my breath. The darkness collapsed around me and squeezed every muscle in my body like a giant snake. The trembling began again.

No. Focus, Hunter, focus. One, two, three.

The trembling stopped. My gut turned to stone. My thoughts fluttered and found feet. "I'm home, Kev. I got this."

Before the tears could escape, I willed myself into "ops-mode"—a place I'd found on my first firefight outside Kabul. Adventure had turned to terror. That night, while patrolling for trouble I'd hoped to find, I discovered youthful invincibility was a myth. We'd been ambushed by a dozen gorillas, and the bullets were whistling inches around me. Bravado and machismo melted into breath-stealing terror until my partner pulled me to the ground and held my eyes in a vampire stare. Ops-mode began to take over. It cleared away the clutter of panic and focused me. It was a state of mind where fear couldn't rule. Terror was reined in. Emotions numbed. All gears on business.

It took over now. *Thank God.* There would be time for emotions later. After I found Kevin's killer. After I balanced the scales. In time. In private. After.

Bond stepped close and smacked my shoulder. "Here's Bacarro, Mallory. Remember what I said."

Bacarro was a dark-haired woman in her midthirties. She emerged through the glare of patrol car lights and stopped near a group of uniformed deputies. In her wake was a short man, five-feet-four or so, with lean, dark Middle Eastern features. He wore jeans and a pullover with a heavy semiautomatic holstered on his left side. Unlike the rest of the cops, he didn't have a gold shield clipped on his belt or dangling from a chain around his neck.

My inner radar pinged when he looked straight at me and narrowed his eyes. Then he said something to Bacarro, turned, and strode away.

Who was he and why so shy?

Bacarro continued her trek to me. She wore an FBI embossed windbreaker and ball cap. Her face, pretty I think, was taut and angry, and her eyes had the gritty redness of dried tears. It was a face that might have resembled mine had I not fought back. She didn't seem to care.

"Is this him, Dave?" Her voice was monotone with a wisp of contempt. "The long-lost brother nobody heard of?"

Terrific, another fan, and I hadn't even opened my mouth.

"Yeah. He's a real peach, Victoria."

"Delightful." She extended a hand to me—odd given her tone.

"I'm Special Agent Bacarro, Special Agent in Charge of the local FBI task force. Kevin was one of my team."

Her hand was cold and clammy. Winchester had an FBI task force? I asked her, "When did Winchester get on the map?"

She eyed me and nodded slightly. "It's more on the map than you know, Mallory. The task force is from the WFO. That's the Washington Field Office. I run a satellite office here. We're part of the JTTF."

I didn't need a translation. Even us spooks overseas knew what the Joint Terrorism Task Force was. Most major cities around the country had them. They were operational law enforcement centers run by the FBI and manned by multiple jurisdictions like the state cops, city cops, sheriff's departments, ATF, Customs. Everyone played a role. Their mission was simple—stop the next 9/11.

Still, Winchester had a terror task force? Had ISIS made a wrong turn on the Beltway and ended up in this tiny town?

She watched the questions on my face but asked a doozy herself. "Why haven't we heard of you, Mallory?"

Good question. "I've been away for a few years. Kevin and I didn't talk much."

"Why's that? Exactly?"

"I don't know." That wasn't a lie. "That's what I came home to find out."

Bond and Bacarro exchanged curt looks.

I threw a chin toward her Middle Eastern pal, who was standing near a group of firemen but watching me intently. "Who's that?"

"Don't worry about him," Bacarro said. "Worry about me."

Funny thing to say. Even funnier since her pal was fixed on me. "I worry about everyone. Humor me."

She turned and watched the Middle Easterner suddenly turn away and disappear between the emergency vehicles. "He's Agent Mo Nassar. Now forget him and let's get back to you."

As I was about to press her further, Bond interjected with, "Where have you been?"

"Exactly?" Bacarro added.

"Overseas. Germany mostly. I'm a security consultant."

Bond's face twisted. "Like, alarms and security systems?"

"Sometimes." But most times it was guns, guards, dogs, and barbed wire. Other times, well, movie stuff like sneaking and shooting and fighting and skullduggery. "Other things, sometimes."

Bacarro eyed me. "Kevin was your brother, huh? Now he's dead. Got any ideas?"

"No." My face turned to fire and the air got thin again. I leaned back on the cruiser's hood and glanced skyward. "Can I go?"

"I know it's rough, Mallory," Agent Bacarro said in a softer voice. "Explain again why you're here. By the river, I mean, tonight. I find it odd."

"Coincidence. Listen, I've been through it already fifty times. I came home to meet with Kevin. I had no idea where he lived, so I pinged his number in a cell phone app and got this location. We used to fish here when we were kids. I came here."

"You pinged him?" Bond glanced at Bacarro. "An app for finding cell phones? How come I don't have one?"

A huge mistake. "It's a big-boy toy, Bond, and—"

He pounced. His powerful paws clutched my shirt and lifted me up and backward onto the hood of his car. "You wise-mouth prick."

"Enough, Dave." Bacarro grabbed his arm and pulled him away. She was as cool as they came. Since joining us she hadn't taken her eyes off me. She watched and listened. She knew how to look for the lie before the lips spoke it. It was about body language and attitude. She listened, not to the answers, but to the word choices, the inflections, and the practiced lies. Good cops—good interrogators—asked basic, straightforward questions. Then they shut up and listened to the answers. They watched for the lies. Special Agent Victoria Bacarro was a pro.

I was in deep trouble.

"Sorry about that, Mallory." She sniffed the air. "Your hair's singed. You were real close."

"No kidding."

She grinned. "So, this shooter blows up the truck?"

"He ran at me, tossed a flash-bang, and whoosh. I smelled gas when I was on the ground just before."

"On the ground ducking gunfire." She glanced at the truck. "Did you see the body in there before it went up?"

I shook my head.

"Okay. So, you found Kevin, got his gun, and fired back?"

"Yes. Dammit, yes. There'll be GSR all over me mixed with his blood. Aren't you going to do a gunshot analysis? Get some lasers out here and start pinpointing the shooter's moves. Once you find out where the shots were fired from maybe you'll find some evidence."

"You know about gunshot residue and crime scenes?" Bond asked. "I didn't think alarm consultants handled that."

"TV."

Agent Bacarro stepped a little closer. "Kevin said some odd things to you and then gave you the address and more gibberish?"

"I couldn't make most of it out."

"Huh." She continued to watch me close. Danger close. "What about this Maya in Baltimore. Any idea who that is?"

"No. For Christ's sake, no. No, I don't know anything. I don't understand anything. I don't know what any of what he said meant. Enough already. Please."

"I get it, I do." Bacarro's cell phone rang, and she stepped away.

"All right, Mallory." Bond checked his watch. "You have to go to the office to sign a statement. Then we're through. One of my men will drive you to a hotel when we're done. We're keeping your rental car for processing. Not that it's drivable. Oh, and don't plan on checking out anytime soon." He started to turn away but stopped and faced me again. His voice lowered and I heard a side of him that eluded me thus far. "You're an asshole, Mallory. But I'm sorry about Kevin. We were friends."

I grunted a "thanks" and stared at the spot where Kevin had died. A wave of nausea swept through me, and I retched bile beside the cruiser. Death, I was accustomed to. Giving a damn, I wasn't.

Bond waited for me to get my feet under me again. "You know, I have this theory about you and the burned-up guy."

Of course he did. "Enlighten me."

"Sure." Bond let slip a dry grin. "Maybe the burned guy is the shooter and you shot him."

"You've got to be kidding me." I shook my head and tried to keep cool as another plainclothes cop, Detective Perry, walked up. He nodded to me and guided Bond a few steps away, where he spoke quietly, but I could still hear them.

"This is weird, Dave," Perry said. "Before your boy got here, some college kids were down along the river. They came across the pickup truck and the body and then left to call 911. They never saw Kevin. I guess he came after. Somehow, things got fouled up and dispatch sent the Clarke County sheriff's patrol to the Route 50 Bridge instead of this one. It was an hour before they realized they got it wrong. Kevin must have stumbled into something between the time the kids left and the patrol arrived. The killer must have returned."

Bond eyed me. "Or never left."

"Give it a rest, Bond," I snapped. "Even you can't believe I killed my own brother."

Bond ignored me and gestured to the old pickup where the crime scene techs were working away. Alongside the smoldering left front tire was the top of a stainless-steel case smeared with soot and charred debris. He focused his flashlight on it. "Figure that out, Perry?"

"No, but let me show you." Perry walked over to the crime scene technician taking photographs. After snapping three or four more photographs, the tech maneuvered the piece of case into a large, clear plastic evidence bag. He handed it to Perry, who then delivered it to Bond.

The case top had a strange inner cavity made of thick gray foam with cutouts. The hinges were torn and twisted as though someone had shot them off. Next to the handle was a modular, digital keypad.

Bond played the flashlight around it. "What's this?"

"A pneumatically sealed case." My brain couldn't stop my lips.

"A what?" Perry asked.

"It pneumatically seals." It was too late anyway. "Air, Bond. It seals the air in and out."

"I know what *pneumatically* means." Bond was lying, of course. Still, he beckoned me over and I obeyed. "For what?"

I shrugged. "How would I know? Whatever it was, though, they didn't want it breathing out in the moonlight."

"Okay, Mallory, impress me. What's a case like this used for?"

"Pharmaceuticals or biological stuff." Then I raised Bond's pucker factor into the red zone. "That's not the big question."

"What's the big question?"

"Where's the stuff that was in it?"

CHAPTER 4

Day 2: May 16, 0600 Hours, Daylight Saving Time
Winchester, Virginia

By EARLY MORNING, I'd given up on sleep. After lying in my bed contemplating the last twelve hours, I decided I couldn't avoid what lay ahead. I climbed out of the lumpy hotel bed and showered. I let cold water wake me and chase the anger and angst from my thoughts, at least for a little while. When I opened my eyes after a long, chilly few moments lost in thought, I realized I had more problems than hunting Kevin's killer. I had a big, complicated problem.

Oscar LaRue.

As I've explained, I was supposed to be in Doha on vacation. Doha is nowhere near Winchester. Like seven thousand miles nowhere near Winchester. There's a funny rule about being a consultant for the CIA. You don't disappear from an assignment without permission. There was another sticky rule to my situation. You don't do *anything* to piss off my friend, mentor, and omnipotent master, Oscar LaRue.

Boy, had I violated the rules.

LaRue was a legend in the intelligence community and had been my mentor for years. It was because of him that I'd visited places like Kabul, Mogadishu, and Damascus while he had tea and crumpets in Washington supper clubs. He dreamed up wild operations, and I carried them out. Most of the time, anyway. Sometimes he dreamed up the operations, and I got all twisted up carrying them out. Strange, LaRue often misplaced my phone number.

Oscar LaRue was my hero.

Sooner or later—probably sooner—old Oscar would find out I wasn't drinking and carousing in the Doha nightlife, and he would be a teensy-weensy bit angry. When LaRue got angry, the world stopped spinning and those around him looked for an exit. But for now, until I was able to find Kevin's killer, LaRue would have to wait. Finding Kevin's killer was my new mission. To do that, I'd have to stay below the radar the best I could. That meant anonymity from LaRue, and that meant anonymity from the cops, too. That might be too late already. LaRue might not be looking for Jon Hunter. I might just have a few days before the men in black came calling to drag me before him for a flogging.

Maybe.

As I dressed, I shook off the thought of the wrath that LaRue would rain on me, and focused on the bile and trepidation building in my guts. Before leaving the hotel room for the waiting cab, I steeled myself for what would be the hardest meeting I'd had to do in my life.

The Frederick County Medical Center campus sits on the west side of Winchester, Virginia, some seventy-six miles west of Washington, DC. Winchester, I learned, was the home of the late Kevin Mallory and had been for ten years. It is small as cities go, perhaps twenty-five thousand residents, give or take. When we were kids, Kevin and I had often visited it when staying at our dad's mountain cabin an hour's drive west of town. The cabin was our retreat away from our Washington suburban home. Back then, Winchester was little more than a rural farm community. Now, commuters and developers reigned.

I made the trip from my hotel to the hospital in ten minutes by cab. By the time I stood in front of the hospital's main entrance, my face was tight and my mouth dry. My hands trembled. An intense battle raged inside me. My brain claimed that too many years had passed. I no longer knew Kevin. We were blood, sure. But that was just a biological connection long ago void as family. My gut, on the other hand, disagreed and threatened to vomit.

Ops-mode was nowhere to be found.

In my reflection in the hospital windows, I tucked in my rumpled cotton golf shirt, straightened my hair with a few finger combs, and pulled on the lapels of my leather jacket, trying to look passable. My reflection didn't hide my terror, but at least I didn't look like the mess that I felt like. Inside the lobby, I found a kiosk for some breath mints—a feigned stall—before going to the reception desk.

"Excuse me," I said to an elderly volunteer across the counter. "My name is . . . *er*, Jon Mallory." It felt like a lie. "I'm here about Kevin."

"Oh yes, Mr. Mallory." She gestured to a row of couches in the atrium waiting area. "Detective Bond said you'd be here. Please wait over there with your family."

My family? Bond?

It took me a moment to find "my family." When I did, it knocked me a step back. Across the atrium on the far row of couches sat a beautiful woman in her late thirties. She had dark, wavy hair and an exotic, Middle Eastern complexion. Her face was pretty but awash in tears and grief. She was five-eight with a curvy, healthy figure. She wore tan slacks and a loose white blouse beneath a shawl. She wiped her eyes and looked at a tall, thin, young man—not quite a man but not quite a teenager—next to her. He, too, had dark, Middle Eastern features, but if they were mother and son, they didn't share any deeper resemblance.

The woman was stunning, and, for a second, that thought bathed me in guilt.

Bond told me their names . . . Noreen and Sam? They sure weren't . . . Noreen and Samuel. It was clear to me now that she was *Noor*—Arab for "light"—and he was *Sameh*, Arab for oh hell, I didn't know. One thing I did know though. They weren't from Winchester. Not the Winchester I remember from twenty years ago.

"Mr. Mallory, they've been waiting," the volunteer scolded. "Go comfort them, for Pete's sake."

Unsteady legs took me across the lobby. When I reached them, Noor looked up at me. Her eyes were red and raining, but had they not been, they would be a heart-stealing green. She never blinked. Her unfamiliarity penetrated and singed me like no bullet ever had. Her eyes were inside me, searching for any semblance of recognition. Perhaps a story she'd been told. Perhaps a photograph she'd seen. Perhaps.

My lips wouldn't part for more than a stutter until I looked away. "I'm Jon. Kevin's—"

"Oh, my God." She stood and studied my face again, my frame, and locked on to my eyes. Somewhere, she found what she was looking for. "You came. Thank God, you came."

Before I could answer, Noor Mallory stepped close and crushed into me. Tears poured from her. Her body quivered. I had never before seen this woman and, until just hours ago, I didn't know she existed. Terror struck me when I realized that, at that moment, we were family.

Steady, Hunter. Steady.

At first, my arms didn't know what to do. Noor's sobs broke through, and I found an unfamiliar urge to hold her. I couldn't remember the last time those feelings invaded me. When my arms closed around her shoulders, the calm that descended on me scared me to death.

Shouldn't I be toppling a tyrant or invading an ISIS stronghold somewhere?

"Ah, Noor. I didn't know about you."

"What did you expect? Mrs. Brady or Mrs. Cleaver, perhaps?" Beneath tears, the slightest of smiles parted her lips. Her words were soft and comforting, with a touch of mirth perhaps, and delivered with only the slightest hint of an accent. "It is fine, Jon Mallory. No one expects Sam and me. We are a surprise. Even to Kevin. That is why we fell in love. At least, that is what I believed."

I looked over her shoulder at the young man glaring at me. "I'm so sorry, Noor. I didn't know Kev was married. I didn't know about Sameh."

"It's Sam," he corrected with a harsh snap. "Sam."

I said nothing. I didn't know what to say.

"No, no." She squeezed me harder. "I know. You two. I do not know where to begin."

"I, well, me either. I'm so sorry."

Noor eased from me and turned to Sam as he stood up from his chair with a slow, exaggerated movement. If he wanted me to know he was unhappy with me, his message was clear. His hands were in his pockets and his head cocked to one side. His stare was cool and brooding. Anger. Bitterness. Indifference.

"Jon," Noor said, "this is Sam, our son."

Sam's response was thick and icy. "I didn't know Dad had a brother." He stepped forward and put a hand on Noor's shoulder. "Where you been?"

"Sam." Noor's eyes flared. "Enough."

I extended my hand and his eyes rejected it. "I'm sorry, Sameh."

"Sam." His eyes cut me. "What's wrong with Sam?"

Damn. "Nothing. I was just, well, I've lived in the Middle East."

"Good for you."

"Sam!" Noor turned to him with a scowl. "Do not be rude."

I patted the air. "No, it's all right."

Sam turned away, and I reached out and touched his shoulder. "If it's any consolation, I was with your dad last night."

"It's not." He strode away.

Silence hung, and Noor's tears returned. I tried to console her but failed. More silence. As I looked around, the room morphed into the waiting room from twenty-six-year-old memories. The morning Kevin and I waited in that room outside Washington, DC. Nothing was different except Noor and Sam. Not the antiseptic smell. Not the murmurs from passing visitors. Not the elderly volunteers with their forced smiles. Not even the anticipation that welled up each time a doctor walked near. It was now as it had been then. Except twenty-six years ago, it was just Kevin and me. We were alone and numb. We'd been silent, reminiscing about Mom and Dad. My thoughts had exploded between sorrow and anger in slow, churning cycles until they told us our parents were gone.

I was back reliving it again. The anger and pain began to well in my eyes, but I shook it off. No. It didn't matter. I knew tears would not come. They never came. Not anymore. Not for twenty-six years.

When Sam reappeared and crossed the lobby, my heart stopped. He walked toward us behind Detective David Bond. Bond's eyes locked onto me like a stinger missile. He looked like a bulldog strutting into the ring for a title match.

"Oh, no. Him?" I said.

Noor watched them approach. "It is Dave. He said he would meet us. Yes, of course, you met last night."

We sure did.

Bond and Sam stopped a few feet away. Sam ignored me. Bond shot icy bullets through me.

"Noor, are you doing okay?" Bond reached out and took her shoulder. "We're ready for you downstairs. I'll be with you the whole way."

"I am not ready," Noor whispered. "But I must."

Bond threw a thumb over his shoulder. "*Follow* us, Mallory."

When Bond led them toward the elevators, I fell in behind obediently. Two floors down in the basement mortuary wing, the four of us—Bond, my less-than-new best pal; me; and the two strangers who were suddenly family—filed into the stark room.

The duty nurse waited until we were positioned near a table and asked Noor's permission to proceed. When she nodded, the nurse folded the sheet back to reveal a face of dark, gray death.

The face may have been Kevin Mallory, but the man was gone.

"Take your time." The nurse vanished.

Bond took a step closer and put one hand on Noor's shoulder and the other on Sam's. Sam pulled away and moved around the table. Noor touched Bond's hand, and that sent a lightning bolt into my head.

Friendship? Compassion? Something.

Stop, Hunter. What's wrong with you?

Bond was impassive. Noor and Sam were frozen. They were not ready for the pale, pasty mask hiding husband and father. I doubted either had ever seen death up close. Now, neither seemed able to connect it with the man they loved.

Perhaps that was good.

I moved closer to the table, stepped around Bond, and took hold of Kevin's shoulder. While it was not for me to identify the body, it was hard to find my brother on the table. Closing my eyes helped . . . a *little* . . .

* * *

... Twenty years ago.

The Alexandria bar was packed, and we had to yell across the table.

"Come on," Kevin growled at me. "Enough of the BS. I spent four years working two jobs and then you dropped out of college and ran away with the circus."

"The Army, Kev. It was the Army."

"Same thing. Your tour is up. It's time to come on home."

"No. I know I promised to finish college, but, well, something else has come up."

Our parents had died when I was still in junior high school. It had been a tragic car accident one night when "last call" came too late at a popular Fairfax club. Kevin was older and took his new role seriously. He'd had a college scholarship and quit his freshman year in order to see me through high school and put me into college later. He never complained. While he wouldn't say it, I owed him. I made him a promise that I'd broken.

"Something else?" He grunted.

"I've left Special Forces, Kev. I'm with another outfit."

"Another outfit?"

"The Agency."

Kevin shook his head as though the words weren't making sense. "What agency?"

All I could do was grin.

"The CIA?" He slammed back in his seat. "You joined the CIA? Are you insane? You'll get yourself killed. You'll never make any money that way."

I sipped my beer. "I'm not worried about money."

"So, you're going to be a mercenary or something?"

"You're the one who sounds like a mercenary. All you worry about is money. I want to live a little."

"You're out of your mind." He emphasized every syllable, speaking each word in a slow, deliberate rhythm. "You promised, Jon. You promised you'd come home after your tour to finish school."

"They made me a better offer. Besides, I'm born for it. They said so."

Kevin got to his feet. He pulled a fistful of folded bills from his pocket and tossed several on the table. "You broke your promise so you could run off and play spy."

Before I could stop him, Kevin was gone.

* * *

Upstairs in the hospital lobby, Bond spoke privately with Noor near the entrance. Sam and I waited near the sofas across the lobby. Exhaustion began to consume me. I'd been almost forty hours without sleep, and while I'd had worse runs, it hit me hard now.

Bond glanced over at me, gave Noor a reassuring hug that lasted too long, and threw a nod at Sam. Without another word, he disappeared through the exit, and Noor made the long, lonely journey to us.

"I'm so sorry." My words were hollow even to me. "If it's okay, I'm going to stay around awhile. I owe Kevin."

Noor wiped her eyes. "Really? Good, I think. Dave said there were others killed last night, too. It is so sad."

Sam's jaw locked. He looked away when he saw me watching. But was it me or the name "Dave"?

I said, "I'm going to look into this. You have my word. Except, I don't even know where to start."

Noor did. "Sand Town."

"Sand Town?"

"Yes, it is a, how do you say, a play-on-words for where many Muslims live," Noor said. "It is not a very nice name, but that is what this town has become. It is outside Winchester in an old farm community that has become mostly, well, those like—"

"Like you?"

She nodded and looked down, embarrassed.

"You don't look so scary."

She allowed a smile. "Perhaps." She turned to Sam. "Sameh knows Bobby—the boy who found the body at the river last night."

Now Sam engaged. Reluctance oozed over his words and made them difficult to speak more than a whisper. "His name is Bobby Fischer."

"Bobby Fischer?"

"Yeah, he's a college guy who hangs around the Old Town Café playing chess."

I nodded. "I want to talk to him."

"We'll see." Sam looked away.

Noor's eyes dropped to the floor again. "I cannot deal with any more now, Jon. There is nothing for you to do here. Let Dave and the police work." She rattled off an address and brief directions to her home. "Come by later if you wish. But, Jon, there is nothing for you to do."

She was wrong. I could do plenty. I'd learned my trade from the Green Berets and on a place called the Farm. Here's a secret— the Farm doesn't have cows or corn or tractors. I'd spent years solving problems and hunting bad guys—guerillas, insurgents, tyrants . . . worse. As it happened, I had free time on my hands. Now, it was time to see just how good I was.

Mourning and sorrow would have to wait. I was going to find my brother's killer.

When I did . . .

CHAPTER 5

Day 2: May 16, 0810 Hours, Daylight Saving Time
Winchester, Virginia

DESPITE REPEATED OFFERS to help Noor with funeral arrangements, she wouldn't accept. I was *just* the estranged brother and
uncle. A stranger. Perhaps more to the point, the guy who showed
up too late. I had to force my feet to carry me out of the hospital
and twice stopped and considered returning. In the end, though,
I knew my place wasn't at their side.

Not yet. Perhaps not ever.

Grow up, Hunter. Life went on without you.

It took me an hour to rent another car. The young rental car
manager, a thin, nervous kid barely out of high school, fumbled
with his computer for ten minutes. His eyes almost popped out
when I told him that my airport rental was at the police impound
lot. My explanation had him speechless. Was it that unusual for a
rental to be riddled with bullet holes? After all, I'd purchased the
extra insurance.

As I sat in my new rental deciding my next move, I thought
about the piece of paper Kevin had slipped me before he died.
The hand-scribed address had been . . . 25783 Christ. Using my
cell phone, I searched the web and found a short list of possibili-
ties but none close by. The closest was a 25783 Christian Run in

Manassas, Virginia, an outlying historic community southwest of DC and about an hour from Winchester.

"Okay, Kev. If it was important enough to waste your last breaths, here I go."

Before I ran off playing detective, one thing had to change. Last night, I rolled into an ambush empty-handed. I almost got my ass shot off and took far too long to respond to the killer's assault to make any difference. Perhaps if I'd been prepared, ready for anything at any moment, like I'd lived my life these past years. Perhaps then things would have been different. Kevin was dead. I'd almost been killed. While Kandahar and Baghdad were worlds away, that lifestyle was in Winchester last night. My world—this world—needed to be in balance.

I needed balance.

A few years after leaving home, I'd rented a long-term self-storage unit in Leesburg. It was a growing community halfway between Winchester and Washington, DC, where I'd stored my few belongings and set up a Post Office box. I never bothered with a permanent residence; there was no point paying for a place I'd never be in. That storage unit contained all that was once Jonathan Hunter Mallory, and a few things that were truly Jonathan Hunter, too.

I drove to Leesburg and made a pit stop at an ATM near the storage place. There, my heart stopped. The receipt groaned that my account balance was *zero*. Ah, zero? I'd socked away a small fortune in a "retirement account" of sorts. The account should have $879,928.66 round about. My account was a little short. $879,928.66 short.

Obviously, the Agency knew I wasn't on R & R in Doha.

My troubles just became serious. I was broke except for my credit cards, and they were under aliases, too. How long before the Agency killed them off? Did they know about my storage unit? All my aliases?

From the ATM, it took ten minutes to drive to the storage complex, remember the passcode to get inside the lot, and reach the rear area where my unit was located. Then it took me another five minutes to remember my unit passcode. I was terrible at numbers, so I used something I wouldn't forget. Except I forgot. It wasn't my birthday, or any of my phony ones, and it wasn't any part of my social security number, former addresses, height and weight, or . . . I got it. It was my zip code in high school. The last time I had a zip code.

Voila, I was in the first roll-up door. I'd installed a second, interior roll-up door made of tougher steel with a high-security lock. This one unlocked using something I couldn't forget or lose—my thumbprint. Once inside, I closed both doors behind me and wormed my way past filing cabinets, a couple pieces of old furniture, and boxes of memory books. Tucked in the rear corner was a heavy, fireproof safe with another entry code I couldn't forget. My palm print.

The locker contained what many survivalists, anti-government loons, and spooks like me called a go-bag. Except my go-bag was a go-safe. It had everything I'd need—clothes, knives, guns, and plenty of ammo. Reviewing my stock, I took a pair of compact Colt Defender .45 caliber semiautomatics, a holster, a few magazines, and extra boxes of ammo. I loaded the mags and slipped them into a small shoulder bag atop the safe. Then I opened a drawer in the bottom of the cabinet and took out a stack of cash. Not much, just a grand of the few there. Emergency money. Just in case the stock market crashed or the CIA decided to confiscate my bank account. I'd prepared pretty well, given my current circumstances.

The six Ps—planning prevents piss-poor performance and poverty.

One of the Defenders went into my shoulder bag and the other into a holster in the small of my back. For the first time since arriving in town, I felt at ease. In balance. Grounded.

Back in my rental car, I dug out the address Kevin had given me, plugged it into my cell phone map program, and headed southwest. Forty-five minutes later, I rolled down an older, run-down street. I'm sure the locals would call it a "mature neighborhood." But this mature neighborhood was littered with run-down town houses, a few small cement block ramblers, and dozens of cars that hadn't seen wax or new tires in decades.

Three houses before 25783 Christian Run, I pulled to the curb and looked around. I half-expected to see police cruisers outside the battleship-gray cement block rambler. The only vehicle there was a large panel van sitting in the drive with its engine running. As I pulled forward, two men came out of the house. The man in the front was a dark-skinned young man, perhaps early twenties, with tight black hair and a narrow jaw. A Middle Easterner. He was thin and gangly and moved hesitantly, stealing glances over his shoulder as he walked to the van.

Khalifah?

The man behind him was tall and wide, muscular and not fat, and he strode close to the first with one hand touching his arm each time he looked back. He had a heavy, perpetual eyebrow and strong, wide cheekbones on white, pasty, pockmarked skin.

A tingle went up my spine. This only happened when something crappy was about to happen, or on payday. Today wasn't payday.

Before I could leave the curb, the bigger man opened the van's side door and prodded the thin Middle Easterner inside. He then jumped in and the van pulled quickly out of the drive. They drove past me without notice, made a right at the end of the street, and were gone.

Instincts took over and I U-turned to fall in behind them a dozen car lengths back. As we hit Route 66 north of Manassas, it struck me that I was doing surveillance for reasons I didn't know, in a rental car with no chutzpah, against an unknown target. I couldn't go to the cops, and really had no reason to—yet. Since the Agency was likely pissed at me, I couldn't call for backup should things get dicey again.

At least I was armed. Overall, this was one of the stupidest things I'd done in a long time.

Thirty minutes later, after a circuitous path around Fair Oaks, Virginia, we entered the parking apron on the west side of a large indoor shopping mall and parked. The van sat four rows closer to the mall entrance than me. The morning traffic was light, but there were a lot of cars in the parking lot. As I parked, two community shuttle buses pulled up and let groups of retirees off near the entrance, and they paraded slowly inside.

The tall, lanky Middle Easterner climbed out of the van and followed the retirees inside. Now, though, he had a bright blue backpack and spoke on a cell phone. He seemed more at ease, too, and moved casually as he disappeared inside.

I checked the .45 holstered behind my back, made sure my leather jacket concealed it well enough, and followed.

Inside was a large atrium near the north end of the food court. The mall was busy with shoppers. A pack of the elderly customers gathered around a coffee shop on the outer rim of the atrium. Everything seemed normal, but the Middle Easterner was nowhere.

Where did he go?

I made my way along one of the grand concourses of shops and stopped halfway. The young man was nowhere in sight. I turned and started back toward the entrance, glancing around trying to catch sight of him.

A lightning bolt sent me diving to the floor. The fireball erupted a millisecond later.

Everyone within fifty feet of the blast was eviscerated. The percussion shattered windows, doors, and display cases the length and width of the ground floor. Damage on the above floors would surely be as bad.

The blast wave struck me even as I dove for cover and sent me backward into a display of children's clothing. I lay there, letting the shock pass. When the ceiling stopped spinning, I staggered to my feet, looked around, and ran into the maelstrom.

Shrapnel shredded bodies. Shattered displays, tables, chairs, and restaurant counters had been blown out of the atrium and littered the boulevard of stores. Stone planters and metal benches had become missiles that devastated everything in their wake. The fireball had topped three stories into the galleries above and shattered the tinted glass roof above the food court. A couple riding the escalator from the second floor never felt the wave of heat and metal that took their lives. A hundred yards away, a twisted metal spike had passed a woman pushing her baby stroller, missed two lovers at a jewelry store, and struck the jeweler. He was dead before he registered the blast. The woman and her stroller stood frozen looking on.

There were bodies and devastated lives everywhere. Shattered glass. Burning wood. Twisted metal. Blood.

Seconds ticked before the first screams began.

Turning in circles, I saw no one nearby I could aid, so I ran for the entrance and fought my way through dozens crushing outward.

Outside, the panel van was gone.

I ran to my rental, weaving around the injured and frightened. After a complete check of the mall perimeter—slow and deliberate—I knew it was hopeless.

The van had disappeared. Probably before the blast. Damn, I hadn't even recorded the license plate number.

Kevin's last breaths had been a warning. He'd strained to give me the address of whoever blew up the mall. *No, Kevin, it wasn't safe.* You tried to warn me. Khalifah, G ... Maya. I failed him.

What more had Kevin taken into death?

Sirens wailed and traffic gridlocked. I considered returning to the mall to aid those I could or at least give the cops a hand and report what I knew.

I couldn't. I was in over my head enough.

Last night, I'd witnessed my brother's murder. I was already on the cops' radar, not to mention the FBI's. There was no longer any way to avoid the crotchety old fart sitting at a desk in Langley, probably counting my $879,928.66 and trying to figure out where I'd gone. Now, I'd just stumbled into a major terrorist attack on our homeland the likes of which no one had seen on our shores for more than a decade.

There was no hiding any longer. I was up to my neck in trouble.

There was something more, too. Something more troublesome. More personal. Kevin had the bomber's address. Although I'd given it to the cops, I had arrived "just in time" to witness a horrific attack—*again.* Two "just in times" in less than twenty-four hours. Both involving Kevin Mallory.

What had he been into? Khalifah. G. Maya in Baltimore. Now this.

There were two things I was more certain of than anything I'd been in years. First, Kevin Mallory got in over his head and had died for it. Second, I couldn't stay below the radar any longer.

Anonymity be damned.

Oscar LaRue was about to know exactly where I had landed.

CHAPTER 6

Day 2: May 16, 1135 Hours, Daylight Saving Time
Mount Weather Emergency Operations Center, Bluemont, Virginia

THE BELL 412 helicopter banked east over the Blue Ridge Mountains and circled the Mount Weather Emergency Operations Center, preparing to land. On approach, it slowed and floated down to rest on the M1-landing pad inside the Center's secured perimeter. The pilot gave the all clear to his only passenger and waited for the short, elderly man to climb down through the side door. As soon as his passenger was clear of the rotors, the pilot waved and lifted the Bell skyward to retrace its route east.

The elderly man, a slender gentleman with thin, gray hair combed neatly back from his forehead, took off his round eyeglasses and polished them with a fine, soft chamois. He had a round, German face and pale skin blemished with sunburn and liver spots—the product of Germanic genes, too much sun, and his more than seventy-five years. He replaced his glasses over wrinkled, dry cheeks, adjusted their fit, and checked his watch.

1135 hours. On schedule. LaRue liked—*demanded*—precision.

A black Mercedes repositioned from the reception building to the helipad. The driver, a striking man of average height with dark hair, jumped out. He walked around the car and opened the rear passenger door. His narrow face and dark skin hinted at his

Southwestern roots and showed more than his fifty-one years. He leaned in close to the Germanic gentleman and briefed him on a bulletin he'd just received.

LaRue's face blanched. "Casualties, Shepard?"

"Two hundred and fifty and counting, sir." Shepard's eyes were stones and the two scars along his temple stood out. "A busy shopping day. There's an urgent call, sir. On the box."

"So, it has begun." LaRue nodded. "Please wait here until I am through."

Inside the car, with the door closed behind him, LaRue tapped a button on the communications panel affixed to the rear of the front seat. He retrieved the call.

"Good morning, Director. What have you?"

The voice was dry, emotionless, and launched into a briefing that turned LaRue's eyebrows upward and his temper hot. The voice continued for several minutes until LaRue cleared his voice and ended the barrage.

"I have just arrived. I have no response yet. I'll need a few hours, perhaps a couple days, to analyze our situation. They have moved prematurely, and we failed to anticipate that. You gave me assurances in Bahrain that I would have the necessary time."

The voice grew louder, harder. Another uninterrupted soliloquy.

LaRue gazed outside at nothing. "I am very clear on the priorities, thank you. You must be clear on their consequences. We cannot move prematurely until we have identified all the terror cells. If we fail to do so, dangerous elements could slip through our grasp. I recognize that the President will want to act, but he must wait until the source of this attack is confirmed and all the cells—"

The voice broke in and LaRue's face stiffened. "I am well aware of the precarious nature. You must also understand that things may not be as they appear. This is precisely why I am here. Is it not? The President must remain patient. The results, well, they could be more catastrophic. They could be wrong."

The voice grumbled something that made LaRue smile a thin, contemptuous smile. "Of course. As of now, I am on a leave of absence. I accept total responsibility. Give me a week to make the assessment. I think you can endure me that long, no? Of course, I will need support. I'm sure no one will voice any objection. My tenure has afforded me this small divergence, no?"

Silence.

"Excellent. You should know Khalifah is indeed present."

LaRue ended the call and tapped on the window. A moment later, Shepard slid behind the steering wheel and glanced into the rearview mirror.

LaRue found Shepard's eyes in the mirror. "Have you brought my things, Shepard?"

Shepard's taut, rippled muscles strained the fabric of his dark suitcoat when he hefted a duffel and lifted it over the seat to him. "Yes, sir. The rest is in the trunk."

LaRue unzipped the bag and surveyed its contents. He opened a manila envelope and fanned out several thousand dollars in currency. Then he retrieved a small ballistic nylon handbag containing a Walther PPK .380 semiautomatic pistol, four magazines, and a silencer.

"Ah, very good."

LaRue sat quietly for a moment and waited until they had passed the security checkpoint and started down the southern slope of Mount Weather. "Shepard, it seems I've begun a little holiday. Your services are no longer sanctioned. Should I arrange for someone else to assist me?"

"Holiday?" Shepard glanced into the rearview again. "Will we be getting dirty again, sir?"

"Filthy."

"Anything I should know from your communication?"

"Our benefactors are worried about the uncertainties."

"Uncertainties?"

"Imagine that. Yes. They do not like uncertainty. If there were not any uncertainties, I would be concerned."

Shepard nodded.

LaRue briefed him on part of his conversation with the Director of Central Intelligence.

Shepard nodded several times and drove on.

LaRue finished his soliloquy with, "There are, once again, too many cooks in this kitchen. Don't you think, Shepard?"

"I was thinking that very thing, sir. An odd mix of loyalties."

LaRue smiled. "Ah, do not confuse loyalty with complicity. Sometimes, despite what the bureaucrats wish us all to believe, the enemy of our enemy is still our enemy."

CHAPTER 7

Day 2: May 16, 1235 Hours, Daylight Saving Time
25783 Christian Run, Manassas, Virginia

A BLOCK FROM the run-down cement block rambler, I pulled to the curb and studied the neighborhood. There was no sign of the panel van. The bombers hadn't returned. Traffic was nil, and the only movement on the street for two blocks was an old woman walking an old mutt. She passed me, crossed the street, and continued down Christian Run back toward the main boulevard.

I was in a precarious situation. Shocking, I know. I'd arrived in town less than forty-eight hours ago and had planned on staying anonymous and under everyone's radar. Murder and terror changed the rules. My empty retirement account did, too. It was clear Oscar LaRue knew I was missing and had taken my money to ensure I popped up my head sooner rather than later. He was sending me a message. LaRue was a controlling SOB.

LaRue and I were pals. Really.

Before I rolled down the street to the rambler, I pulled out my cell phone. "Dammit, Kevin. Now we're both in the shit."

First, I turned the phone's GPS back on—something I'd turned off soon before I'd left Doha. Next, I dialed a telephone number from memory and waited for it to connect to a mindless answering service buried somewhere in Langley, Virginia.

"This is Hunter from Doha." I rattled off my contractor ID number and a code word that signaled I was not under duress. "Hiya, Oscar. Sorry for leaving without talking to you. I'll explain later. For now, I'll trade you $879,928.66 for Khalifah and Maya in Baltimore. Hugs and kisses."

I tapped off the call and put the rental in drive.

Before my wheels rubbed up against the cement curb in front of 25783 Christian Run, my message was delivered. A computer encrypted my phone message, pinged a satellite overhead, confirmed my cell phone's exact ground position, and transferred my message to a cell phone somewhere in the world. What transpired in the few moments thereafter was anyone's guess. Mine was that I had less than sixty minutes to do what I needed here.

So I did.

I slipped out of the rental and looked around. From a haphazard gaggle of trash cans nearby, I pulled a pizza box off the pile and walked to the front door. I rang the doorbell and juggled the empty pizza box precariously atop my .45 semiautomatic.

No response.

I knocked.

Nothing.

After stolen glances around the neighborhood, I walked around the rambler's corner and disappeared through some overgrown shrubs. Beyond the shrubs, I shouldered in a tall wooden fence gate, ditched the pizza box, and found a rear yard of dead grass and weeds surrounded by a six-foot-high privacy fence—a lawn long ago abandoned.

No one around.

At the rear door, I banged loudly. I checked the door. Locked. On my tiptoes, I peeked in the small, eight-inch-square door window but saw nothing but an empty mudroom.

Normally, in situations like this, I'd wait on a breaching team and drone surveillance. We'd sweep the area, make sure no hostiles were waiting in ambush, and crash through the door with fire superiority.

I had none of that.

What I did have was a heavy, folding survival knife that took only a few seconds to force the cheap rear door lock and pop the door open.

I followed my .45's front sights through.

Two turns later, out of the mudroom, through the tiny, sparkling-clean kitchen, and into a scantily furnished living room. There, the reason no one had answered the doorbell was clear.

The residents were no longer home. Well, they were there, but they were no longer living.

An older couple was there. I always had a hard time with the ages of Arabs, especially those living in the small Middle Eastern villages. Life was too often hard, and the sun and weather aged them beyond their years before they were thirty.

This couple was no different.

They were most likely husband and wife, and from the few framed photographs on the table beside them, they were also Mom and Dad. Mom and Dad sat head to head in the center of a badly worn sofa against the far wall. Blood had emptied from them and pooled on their laps, chest, and sofa cushions. Their hands were bound in front of them and their throats had been cut. Death had taken no time at all.

Bloody footprints crossed the room and led into a dark, narrow hallway.

I took a breath, listened to silence, and followed the fading work boot tracks to the last door at the end of the hall.

Oh, hell no.

A young girl of maybe sixteen or seventeen lay facedown on a mattress near the window. The room held a frameless bed and a single dresser that was untouched and showed no signs of robbery. The blinds were drawn, and I had to strain to see the details I regretted seeing at all.

The girl had been raped. Brutalized. I wasn't an expert, but her body was a road map to her end. What had been a modest, dark dress was torn and bloodied around her. Part of it had been used to bind her hands over her head. There was bruising and contusions from a beating she'd probably taken trying to stop the inevitable. Her ankles showed the bruises of handprints as though one had held her down while another savagely took her.

At the end, there was only the knife across her throat that ended her terror. Those last few seconds were perhaps solace from the savagery she'd endured.

Bile rose in my throat. I retreated to the hall, where I found a tidy bathroom and fought back the retch.

After searching the remainder of the small house, I found nothing but an old, crumbling home kept neat and clean by the family who lived within its walls. There were no hidden weapon stashes, explosives or their mechanics, or even a bomb-maker's workbench. The refrigerator was nearly empty. The cupboards held the packages of a newly settled Middle Eastern family trying to assimilate to their new Western world—bagged rice and flour, a near-empty jar of peanut butter, fresh-baked flatbread, containers of dried beans, and fresh fruits. Nothing extravagant. Simple country foods that were as close to those they'd had in their cupboards back home. Wherever home had been.

This was the family of the young man who'd bombed the mall. An old black-and-white photograph on an end table near Mom told me he was their son. There were no clues as to who the other men had been. Had the son gone voluntarily? It hadn't seemed so when they walked him to the van earlier, but at the mall, he seemed calmer and in control. He'd walked inside without escort and had done the deed presumably unbridled by any captors.

Yet here, behind him, his family had been butchered.

If they were hostages used to force the son to commit the attack, they were executed as witnesses soon after. If they were not hostages, had the son fallen within the evil spell of the other men?

I'd seen this tactic before. I'd picked up these pieces before. I'd seen it from ISIS, the Taliban, and the Mujahideen before them. But they were in the age-defying villages of Afghanistan and Pakistan. Places where law was void and tribal power was often at the tip of a scimitar. Life was not supreme and radical Islam allowed no peace before death. Violence was a tool, death a means to an end, and terror a playbook.

But this was home. This was America.

Bile rose in my throat again as I holstered the .45 and looked at Mom and Dad on the couch. Dear God, why? The hate and violence was not *"over there"* any longer. It was here. Here and now. Right now.

A terrible feeling struck me. Those who did this. Those who brutalized this family. They were just getting the party started.

CHAPTER 8

Day 2: May 16, 1330 Hours, Daylight Saving Time
25783 Christian Run, Manassas, Virginia

AFTER SWITCHING MY cell phone GPS off again and backtracking out of the single-level rambler—there was no need for Oscar LaRue to catch up with me quite yet—I moved my rental car two blocks down Christian Run and waited for the cavalry.

I didn't have to wait long.

First, a dirty, dented four-door work truck rounded the corner a block ahead and made a slow pass by the rambler. There were four men inside, and the back of the truck was laden with ladders and equipment of home tradesmen at a local job site. Then the truck returned and pulled into the rambler's driveway. The four men climbed out, carrying tool kits. They immediately went around the house through the side shrubs where I'd entered earlier.

Minutes later, two white vans with door panels that read "American-Made Renovations" rounded the corner and pulled up to the rambler's curb. Six men climbed out and retrieved tool kits from the rear of the van, then they moved to the front door. One of them tapped his ear, nodded, and the workmen pressed through the door and disappeared inside.

Anyone in the neighborhood who noticed the workmen descending on the house might have wondered how the new Arab family inside had the means for renovations. Of course, none would have noticed the earwig communication pieces or the unusually bulky work clothes the workmen wore—coveralls that hid Kevlar body armor and protective breaching gear. The tool bags did not hold tradesman's hammers, screwdrivers, and power tools, but MP-5 silenced machine guns, tactical armaments, and other assault paraphernalia.

I strained to make out the men. Not among them was the short, scuffling man with Germanic features and ever-smudged eyeglasses. He was absent.

By the time any neighbor had given a second thought to the construction crew, the CIA tactical response team was already inside assessing the body count and meticulously scouring the home for intelligence. A few moments later, a tall, thin man wearing a white hard hat walked outside. He spoke into an encrypted cell phone and scanned the area in slow, careful movements. Twice he glanced skyward and once threw a thumbs-up.

I started my rental and slowly made the trip past the rambler. White hard hat and I made eye contact. I nodded and headed for the highway and the drive back to Winchester.

Officially, I was back on Oscar LaRue's radar.

CHAPTER 9

Day 2: May 16, 1345 Hours, Daylight Saving Time
Old Town Winchester, Virginia

"SHOULD THEY TAKE Hunter into custody, sir?" Shepard asked LaRue across the coffee table. "They can recover him in twenty minutes."

"No." LaRue snapped his hand up. "I did not anticipate him moving so swiftly, but he's on to something. Let him run awhile and see where he leads us. He knows he is no longer invisible. He called for assistance, after all."

"Yes, sir. But . . ."

"No." LaRue stood and walked across the hotel suite to gaze out the window into Old Town Winchester. "You have concerns, Shepard?"

"Hunter is acting reckless. I will forgive him for now. His brother's death has dulled his common sense. Assuming he ever had any. But I worry he might start bouncing all over, considering the consequences."

LaRue smiled a rueful smile and turned back around. "Yes, consequences."

"He might also trip into things he shouldn't. After all, he's not supposed to be here at all."

LaRue continued to smile.

"Is he, sir?"

LaRue removed his eyeglasses and began polishing them with a chamois from his shirt pocket. "I want Christian Run processed within an hour. Retrieve any links to our concerns and leave the rest a crime scene. It'll take the Bureau that long to sort out the mess at Fair Oaks. One hour. No more. Monitor the authorities, Shepard. If there is any sign they have discovered Christian Run sooner than one hour, extract our team."

"Yes, sir."

"I'm going for a walk." LaRue headed for the suite door. "One hour, Shepard. No more."

"What about Caine? What if Hunter..."

"Ah, yes, Caine." LaRue stopped and turned back to Shepard. The smile was gone and in its place was a solemn, dark frown. "We will act on Caine at the proper time. You are correct. Hunter will flail here and there. When the time is right, I'll rein him in. Until then, let him flail. It might be to our advantage."

"So, he's bait."

LaRue lifted a chin. "Bait is for the unknown, the unwilling, non-volunteers. Hunter stepped onto the field voluntarily. He is not bait. He is a decoy to flush the prey."

"A pawn." Shepard caught the old spymaster's eyes.

"We are all pawns, Shepard. But, we can choose when to become knights."

"Sure, sure." Shepard forced a laugh. "Whenever you—the king—allow us to. The key is to stay alive long enough."

"Precisely, Shepard. Precisely."

CHAPTER 10

Day 2: May 16, 1400 Hours, Daylight Saving Time
Winchester, Virginia

THE DRIVE BACK to Winchester was painful. Inside, my guts churned and my aches and pains from having been blown twenty feet into a display case began to take their toll. Besides the pain, there was disappointment—in me. Kevin had tried to warn me, and I'd failed him. I'd given the information to the police, but they hadn't acted. Hundreds were dead. I hadn't acted either. I'd simply been an observer—*again*. If this had been Kabul or Baghdad, my senses would have been off the charts and I would have, perhaps, anticipated the pending violence. But no. This was Virginia—the States—suicide bombers didn't live here. Right?

Wrong.

My senses were dulled by the earth beneath my feet—home turf. What if I'd tried to take the bomber? What if I'd called Bond or Bacarro and warned them what I was watching? What if I'd simply called 911 and reported the panel van and suspicious acts?

What if? What if? *Damn.*

Then, there had been 25783 Christian Run. The old couple. The young girl.

Damn. Damn. Damn.

I didn't need more cops and Feds and interrogations, so I returned to my cheap hotel east of Winchester and dropped into bed. It was too late now, anyway. The tactical team would handle Christian Run the way Oscar LaRue deemed necessary. The FBI would be along soon enough. For now, I'd leave the bad guys to the good guys. Whether that was the right choice or the wrong choice, it was my choice.

I had other things to do. I didn't need the cops crawling all over me asking the million-dollar question—what were the odds I'd accidentally fallen into two bloody crime scenes in less than twenty-four hours? It was bad enough Oscar LaRue knew where I was. Him, I might be able to negotiate with. Handcuffs and a jail cell were not negotiable.

I was exhausted. Late-night gunfights and suicide bombers will do that to you. Yet, sleep evaded me again. First, there was tension and angst. Then silence. There were no indistinguishable voices. No running feet. No gunfire in the distance. Just silence. Strange, foreign, empty silence. It was deafening. Lying there, memories took me back to age seventeen and my battles with Kevin. We fought over everything. More like a father and son than brothers. He won like a father. I rebelled like a son. In the hotel air-conditioning, I lay in sweat and wished for that urgent call to arms that so frequented my past.

Crisis. Action. Reaction . . . *incoming*. Something to feel at home. Anything.

Relax, Hunter, you are home.

I gave up on sleep and took a long, cold shower. The two cups of bitter hotel-room coffee, a quick change of clothes from my duffel, and I felt almost human.

I checked my cell phone. No messages. Oscar LaRue was content to have me at arm's length. That couldn't be good.

No cops at my door meant my name wasn't on a police BOLO or arrest order requiring some bureaucrat to bail me out. That has never happened to me, mind you. I'm just saying.

Consultants like me—those who operate under fuzzy government contracts—are a strange lot. Government agencies with nicknames like "the Outfit" and "the Company" contract with the likes of me to provide all manner of services, many of which they prefer to be handled by someone other than US government employees. They do that for lots of reasons. The biggest is the old cliché—*plausible deniability*. Simply translated, they want you to do certain things—things they don't want spoken out loud or on the record. Things they don't want their name on. But things they really, really want done. That way, if something bad happens, they can throw up their hands and shout, "It wasn't us!"

When I got an "assignment," like chasing down stolen war treasures or hunting faces on a deck of playing cards, Uncle Sam didn't want complications. Of course, we're talking the Middle East. Complications are on the menu under appetizers, entrées, and dessert. Complications are just part of the equation. Complications like trained Afghan troops who become insurgents by night and kill their comrades. Stolen treasures can wind up in the hands of bad guys who sell them for the money to pay the wayward Afghan troops who turn on their comrades. Faces on the playing cards can be found in the most embarrassing, delicate places like an ally's safe house, and require "special handling." When these things happen, old Uncle wants to wash his hands of anything "untoward." *Untoward* is why they have consultants. We're one tax form short of being Uncle Sam's employee and two toes shy of a mercenary.

Potato—*potahto*.

Unfortunately, Uncle gets upset when one of his illegitimate nephews disappears from the playground without permission.

He gets downright nasty. Nasty like you got caught smoking dope with your boss' daughter . . . in your boss' car . . . after curfew . . . naked. That's never happened to me, either. But, I am said nephew, and I was most assuredly in deep trouble. Finding a crime scene littered with the family of the recent suicide bomber in hometown USA was not exactly the way I wanted to contact my boss and mentor, Oscar LaRue, and whisper that I was home and okay. Hopefully, he'd be too busy with his cloak and dagger to visit, and maybe I still had a few days to find Kevin's killer before Uncle came knocking on my door with handcuffs and a blindfold.

Sure, I'm being melodramatic. *I hope I am.*

The sunlight was bright and the day blue and breezy. I'd forgotten just how beautiful a Virginia spring could be. Even on this day, my gut churned when Kevin crossed my thoughts and Noor's face played in my vision.

Noor. I had to help.

I typed her address into my cell phone and climbed into my rental car.

It took me thirty minutes to wander northwest of town and find her place just off the county highway. I bumped along a secondary road until the sexy lady inside my cell phone told me to make my turn in a quarter mile. A few seconds later, the only mailbox I'd seen for a mile appeared. The closer I got to the driveway, the sicker my insides felt. I pulled around Noor's mailbox and bumped down the long gravel driveway toward her house. My meager breakfast threatened to reappear, and twice I nearly retreated. I checked the map program three different times to ensure I was at the right house.

Really? I needed a map to find her house?

I'd never been there before. I'd never seen photographs or read letters or chatted on the phone about "their place." Kevin's life—my

brother's world—was more foreign to me than many Afghan sol-
diers I'd trained. With them, I knew their homes and what made
them tick. Most of the time. Ahead, the two-story, gray-and-white
American Foursquare grabbed my lungs and *squeezed.*

What was I doing? I glanced in the rearview mirror and momentarily hoped the men in black would find me and take me
away before I parked.

No such luck.

The driveway was a few hundred feet long, and I needed every
foot to quell the rebellion raging between my gut and my brain. As
I parked, my stomach twitched like a schoolboy at his first dance.

Noor's property was secluded a mile from the closest residence.
It was an older home surrounded by trees and farm fields, giving it
a rustic, country appearance. To the right, east I think, was an old,
single-story barn with a small, weatherworn farm tractor parked
in front. To the west, a stone's throw from the house, was a two-
story garage with curtained windows and an outside staircase to
the second floor. To the side of the house was a fenced-in field
that extended several acres beyond. Another post-and-rail fence
enclosed two large corrals and four horses.

Kevin was a cowboy?

Suck it up, Hunter. You wouldn't know. Get over it.

Thinking about Noor and Sam Mallory made me slip my .45
out and tuck it under the front seat of the rental car. It was against
every fiber in my body to lose the weapon, but meeting her for
only the second time in my life wearing a gun might not get me
the warm welcome I hoped for. I wasn't sure how much Kevin
had told her about me, but walking into her home while packing
a gun was surely not something she'd take easily. She needed to
get to know the kinder, gentler me first. I'm sure there is one hidden somewhere.

"Noor?" I called out, heading onto the front poor. "Noor?"

I knocked and peeked in the large front window. There were no lights on. No movement. No household sounds. I wandered around the side near the barn to a stone and brick patio. There sat an immaculate yard, patio, and sunporch, all creatively designed and furnished with expensive things. Several lawn chairs, a fire pit, and an old gas barbecue grill waited for a weekend party that wouldn't come for a very long time. The setting belonged in the pages of a country life magazine.

Kevin was doing all right for a copper.

At the sunporch, I peered inside. There was an inside door that looked like it led into the kitchen. The inner door was ajar and I could hear faint sounds inside.

"Noor? It's Jon, Noor."

The noises ceased.

"Noor?" It sounded silly, but I called out, "It's Kevin's brother."

I opened the screen door and stepped inside. "Noor?"

In the kitchen, I found a flame on the stove below a pot. A line of ingredients—for homemade spaghetti sauce, I think—sat on the countertop beside an empty, smoking pot. I turned the burner off.

"Noor?"

A faint, almost imperceptible sound—the creak of a chair on hardwood—came from somewhere down the hall ahead of me.

Muscle memory sent my hand behind me, but there was nothing waiting there. My .45 was in the car. I looked around but there were no obvious weapons visible in the kitchen. No knife rack or cast-iron fry pans. Nothing. Too many cabinets and too many drawers made a quick search impractical, so I grabbed the first weapon I found—two giant cans of whole tomatoes.

If my pals in Kabul could see me now.

At the end of the hall, I stopped beneath an archway leading into the living room. It was a comfy room with two overstuffed chairs and a couch facing a massive fieldstone fireplace. The window blinds were drawn and the room darkened.

Noor.

She sat to my left on a wooden straight-backed chair. She faced the far wall to my right. Her hands were folded on her lap. Her face was pale—ashen—and her eyes fixed across the room.

When I eased another step closer, her eyes exploded—wide and afraid—and darted from me to the far wall.

There, barely ten feet away, stood a man. He was holding a gun.

CHAPTER 11

Day 2: May 16, 1620 Hours, Daylight Saving Time
Noor Mallory's Residence, Frederick County, Virginia

CANNED TOMATOES, ESPECIALLY the 28-ounce size, are good for a lot of things like stews, sauces, and, my favorite, chili. Now, they were for artillery tartare.

I slid left into the living room and hurled one heavy can at the assailant. He reacted as I anticipated—he twisted himself out of the can's path, swung his left hand up to protect his face, and fired his pistol at the spot where I'd been. His defensive reaction put him off-balance and the shot went wide into the wall a foot from me. Before he could recover, I spun around like a baseball pitcher catching a runner off first base. At the apogee of my turn, I hurled the second tomato can. It slammed him in the right eye, and he staggered backward against the fireplace.

I was on him before he recovered. My groin kick connected solidly. *Rule two of mortal combat—fair play isn't required.*

As my kick landed, I grabbed his gun hand, slammed it backward against the fireplace stones, and twisted. The gun fell. I drove a knee into his midsection. He faltered to keep his balance. Still holding his gun hand, my right elbow cracked into his temple. Air exploded from him and his eyes rolled back.

He dropped facedown on the hearth.

"Jon!" Noor cried.

"Stay back." I retreated a step and grabbed his gun. "Are you all right?"

A pause; then, "Yes, he did not touch me."

"What'd he want?"

"I do not know. I came home and found him searching my house. He asked nothing. He did not seem to know what to do with me. He never spoke to me."

Lucky. "Where's Sam?"

She walked across the hardwood and opened the window blinds. "He left on his motorcycle just before this man came. I do not know where he went. He never tells me."

Double lucky. I knelt down on one knee beside the assailant and rolled him onto his side. He was young, pale-faced, and bald. His features were hard and strong—burly and robust. He was clean-shaven and had no distinguishing marks—no tattoos or scars or eyepatches. Okay, eyepatches would make him a pirate, but there wasn't anything that stood out about him. He wore jeans, cowboy boots, and a black t-shirt beneath an old, dark-green military field jacket.

"Who is this man?" Noor asked. "Why is he in my house?"

I reached for his wallet. "I'll ask him. If he's a good boy, he might be able to walk to the police car later."

"I will call Dave."

Oh sure, call Dave. "Wait a few minutes, Noor. He might talk to me faster than them."

"But . . ."

I looked back at her. "Trust me."

"*Otyebis.*" The assailant's left hand slashed up. He had a knife from nowhere that sliced across my shoulder. His strike surprised me, and he followed with a kick to my knee. His boot heel knocked my leg from beneath me, and I teetered off-balance. He rolled away and landed a hard, head-rocking heel into my jaw before I hit the hardwood. He was on his feet and out the door before my eyes refocused.

Stunned at first, I checked my arm and found only torn jacket fabric and a faint cut beneath—no more than a scratch—across my shoulder.

I went after him.

At the kitchen door, I saw him disappear behind the barn. I followed with his 9-millimeter pistol out and ready. At the barn's corner, I scanned the woods as the roar of a distant motorcycle told me I was too late.

The chase was over before it started.

It had been pure luck to take him in the first place. He could have easily killed Noor and then me, had it not been for an old adage I'd learned on my first tour in Iraq—the last one to move dies. When ambushed, you assault. Surprise often wins the battle.

Noor's living room had been the ambush. I assaulted. Had I been armed, he'd be dead now. He survived my artillery barrage of whole tomatoes. Unfortunately, he'd also used an old tactic that I'd learned in the Army—play possum until the enemy is off guard. Then counterattack. I screwed up.

Rubbing the slice on my jacket sleeve, I knew I was lucky to be alive. A few inches to the left and he would have taken my head off. Still, I'd learned something very important.

"*Otyebis*" was slang and my knowledge of idioms was rusty, but I was sure the man had told me to fuck off—in Russian.

CHAPTER 12

Day 2: May 16, 1650 Hours, Daylight Saving Time
Old Town, Winchester, Virginia

"Follow," ordered LaRue, as he sat back and sipped a cup of tea. "Are we prepared to intercept?"

Shepard tapped the keyboard that sat atop the table in front of him. The table was a combination command station and dinner table. It was littered with an empty lunch tray, a still-steaming pot of Earl Grey tea, and a carafe of coffee. Across the room, the large 52-inch TV screen tracked the small image of a lone man on a motorcycle driving through the country. The bike weaved around a farm tractor on the dusty county road and accelerated around a turn. A moment later, the words "Tracking" flashed on the screen and a bull's-eye encircled the motorcycle as it made its way southeast toward Winchester. Across the bottom of the screen, like a late-breaking news story, the motorcycle's position in satellite GPS longitudes and latitudes appeared, then translated into road names, compass bearings, and distance from the command center.

The command center was LaRue's three-room suite at the George Washington hotel in downtown Winchester. It came complete with room service, fresh linens, and state-of-the-art surveillance.

LaRue rarely traveled second class.

"Yes, sir," Shepard said. "A team is standing by."

"Execute."

The unmanned aerial vehicle, or UAV, banked sharply and leveled above the motorcycle some one thousand feet overhead. Unlike the larger, sophisticated military or intelligence drones used in Afghanistan and Syria, this UAV was only four feet in diameter—barely larger than a home enthusiast's radio-controlled replica. Shepard had nicknamed the device "Tweety." Now Tweety banked left to maintain its position above and slightly behind the motorcycle that had just escaped Noor Mallory's farm.

Shepard spoke quietly into a headset to two men eating lunch at a roadside convenience store three miles ahead. An instant later, Tweety's feed was relayed to their cell phones.

"Ready, sir."

"How long has our boy been in the area, Shepard?"

Shepard grinned. "Less than twenty-four hours, sir."

"My, my." LaRue removed his eyeglasses for a cleaning. "He does tend to stir things up rather quickly."

"You're surprised, sir?"

"Oh, no." LaRue slid his eyeglasses back on and reached for his Earl Grey. "If it were not so, *then* I would be surprised."

CHAPTER 13

Day 2: May 16, 1700 Hours, Daylight Saving Time
Noor Mallory's Residence, Frederick County, Virginia

"I CALLED DAVE," Noor said, nervously pacing the kitchen. "He cannot make it, so they are sending someone else. There has been a terrorist attack in Fair Oaks. It's awful."

"Yes, I, ah . . . heard." *Should I tell her?* "Did Dave say anything about it?"

"I did not speak with him. Everyone on the task force is very busy."

"Where's your television?"

She gestured above the refrigerator to a small television and picked up a small remote. She switched the TV on.

Every channel had the story. Every channel was the same. Fire trucks, police, FBI, and dozens of ambulances surrounded the shopping mall I'd been at just hours before. Smoke and flames billowed out the top of the four-story structure. Chaos consumed the picture. Bodies and injured consumed the reporters. Fear consumed the audience. On the bottom of the screen, the ticker commented on various sources, but the last one I caught sent a chill—"*President calls for calm. Puts nation on highest state of alert since 9/11. Military at the ready.*"

Military at the ready meant the Joint Chiefs were reviewing one of a hundred or more special operations plans put together after 9/11 for just this contingency. All around the world the DefCon—Defense Condition—was prepared to nudge upward to DefCon 3—increased readiness. One step closer to war. Special Operations units supporting the Middle East would be packing up and readying to board transports to the region. Those in the region—my brethren—would be primed and ready to fire at whatever targets the Joint Chiefs dictated. Everyone would be on pins and needles. Someone's hand would be on the trigger— waiting on the President's orders. This President was not known for his patience in these matters. All he needed was the right target and—*Boom*—there we go again.

"This could get ugly," I said to Noor. "Fast."

Noor's hands went to her face. "I cannot believe this. Not here. Not again."

"Believe it, Noor." Should I tell her what I'd witnessed? "We should talk."

"Talk? Yes, we should." She flipped off the television. "And you, Jon Mallory, what kind of business consultant are you?"

Huh? "What do you mean?"

"No, no, thank you for saving me." She came to me and wrapped her arms around me for a brief embrace. She lingered for a moment—perhaps a moment too long—before retreating across the room. "I did not know business consultants could fight as you do."

What exactly had Kevin told her about me? Business consultant? Are you kidding me?

I smiled and diverted her attention. "Are you sure you're okay?"

"Frightened but fine."

"That guy never said a word to you?" I flexed my arm a few times and massaged my knee where the assailant kicked me. "What was he doing when you walked in?"

"He said nothing. He was searching Kevin's den. He turned, pulled his gun, and forced me into the living room. He spoke on his cell phone, but I could not hear. He spoke very low. His words were foreign and I could not say what language. I was very frightened. Then we sat like we were waiting for something or someone."

"You've never seen him before?"

She shook her head. "No, but he is a dangerous man. Even when we heard you come in the house, he was relaxed. It was as if he knew everything that was about to happen. I remember men such as he."

"Men like him?"

"In Sāri. Where I was a young girl." She looked away. "He was evil. He had done evil many times before."

She was right. He wasn't startled when I came in. He could have easily shot me the moment I appeared in the living room archway. Instead, he just waited, watched me. Waited for what? Reinforcements?

"We got lucky, Noor."

"Yes, of course."

"He . . . didn't find what he came for. Why else would he make a phone call after grabbing you?"

"Oh, I understand. He was reporting to someone?"

"Yes." I stood and raised the assailant's 9-millimeter. "I better take a look around the house. Just to be sure."

She stood. "I do not wish to be alone."

Outside, we found only locked doors and windows, a wheelbarrow full of gardening mulch, and a rake left facing up in the grass that attacked me and left a welt on my cheek. There were no knife or pry bar scratch marks around any of the door or window locks. No cracked or broken glass where a thief broke in. There were no forced locks, broken hinges, or other signs of nefarious deeds. There was just nothing. I checked the two-story garage, but the doors were locked and showed no signs of tampering. The barn was unlocked, but there were no thieves hiding inside. Just a custom-built three-wheeled motorcycle trike shined and ready for the road.

Kevin was a cowboy and a biker? To think he called *me* a risk-taker?

Twenty minutes later, we returned to the kitchen.

I said. "Were your doors locked, Noor?"

"Yes, of course. No one around here locks theirs, but Kevin insisted." Tears welled in her eyes. "He was never here. Even when he was not working, he was not here. So, I was extra careful."

"It's okay, Noor. Let's check the inside."

"Yes, good." She pointed down the hall. "I will follow you."

She narrated the rooms as we searched the downstairs. Their home was warm and friendly with a side order of expensive antiques and good taste. The kitchen was small and modestly furnished. The main downstairs hall traversed the entire length of the house. It began at the front foyer beside the large living room. Around overstuffed furniture, the walls were covered with bookshelves loaded with books and a plethora of knickknacks and framed photographs. There was a small dining room with family photos on a cherry hutch stuffed with family heirloom dishes and crystal. On the back wall hung an elegantly framed set of photographs of an elderly Middle Eastern couple—Noor's family.

She checked each room's drawers and cubbies. Each time, she gave me the "nothing's missing" headshake. With each room, my breath became more evasive and my heart beat faster. But not from trepidation that a henchman lurked close. It was Kevin and Noor's life. The Mallory home. It was filled with memories and remember-whens. With each step, my breath labored and my body threatened to turn and run. Photographs were everywhere. Frame after frame of reminiscences. Weddings and outings. Big gatherings where Kevin's was the only familiar face. Camping trips. Waterskiing. Target shooting at the range. Teaching Sam to drive. Sam on his motorcycle. Kevin on his. Kevin here. Kevin there. Kevin alive.

The wooziness invaded me. By the time we reached Kevin's den in the far corner of the house, my wounds were deep and severe. The room had hardwood floors, tall, low windows, and a high ceiling. An old wooden teacher's desk sat centered on the rear wall facing the doorway. On the side wall stood a file cabinet and a shelf where a fax machine sat idle and piled with papers. Along the other wall, bordered by two antique floor lamps, was an old leather recliner that faced the windows. There was a twelve-gauge pump shotgun and a bolt-action scoped rifle resting in a gun rack behind the desk. This was a man's room. But the deeper I looked, the emptier and sadder it became.

The man was missing.

Emotions descended—a foreign feeling. Kevin's dusty bookshelves pulled me to a photograph of him, Noor, and Sam at some celebration. Sam was a young teenager, perhaps fifteen. Smiles all around. Even though family photos and bric-a-brac adorned every shelf and cranny around me, not one memory was familiar. I shared nothing. There was a void in the room, and it was me. There were no photographs, no postcards. There were no souvenirs from my exotic travels. Nothing. This place—this home—and family and I were strangers.

Shame drowned me.

Grow up, Hunter. You blew it.

"Jon?" Noor stood in the doorway as I tried to clumsily wipe a traitorous tear from my eye. "Are you all right?"

"Absolutely. Not a scratch." I flexed my left arm and noted the knife cut across my sleeve and the thin, shallow cut below. "Well, not a big one." A photograph on the bookshelf bade my attention, and I picked it up. It was of a rustic pine-board hunting cabin surrounded by birch trees and firewood piles. "Dad's old hunting cabin. We had good times there."

Memories cascaded in and swirled around me like a kaleidoscope. Yet, despite the years we'd spent at that cabin, this photograph had neither of us in it. It only captured the empty, lonely cabin secluded in the Shenandoah Mountains in mid-fall. A lonely photograph vacant of life.

"I am so sorry, Jon." Noor's voice was meek. "We sold the cabin a year ago. Money. Please, we had no choice. I am sorry."

A gut punch. "He should have told me. I would've helped."

"You did not know him, did you?" She looked away.

Ouch. I changed the topic. "How about some coffee?"

"Yes, coffee." She turned and walked out. "I can feel him here, Jon. Maybe you can, too."

Would I?

She disappeared down the hall.

I had no idea what I was looking for. I wasn't a detective. Nothing in my training was going to help me sleuth around Kevin's things and find the "Ah ha!" piece of evidence. Now, if, let's say, a balaclava-wearing thug were hiding in one of the filing cabinets, I could handle it. Or if Noor had issues with a West Virginia tribe of anti-American, gun-slinging roughnecks, oh yeah, I'm your man. But a detective? Nope.

After twenty minutes of searching, I had found nothing.

I turned and found Noor watching me from the doorway. Her face was sad and angry at the same time. "What is it?"

"I cannot reach Sam. He is not answering his cell phone."

"Maybe he's on his motorcycle and can't hear the phone." She shrugged.

"It's convenient he was gone just before the intruder arrived."

"Convenient?" Her eyes nailed me. "What are you saying?"

"Ah, convenient was the wrong word." Jeez was I a jerk. "I'm surprised he left, considering what's going on."

"Surprised?"

"Never mind. Look, did Kevin ever mention anyone or anything? A book, a place, or anything that he called 'G'?"

She thought a long time and shook her head. "No. I have not heard that. Why?"

"What about Khalifah? Or have you heard anything about Maya in Baltimore?"

"No, should any of this mean something to me?"

I told her what I could make out of Kevin's last words, but before I finished, her eyes darkened. "I thought maybe—"

"Maybe what?" She folded her arms and looked to the ground. "First, you distrust Sam. Now, you hear a Muslim name and because I am Iranian I must certainly know every Muslim in the country? Is that it, Jon Mallory?"

Huh? "No, wait, Noor. I asked because—"

"I do not know any Khalifah or what 'G' means." Then she hit me hard. "I do not care what Kevin told you. Sam is not responsible for any of this, and being Iranian does not mean I am, either. Please wait on the police outside."

What? "I don't understand what you're upset about, Noor."

"Please go."

Outside, it struck me that I'd just learned the most valuable survival lesson of all. When confronted with danger and tumultuous events—regardless of the risks—never, ever piss off a beautiful woman.

CHAPTER 14

Day 2: May 16, 1815 Hours, Daylight Saving Time
Noor Mallory's Residence, Frederick County, Virginia

ALTHOUGH NOOR WAS unhappy with me, she saved me from a trip to the sheriff's office for more hot lights and thumb-screws. The deputy couldn't hold me responsible for the home invasion. I'd probably saved Noor's life, and the sheriff's office promised to keep a deputy outside the house for a few days. So, after answering more questions and searching the house and surrounding area again, the deputy delivered the ritual, "Don't leave town."

I had no plans to.

There was nothing like a good life-and-death fight to get the creative juices flowing, so I decided to get to work. I've read plenty of Dick Tracy, Scooby-Doo, and the Hardy Boys. You know, the classics. I'd learned that all good detectives returned to the scene of the crime. No, that was the killers. Well, the detectives had to, too, or they wouldn't know that the killers had.

I drove east out of town and headed back to the Shenandoah River.

At the bottom of the hill at the Route 7 Bridge, where Kevin was murdered just hours ago, a Clarke County sheriff's deputy blocked the road and directed traffic back through a cut-through between the east- and westbound lanes. As I approached, he waved me to a stop.

"Road's closed, sir." He threw a thumb over his shoulder toward the bridge. "You'll have to turn around and detour through Berryville."

I played dumb. "What's up, Deputy? An accident? Not more terrorism like the mall this morning?"

He shook his head. "No terrorists out here, sir. Who'd come all the way to a small town like Berryville? Nope, crime scene from last night."

"Crime scene? That cop who was killed last night?" I lifted a gun-finger and scowled. "I hope you guys kill the bastard."

"We're working on that." He gave me directions to a secondary road behind us, but I wasn't listening. "Thanks. Good hunting."

The deputy smiled and directed me through the crossover, and off I went.

He was lying. They didn't need to divert traffic, and hadn't last night, just to finish processing a crime scene. Something else was unfolding. I backtracked to a small gas station up the road, tapped into my GPS, and found a private farm lane just up from the roadblock. Minutes later, I turned off Route 7 onto a gravel and dirt track that paralleled the river for miles. An eighth of a mile in, I found another dirt road that headed for the river. I took it to a small clearing at the end. From there I went on foot down the slope toward the Shenandoah. In another hundred yards, I found a deadfall of trees with a clear view of the boat launch just upriver and knelt down to watch the circus.

Panic had closed the road.

FBI sedans were parked on the bridge with several local deputies, detectives, and agents peering over the edge. Below, around the boat launch, was a team of peculiar astronauts milling around a large, billowing white tent where the burnt pickup truck had been last night. I say astronauts, but I knew biohazard suits when I saw them. There were four of them outside a huge biocontainment tent. The suits were gray, baggie ensembles with elbow-length black gloves and knee-high boots. They wore space-helmet-like hoods and carried equipment I'd never seen before. Whatever they were doing, they had prepared the old pickup for a journey. Parked along River Road, backed into the boat launch, was a black, unmarked tractor trailer surrounded by several armed men. Each wore a windbreaker that read FEMA—Federal Emergency Management Agency. FEMA was the US agency responsible for national crises such as natural disasters—hurricanes, tornados, floods. They were also the agency responsible for unnatural disasters. Man-made ones—like, *er*, chemical and biological *oops*.

As soon as I returned to my hotel room, I planned to stand with the lights off and see if I glowed in the dark. What the devil was going on?

Even without binoculars, I saw a familiar face on the bridge overlooking the scene. Special Agent Victoria Bacarro stood with that slender Arab I'd seen last night—Agent Mo Nassar. Me being the inquisitive guy I am and her being so keen on me forgetting about him meant I was most certainly not going to forget anytime soon. There was something about Nassar that made me want to look over my shoulder a lot, and the last time I felt that, I got shot. In the dark. In the back. Twice.

"Now, what are you two up to?" I said to no one as they walked along the bridge toward my side of the river. "Ah, crap."

The Arab suddenly stared in my direction. They both focused on the hillside where I was, if not on *me*. They exchanged words and their pace quickened. Bacarro pulled out a radio or cell phone.

"Double crap."

It was time to follow old Bill Shakespeare's advice and exit stage left. Fast. Quick-fast.

I did.

No sooner had I made it to my rental car when voices came through the trees. I didn't want to spend another moment answering questions with Bacarro's people, so I floored the rental back up the hill, disregarding its cries of pain and torture as it crashed over rocks and ruts. Ten minutes later, after two side roads and a few dings and dents on my rental car, I lurched out onto Route 7 and sped back to Winchester.

What was in that pickup truck that Kevin's killer had to torch it and FEMA's biohazard team was needed? Did I have days, or perhaps hours, to live?

What had Kevin known? What was he into? Terror bombings and biohazards?

I needed a shower. A very long, hot, soapy shower. Maybe three or four. And a drink. Yes, definitely a drink. Not that I needed a drink to know that I was over my head and alone in whatever Kevin had pulled me into. No. I needed a drink—or two or three—before I made the call to Oscar LaRue.

That call, like hypodermic needles and the IRS, scared the crap out of me.

CHAPTER 15

Day 2: May 16, 1815 Hours, Daylight Saving Time
Arlington, Virginia

CAINE SPENT TWO hours dry-cleaning himself—taking evasive maneuvers to shake any potential surveillance—on his way to DC. He drove to Reston, double backed twice, and took the Metro to the District. From the Mall, he hailed the first of two cabs and hopscotched across town to DuPont Circle, where he went on foot to a Metro stop and jumped another train. Forty-five minutes later, he hailed another taxi to Arlington, Virginia, where he got out in front of the Islamic Foundation for Cultural Understanding, known locally as the IFCU Mosque, and walked the last block to an underground garage and up the stairs to the second-floor suite 2E belonging to Hafez & Fasni, Public Accounts. Before entering the suite with a key, he checked the weight beneath his left arm and flipped the silenced semiautomatic's safety off.

"You're late," said the man Caine knew as Khalifah in a curt tone. "We've been waiting fifteen minutes. We were concerned."

"Traffic." Caine neither offered nor received any handshake or greeting. "I don't like meetings like this. I've warned you before. What's this about?"

Khalifah started to speak when a tall, sturdy man with dark, sunken eyes stood. The man came around from behind the office desk and spoke with a thick foreign accent. "There has been an unfortunate development."

Caine didn't ask. He didn't have to.

The Foreigner continued. "Yes, your failure at the river."

Caine bristled. "My failure? Khalifah should answer for that one. You sent me here, *Comrade*, to look after your interests. I can't when the rest are reckless."

"Reckless?" Khalifah said. "I fail to see . . ."

"Of course you do." Caine considered the Foreigner—the man who'd hired him three months before through an Iranian middleman. Since then, he'd met the Foreigner only twice. Once upon arriving in the United States to begin his assignment, and once a week before when the assignment had changed from babysitting a band of thugs who smuggled men and material into the country for a high-stakes poker game.

"You should take care, Caine. Everyone is expendable." The Foreigner lifted his chin and smiled dryly. "Even one such as you."

Caine forced a laugh. "You hired me to manage your crew. Then you changed the rules and demanded I take orders from him"—Caine threw a chin at Khalifah—"to help execute some crazy-ass plan. None of that was ever in the deal. Just what am I doing here? I don't babysit for anyone."

"Babysit?" Khalifah sliced the air with his hand. "Had you been babysitting Saeed, we never would have lost that shipment."

"You were reckless, Khalifah," Caine said. "If you'd told me what you were doing to begin with, I could have dealt with it personally. I have no control over Saeed and his cell, and I don't know about other cells. Your carelessness—"

"Carelessness?" Khalifah thrust a finger at him. "Reckless? That shipment was lost because of you."

"I saved it from discovery. Mallory is your disaster."

"Enough." The Foreigner held up a hand. "This solves nothing. Caine, you will be brought into the activities of the other groups when the time is right. Until then, you are to focus solely on the big prize. The final strike. He will worry about Saeed Mansouri." He jutted a disfigured finger toward Khalifah. "Once Saeed has executed his final mission and moves to support you, I will give you control over all the groups. Not until. Your current target is far more important and will take all your concentration."

"How am I to know what the other cells are doing?" Caine's face tensed and his words were curt. "How am I—"

"Khalifah will concern himself with the others for now." The Foreigner hardened his voice. "Do I make myself clear? You all— you and Saeed—take your orders, and your money, from me. Mine is the only voice you need concern yourselves with."

Caine nodded. "As you say. For now. But if this begins to unravel, I want control or I'm out."

"Agreed," the Foreigner said. His voice lowered. "Sokoloff is missing. Find him. Find him before the Americans do. If he is in their hands, eliminate him. If he is not, bring him to me."

Khalifah nodded and eyed Caine. "You handle that. I'll deal with Saeed's people. They're behind in their planning."

Caine didn't like answering to Khalifah. "Isn't that backward? Considering your reach, shouldn't you be hunting Sokoloff?"

"No, he should not. No more unnecessary risks in the field." The Foreigner considered Caine for a long time. Finally, he nodded and returned to the desk across the room. He turned back, lit a cigarette, and inhaled deeply on the dark, rich tobacco. "The scientist I sent you, Al Fayed, must prepare the incoming product to my standards. It must be done within three days."

"Working with that stuff isn't like making tea," Caine snapped. "He's under pressure. Perhaps if you let him see his family . . ."

"Three days." The Foreigner folded his arms. "That is all there is. Sooner is much better, no?"

Caine remained silent and shrugged.

The Foreigner cocked his head. "When the time comes, Saeed's men will move the product to a staging area and he and you will join forces. You will all await my order to proceed to Baltimore. After that, Caine, you will clean up *everyone* behind us."

"That's all of it, then?" Caine asked, glancing from the Foreigner to Khalifah. "I thought there were more groups. I thought this was a larger operation."

Khalifah raised a hand. "There is more in the works, shall we say. It's not your concern. You focus on your task, and I will focus on Saeed."

Caine shrugged. First a project manager. Then a babysitter. In the end, a cleaner. For all that, he would be paid two million dollars.

"Are you clear?" Khalifah didn't wait for Caine's response and turned to the Foreigner. "How long will the final preparations take?"

The Foreigner considered both of them in turn. "Operation Maya is not for the shortsighted. It will depend on the Americans, no?"

"If you say so," Caine said. "I don't understand all these small operations scattered about. They have no rhyme or reason to me."

"Ah, but they do, my friend. They do." The Foreigner smiled a broad, forced smile. "Sometimes, when you wish to pick your berries and a bear is in your way, you poke the bear from another direction. When the bear charges off in that direction, he will no longer be interested in your berry patch."

Khalifah exchanged uneasy glances with Caine. "I don't care about berries. I just care about—"

"Yes, of course." The Foreigner removed two thick envelopes from his jacket pocket and handed them over. "You are both simple men, not confused by politics or ideology. That is how men such as yourselves should be."

When Caine took the envelope, he noticed the accented man's left hand was missing his ring finger.

The Foreigner noticed Caine looking at his hand. "Often when you poke the bear, the bear bites back."

CHAPTER 16

Day 2: May 16, 2045 Hours, Daylight Saving Time
Winchester, Virginia

AFTER RUNNING THE hotel out of hot water and fresh towels, not once but twice, I tried to grab a quick nap, but sleep was elusive as ever. Visions of Kevin lying in the mud. The flash of the old pickup truck bursting into flames. The carnage at the mall—bodies, debris, blood—and the family in Manassas plagued me. It all plagued me. Every time my eyes closed, all I saw was guilt. Memories wouldn't stop haunting me. Regrets wouldn't exonerate me.

Time for that drink.

The Old Town pedestrian mall is a four-block area of central Winchester. The mall is frozen in time somewhere in the late 1800s. The black iron streetlamps, brick streets, and nineteenth-century courthouse looked like one of Mort Kunstler's paintings. Framed glass windows and hand-painted signs lined the street where no cars had driven for decades. A couple shopkeepers wore white aprons and fussed over window displays. They waved and called for me to shop.

The Old Town Café was a cozy bistro in the epicenter of the pedestrian mall. It sat on the corner where both main streets, Loudoun and Boscawen, crossed south of the historic courthouse square. Across from the café, I took up a position in a doorway where I could observe. The large, front glass windows displayed hand-painted burgers and fries. Outside, a half dozen tables covered with the traditional red-and-white-checkered tablecloths were occupied by patrons or littered with dirty dishes. A cook lingered outside the Boscawen Street–side door nursing a cigarette. That exit would make an alternate escape if trouble found me inside.

Come on, Hunter, this isn't Kandahar.

Since Abu-Bahoo the International Terrorist and his band of seven masked dwarfs weren't hanging around polishing their scimitars, I walked over and went inside. To my surprise, Sam Mallory was perched atop a counter stool sipping a cup of coffee at the far end of the café. He was talking with a tall, robust man of perhaps sixty-five. The two were in deep conversation, and the older man was leaning on the counter and tapping it to make some point. He was balding and his remaining hair was thin and gray and curled around his ears. His frameless glasses were perched on a wide nose and his gray, tired eyes looked out from behind them. He wore a white dress shirt with a gold tie undone and dangling from his neck. His expensive-looking suitcoat lay over the counter, half-covering a briefcase.

I walked over to Sam. "Hi, Sam. How are you?"

He looked up and his face tightened. "You?"

"Sorry to disappoint." I glanced at the older man. "Hello."

"I'm Edik Yurievich Petrov." The man jutted out a thick, meaty hand. "You are Jonathan Mallory, yes? I am sorry for your loss."

Edik Yurievich Petrov was clearly not a native Winchesterian . . . Winchestrite . . . he wasn't from here. He was Russian. Very Russian. His eyes were soft and friendly, and I took his large hand in what turned out to be a crushing handshake. I tried my best Russian greeting. "*Dobryj večer.*"

"Ah, yes. *Zdravstvujte.*" His eyes lit up, and he crunched my hand harder. "You speak Russian?"

I shrugged. "Not much. But I ran into someone this morning who did. Tell me, Edik, what does *otyebis* mean?"

For a second he eyed me. Then, with a big laugh, he slapped the counter. "Ah, you play with me. You know it means, ah, to 'fuck off,' yes? Forgive my crudeness."

I winked. "I do. Are there many ethnic Russians here?"

"Some, yes. Why?"

"Just curious. You knew my brother, Kevin?"

"Yes, of course. A good man." He handed me a business card from his shirt pocket so fast I thought it was spring-loaded. "I'm an entrepreneur. An accountant by trade. My partners and I own enterprises in the area. This is one."

I pocketed his card. "How did you know Kevin?"

"From here. We have the best coffee in town." He turned and snatched up his jacket and briefcase. "You speak with your uncle. I will not intrude." He nodded to me, patted Sam on the shoulder, and wandered into the kitchen.

Sam didn't waste a second. "You really upset Mom."

"Sorry. Are you waiting for—"

"Bobby. The guy I told you about who found the first body at the river last night." He ordered more coffee and a cup for me from the thin, blond waitress named Kelley. Kelley danced when he spoke to her and went for the pot, leaving another patron waving his cup in the air as she twice passed him.

I watched her go. "Is your mom okay?"

"Not really. She told me what happened. Thanks, I guess, for protecting her."

I said nothing.

His mood turned darker. "She says you think I'm up to something. Everyone thinks stuff like that. I bet they'll think I had something to do with Dad's murder."

"No, Sam." I put a hand on his arm. "I don't."

"Right." His face darkened. "I know what others say and think. Maybe you, too. I was born in DC. Mom was born in Sāri, north of Tehran. But she's an American now. So—"

I threw up a hand. "Whoa. We're family, and that's what matters." When Sam looked away, I added, "Do folks around here give you a bad time?"

He shrugged. "Sometimes. Heck, after the mall bombing today, it'll be worse. Those who don't think we're terrorists think we're refugees. Mom was a refugee once. She escaped when she was a teenager. Not me. I'm American."

"Me, too." I winked. "Small towns can be like that, Sam."

Silence separated us for several moments.

Sam broke it. "Bond showed up after you left. He told Mom he was going to deal with you." Something about that statement made him smile.

"I look forward to it." I leaned on the counter. "You should be home with her. Just to keep an eye on the place."

"Bond's there." He locked eyes on me. "Why should I trust you? I don't know anything about you. You think you're gonna find Dad's killer?"

Yes, I did. "I'm going to help you and your mom if I can. For a while at least. It's the least I can do for your dad."

"Whatever." His eyes lowered to his coffee cup, hiding there.

Kevin's den told me how much Sam meant to him. My memories of Kevin and my dad turned painful, knowing they were forever gone. My best memories were at our cabin in the mountains. That was gone, now, too.

"You know, Sam, your dad and I loved to fish up at the cabin. It's the only place we got along sometimes."

"Fool's Lake." He turned on his stool and faced me. The anger disappeared, and he smiled a faraway smile like a memory found him. "Dad and I went there a lot. But it's been a while."

"Too bad it's gone."

"It's not." His eyes went narrow. "Mom doesn't know, but Dad didn't sell it like he said. They fought about it for weeks last year. All over money. Then the money trouble stopped, and he said he sold it."

Kevin lied? "How do you know he didn't sell?"

"I followed him up there." He folded his arms. "One night a couple months ago, he went there. I left after midnight, but he must have stayed until morning. He did that a lot. He was up there just last week."

Why would Kevin do that? Nothing about his home suggested he had money issues. Nothing. If money was tight, how'd he fix that and not sell the cabin?

I asked Sam those questions.

He shrugged. "I don't know. But things got better after he lied about the place. Anyway, he lied a lot."

"He did?"

"Yeah, he did." Something in Sam's voice told me he had a litany of anger he wanted to unleash. "Plain and simple."

"Come on, Sam. Say what you want. I'm listening."

He returned to his coffee, and just when I thought he was going to unload on me, he threw a chin toward the café's windows. "There's Bobby Fischer."

Bobby, whom Kelley explained was Bobby Kruppa, not like the chess champ, as Sam believed, was a round-faced kid of about twenty-two. He looked more like a recluse than a college student. His uncombed, sandy hair covered his ears. He wore a baggy t-shirt with the logo of some rock band I'd never heard of and didn't want to. His jeans were shabby and old, and he'd lost his razor months ago. It was probably on his bathroom sink next to his comb. Bobby was about five-six or -seven and lumpy in places, but he carried himself well. He sat outside on the patio and set up a rolled chessboard and chess pieces.

"Introduce us, Sam."

He grunted something and led me outside.

As I walked from the café, I noticed an attractive Middle Eastern mother and her teenage daughter at one of the outside tables. Mom was in her midthirties and had black hair and dark features. Her daughter, slim and pretty, was about seventeen or eighteen, I'd guess, and shared her mother's beauty and buxom figure. Both were dressed casually with colorful scarves around their necks but not worn around their heads like traditional hajibs. Except for their Arab features, they fit into the café like the other few locals. Mom noticed me looking at them, smiled faintly, and politely looked away.

Sam dropped into a seat at Bobby's table. "Bobby, this is who I told you about." He looked over at me. "I don't even know what to call you."

"Jon is fine, Sam. Skip the uncle thing."

"I planned on it."

What a shit.

Before long, I sat across the chessboard beneath the corner streetlamp playing black. Sam sipped coffee next to us while Bobby maneuvered a white pawn into the center of the board. I knew I'd be little more than target practice, but winning was not my strategy.

Winners talk more.

Of course, I sucked at chess, too.

After he destroyed my opening moves, Bobby asked, "What do you want to know? I've told the cops everything. I'm not supposed to talk about it anyway."

In three more moves, he took control of the board. My strategy was to run away and let him chase me. It would give me time to get every bit of information I could. Unfortunately, his strategy was my swift and total destruction.

It might take me a few games.

"Trust me, Bobby. No one will know we spoke." I nodded confidently at him. "You found a body at the river last night, right? But it wasn't Sam's dad?"

"Yeah." Bobby glanced at Sam in-between sacking one of my rooks and laying waste to a knight. "There's not much to tell. Check in three."

I stared at the board and saw nothing. "In three?"

He continued. "I was farther along the river with my girlfriend, Lacey. You know. We heard thunder and saw some lightning flashes upriver at the boat launch. She got nervous, so we left. She's only seventeen and her dad would've had a shit fit. Driving out, we saw a pickup truck at the boat launch with its lights on. When we looked, there was a dead guy in the back."

Sam listened to Bobby and twice looked away. It was churning up feelings, but he was handling it well.

I moved a pawn deeper into the board and swear it screamed in terror. "Kevin's SUV wasn't there?"

"Nope. Just that pickup." Bobby took the pawn and lined his bishop on my queen. "Saw an arm draped out of the truck bed. Oh, and at the sheriff's office, I overheard one of the detectives say the dead guy we saw was a snitch. That's probably why he was killed."

"An informant? Interesting. Did you see anyone else around?" Each sacrifice got an answer, so I moved another piece into the slaughter.

"No." Bobby looked from the chessboard to me with a grin. I'd sprung his trap.

"What next?" I asked.

"I tried to call the cops, but I couldn't get a signal. We drove toward Winchester and called from a gas station up the road. We waited there for them. I guess while we were gone, Sam's dad showed up and got killed, too. By the time the cops got to Lacey and me, all that stuff happened to you. But I didn't see Mr. Mallory or you. We were already gone."

"That's it?" Sam snapped back in his chair. "Come on, Bobby. I know there's more."

Bobby shrugged. "I was scared to death, man. Lacey locked the doors until I got back in."

"Probably Dad." Sam's face paled. "Probably."

Bobby's words struck me. "Lacey locked the doors until I got back in." I let the comment lie while Kelley refilled our cups with steaming, fresh coffee. She lingered to flirt with Sam. After a few coughs and grunts from me, it took a five-dollar tip to send her away.

Bobby killed off my remaining rook and glanced up. His face went from triumph to horror and his mouth slammed shut. He placed his captive down alongside the board and leaned back.

"Oh no, not them." Bobby's face was terror.

I followed Bobby's stare across Loudoun Street. Two dark-skinned men headed for us. As they passed beneath a streetlamp, they would have been at home in Kabul or perhaps Tehran as much as here now. They walked confidently. They wore jeans and wool sweaters beneath old, tattered sport coats—common dress of the Iranian youth I'd encountered on my many jaunts around the Middle East. They laughed and gestured to us—and my Arabic is pretty limited like *Salâm, shab bekheir—good night, asheghetam—I love you* (don't ask), and *Ma'assalama—good-bye* and some curses—but I doubt they were reciting Frost.

I was about to meet some out-of-towners.

With each step they took, Bobby sank. One of them gestured at him with a three-finger jab in some pagan gesture. It was bullets to Bobby. I watched him melt as they neared. He couldn't break the larger Arab's stare. Bobby had a death grip on the sides of the table, and I could see his pulse raging along his neck.

Sam sat back, unfazed, and sipped his coffee.

I tried to calm them. "Bobby, relax. Maybe they're collecting for the local widows and orphans."

Bobby didn't even smile.

"It'll be fine," Sam said. "Trust me." Bobby tried to stand, but Sam grabbed his arm. "It's okay, Bobby."

I moved a chess piece—a pawn. "Everyone stay cool."

The two Arabs strode onto the patio. They hesitated at our table, leered at Bobby, and sauntered over to the Middle Eastern woman and her daughter, who were still eating ice cream nearby on the patio.

"Look, I'm a lovable guy." I tapped the table to break Bobby's stare. "We'll all make friends. You'll see." I turned to watch the two speak rapid Arabic to the woman. She nodded and kept a hand on her daughter's arm. Her face showed something odd—not fear but obedience. She stared at the table and refused to look up.

The larger of the men suddenly slapped the woman on the back of the head and yelled loudly at her, pulling her hijab from her shoulders and forcing it over her head. The woman's daughter quickly followed suit and repositioned her scarf in the traditional manner of modesty. Finally, the mother stood and pulled her daughter to her feet. Before they left the patio, the larger Arab slapped the woman again on the back of the head and bellowed profanities at her.

Mom and daughter hurried from the patio into the darkness down the street.

Bobby looked like he would vomit when the two Arabs strutted to our table and stood alongside it, hovering above him. They crossed their arms, kept their eyes on Bobby, and joked between themselves.

Steady, Hunter, steady. The weight of my .45 in the small of my back made me breathe easier. *Don't make things worse—widows and orphans.*

CHAPTER 17

Day 2: May 16, 2045 Hours, Daylight Saving Time
Western Loudoun County, Virginia

LaRue stood at the stair landing and watched the two men across the cement basement. There, Shepard stood above Noor Mallory's assailant, who had tried without success to avoid his present predicament. Little had the man known that Tweety and two security teams had awaited him along a dusty country road five miles from Winchester. Adrenaline caused the man to attempt an escape. Resistance caused the bruises that began to show now.

The powerful assailant sat in a metal straight-backed chair. His arms were behind his back with his fingers and wrists duct-taped so as to be immovable. His feet were tightly bound to the chair legs, both secured with zip ties and more duct tape. His limbs and torso were also tightly bound to the chair, which was itself bolted to the floor. He was incapable of so much as a twitch. The only thing the man wore was a black hood, which was pulled securely over his head to ensure total darkness, and heavy, noise-canceling headphones deprived him of all sound. The ensemble ensured he was immobile, void of light and sound, and unable to receive any stimuli unless his captors wished it.

There would be time, much time, for the demons of sensory deprivation to seize him.

LaRue understood those demons. It was his means of interrogation, preferable to more arcane, brutal methods that employed violence and left scars. Methods that often facilitated death.

"Shepard, let us have some dinner. Shall we?"

"Dinner?" Shepard regarded their captive. "What about him?"

"Time, Shepard. Just give it time. We will have what we need."

Shepard narrowed his eyes on LaRue. "Sir, the FBI is tracking a few dozen groups. NSA says the Islamic chatter does not indicate any unusual activity. None of the known threats are on anyone's radar. We stand alone with what we know."

"Ah, you need assurance?" LaRue removed his eyeglasses for a polishing. "Sometimes, Shepard, surveillance and intelligence chatter do not return the only meaningful results. Some rely too heavily on electronic wizardry. Let us see what our guest brings us, shall we?"

"Yes, sir. How long do we wait?"

LaRue contemplated the question. "Tomorrow, I think. We shall hope for tomorrow."

"Until then?"

"Patience." LaRue climbed the stairs. "Well, patience and perhaps Chinese takeout."

CHAPTER 18

Day 2: May 16, 2200 Hours, Daylight Saving Time
Old Town Winchester, Virginia

"WHAT DO YOU think you are doing, chess boy?"

The larger Arab kicked the side of the table and toppled chess pieces. He laughed and spit a gooey mass of intimidation onto the middle of the board.

"Hey, chess boy." The big Arab nudged Bobby's arm. "What are you talking about with this old man?"

Old man? "*As-salamu alaykum.*" I offered them "peace be upon you"—the traditional Arabic greeting.

Neither Arab looked at me. How rude.

"Not speaking, chess boy?" the larger Arab said.

"Nothing, Azar." Bobby's voice quivered. "We're playing chess. That's all."

Azar. At least he had a name. Maybe it was Azar the Magnificent or Azar the Great—wordplay kept me calm. Sometimes.

I looked at Sam, who watched Bobby. He showed no concern. What did he know that I didn't?

Considering the events of the past twenty-four-plus hours, I needed to keep things calm and cool. No fuss. No mess. *Nirvana*—grace, not the rock band.

"So, Azar, where are you from?" I asked, smiling. "Kabul? Cairo? No, I'm thinking—"

"Detroit." The word was overly heavy and poorly pronounced.

No, Azar and his pal were not native Detroiters. My accent meter pegged on Iran.

Azar kicked the table again. A few chess pieces leaped to their deaths onto the patio. "Chess boy, you need to speak with us. Now. We want a private game."

"No," Bobby whispered. "Everything's cool, Azar."

"Fariq does not trust you. Neither do I."

Fariq, the shy one, grinned and looked at me. His eyes were dark, and behind them, hate seemed ready to boil over. He had one hand in his raggedy sport coat pocket gripping something—a knife, a gun, something that would make me bleed.

Bobby started to speak, but I touched his arm as I slid my feet away from the table and focused on Fariq. "Look, fellas, chess boy is with me. We're minding our own business and you should, too. *Motevajeh?*—Understand? Walk away. You know, *Borow kenâr.*"

"Leave?" Fariq's eyes flared as his left hand reached into his rear jeans pocket. "You must leave, *madar ghahveh.*"

I wasn't sure, but I think Fariq just called me a bitch. Hmm, I saw this scene in a bad B-rated movie once. If I didn't get control soon, things would get nasty.

Easy, Hunter. Don't do anything stupid.

"You walk, old man." Azar smiled a crooked, toothy smile. The mood changed when he and Fariq flipped open wide-bladed pocketknives and aimed them at me. "You do not understand who you are interfering with, old man."

My .45 begged to come out and join the fun, but I resisted. *One, two, three. Steady.*

"Come on, guys. This isn't necessary. We're just playing chess. How about I buy you some ice cream? Two scoops."

Azar snapped forward, pressed his knife beneath my chin, and forced me to my feet. "Chessmate, old man."

"That's 'checkmate, old man.'" The words slipped out before I thought—not uncommon.

Rage. Azar jerked his knife back and swung it in a vicious arc. The knife stabbed through the vinyl chessboard into the tabletop and sank halfway to its hilt. He held it there, grinning at me as violence churned in his eyes.

Bobby pushed back from the table and sucked in air.

Sam raised a hand. "Azar, no."

Fariq slashed his knife back and forth as adrenaline fueled him. He jabbed toward Bobby and laughed. He jabbed again and again.

I fought the urge to pull my gun and kill this little twerp, but a gunfight in the middle of Old Town was not a great idea. I've seen maniacal grins from toothless al-Qaeda terrorists and one-eyed barkeeps. Azar's and Fariq's were worse. Fariq toyed with Bobby, poked and prodded with his knife. One stab drew blood across Bobby's cheek. Azar focused on killing me. But anger often fuels mistakes and creates vulnerability. Now, if I was wrong and Azar was a controlled killer, I'd never realize my error.

Calm. Steady. Focus. One, two, three.

"Stop this! Stop this now!" Edik Petrov exploded through the café door with his arms flailing. "Azar, no more. Not at my place. You go. Go now."

Azar whirled around and slashed his knife through the air toward Petrov. "Keep away, Edik. Go back inside. This is not for you."

Petrov braked six feet away. "You must stop. I don't want this here."

I took a breath and assessed my situation.

Special Forces CQB—close quarter battle training—includes combatives. That's the meat and potatoes hand-to-hand stuff. Contrary to what Hollywood thinks, not all SF guys are black belts in karate or kung fu masters breaking bricks with their minds. But we can get the job done. We're taught the ancient martial art of KISS—keep it simple, stupid. When it's life and death, spinning back kicks and fancy Bruce Lee chicken-dancing will get you fitted into a body bag. You strike first and fast and with lethality. You go for the kill. When you're up against multiple opponents, speed, surprise, and violence-of-action decide who's going home.

Action. Fariq grabbed Petrov's arm. Azar lunged at me, blade first.

Reaction. I snatched Azar's outstretched knife-hand wrist with my right hand and yanked him toward me. His momentum allowed me to pull him off-balance as I stepped out of his path. Before he could react, I grabbed his elbow with my left hand, levered his arm up and over his wrist, and twisted his hand backward until he cried out. The knife dropped away. My heel drove into the back of his knee. He started down and I slammed his face onto the table amidst the remnants of chess pieces. But Azar's superior strength allowed him to rise quickly, so I grabbed Bobby's steaming cup of coffee and smashed the cup into his face. Scalding coffee cascaded into his eyes, nose, and cheeks. His scream was as maniacal as his grin—almost.

I finished him with a powerful knee to the side of his head. His lights flickered and went out.

Fariq shoved Petrov away and charged me.

I lunged forward, drove my instep into his groin, and, as he dropped down clutching his privates, I pounded a shattering right hook into his jaw. Still, his arm slashed back and forth, trying to fillet me with his knife. I blocked his last slash, grabbed his arm, twisted, and landed another knee to his head. The knife beat him to the ground, but he joined it a second later.

Moments lingered before Fariq and Azar began to stir. When they did, Fariq tried to get to his feet and revive his attack.

Sam jumped between us. "Enough. No more."

Petrov jumped in and held his arms out between us like a referee.

"Old man," Fariq groaned and looked past Sam at me. "Another time, *madar ghahveh*. You will soon bleed."

I looked from Azar to Fariq. "Go."

Petrov went to Azar, grabbed him by the arm, and helped him to his feet. "It is over. Go. I will not call the police if you go now."

Fariq took Azar by one arm and hefted his weight against him. He looked at me with murder on his mind. "You will die. You know this, right? You are one of the dead."

"So many people wish that were so." I wasn't lying. I stopped and picked up Azar's knife. "You'll get this back when you learn to play nice."

Fariq aimed a gun-finger at my face, growled something, and the two limped down the street into the shadows where they'd emerged.

Petrov sighed and straightened the table. "They are dangerous young men, my new friend. You should go. I must calm the customers inside." He returned into the café, where customers stood at the windows, watching.

I turned to Bobby and Sam. "Okay, Bobby, those two have a beef with you. Anything to do with the river?"

He stared after Azar and Fariq. "No. I don't know what they want."

"Bull." I reached for Bobby's shoulder, but he recoiled from my touch. "No one will hurt you. I promise."

"The cops can't help. Neither can you." Bobby backpedaled more, turned, and ran away.

I looked at Sam. "Care to tell me how you know these two?"

"It's not my fault." His face twisted. "None of this is my fault. You can't blame me. Leave me alone." He followed Bobby into the night.

CHAPTER 19

Day 2: May 16, 2215 Hours, Daylight Saving Time
The Darby Farm, Rural Frederick County, Virginia

THE DARBY FARM sat nestled in the climb toward the Appalachian Mountains ten miles west of Winchester off State Route 50. The farm lay in a tiny draw valley—some of the locals called it a "holler"—and it had been gone from local memory for at least ten years. Crumbling roofs, peeling paint, and overgrown pastures were all that remained. During the Second World War, the farm was the once-thriving source of West Virginia beef and produce. That was no more. Now, it sat as a crumbling shell of what it once was.

Its newest tenants—unpaying visitors, really—were neither farmer nor country folk. Not *this country* folk, that is.

Caine turned off the old pickup truck's headlights before he turned off Route 50 and onto the rutted gravel road. He wound through the dying apple orchard toward the main farmhouse and outbuildings.

Easing slowly forward, he pulled the pickup around the rear of the ramshackle barn and killed the engine.

In Farsi, he said to the two Iranians sitting on the seat beside him, "You two bring your friend into the root cellar. Wait there for me. Make it quick."

The two men, cousins and inseparable since arriving in the United States, had been with Saeed Mansouri from the beginning. Often, with regret. This was one of those moments. The eldest nodded and slipped from the truck. A moment later, he and his younger cousin had hefted the rolled canvas package with their friend wrapped inside. They carried the package from the truck bed and disappeared into the darkness.

None of Saeed's men knew Caine. Neither did the Foreigner's men. They only knew what he allowed them to. What they should know. Part of his survival was the aura of the unknown. What your enemies didn't know, they feared. Fear kept these men wary. Fear that he was the *alqatil*—the assassin—who struck at will. They knew he came from the darkest sources somewhere in their world before this country. He had worked for organizations—for dangerous men—whose goals were accomplished by fear and intimidation—terror. Goals they understood and knew well. Caine's talents were reputed to have taken down cities and countries, even reversed Western gains in Syria, Afghanistan, and Iraq. That knowledge spread through his clients like a virus.

Caine had killed often and violently. He had no compunction against killing again. His reputation was a man without governments or causes. His was a trade of the most basic common denominator—profit. That's all Saeed's and the Foreigner's men needed to know. Anything else was simply irrelevant.

Caine hefted a heavy, green, military-style rucksack from behind his driver's seat and followed at a distance.

Secluded two hundred yards beyond the barn, concealed by an outcropping of apple trees and thick brush along a hillside, an armed sentry sat on a large rock. Standing beside him were the two Persian cousins. They were hefting the heavy canvas wrapping containing their dying comrade—a young twenty-five-year-old who had the misfortune of being in the wrong place at the wrong time when a stainless-steel case was breached and unleased the unthinkable into the night air.

The lone sentry stood as Caine approached. "*Salaam*, Caine. I keep my eyes out. No one went in."

"Good." Caine shifted the rucksack's weight. "Then you have done what I told you."

"*Baleh.*" Yes.

Caine held up a hand for the cousins to remain behind and moved through the brush to a bulkhead door obscured from view had he not known it was there. He propped open the rusted metal door and descended a steep flight of heavy oak steps into the earth. Twenty feet down, a single propane lantern hung overhead, and he struggled in the darkness to light it. Finally, it flickered and shined through the fifty-year-old iron door in front of him.

He bent down and examined the door frame. There, he found a short, thin piece of tree branch positioned between the door frame and door. If the door had been opened, the twig would have fallen. A trick of Cold War spies and pulp fiction novelists.

The twig was intact. The treasure inside was secure.

With a key from his pocket, he manipulated the heavy security lock and tugged on the iron door. With effort, he pulled it open and slipped inside. He found the second lantern and lit it, bathing the root cellar in fluttering light. The room was about twenty feet square with wooden shelves on two sides. The walls were timber. The floor was fieldstone. Along the far wall was a workbench where a heavy steel chest rested. Beneath the bench were four large five-gallon cans of gasoline, cases of machine oil, and sundry storage boxes.

Everything was as he'd left it.

He opened his rucksack and withdrew a bulky case with a strange digital keypad beside the handle. He set it on the workbench and punched in the combination. Inside were three stainless-steel cylinders, each nearly two feet long and six inches wide, berthed within protective foam cavities. He removed the cylinders and laid them on the bench beside the case. His movements were careful and practiced. The contents of the cylinders would kill him should he make any wrong moves. Like a venomous snake, the contents existed for the kill.

Next, he manipulated both combination locks on the chest, and with a long, pensive breath, opened the lid and exposed the foam liner.

There were three cavities cut into the protective foam, holding heavy cylinders identical to those from his rucksack. It took him only a few moments to swap the cylinders. Before he secured the case back into his rucksack, he took out his pocketknife and carefully carved three notches into the side of each tank.

Afterward, he secured the steel chest atop the workbench, slipped the case back into his rucksack, and called for the cousins.

A moment later, the two Persians descended the stairs, struggling with their canvas coffin.

"Lay him down there in the corner," Caine ordered and watched the two Iranian men maneuver the canvas roll across the room. He pointed to the steel chest on the workbench. In Farsi, he said, "Take that to Doc and tell him to lock it up very carefully. Don't open it. Don't drop it. Don't even breathe on it. Understand?"

"*Baleh.*" The older cousin looked from Caine to the canvas roll. "*Alhamdulillah*"—Praise be to Allah.

Caine waited until the cousins left with the steel chest. Then he went to the rolled canvas and pulled part of it down, revealing a frail, withering body. He could hear the man wheezing inside. A painful breath. A raspy, dead cough. The end.

"You saved us at the river." He withdrew a small-framed semiautomatic from the small of his back. The pistol had a stubby silencer affixed to it. "No good deed goes unpunished. *Salaam.*"

Three minutes later, Caine locked the heavy iron door and ascended the stairs to the sentry. He was barely away from the entrance when the smoke began billowing out.

"Stay clear of the stairs. It's going to get smoky and hot."

"*Baleh*, Caine." The sentry's eyes were round and fearful. "*Baleh.*"

"No one gets close until the smoke's gone. If they do, I'll bury you inside."

CHAPTER 20

Day 2: May 16, 2230 Hours, Daylight Saving Time
Old Town Winchester, Virginia

ON MY WALK back to my rental car parked along a side street adjacent to the Old Town Walking Mall, my inner radar began pinging and my eyes began swiveling around looking for the reason. In the shadow of a building, I slipped my .45 semiautomatic out and held it close to my side so not to attract attention. As I did, I noticed a dark-colored Mercedes three cars ahead of me on my side of the street. A few steps from the front of it, the door opened and a dangerous man stepped out and faced me.

Dangerous was an understatement. He was a skilled assassin and a professional mercenary. His skills in combat were twice mine. Yep, hard for me to admit that. I'd learned much from him. He was average height with dark hair and a narrow, dark-skinned face. Without light I knew he had two scars along his left temple but couldn't recall the story of how they came to be there. The last time I'd seen this man was nearly six months ago just outside Kandahar. He'd been sitting across the table in a dusty café waiting to deliver a message to me.

This time was different, though. This time, he held his hand inside an overcoat strategically draped over his arm. He would be holding a weapon. My guess was a silenced .22 in case anything untoward happened.

"Well, Shepard. I've been expecting you."

"Hello, Hunter." Shepard gestured to the rear door. "He wants to chat."

"I know he's pissed at me," I said and gestured to the coat draped over his arm. "He's not *that* pissed at me, is he?"

Shepard allowed a thin smile. "You've made enemies around here, Hunter. I'm not taking chances."

Did I mention he was a smart guy?

As Shepard returned to the driver's seat, I climbed into the rear seat of the Mercedes and came face-to-face with a short, thin man with thinning gray hair and a round, friendly Germanic face. This was, of course, my friend, mentor, and omnipotent master, Oscar LaRue.

LaRue hid his physique inside khakis and a starched white dress shirt without a tie. His aging blue eyes considered me through his round bifocals that were in constant need of cleaning. Don't let his slight appearance fool you. LaRue was a hardened intelligence operative as lethal as they come. Though he rarely pulled the trigger or threw the switch. That's what Shepard and I did. No, he gave the orders.

That required more than guts. It required strength. But in his day, decades before, of course, he was a machine. A deadly, brilliant machine.

"Well, Hunter, you have made quite an impression around town. This is Winchester, not Doha. You cannot go around shooting and fighting and getting into trouble."

"I'll make a note." I settled into the leather seat and turned to face him. "You owe me $879,928.66."

"I know." He grinned and removed his eyeglasses for a cleaning. "Now, however, I require an update."

LaRue and I had known each other forever. We met at Fort Bragg when I was young, brave, and stupid. I was toughing through the Army's elite Special Forces training to earn the long tab and a Green Beret. LaRue had been recruiting for his CIA operations and trolling for new cannon fodder. Somehow, I was on a shortlist and had volunteered—*unknowingly*. For years, I'd followed him on one wild ride after another, in and out of the Middle East, Northern Africa, and even a few testy episodes inside the former Soviet Union. Our years and adventures formed a bond. He was my CIA mentor and my greatest benefactor for paying jobs—good paying jobs.

I liked to think he lived vicariously through me. Or, I was expendable.

"How about you get my money before I update you, Oscar?" I said. "You know, in good faith."

"Good faith?" He gave me a curious smile. "You left Doha without even discussing it with me. Where was your good faith then?"

Touché. "Look, Oscar, my brother—"

"Yes, yes, of course. I am sorry." He flipped on a small interior reading light that wasn't bright enough to penetrate the tinted windows. "You have gotten crossways with the authorities and riled some very dangerous people. Is there anyone who does not want you killed? No, of course not."

I said nothing.

"Considering your brother's murder, I will overlook all that."

"Thanks."

"However, there is one thing." A steel finger stabbed the air and the lashing began. "One of my people does not disappear without my notice. I was at Dulles airport when you arrived from Frankfurt." He looked away dismissively. "Your passports are compromised."

"I'll look into it."

"You disappointed me, Hunter."

"It's a curse."

LaRue folded his hands on his lap and looked out the side window away from me. "So, you're through? Retired? Or shall we simply call it what it is—*unemployed*?"

Here we go. "You're here, so I guess I'm not unemployed."

"No, not yet. But you will have to pay for your error in Doha." He turned to face me now. "Leaving the theater abruptly, without authorization, caused me issues. I am responsible for your performance *and* your income."

"Yes, missing income." I hate it when he's right. I explained to him about receiving Kevin's letter and returning home late just in time for his murder. "I'm sorry, Oscar. I expected to be back before my R & R was up. Things spun out of control. But the moment I realized what was happening, I called you."

"Yes, you did. I have been concerned you would embarrass me."

Embarrass him? "Well, I nearly got killed at the river. I was blown up at the mall. I tangled with a Russian thug, and got into a brawl with two Arabs just now. Did any of that embarrass you?"

"Not yet." He removed his eyeglasses for a polishing. "Begin at the river. Leave nothing out. But do not be redundant. You know I hate that."

"You reminding me is redundant."

He frowned. "Begin."

I did. It took me nearly thirty minutes to go through the details of the past twenty-four hours. I started with Kevin's murder and the events at the river. Then we discussed the mall bombing, my discovery at Christian Run in Manassas, and my message to him. In all, the two things that made his eyes widen were the Russian who took Noor captive earlier and the FEMA biohazard crew at the river.

When I was through, he sat silent with his hands folded and his eyes seeing nothing out the window. After several moments, he turned back to me, and his face was grim.

"It is worse than I feared. Much worse."

Huh? "Which part?"

"Tell me again what Kevin said to you at the river."

I thought about that and told him. "He mentioned Khalifah and gave me the partial address to Christian Run. He also said something about finding G and that 'it's not them.' Oh, and he repeated 'Maya in Baltimore.'"

He turned away from me again. "You are certain of these words?"

"As much as I can be. He was dying, Oscar."

He lifted his chin and removed his eyeglasses to rub his eyes. "You are sure the intruder at Noor Mallory's home was Russian?"

I remembered LaRue spoke Russian. "He said *otyebis*."

"Understandable." He allowed a thin smile. "I would not worry about him any longer. He has been removed from the game."

The game? "Ah, what's that mean?"

"We have him."

"What? How'd you get him? You just got into town . . ."

He gazed out the window again. "Some of us move a bit faster than others, no?"

"Oh, come on, Oscar. Give me a break. I've done pretty well for only being on the ground a day or so."

"Bravo for you. Imagine what you could do with patience and polish." LaRue narrowed his eyes on me. "Now, let's be clear on your situation."

Situation? "How about a few answers first? Then my money."

"Of course. But first, you must earn your place back on my team." He faced me again. "One must pay penance first. There is a cost for you leaving Doha."

"Let me guess, the cost is $879,928.66."

"You can earn it back."

"I already earned it."

He looked at me with his chin up and his eyes locked onto me.

I was had. "Okay, Oscar, but if your assignment entails deserts or routing out former Arab dictators, count me out. I gotta stay here for a while. I'm officially retired from overseas skullduggery. I'm going to find Kevin's killer."

LaRue signaled Shepard to drive. "Kevin identified 'Khalifah.' Extraordinary coincidence."

CHAPTER 21

Day 2: May 16, 2330 Hours, Daylight Saving Time
The George Washington Hotel, Winchester, Virginia

EXTRAORDINARY COINCIDENCE? IF Oscar LaRue said something was an "extraordinary coincidence," then it was not an extraordinary coincidence.

"Come on, Oscar," I said, sipping the drink Shepard made me
from the suite's bar. "You know a lot more than you're saying."

He continued to pace the room. When LaRue paced,
world-changing events loomed. He paced for days when the Ber-
lin Wall was built and when it fell. Actually, I think he pushed it
over. "Khalifah is precisely why I am here."

"Khalifah? A terrorist in Winchester? Why?"

He frowned as though I should know already. "Perhaps this Maya."

I already thought of that. "I think Maya is someone in Baltimore."

"Perhaps. Khalifah is a dangerous operative from the Middle
East. He is here to undertake some extraordinary attacks against
us. Maya must be part of it."

I leaned against the counter in the kitchenette and stared at
him. I knew why I returned to Winchester. My brother sum-
moned me to fix old wounds. It was totally coincidental. But
LaRue? He was here for business, and if I knew one thing about
working with him, his being here at the same time as me was

no extraordinary coincidence. The question was, was my being here one?

I said, "Tell me about Khalifah."

"Yes, yes, of course." LaRue leaned back and folded his hands on his lap. He thought deeply for a long time before beginning. When he did, a chill ran through me like the north wind.

"Khalifah is an unknown, but a dangerous, lethal one. He first appeared in Middle Eastern intelligence connected to splinter terror cells. Hits in Istanbul, Athens, Kabul, and even the Saudi Kingdom. Always American targets. Always successful. His presence here, if true, is troubling. He is a master at deception and has eluded all attempts to identify and stop him."

"You know nothing more? Why haven't I heard of him if he's such a big shot?"

Shepard was sitting across the room and stood. "Don't feel bad, Hunter. He just read me in today."

"Neither of you had a need to know." LaRue returned to a cup of tea he'd been nursing for fifteen minutes. "It is troubling that Khalifah and Caine have taken interest in this area. Troubling indeed. But, perhaps Maya is the answer."

Caine? "Who's Caine?"

LaRue looked at me as though he were deciding to answer. With a sigh, he continued. "Caine—presuming it's the same man who disappeared from Syria two years ago—is connected to more terror plots than Bin Laden ever was."

Oh, that made everything clearer. "What's his role in this? He's obviously not an Arab."

"Caine is a mercenary. An assassin for hire." LaRue thrust a finger into the air to make his point. "Two years ago, he met with key ISIS leaders in Germany and then appeared in Pakistan. We tracked him into Karachi before we lost him. He reappeared in

Syria. After several months in and out of Damascus, he vanished again. Our sources tell us he came here to the States."

I know I've been gone awhile, but how had Winchester become a terrorist hot spot? I asked LaRue that very thing.

"I do not know." He removed his eyeglasses. "We will find out. We must learn how many cells there are and about their targets. It is the where and how that is most significant."

Oh hell, I'll have that by tomorrow. *Not.* "How is it you know Khalifah is here but nothing about him?"

"He is a double agent, almost assuredly. Since his emergence several years ago, we have been unable to identify him. For a long time we believed it was a cover name for one of the al-Qaeda operatives or perhaps a double agent within one of our allies' intelligence agencies. I believe he infiltrated the Saudi services, but I cannot prove that. He and Caine are, for all intents and purposes, phantoms."

Delightful. I wasn't chasing Kevin's murderer, I was chasing ghosts.

Shepard walked over. "Mossad confirmed that Caine was dispatched from Damascus to join a domestic US operation involving Khalifah."

Mossad was Israeli intelligence. They didn't get it wrong very often. "Did they say what they were up to? Or where?"

"No. The attack at Fair Oaks confirms, at least to me, their presence." He abruptly left the room and returned with a file. From inside, he produced a single grainy photograph that looked like a copy of a poorly taken passport photo. He handed it to me. "This is Caine. We have nothing to show you on Khalifah. Not even a photograph."

Caine was a narrow-jawed man, perhaps German or central European, with hair pulled back tight on his head. He had dark, dangerous eyes, and a distant, empty stare.

"He's an evil-looking bastard," I said. "He wasn't one of those I saw on Christian Run, though, or the guy who attacked Noor, either. What did your team find at Christian Run, Oscar?"

LaRue lifted his chin again. "The mall was a suicide attack. The victims in the home were his parents and sister. They were dead before the bombing took place, we believe. It is also possible the young bomber had no idea what he was doing."

"That's an ISIS and an al-Qaeda tactic," I said. "Take a man's family hostage and force them to act."

"True. But that terror cell is not the only concern." LaRue looked solemn. "Khalifah's presence suggests there are more attacks coming. More significant ones, too. More cells. You must find him, Hunter. That is precisely your mission."

LaRue's use of "precisely" meant he was not telling me everything. There was a lot more to my mission than what he *precisely* said. "Precisely" and "extraordinary coincidence" were his tells.

"Sure, but CIA doesn't operate domestically. So, what if—"

"There is no 'what if.'" He frowned. "It's complicated."

By complicated, he meant illegal. The National Security Act of 1947 created the CIA, among other things. Part of its birthright was a prohibition from operating in the United States. After all, no one wanted our government spying on its own people, right? Ha.

"Ah, no. If I'm going to break the law, I'd like to be in on why and know that you won't get amnesia when I call you from prison."

For a moment, he glared at me as though I'd just taken his lunch money. Then, he waved dismissively. "You will not be operating under Langley. The rules are therefore murky."

Murky? I'd say as clear as chili. With LaRue, things were never simple and precise. This one had murky and ugly written all over it. Chances were I'd end up shot.

I said, "Why me? You have assets already here that can do this."

"Think about it, Hunter. It should be crystal clear."

I did and it wasn't. "Because Caine and Khalifah are involved in Kevin's murder."

"Precisely."

Oh, I got it now. "I can chase after Kevin's murderer and not raise eyebrows as a CIA consultant."

"*Former* consultant." LaRue raised a finger to stab that point into my forehead. "Caine's an assassin trained by Mossad before the Syrians turned him. His arrival in Winchester and Kevin Mallory's murder is no coincidence. Neither is the mall attack. Neither is Khalifah's presence here. You can have your revenge and we can have Khalifah."

I thought long and hard on that. It worked for me. "Okay, Oscar. That's easy enough."

"Ah, it will not be easy. There are many more factors to consider." He stood and walked to the window to gaze out at nothing. More melodrama. "For now, I don't want to burden you with too many details. We both know you don't do well with details."

Ouch. "Got it. I'm to find Khalifah and identify his targets."

"Correct," LaRue said without turning.

"You and Shepard are all the backup I have."

He nodded.

"I can't tell anyone because we're operating off the grid and we're not sanctioned by the Agency."

Another nod, this one slower and disconcerting.

"What about my $879,928.66?"

He held up a hand. "You will receive an allotment from your retirement account with each successful assignment."

Wait, what? "You stole my money and I have to earn it back in allotments?"

"The Patriot Act, my boy." He folded his arms. "When you disappeared, they considered you a possible threat."

A threat? "Bull. It's leverage."

LaRue said nothing.

"I have no choice, do I?" I knew the answer, yet his silence was still irritating. "Any last advice?"

He turned and looked at me with solemn eyes. "Don't get killed."

Better advice was never spoken.

CHAPTER 22

Day 3: May 16, 0130 Hours, Daylight Saving Time
Fool's Lake, 21 Miles West of Winchester, Virginia

FOOL'S LAKE WAS not truly named Fool's Lake, but as a boy, it was my retreat. Before my parents died, it had been a hideaway for Dad, Kevin, and me. I don't recall Mom venturing there more than once. The stark conditions kept her away. I often thought Dad kept it stark for that reason. After their deaths, it was the place where Kevin and I found comfort. It was the place we made peace. No matter what we fought about or for how long. Fool's Lake was neutral ground.

After the day's events—hospital, the river, and my introduction to Russian housebreakers—Fool's Lake was the solace I needed.

Before I was born, Dad had found the old log and pine board cabin in the Shenandoah Mountains twenty miles west of town that sat on top of the Virginia–West Virginia line. I had no idea what Fool's Lake's name truly was, but my father had called it that after an entire summer trout fishing the secluded waters. Needless to say, we had very few fish fries. It dawned on him that in the many years there, he caught more fish from the small town market at the foot of the mountain than the lake. Regardless, winter was for hunting and campfires and stories. Summer for fishing and hiking—and more campfires and stories.

Always the stories. Passed down from my grandfather to my father, then to Kevin and me. Now, who was I going to pass them down to? Sam?

I made the trip out on Route 50 until I'd reached the township road I knew only from memory. Then I bumped along the mountain for five miles until I found the correct turns that led to the cabin.

Our place was the only one on Fool's Lake. While it was about twenty-one miles as the crow flies from town, it's closer to forty as the rental car drives. It took me over an hour. When I pulled through the pines and stopped in front of the small, four-room cabin, the memories overwhelmed me. I couldn't get out of the car. It was after one thirty a.m. and there were only my car lights shining on the cabin. In front of me, I saw my life unfold with an eerie clarity. Inside, Kevin and I sat at the small kitchen table playing cards with Dad. Laughter and loud voices. It was difficult to recall that I'd had a normal childhood—for a while. Until it was snatched away by a late-night driver filled with whiskey and beer.

Rebellion helped me cope. At least, that's what I told myself. But it also pulled me from home and carried me far from Kevin.

Now, it served me loneliness. The loneliness that came with being the last of my bloodline.

It had been nearly twenty-six years since I'd played rummy with Dad and more than twenty since I'd fished with Kevin. On our last trip, Kevin and I came for my summer break before I left for college. We'd fought terribly about school, and we both hoped the mountains would quell the anger. It hadn't. A year later, I left school and enlisted in the Army.

I hadn't been back since.

Now, those memories pained me like no combat wound ever had.

Deal with it, Hunter. Suck it up.

Rickety porch stairs groaned beneath me, and my breath caught with each one. I fished the key from the birdhouse that still hung from the porch roof, and unlocked the door. It took me a few minutes using my cell phone flashlight to find matches and light the candles on the fireplace mantel. A moment later, I found the kerosene lanterns and bathed the main cabin in flickering light. I succeeded in doing all of that without bruised shins or broken toes.

To think, Kevin said my CIA training was worthless in civilian life. *Hah.*

As soon as the second lantern lit, I wished the darkness would return.

"Why am I here?" Great question. But not as good as my next. "What am I supposed to find? Evidence? A secret videotape of Kevin's murder?"

Bourbon.

It was where it always was. A half bottle of cheap Kentucky courage waited beside a full bottle of expensive Macallan Scotch—the-several-hundred-dollars-a-bottle expensive—in a cabinet above the sink. *Now, when did Kevin develop such expensive tastes?*

I grabbed the bourbon and a dusty coffee mug. A triple pour later and the bourbon seared my nerves all the way down.

At least some things were friendly.

The cabin was unchanged—rustic and homey—a memory as finite and pristine as the first time through the door. There was old pine-beam furniture with worn cushions, a couch, two straight-backed chairs in the center of the main room, and a rocker in the corner. A comfy, overstuffed leather chair still sat front and center, facing the fireplace. Its springs were so shot that its cushion rested nearly on the floor. Wood was stacked beside the fireplace on both sides. Dad had always insisted that at the end of each visit we left the cabin ready for us to return with readied candles, stacked firewood, and clean, covered beds. A few cheap outdoor mountain scene prints hung on the walls. An eighteen-point buck head oversaw the room from above the fireplace—Dad's pride and joy. But he hadn't bagged that prize after cold winter hours stalking it. He'd found it at a local yard sale down the mountain one spring weekend before his death. The sagging, dilapidated leather chair was part of that negotiation.

That was not, however, the story told to visiting friends.

"God, Kevin, how did this happen? Why aren't we fishing and drinking right now?"

Kevin did not answer.

The rooms were simple, and I visited each, including the bathroom and two bedrooms. Both beds were made with old Army blankets and feather pillows covered by old bedsheets. It was impossible to tell when the last time anyone had laid their heads there. Each had its own small fireplace and was furnished with the basics—beds and antique pine dressers that smelled of mothballs, nightstands with wind-up alarm clocks, and candles stuck in old metal coffee cups strategically positioned around the room.

The small kitchenette in the rear of the cabin had a stove and refrigerator powered by a gas generator secured in the wood-shed out back. The cupboards were bare but for the bourbon and scotch. As I surveyed my youth, my stomach churned and emotions gut-punched me like a boxer in the clutch. Faces and conversations careened throughout my thoughts. I fought back. I was a tough guy. A warrior of sorts, not unaccustomed to violence, killing, and the gloom they brought. That was war, and, well, it was the job. This . . . this battle of memories and remorse was different. This cabin had never seen tragedy. It was a warm retreat from it. A safe haven. Oh, it had known our parents' death. But it hadn't mourned them. Instead, its walls replaced their arms for our comfort.

This was different. This was cold, unnecessary violence, not a tragic accident. It was malice. Evil.

Did these walls feel as I?

I snatched my bourbon and escaped to the front porch. Only a finger remained by the time I closed the cabin door.

Grow up, Hunter. Shit happens. One, two . . . oh crap . . . ten.

The mountain night was alive with crickets and birds and Bigfoot. A breeze lapped the lake against the rocky bank and soothed the fringes of my angst. The bourbon did the rest. There was something about nighttime, even in Afghanistan and Syria, that I loved. Stillness. Solitude. Something. Maybe I was a vampire who thrived in the darkness. Maybe.

Then reality struck. Kevin was the last of us to stay here. Recently, too, from what Sam said. Kevin was the last of us, too. I wasn't sure I counted anymore. I'd abandoned him. Abandoned our name. Hell, I abandoned me a long time ago.

Kevin was gone and his last words drifted into my thoughts— *Khalifah. G. Not them.* What did it all mean? I ran his whispers through my brain a hundred times and . . . wait . . . *Hunter*? Kevin had said "Hunter." Kevin never called me Hunter. Never. In fact, he didn't even know I used that name. To him I was simply Jon Mallory. He scoffed when I confessed my aliases, and that one was not among them.

"Only criminals and spies hide who they are," he'd scoffed. "One is no better than the other."

Yet, he had said, "Hunter."

I pounded the remainder of the bourbon down and returned inside. My first act was another two fingers in my mug, and next, I went to find my old yellow Labrador Retriever.

Hunter had been Dad's inseparable companion. Two years before Dad died, Hunter had succumbed to old age—he was fifteen—while warming himself on the hearth one cold November evening. He lived to swim in the lake and stalk deer and rabbits for dinner. He was no better a hunter than Dad. He was good for two things—eating and sleeping. In that order.

Outside in the rear yard beside the woodshed was a three-foot-high stone statue of a Labrador Retriever. It was the spitting image of good ole Hunter. Dad found it at a boutique pet store somewhere in Winchester and kept it on the fireplace hearth for years until Hunter died. The stonework became Hunter's headstone. The grave was below, covered in a knee-high stack of firewood. Below ground was a large piece of slate that protected Hunter's remains.

It took ten minutes and dozens of shovels full of wood chips and earth before I felt the slate slab beneath the toe of the shovel. With some effort and a little sweat, I lifted the slate clear and shined the lantern into the shallow cavity. There, wedged in the dirt, was a dirty rusted metal cashbox.

"Well, Hunter. You always were Dad's favorite."

I retrieved a heavy, ballistic-nylon duffel bag from the hole and brushed off the dirt and debris with my hand. The zipper was stuck from the dirt, but after a moment I convinced it to open. The lantern provided enough light to know I was totally and utterly confused.

Inside was a stash of money—at least ten thousand bucks—a set of unmarked car keys, a plastic freezer bag with something balled up inside, and a heavy bundle wrapped in a paper bag. Hefting the paper bundle, I knew what was inside, and I unfurled it.

A Bersa .380 semiautomatic pistol tumbled into my hand. The magazine was still inserted into the butt and, when I checked, I found three rounds left. Four missing. Most unnerving was that the end of the barrel had been modified with threads for a silencer.

But it was the plastic bag's contents that sucked the wind out of me. There were three Canadian passports with the photographs of Kevin, Noor, and Sameh. Except those were not the names on the passports. They were aliases and the passports were high quality and pristine. I know these things—after all, I have several sets myself. Last, there was a computer USB thumb drive rolled in a small manila envelope.

There were no notes. No explanations. No clue of what evil Kevin had secreted there. The scary things were there. Just not the "why."

"Jesus, Kevin. Were you running away or is this a rainy-day kit?" I finished my last finger of bourbon and stared at my booty. No, this wasn't a rainy-day kit. This was a smaller version of what I had back in my Leesburg storage unit. This was Kevin's go-bag. For me, the go-bag was a quintessential item for emergencies. Havoc tended to follow me and, in my line of work, having a quick escape and the means to get the heck out of Dodge and take on a new identity was as important as my missing retirement account.

But why did Kevin need that? He was a cop, after all. What had he stumbled into that required a go-bag? Obviously, whatever it was got him killed. He waited too long to dig up this duffel and "go."

My gut churned again. "Kev, what have you gotten us into?"

CHAPTER 23

KHALIFAH WAITED AN extra fifteen minutes at the little downtown café, sipping a double espresso and enjoying a chocolate croissant. He'd chosen a table in the corner near the large picture window that gave him the long view down King Street. On the next corner, easily within view, he could observe both entrances to the antique shop that specialized in local 1800s pieces.

Khalifah sipped his espresso, adjusted his *taqiyah,* and played his *mas'baha*—prayer beads. His attention was on the intersection a half a block away. Only the antique store's side-street entrance gave access to the second-floor business office rented to a local attorney some months ago and only occasionally visited. Its double entrance, one into the antique shop and the other to the narrow stairwell leading to the office, shared a wide foyer with heavy oak-framed doors. Once inside the foyer, anyone outside had no view of who entered the shop and who ascended the stairs. Likewise, until a visitor entered the shop's stained-glass-windowed door and jingled the overhead bell, no one inside the shop would observe visitors to the second-floor office.

It had been thirty minutes since the tall, wiry Iranian and his bulky companion—both dressed in Western business suits—had walked from Market Street up the block and made the turn into the side-street entrance. By the time the two men reached the second-floor offices, they were restless and edgy, pacing perhaps and chancing glances through the window blinds looking for his approach.

With a last glance at his watch and an extra two-dollar tip on his table, Khalifah casually strode from the café and walked the half a block. At the corner, he crossed the street and continued past the antique shop's side-street entrance. As he strode, he cautiously observed the parked cars and other shop windows and eateries for any rogue surveillance his contacts failed to warn him of.

There was none.

Twice Khalifah crossed the street, double backed, and finally returned to the corner adjacent to the antique shop. There, he waited curbside as though contemplating which shop to visit. As he scanned the street, he saw a gray Dulles airport taxi idling half a block away. He made casual eye contact with the driver, a thin Arab man, before he slowly rubbed his eyes. A second later, the taxi pulled away from the curb and made the turn in front of Khalifah before heading west out of town.

Nothing unusual to see.

Ten minutes later, assured the two Iranians were as jittery as expectant fathers, he double backed, crisscrossed the street twice, and entered the antique shop through the main entrance. Five minutes later, after pondering shelves of old books, he exited into the foyer, and climbed the stairwell to the second-floor offices.

He didn't knock. He just strode into the partially furnished phantom attorney's office that bore no name on the front door.

"It is about time, Khalifah," Saeed Mansouri growled, turning from his position near the front windows. "I do not like waiting. Not even on you."

Khalifah closed the door behind him and moved to the center of the room between Saeed and his bodyguard. He considered the muscular Persian guard before turning back to Saeed.

Saeed Mansouri was a tall, thin man, even by Persian standards. His shoulders were wide and his arms sinewy and strong. His face was narrow and hard, and he wore a tight-cropped, neatly trimmed beard. His Persian olive skin showed the marks of youth marred by violence. Gnarled, reddish scars adorned his neck and arms and peeked from beneath his tieless dress shirt. The wounds, the remnants of weeks in captivity by a warlord on the wrong side of the Ayatollah. Had it not been for his special benefactors—the Iranian Revolutionary Guard Corps—his head would have rolled to the ground without mercy. When the IRGC *Pāsdārān* commandos, "guardian brothers," rescued him just days before his execution, his first act after quenching his heaving thirst with water was to kill every man who had held him. None escaped him.

His bravery, tenacity, and, above all, brutality earned him his own command in this foreign incursion onto American soil. The dream of every IRGC *Pāsdār*.

"I care not what you like or dislike. You will wait as long as necessary for me to ensure our security." He threw a thumb toward the bodyguard. "Is this him? Was he responsible for those at Christian Run?"

Saeed grinned and rolled his hand in the air like a sheik granting a favor. "Yes, this is—"

"Enough." Khalifah snapped. Then he turned, took two long steps toward the bodyguard, drew a short, narrow stiletto from his pocket and thrust it deep into the man's ribs just below the heart. His other hand snapped up and covered the Persian's mouth before his cry erupted. He twisted his blade, first left, then right. With a grunt, he angled it upward into the man's heart.

It was over in seconds.

"What is this?" Saeed blurted and reached beneath his jacket, but his hand stopped short of his weapon when Khalifah turned on him. He slowly lowered his hand—empty. "Explain this."

Khalifah cleaned his blade on the bodyguard's suitcoat before turning back to Saeed. "He was an animal. Killing the mother and father is one thing. We had no choice. But what he did to the little girl was wrong. He was an animal. I do not condone such defiling acts of barbarism."

"You kill him for this? What difference did the bitch make?"

Khalifah raised his hand for silence. "All the difference. But that is not all, Saeed. He was followed to the mall. He was compromised. *We* were nearly compromised. Next time, I will come for you."

Saeed's face darkened and his eyes grew angry and hard. "Do not tell me how to command."

"I'll tell you everything I wish." Khalifah moved close to him and held his blade level with the man's chest exactly where he'd plunged it into the bodyguard. "You will listen, Saeed. You will act. You will do these things at my command."

The air between them was ice.

Finally, after a long contest of wills and unflinching eyes, Saeed raised his chin. "What is it you wanted of me this day?"

"Ah, finally, an intelligent conversation." Khalifah reached into his pocket and withdrew a USB flash drive. "Your new instructions. You must wait until after noon today before using the passcode, or the information will be destroyed. You may read it once. Then it will be bleached."

Saeed took the computer drive. "I understand."

"There are two more families. Two more new targets. You will take Sadik Samaan in Alexandria, first. The second will be a combined effort with our last attack. The instructions are all there on the computer stick."

Saeed looked at the USB drive. "*Baleh.*"

"Now, Caine will be ready in three days. You must complete these tasks in that time."

"Caine." Saeed stepped back, spit on the hardwood between them, and threw a glance toward his dead bodyguard across the room. "I take my own men a thousand times over him. You put too much faith in that Westerner."

Khalifah shook his head. "He's not my man. He is the Foreigner's choice. But we are in the West. Caine has value."

"Keep him away from me. If you do not, I may gut him like a pig."

"No, you won't." Khalifah cast his eyes on the Persian. "Now, there is one more thing. Another cell."

"Another cell? I do not understand. I was told—"

"Plans changed." Khalifah explained the new mission and watched Saeed's face contort with delight. "Do you understand?"

Saeed Mansouri couldn't contain his pleasure. "My friend, yes. This is a brilliant stroke. Brilliant. A fifth attack. They will not see this coming."

"You have three days. When the time is right, the third attack will begin, and I will facilitate it. Until then, it is yours to develop and ready for me."

Khalifah turned and walked to the door. "Wait fifteen minutes to leave. I'll have others come in later tonight and clean up."

"Of course, Khalifah. *As-salamu alaykum.*"

"*Wa alaykumu s-salām.*"

* * *

Earlier, as Khalifah had walked circuitously from the corner café down the block and back to his meeting, he'd noticed the taxi's departure coincide with his arrival at the antique shop. None of the shoppers and local shopkeepers took notice of anything unusual. Had they, some might have found it coincidental that the taxi's left turn signal coincided with Khalifah's itchy eyes. If anyone were curious and watched the taxi closely, they might have seen the thin Arab speaking to no one as he made the turn in front of Khalifah. They would not have seen the driver's concealed hands-free microphone inside his shirt that was wired to a thin radio clipped on his belt just behind his holstered semiautomatic.

Still, no one's curiosity had been aroused.

That was what Mo Nassar had counted on.

CHAPTER 24

Day 3: May 17, 0715 Hours, Daylight Saving Time
Winchester, Virginia

THE NEXT MORNING, I woke to pounding loud enough to wake the dead on my hotel room door. I, having had only a couple hours sleep again, was near dead. Last night, my adventure at the cabin was fruitful but scary. After I found the gun, money, and other treasure beneath old Hunter, I'd paced the wooden cabin floor, wondering what my long-lost brother got himself—and now me—into.

I found no answers.

Afterward, memories from my childhood consumed me again. They were bittersweet and most of them caused my insides to churn and torment me. Remembrances were warm at first. Visions of happier days and laughter. Then, like a schoolboy remembering a love who'd broken his heart, those memories turned painful.

At four a.m., I dropped into my hotel room bed.

Now, someone was outside my door earning a busted lip.

I tripped over my running shoes and stumbled to the door's peephole. It took a little while to focus through the tiny glass. *Oh crap, what did I do now?*

Maybe Detectives Bond and Perry were here to take me to breakfast. You think?

No, breakfast was out. The handcuffs would get in the way.

* * *

My reception at the sheriff's office was no better. After an hour of "good-cop, bad-cop, quiet-cop, raging-cop," irritation set in. To me, not them. The interrogation room was too bright, too stuffy, and too crowded. I was tired and mentally spent. In the past thirty-six hours, I'd been through everything imaginable except a small coup.

Generally speaking, I was in a bad mood.

"Mallory? Let's start with that." Annoyance shrouded Bond's voice. "Jonathan Mallory graduated high school in Fairfax in ninety-two. Then poof. Nothing."

"Poof?" Oh right, the CIA "poofed" me.

Perry banged his hand on the table. "We ran Jonathan Mallory from Fairfax through the computers. There's nothing to speak of. No credit cards, no addresses, nothing. After high school, you did what?"

"Hey, look. I pay cash, I move around a lot. I stay off the grid."

"Shut up." Bond leaned across the table. "I talk. You listen."

I nodded. Silence was my best defense. Unfortunately, silence was not my best strength.

Bond folded his arms and flexed bone-breaking muscles. "After your cage match at Noor's house, you tangled with two Sand Town bad boys. You beat the crap out of them. How come? Didn't they want to have a gunfight?"

I smirked. Bond was a funny guy.

"We're not even going to talk about the address Kevin Mallory gave you," Perry said. "Speaking of Kevin, you claim to have witnessed his murder. Right near a dead guy you never saw."

"Claim?" The heat surged across my face.

"We've got an interesting theory." Bond dumped my license and credit cards on the table before me. Then he flipped one over and it was a fifteen-year-old driver's license with the name Jonathan H. Hunter on it. "Want to hear it?"

Now where did they get Jonathan H. Hunter from? I thought the CIA poofed me good. Obviously, the poof was a little short.

"It's why you lied about your name that gets us wondering." Perry was watching me close now, like a jackal about to pounce. "We ran the name Jonathan Hunter, too. Funny, he's as much of a mystery as Jonathan Mallory. You show up in Winchester two days ago. Before that, poof."

"Where you been?" Bond moved closer. "The computers can't find you."

Perry came around the table and leaned over my shoulder so close I could taste his mouthwash. "Then we ran your prints. We got nothing."

Poof.

"Look, guys, it's complicated. My legal name was Jonathan Hunter Mallory. When our folks died—Kevin's and mine—I used my middle name instead of Mallory. I was young. I rebelled. It's how I coped." That wasn't a lie.

"You just happened to have phony ID?" Bond slammed his hand on the interview room table so hard my fillings vibrated. "Noor never met you, either of *you,* before yesterday."

My radar pinged. Bond was a gruff guy. Equal bite and bark. But when he said "Noor," he softened. I was already in enough trouble, but the way he said "Noor" sealed it.

I tried to soothe the beasts. "What could she know? I just met her yesterday."

"Kevin never told her you used a different name. You were with her yesterday and you never brought that up? She said you and Kevin had bad blood." Bond was all confidence now. "People kill over less."

I looked at him and tried to keep my temper in check. The urge to snap his neck was simmering.

"Want to explain?"

"No."

"You come home and now he's dead." Perry pressed. "No more problem. See what we see?"

"You don't see anything." I jumped to my feet. "You're fishing for a suspect, and I'm an easy catch." Perhaps the condescending attitude wasn't wise. "Respectfully, that is."

"Prove you're Kevin's brother," Bond said. "Then we'll talk about all the killing and fighting that happens around you."

"You handled yourself pretty good, Mallory, *er*, Hunter." It was Perry's turn to be the good cop. "Kelley the waitress said you karate'd those boys. Those two Sand Towners came at you with knives, and you kicked their asses. Then there's the intruder at Noor Mallory's house. Where'd you learn that martial arts stuff?"

"The Internet." I regretted the words the moment they came out—again. "Listen, what do you want from me?"

"The truth!" Bond shoved the table out of his way. "We checked the airlines. No Jonathan Mallory or Jonathan Hunter came into the area in the past month. You're going to get real cozy with some drug dealers and gutter-trash in lockup. You can practice karate or do the chicken dance with them. Ever been a gangbanger's bitch?"

"No, but I bet you like it." *Damn, I did it again.*

Bond came at me, but Perry grabbed his arm and backed him to the door. There, they whispered and strategized my path to death row. I sat silent, difficult as it was, adding up my mistakes since arriving home. Mistakes enough for a hangman's noose.

Bond moved the table back in front of me and found a calmer tone. "How about the .45 we found in your hotel? You got a permit?" Bond already knew I didn't. "We're running it through ballistics."

"Permit? No. But owning a handgun is not a crime and doesn't require a permit unless you're carrying it concealed in this state, right?"

Bond stared.

"So I'll expect it back when I leave. That will be very soon."

A voice from the past boomed into the room. "Good morning, Jon. The desert too hot these days?"

I looked at the speaker and then at the large two-way observation mirror below it. The voice was familiar, but I couldn't place it.

The voice said, "Don't you think you should come clean? I'm sure you're leaving out the good parts."

That voice . . .

"Please, Detectives, don't let me interrupt. Jon was about to tell us about the gun and all his aliases. It won't be the truth. But it'll be colorful."

I looked at Bond. He watched me like a tiger that smelled blood. I tried hard not to give away any body language, but I twitched like a fox before the hunt.

"You've been busy." Now, the voice came from the open interrogation room door. "Cut the bull. You can tell me, and then, of course, you'll have to kill me. Isn't that how it is, *Jon Clayton*?"

Jon Clayton? I hadn't used that name since . . . Riyadh. Ten years ago.

A tall, distinguished black man in an expensive vested suit walked into the room, and I felt like I'd just been caught in church with my zipper down.

Damn, they got me again.

CHAPTER 25

Day 3: May 17, 0715 Hours, Daylight Saving Time
Eastern Frederick County, Virginia

LaRue sat in a metal folding chair sipping a cup of Earl Grey. He watched the three men in the far corner of the stark, barren basement. Two of the men were dressed casually in jeans, sneakers, and polo shirts. Both were armed with semiautomatic pistols. The third man, a young, pale-faced man, sat on an inverted metal bucket with his hands bound behind him. His black t-shirt was soaked in sweat. His feet were bare. His cowboy boots and military field jacket lay in a pile beside him. Yet despite his hours in isolation and discomfort, his eyes were still defiant.

LaRue watched and began to nod. He'd reached a decision. "Regrettably, Shepard, events require us to expedite the interview. Proceed."

Shepard stood facing the man. He gave him a long, slow drink with a plastic water bottle. Then he wiped the sweat from the man's face with a towel. His offerings were solemn and controlled. "We're not asking a lot. Just your name."

Silence.

Shepard offered him more water and the man drank. "Baby steps."

The man spat the water into Shepard's face.

"We won't be pals." Shepard rose and retrieved a large suitcase from behind LaRue. He opened the case, withdrew an electronic device the size of a microwave oven. The control box was complete with a round, blunt saucer mounted on a pedestal that resembled a tiny satellite dish. He positioned the dish on a chair ten feet from the man and aimed it at him. He turned dials and switches and activated the control box.

The man looked on indifferently.

"How do you like your meat? Medium or well?" Shepard turned a dial on the control box and waited.

The man's eyes widened and snapped shut. He broke into a sweat and began panting, fighting the urge to scream. A few seconds later, his teeth clenched and muscles flexed and vibrated. His body wiggled for freedom above the metal bucket. He twisted and turned, but there was no escape. Finally, he lost his fight and screamed.

"*Ostanovite, pozhaluysta!*"

LaRue looked on.

The Active Denial System, or ADS as the research papers referred to it, projected a focused beam of electromagnetic radiation at the man. The beam excited the molecules just beneath his skin. The resulting sensation was that his skin was on fire and melting away. It was not. If used in limited engagements over limited time, no permanent damage was done—*physically*. Scientifically, that was the intent. Originally designed as a defensive antiriot device, creative uses of the ADS were another matter.

"*Pozhaluysta, ne, ne boleye.*"

LaRue raised a hand. "*Ja ponimaju*—I understand. *Ya plokha gavaryoo pa rooskee.* But you are *Sluzhba Vneshney Razvedki*, SVR—my Russian is bad—but you are from the Foreign Intelligence Service of the Russian Federation, the SVR. Shall we try English?"

The *Sluzhba Vneshney Razvedki* has the distinction of being to Russia what the KGB—The Committee for State Security—was to the former Soviet Union. The SVR's mission is foreign intelligence and security. It accomplishes this mission through what has traditionally been dubbed cloak and dagger. Often, however, there is more dagger than cloak. The SVR, like the former KGB, is not squeamish about violence.

Shepard turned the device off.

The Russian's head dropped low. His body quivered and saliva dripped from his mouth. After several moments, his panting subsided and his breathing returned to normal.

LaRue slid a metal chair close to the Russian and faced him. "Now, if you please, explain to me what SVR is doing in our lovely town of Winchester."

The Russian's head rolled from side to side and he mumbled in Russian.

"English, if you please." LaRue gently touched the man's knee. "It has been too long for me. I would hate for my associate to make you uncomfortable again."

"Grigori." The Russian's head lifted and his eyes were defeated. "My name, sir, is Grigori Sokoloff. You will wish to know of *Operatsiya Maya*."

CHAPTER 26

Day 3: May 17, 0845 Hours, Daylight Saving Time
Frederick County Sheriff's Office, Outside Winchester, Virginia

"Artie Polo. How are you?" I looked across the interrogation table at the man I hadn't seen in ten years. "You look good. New suit?"

"You're still a smartass, but not still Jonathan Clayton. What do I call you?"

"It's Jonathan Hunter. It used to be Mallory. Long story." He had me cold. "Just call me Hunter."

Artie shook his head. "Everywhere you go, carnage follows."

That was harsh.

Artie was a distinguished man in his late thirties, perhaps early forties. His features were tight and muscled, and, as always, he was dressed as if he'd just walked out of a fashion magazine. He wore a goatee that was new since I'd worked with him in Riyadh—yes, as Jonathan Clayton—and it made him look more refined and intelligent. Artie was the first in his family to graduate high school, let alone college, and the first to reach twenty without a parole officer. Detroit is a tough town.

"Artie, you used to be fun."

"You used to be Jon Clayton."

Touché.

Artie eyed me, probably deciding where to insert the executioner's needle. He'd listened to my interrogation. He knew every truth and every lie. Artie knew more about me than most people. That's why I never played poker with him. He could spot a bluff three cards deep. I tried to remember what lies and any half-truths I'd given out so far. I'd have to answer for them now.

Time to play nice. "Yeah, about the name thing, Artie—"

"Save it." He laughed and extended his hand with surprising warmth. "You look good. Whoever you are."

"Just call me Hunter." I gestured to Bond and Perry in the doorway. "Your friends are a little tense. You know me, I hate confrontation."

"Know you? I'm not sure I ever knew you." He rose from his chair and gestured for Bond and Perry to join him in the hall. I couldn't hear what he said, but Perry shook his head and Bond glared death threats at me. Both detectives left cursing.

When the door shut and Artie sat back down, I asked, "Everything okay?"

"No, it isn't. Terrorists hit the mall outside Fairfax this morning and killed several hundred people. We're still sorting body parts. The one lead we had led to that Middle Eastern refugee's house at the address Kevin Mallory gave you."

Oops. "Did you take out the cell?"

"No. All we found was the family. All dead. Strange, too. It looks like a terror cell grabbed the family and forced the bombing. They killed the family anyway. What a mess."

"That's an ISIS thing, Artie."

"Yes, I know." He eyed me. "We're still working the scene. We hope to get more."

As much as I wanted to spill what I knew to Artie and help out, if LaRue didn't want them to know, then I wouldn't. I was on my own for now—Shepard and LaRue notwithstanding. Silence was key. If I wanted Oscar LaRue to leave me with my balls in place, that is.

LaRue was a complicated guy.

"Look, Clayton, *er*, Hunter—" Artie threw up his hands. "Our phones are ringing off the wall after the mall bombing. Isn't it a coincidence all this happens when you roll into town?"

"I can't help you there, Artie. This is Winchester, not Fairfax County." The look on his face told me he knew the geography. "Kevin gave me a partial address, and I gave it to you guys. That's it."

"How did you know it was only a partial?"

Ah, good question. "Come on, I looked it up myself. I couldn't find anything that matched so I left it alone." Okay, a teeny-weeny lie. "Trust me."

"Trust you? You and trouble are one." He cursed and changed the subject. "What happened last night? Hell, what happened the night before? No BS, Hunter." He pushed himself back in the chair. "Not like last time."

"Come on, don't be like that." I tried my best smile. "It wasn't my fault the Saudi cops grabbed you."

"It took me days to get out of that mess. You have no idea what it cost me, and LaRue didn't help at all. Is he lurking around here?"

"I can honestly say that I have no idea." That wasn't a lie. Not really. With LaRue, he could be under the table spying on us and we wouldn't know it.

He crossed his arms and looked me over. "Really?"

"Come on, Artie. I'm not involved in any of this."

"Involved in what?"

"Nothing. I mean I'm here alone." Damn. "I mean, I came home for a visit. The last time you and I—"

"The last time you almost caused an international incident. It was me, not you, who cleaned up that mess. So give it up, Hunter. What are you doing here?"

Ten years or so ago, Special Agent Arthur Polo had worked a case in Riyadh. I was there, too, and I found myself in a little *debacle.* I had shot one or two people, perhaps a couple more. Okay, it was more than five and less than ten. I was on the trail of an al-Qaeda operative ID'd by my asset. "Asset" is "snitch" in cop talk. A local Saudi cop, also one of my assets, double-crossed me and arranged for me to be kidnapped or killed, or kidnapped *then* killed. Unbeknownst to me, Artie was hunting the same bad guy and had been double-crossed, too. We were both held at a run-down hotel but broke free and shot our way out. I caught the next plane to Kuwait. Artie had to stay and clean up the mess. Since he was officially there on FBI business, and I wasn't officially in the country, he lost the coin toss. He also had fewer friends. I, thankfully, had my hero, LaRue.

"Out with it, Hunter. What are you doing here?"

"Okay." I leaned forward. "See, there's my Sadie back in Riyadh."

"Sadie?" He laughed and threw his hands up in surrender.

"She's my best girl."

Artie smiled. "Forget Sadie. Straight, Hunter, what are you doing here?"

"I came home to see Kevin. You know the rest."

Artie cocked his head. "You still CIA?"

I grinned. "I'm a consultant with the State Department helping rebuild faraway nations and win the hearts and minds of their peoples."

"Of course you are." He got serious. "I'll check with our agency liaison. Just to be sure. I didn't know Kevin had a brother. What happened between you two?"

I lost my voice. The question punched my gut with brute force. It took me a few moments to fight the bile back. When I did, I stood up and walked across the room. "Heck if I know, Artie. I was headed to Winchester and pinged Kevin's phone. I had no idea where he lived."

"You didn't call?"

"No, but he was expecting me. He just didn't know when." I waited for Artie to roll his eyes again. "Anyway, all hell broke loose when I got there."

"Nothing out of the norm."

He hit a nerve. "Except Kevin's dead."

The words sent lightning through the air.

"Sorry." Artie lowered his eyes. "I didn't mean it that way. Tell me about the break-in at Noor Mallory's place."

It took me a few minutes to repeat the events just as I had for the deputies yesterday.

Artie took it all in. "Any ideas?"

"He searched her place, but mostly Kevin's den. Don't know what or if he found anything. Artie, the guy was Russian."

"Russian? How do you know that?"

"*Otyebis*." I translated next.

He frowned. "We've got deputies on Noor's place for a while. She'll be safe. What was he looking for?"

"I don't know. But I don't think he found it. He sat there like he was waiting for someone. He made a cell phone call, but she couldn't hear it. Then I showed."

"That's it?"

I nodded. "He almost cut my head off."

"That I understand."

"Funny."

"Noor has no idea what it was about?"

"None."

He changed the subject. "What about the café last night?"

"What about it?"

"Kruppa's our witness."

"And?"

"What about Fariq and Azar? They're the two you beat up. What did they want with you?"

I shrugged. "No idea."

"No idea?" He cocked his head. "What did Kruppa tell you?"

"Same thing that was in the paper."

He started slowly shaking his head. "You just happened by?"

"To play chess. You know, minding my own business."

"I don't know what's more BS, you playing chess or you minding your own business." Artie shook his head. "What's with this name game, Hunter? Is that for Company business? First, assuming you *are* Jon Mallory."

"Yes, Artie, I'm Kevin's brother." I didn't want to talk about Bobby Kruppa anyway. "No, I'm not on Company business. I am still legally Jon Mallory. I'm sure you used aliases over there, too."

"Never." He eyed me. "I've known Kevin for over a year. He never mentioned you."

"He's been my brother all my life, and he never mentioned you, either."

"Sure, sure. Okay." Artie aimed a bony finger at me. "Why the bad blood between you two?"

Fair question. Instead of answering, I asked one myself. "Artie, who is Khalifah? What does 'G' mean?"

For a moment, a flicker of something—not quite panic but more than concern—flashed on Artie's face. "You tell me. You're the spook."

The interview room door opened and Agent Victoria Bacarro entered. As she did, I noticed Mo Nassar from the river just outside the door looking in. He held my gaze until the door shut. That eerie tingle crept up my spine again.

"Artie, is your pal Nassar a spook?" I watched him for a lie. "Don't tell me 'he's nobody.'"

"He's nobody." Artie was a terrible liar. Mo Nassar was most assuredly a spook. Perhaps like or unlike me. I knew because, like dogs, we can sniff each other out.

My attention fell to Agent Bacarro. There was no rainy darkness to shroud her now. She had strong features—not manly, but firm and sturdy—with a light olive complexion and dark shoulder-length hair pulled back. Her business suit couldn't hide her well-shaped curves that begged my attention. For professional observation and analysis, that is.

Now, this was an FBI agent. Or a supermodel. Maybe I worked for the wrong federal agency.

"Hunter," she said, leaning against the wall, "please continue. Artie explained our security consultant from Germany is actually CIA from Afghanistan. I just had to say hello."

I glanced at Artie. "I thought only I called you Artie."

He silently mouthed, "*Screw you.*"

Bacarro locked her eyes on me. "I'm very interested in how you arrived just in time for your brother's homicide. It's a little ironic, considering your profession. Don't you think?"

"That's not irony, that's bad luck." I stood. "I'm not an assassin. I'm a consultant."

"Easy, Hunter." Artie motioned me back to the chair. "No one's accused you of anything."

"No, that's right." Agent Bacarro took one of the spare chairs against the wall and sat backwards in it. "Noor says you had issues with Kevin, but then he called you home."

Artie hooked a thumb at me. "Hunter was just about to explain, Agent Bacarro."

The words caught in my throat, but I got them out, unable to look at either of them when I did. "He sent a letter to a drop box I use. It's hard to get mail when you're on the move, so it took two weeks to find me overseas. I started home a few days ago."

"Do you still have the letter?" Bacarro asked. "What did it say, *exactly*."

"He asked me to come home. I figured he wanted to fix things up. We're not getting any younger."

"That's it?" Artie probed my face for a lie. "You sure?"

I nodded.

He let me simmer while he and Bacarro had a telepathic discussion. He finally asked, "Any ideas who killed him?"

"Khalifah or the guy at Noor's yesterday. Maybe whoever 'Maya in Baltimore' is? They could all be the same person. Maybe they're looking for this 'G,' whoever he is. You guys got anything?"

"The investigation is ongoing and we're following every lead." Bacarro delivered the FBI mantra. "We cannot comment."

"Bull." I leaned back and forced a fake, hoarse laugh. "The newspaper has a big story."

"We have nothing." Artie threw a curt glance at Bacarro. "Not a damn thing. The truck at the river was stolen months ago, and it's a dead end."

I looked from one to the other and asked a direct question that should get me a direct answer. "What's coming out of Sand Town? Seems like that's a logical place to start looking for a killer, right?"

"You'd think so, yes," Agent Bacarro said, glancing at Artie. "But we can't go rousting refugees and locals just because they look like bad guys. That's called profiling, Hunter. We don't do that."

More bull. "You don't have any probable cause or anything to get you into Sand Town?"

"You let me worry about that," Artie snapped. "We're the FBI. We move on evidence, not street gossip. When, or if, we get any for Sand Town—Sandy Creek—we'll move on it."

"Sure, Artie, sure." I riled him and didn't want to let go of the bite I had. "Who's Khalifah? Every time I say the name, you guys flinch."

"It's classified," he said. "Still, we don't know much about him. It suffices to say he's an ISIS asset."

"In Winchester?"

Agent Bacarro nodded. "We don't know. Maybe. Maybe he's still in the Middle East and calling the shots from there."

I let that sink in. "So, why is Kevin's murder FBI business? Task force or not, the Feds rarely worry about pesky murders."

"Because he's been working Sand T—" Artie caught himself again. "The Muslim community that's developed out in Sandy Creek. You got into the scuffle with two of them last night. We're working some other related activities. The BCI assigned Kevin to us. He worked for Agent Bacarro. She works for me."

Bacarro added, "When one of our own goes down, the FBI takes it seriously. We're working it with the State and locals. But we're lead."

"Got it. You're in charge and following every lead. You cannot comment further. Sorry I asked." I was, too.

Agent Bacarro leaned forward and did this funny thing with the corner of her mouth. It would have been sort of sexy if she hadn't ruined it with more questions.

"What about the forty-five semiautomatic Bond took from you?" she asked.

I shrugged. "I can get my hands on a gun—legally. That is, if I need one."

"Do you need one?" Agent Bacarro folded her arms.

Was she paying attention? "Look, someone tried to kill me as soon as I arrived here. They already killed my brother. Next, someone took Noor hostage. Last night, two other somebodies tried to fillet me."

"You're surprised?" Agent Bacarro glanced from Artie to me. "I just met you and I want to kill you."

I liked her.

Artie's eyes focused on me again. "Look, Hunter, I understand you want revenge for Kevin. But that's not justice. This isn't the Middle East. CIA rules don't apply here."

I leaned back. "Potayto, potahto."

"No." Artie aimed a long, slender finger at me. "We'll do this our way. The legal way. No street rules."

"Meaning?"

"I can read your mind," he said in a dry voice. "You're going to cause mayhem. That's a very bad idea. This isn't Riyadh or Baghdad. There are police and laws and warrants and courts. You can't go around shooting things up. We have to be accountable."

"Of course, Artie, accountable."

"Ah, Christ, Hunter, don't even think about it."

"No, I get it." I leaned back. "Honest. Besides, I'm only here for a few days."

"Quit the Agency? Tired of the cloak and dagger?"

I shook my head. "Just a little R & R."

"LaRue isn't hiding in the shadows somewhere?"

"I already told you, Artie. I haven't seen him."

Artie pressed. "Really?"

I made an exaggerated X over my heart. "You have my word."

"Why am I worried?"

I pushed a little more. "So, what about the crispy guy in the pickup truck?"

"No comment. You have no comment either, for the papers or anyone else." Bacarro raised her chin the way FBI agents do when they want to look authoritative. "I mean that, Hunter. No comments from you."

"My mistake." Why were they playing so many games? "Can I talk about the hazmat team at the river yesterday?"

Bacarro's mouth snapped closed so loud I heard a filling loosen. Artie's very African-American face turned Caucasian.

Had I struck a nerve?

Artie's eyes zeroed on mine. "You're getting close to the Patriot Act, Hunter."

"I've been told that before." The Patriot Act might land me in a jail cell for eons without benefit of lawyer, due process, or freedom until old age erased any memories of the aforementioned biohazard cleanup team and crispy body at the river. The Patriot Act had already confiscated my retirement fund.

Artie and Bacarro locked eyes and had a conversation without moving their lips.

I eased their minds. "No worries, guys. We're all in this together. My lips are sealed. I'm one of the good guys."

Artic shook his head. "Now we're in trouble."

"All right, then, Hunter," Bacarro said and walked to the door. Before she left, she turned around and fired a shot across my bow. "We'll hold you to that. If you open your mouth, you're going to jail for obstruction. Got it?"

"Got it."

Artie stood and came around the table. His eyes dropped, and for a minute, he looked sad and far away.

I leaned back. "You're not going to hug me or anything, right?"

"No." He touched my shoulder. "I'm truly sorry about Kevin."

"Thanks." Then I ruined the mood. "It's good to be working with you again."

"We're not working together." Artie stabbed my shoulder with a finger. "Get that through your stone-head."

"Right, we're not working together." I smiled. "Got it."

"Dammit, Hunter, you never change."

CHAPTER 27

Day 3: May 17, 0945 Hours, Daylight Saving Time
Sandy Creek—Sand Town—Rural Frederick County, Virginia

SANDY CREEK, VIRGINIA, was once a small farming community twelve miles southwest of Winchester nestled among the rolling hills leading deeper into the Shenandoah Mountains. It had been decades since the farms sold out or went bankrupt and the only steady employer, a textile mill, closed for good. What remained until a year ago were vacant houses, a small grocery store and lunch stop diner that served the occasional tourist driving the mountain roads, and a few run-down businesses that hadn't had customers for a generation.

A little over fourteen months ago, a developer moved into town and began refurbishing the homes into livable—albeit barely—properties. A few months later, a wave of Middle Eastern refugees began populating the dying town. Business started to rekindle. The grocery store began to cater to the new clientele and the small diner turned into a tea shop offering a taste of the locals' homelands.

Within six months, the town was nearly repopulated with Syrians, Afghanis, Iraqis, and other Middle Easterners. Two months later, Sandy Creek was rarely spoken and Sand Town became its moniker.

Not everyone in Frederick County was happy to see the town revitalized.

Caine was no stranger to Sand Town and left the diner on foot. He walked across the road to a two-story, four-bay cement block garage. There, an older Iraqi mechanic and his eldest son were working on one of two school buses parked inside the garage.

As Caine approached, the older man shooed his son away to the rear of the garage. The man waited until Caine stopped beneath the open garage door before he turned and acknowledged him.

"*Salaam*," the mechanic said, bowing slightly. He continued in Arabic. "We are not finished yet. I am waiting on the remaining parts."

Caine surveyed the first bus—Bus 219. Alongside it were a series of long pipes and a box of spray nozzles similar to fire sprinkler heads. Caine replied in Arabic, "What are you missing?"

"Connectors and air compressor controllers. The wiring for the controls. I am not a plumber or an electrician, I am a mechanic. I do my best to meet Khalifah's demands. But what he asks is difficult."

"Khalifah has not asked anything. He commands." Caine glared at the man. "Do your best. I'll check on your supplies."

The older mechanic looked to the ground for a long moment. When he looked up, his eyes were teary and his face pale and meek. "Will he and Saeed Mansouri understand it is not my fault? Will he not hurt my family?"

"I don't know what Khalifah understands or not. Saeed is a thug that Khalifah has on a leash." Caine turned to go but stopped and turned back around. "I will see he does not hurt your family because of this delay. Make certain there are no others."

"*Shukran. Shukran.*" The mechanic ran to Caine and took his hand in both of his, thanking him over and over and nearly pulling Caine off-balance. "I am in your debt."

"Yes, you are." Caine pulled free. "Remember that, too."

CHAPTER 28

Day 3: May 17, 0945 Hours, Daylight Saving Time
Frederick County Sheriff's Office, Outside Winchester, Virginia

BY THE TIME Artie arranged for Bond to release me and even return my .45, it was after my breakfast time and I was starved. Cop coffee and plastic-packaged, stale donuts didn't count as the most important meal of the day. So, I wandered Old Town until I found a nice sidewalk breakfast café, took an outside table, and ordered a heaping breakfast. The server, an older woman with pulled-back gray hair and a plump, puffy face, poured me coffee with a wide, friendly smile, and disappeared. Between sips, I sat and watched the people around town.

I half-expected Bond and Perry to be hiding behind newspapers and cheap sunglasses nearby. But no, they were nowhere to be seen.

I sipped my coffee and Kevin joined me at the table—memories, conversations—regrets. The ache was gone. Most of it. I kept it at bay by focusing on what was ahead. Thoughts about the old times were bittersweet. Some memories made me laugh. Well, now I could laugh. Once, Kevin had to get the neighbors to drop trespassing charges against me. I was fifteen and had broken into our neighbor's garage. Inside, there were secret radios and stolen government secrets. I was sure that Mr. Chan Lee was a Chinese spy—a clandestine agent plotting to overthrow our government. Much to my dismay, Mr. Lee was not from Beijing, but Buffalo. He was not a spy. He was a dentist. I spent the entire summer mowing lawns for restitution.

Ah, the good old days.

When I looked up from my coffee, Noor Mallory loomed above me. She was stone-faced and her eyes dark and cold. I'd spent a few days held by Afghan warlords while they decided if I would be a guest at dinner or cut into little pieces. The look on her face made me reminisce for those days. I was never good figuring out women, but I think she was upset with me.

"We must talk. Now, I think."

Oh crap.

She didn't wait for an invitation and sat across from me.

"Um, sure." *Okay, Hunter, don't screw this one up.* "Everything okay? Are the deputies still at your home?"

"Yes. Sam did not mention the fight last evening. Dave told me."

"He didn't?" My heart sank. Of all the people I didn't want to disappoint, it was Noor. "Look, things got a little out of hand."

She glared at me. "I cannot have Sam involved in such things. He has enough problems."

I held up my cup and flashed my best puppy dog eyes. "Coffee?"

"No." She glanced at her watch. "I have more funeral arrangements."

"Please, Noor. Give me a few minutes. Okay?"

She lowered her eyes. When she raised them, they were a little softer. Still angry as hell, but a softer angry as hell. "Fine. Tea."

I beckoned for my server, who arrived at the table carrying a carafe of coffee. "How about more coffee and some tea for my guest."

The puffy-faced lady stared at Noor. She refilled my coffee but never took her eyes off Noor. "Tea? Let me check on that." She snapped a dry, nervous look at me and walked off.

Noor followed her with her eyes. "Tell me about the fight, if you please."

"I'm sorry," I said before she could reload. "That fight wasn't my fault and it never fazed Sam. I think he knew those guys."

"What is it about Sam you do not trust?" She slapped the tabletop with a bang. "You think he is involved with them, too? Why, because they are not from here? We are not from here? So we must all be involved somehow?"

"I'm not saying that." Though, the thought had seeped into my head. "He did know those two, Noor. They're trouble, trust me. I'm worried about Sam."

"I, too, am concerned." She played with a paper napkin on the table and used the distraction to keep from looking at me. "He has not been home today, and he is not answering his cell phone. Bobby called me and cannot reach Sam either."

Interesting. "What did Bobby want?"

"I do not know. I do not like him. Kevin did not either and warned Sam away."

Bobby and Sam had some explaining to do. Neither of them mentioned any issues with Kevin. Sometimes, people lie outright. Other times, they lie through silence. Either way, lying was lying.

"Give me Bobby's number." She did, and I added, "Where's he live?"

She thought a moment. "Near the university. One of the small hotels they made into dormitories. Yes, I have seen him there."

I started to ask another question when she ambushed me.

"Now, why did you lie to me, Jon *Hunter*?"

Jon Hunter? Lie? I didn't lie, I . . . oh crap. Lying was lying. "I didn't mean to. My past isn't important. I wanted you to get to know me first. Obviously, Kevin never told you about me. Not the real me, anyway. I thought I'd wait until a better time."

She folded her arms. "There is time now."

Now?

Noor looked at me for a long time. Her green eyes were both beautiful and dangerous. "Why do you not use your real name? Dave asked. I do not know."

"Captain Amazing was taken." She actually smiled. "I often use cover names for my work with the CIA."

"CIA?" The letters were bitter as she spit them. She pushed back a little from the table. "You are *CIA*?"

"Ah, well, sort of." I guess Bond forgot that part. "I used to be, I mean. Not anymore. I'm a consultant."

"Kevin never told me." She looked away as tears welled in her eyes. "He said you were in business. He was always vague. I believed it was your bad blood that kept him silent."

"Noor, it's not important." I reached for her hand, but she pulled it away. That stung. "I've been overseas for years. Kevin didn't know much about me, either."

"He did not speak of you. Except . . ."

"Except?"

She started to reply when my breakfast arrived without her tea. I looked up at the server. "Ma'am, how about that tea?"

The woman looked from me to Noor and back. "All out. Sorry." She turned to go.

"You're out of tea?" *Oh, hell no.* "How about some coffee for her, then?"

Noor raised a hand. "Jon, please. I am fine."

The server glanced at me with fangs and a sour face. "See, she's fine."

"I'm not fine." I returned puffy-face's stare with ice. "What the hell's wrong with you? Bring some coffee. Now. *Please.*"

The server started to reply, hesitated, and relented. "Yeah, sure, coffee. Okay." She retrieved a cup from another empty table, filled it from her carafe, and dropped it on the table hard enough to spill.

"Anything else?"

"No. This is fine. Thank you." Noor waited for her to leave and caught my eyes. "Let this go, Jon. It is not worth it."

Let it go? "Noor, do you know her? Is there a problem?"

She shook her head. "I do not know her. I do not need to."

"What then?"

"Surely you must understand? These are your people. These days, we are all from Sand Town, no?"

My people? "Ah, no. But they're yours. You've lived here a long time."

She lowered her eyes. "Yes, I have. But you see, yesterday, I was the sorrowful local widow of a murdered policeman. Today, after the horror at the mall, I am just another scary Muslim who must be from Sand Town. Yesterday, hugs and well-wishing. Today and tomorrow will be ignorance and stares."

Jesus. Was she right? I looked after the server and the spilled coffee. Yes, she was.

"Noor, I'm so sorry."

She turned away and let the silence simmer. After a few long, unnerving moments, she turned back to me. "Kevin told me once he wondered if you'd ever come home again. That was months ago."

Months ago? I received the letter two weeks ago. "Did Kev say why he wanted me home?"

"He was not, I mean, he had not been himself." She was crying and her last words were a whisper. "We did not talk. His comments about you were all he'd said in weeks to me."

I ate a little breakfast and let her have a moment. It took both eggs and half my steak before it was safe. "Was Kevin in trouble?"

"Something was wrong. I do not know."

She was lying. She knew something. "Noor, you have to be straight with me."

"Why?" Her green eyes flashed. "You have not been honest with me. You were never in our lives. You return and Kevin is murdered. Maybe if you returned sooner."

There it was. She wasn't even aiming and she hit me right between the eyes. Maybe if I'd come home when I first got his message, he'd be alive. Maybe if I'd met him a few hours earlier instead of procrastinating, he'd be alive. Maybe if I'd stayed in touch all these years . . .

Maybe. Maybe. Maybe. Damn.

Her eyes flooded and she reached for my hand. "That was unfair. It is not your fault." She clutched my hand and drew it close. Grief accomplished what I could not. "I am sorry."

I held her eyes and tried to speak. At first, words wouldn't come. Finally, all I could manage was, "Noor, I'm home now."

"Please," she whispered, "what happened between you two? I must know."

What indeed? Kevin was angry every time we spoke. Our telephone calls lasted a couple minutes. The last I'd actually seen Kevin was at that Washington bar. It had ended badly. The images were as clear as yesterday, and the happy hour partiers and jukebox music were still vivid in my mind. Since then, our connection had been just phone calls here and there. They always ended in anger.

"Noor, he was obsessed with money. He wanted me to go to college so I'd make more money afterward. All I really wanted was, well, some adventure." I sat back and hoped my feeble explanation would satisfy her. It shouldn't. It didn't satisfy me. "We were in different worlds. That sounds cliché, doesn't it?"

"Money, yes. Yes, it was always money." Those green eyes found mine again and their anger turned soft and sad. "Different worlds. Kevin and I were like that, too. For so long now." Tears again. "What took you so long? It has been two months since, ah, since he wrote."

"I just got the letter a few weeks ago."

"I see." She blinked a few times and wiped away the tears.

I still held her hand. "Tell me everything."

Her face darkened with painful memories. Some of them must have been more than painful—devastating. She played with her coffee cup, looked around the café, and bit her lip.

Finally, she looked at me again. "The other night when Kevin was murdered, Dave came and told me. I will never forget."

Noor and Dave spoke about each other with such familiarity. It stung. "How about Artie Polo and Victoria Bacarro? Have you spoken with them?"

"I do not like Bacarro."

"She doesn't like me, either," I snorted. "You two have that in common."

She dropped her head and let slip a laugh. "Perhaps."

I got serious again. "Any idea who killed Kevin or why?"

"Perhaps that man at my house?" She looked away. "I do not know. Kevin worked so much. He would come and go. He told me nothing. We fought. He and Sam, too. Kevin was not always easy to be around."

I fidgeted a little. "I remember."

"Why did it happen, Jon? Did he say anything to you before he died?"

"Yes, but nothing I understood." I thought about Kevin's last words. "Noor, you never answered me before. Not really. Do you know what he meant by 'G'? Did Kevin ever mention the name Khalifah or Maya?"

She shook her head. "No. I have not heard any of that. I swear."

"I'll work on it."

She frowned. "Kevin was killed where he and Dave went fishing."

The thought of Dave and Kevin drinking beer and telling stories at our favorite fishing spot sent a spear jabbing my gut.

"Were they close?"

"Once, yes. Not the past months. Kevin said it was work. He fought with everyone except Bacarro."

"She and Kev were close?"

Noor flushed. For a long time, she sipped her coffee and avoided my eyes. When she finally looked over her cup at me, her voice was strained. "Yes. Close. Only her."

I wanted to pursue that but thought better. "Kevin wasn't getting along with anyone?"

"No. He was quitting his job."

"What?"

"There were strange calls on his phone bill. When I asked him about them, he said he was talking with someone about a job."

"All he ever wanted was to be a cop."

"It was the money." She looked away. "He said security contractors made much more than he. He always worried about money. He wanted Sam to go to college, and well, we cannot afford that. That is why we sold the cabin."

No, you didn't sell the cabin. I let that slide, too. Now was not the time to blindside her. It was another lie by silence, but one I could live with.

"I'm going to get to the bottom of this, Noor. Artie Polo and I . . ."

She looked down. "*Him.*"

"What's wrong with Artie?"

"Jon, come to the house tonight." She squeezed my hand. "We will talk more. I need time."

"Okay, sure. But tell me about Artie?"

"Tonight." Whether it was caution or grief in her eyes I didn't know, but it was there now. "Please?"

"Okay, sure."

She stood to leave, and I asked a nagging question. "Who was Kevin speaking with about a job?"

"Petrov. Edik Petrov."

CHAPTER 29

Day 3: May 17, 1045Hours, Daylight Saving Time
Old Town, Winchester, Virginia

EDIK PETROV?

After Noor left, I pulled out a fistful of bills from my wallet and caught the puffy-faced server watching me. I smiled and dropped about 120 worth of bills on the table. 120 *Afghanis* that is. That's about two bucks in good ole American sawbucks. That's more than the old bigot deserved. After all, she probably spit on my eggs, too.

I headed for my rental.

As I approached my car, I noticed something tucked beneath one of my windshield wipers. I thought it was a traffic ticket—Bond harassing me. Then I realized it was a small piece of paper, rolled tightly and jammed beneath the wiper blade so not to be noticed easily. I retrieved it and read it. "*They no stop the mall. We must talk. 10 2-nite behind Handley Library. I watch you. No police. G.*"

The mysterious "G" was a person, after all. He was involved with the terror attack at the mall and Kevin was involved with him. Terrific. I looked around but no one seemed to notice me, so I pocketed my note and drove to the hotel.

The "Do Not Disturb" sign was already on the door when I reached my room.

Now, who put that there? Perhaps a lingerie model was waiting inside with no morals and free cookies? Nope. Agent Victoria Bacarro wasn't a lingerie model and she hadn't brought me cookies, but she'd do.

"Victoria, how nice." I shut the door. "You should know that I'm not cheap. I'm easy, but not cheap."

She sat in the wingback chair in the corner of the room. Her feet were propped up on my bed. She wore the same navy blue business suit and the light, white cotton shirt as earlier. Her jacket was open and I couldn't help but notice her butt inside. Pistol butt that is. I also couldn't help but notice her other concealed weapons hiding farther up. Take nothing from that comment. I'm a trained observer.

She half-grinned, half-frowned. "Are you always a consummate smartass, Mr. Hunter?"

"Consummate, absolutely. Please, it's Jon, or Hunter. No mister. But definitely consummate."

"I see." Her eyes penetrated me. She caught me peeking at her gun, so she casually allowed her fingers to rest on the holster. "I want to follow up on this morning. You don't mind, do you?"

"Of course not. After all, we're all after the same thing. Aren't we?"

"Are we?"

"Kevin's killer. You want to arrest him, and I want to serve him to the worms."

"Then we do want the same thing." She looked me up and down. "I'm here off-the-books."

I winked. "Sure, I work like that a lot, too. Why are you?"

"Because even though I'm the task force chief, I prefer to do things on my own this time."

This time?

"Two things interest me, Hunter." She shifted in the chair. "First, you assume Kevin's killer is a man. Why?"

Interesting comment. "It could be a woman. If so, she's a nasty bit . . . one." She sized me up again and gave me a warm, tingly feeling. "What's the second thing, Vicky?"

"Agent Bacarro."

"Victoria."

"You are so much like Kevin in some ways." She allowed an almost imperceptible smile. "Not even close in most."

"You don't know me yet."

"No, I don't." She raised her chin. All FBI agents raise their chins when they get serious. "Artie says you were Army Special Forces. A Green Beret."

I nodded.

"You're a killer."

Wow, really? "Well, not like it sounds. But, yeah, I can do the job."

"You must be good. The CIA wouldn't use you as a consultant if you weren't." She leaned forward and locked eyes with me. "Are you, Hunter? Are you good at killing?"

I didn't like where this was leading. "Yes, Victoria. But you've been trained to kill, too."

"It's not the same." She stood. "You stopped Noor Mallory's intruder with a can of soup."

"Tomatoes."

"Whatever." She zeroed in with one eye. "You can kill with guns, knives, and hand-to-hand. Even tomatoes."

I didn't answer. I didn't need to.

"Any other skills?"

"No, you're doing okay." I tried to see beyond her eyes, but all I got was static. "I just don't know what you want from me."

She walked to the window and opened the blinds to look out into the parking lot. I hoped it wasn't a signal for a SWAT team to bust in the door and remove my spleen with a spoon. "I need to know who you really are. I need confidence that you're Kev's brother. Proof, Hunter. I need proof."

She hit me right in the gut and never threw a punch. "I am, Victoria. Ask Noor."

"I did."

"And?"

Curveball. "Noor is Iranian. Did you know that?"

"I noticed."

"Sameh, too. But they're not related. Not by blood, I mean."

What was she playing at? "Sam was born here. Noor escaped Iran years ago. I'm not up on the details."

"They're still Iranian."

"I know the geography better than you. Your point?"

"Just thinking out loud." She faced me with folded arms. "Noor *thinks* you're Kevin's brother. She's never seen a photo or a letter. No proof."

No, there really wasn't proof, was there? "Artie can vouch for me."

"Artie knew Kevin. He knew you." She shook her head. "You never told him about Kevin. Kevin never mentioned you to anyone. Not even me."

Not even her? "Something you want to tell me, Victoria?"

"No." She slowly walked to the dresser and looked at me through the mirror—classic vampire test. "CIA needs to vouch for you, but our liaison won't. I need identification that connects you and Kevin. Relatives? Anything?"

I had none of that available. "Look, Victoria, I left Virginia as a kid. I'm sure if you dig around enough, you'll find someone who remembers me. But, after our folks died, we stayed to ourselves and had few friends. They'll remember the name but probably not the face. I don't know what to tell you. Go pull my birth records and match me up to my military records. The FBI can do that much."

"Your military records are classified. The Army won't budge. Seems someone has a hold on them."

I know who that was. LaRue. "You know I didn't kill Kevin, so what's your problem?"

She turned from the mirror and crossed the room to me. She stopped a foot away and did the FBI mind-probe. It didn't work because she'd have to zoom into my eyes and they were focused too low.

"Because it's important to me, Hunter. Because I'm the goddamn FBI and I want proof." She took a breath and softened. "No, I don't think you killed Kevin. But that's not because you claim to be his brother. It's the evidence. You say you're a CIA consultant and Artie backs you up. But that's all I have. Nothing else. No records. No witnesses. No proof. I need all of that. I need to know you're Kev's brother."

Kev's brother? Did I hear something in her voice that wasn't there?

I looked straight into her FBI-vampire eyes. "You know, Victoria, your slinking in here isn't exactly FBI protocol, is it?"

"No, it's not." She retreated to the window again. "But these are not normal times. I'm responsible for this case. Things have gone bad. I need to know who I'm dealing with. You were with Kevin when he died. I need to trust what you told us. I need to trust *you*. That, Jonathan Mallory Hunter, begins with knowing just who you really are and what you know."

I'd swear she had a shudder in her voice just then. Emotion. Maybe a little self-pity. But I was exhausted and didn't want to misjudge her. It might get me in more trouble than my mouth does. Inconceivable as it was.

I said, "It's Jonathan Hunter Mallory, actually. That's what's on my birth certificate. That's what's in my classified Army file. Give me a week and I'll hand-deliver all the proof you need. All of it. Records. Witnesses. But I need a week."

"Why a week?"

I said nothing.

"Because you're AWOL from the Agency."

"Perhaps." Well, that was no longer true, but I couldn't admit that.

"What happens when they find you?" She allowed herself that thin smile again. "Do they shoot you or something?"

"Or something." I grinned. "I'll have to face the music, and the conductor is a real prick. Worse, I'll have to leave for a while to sort things out. That would mean—"

"You couldn't hunt Kevin's killer." She held my eyes like Dracula. Well, a sexy, hot Dracula—Draculette. "That's your plan, right?"

"Exactly."

"All the coincidences are fascinating, don't you think?"

"Coincidences?"

Her eyes considered me and she picked her words carefully. "You're a CIA spook operating in the Middle East. Your brother, whom you've not seen for years, marries an Iranian refugee and adopts an Iranian boy. Then, Middle Easterners launch a terror attack just after Kevin is murdered in front of you. You're a CIA Middle Eastern counterterrorism operative. It's like you and Kevin were cosmically connected. The cosmos brought you here."

"The cosmos?" What the heck did she smoke? "Victoria, you're seeing shadows where there aren't any. Kevin brought me back home, not some astrology chart."

"Food for thought." She stared at me, and her eyes got inside my head and roamed around awhile. I could feel her probing, seeking, chasing answers. I tried the hypnosis thing that commands obedience. All I got was more static and the weather channel.

Finally, she went to the door and opened it, then turned and faced me. There was no thin smile. No dark, probing eyes. There was relief.

"Okay, you're Kevin's brother." She left and closed the door behind her.

Damn, if it was that easy, I would have hypnotized her before.

CHAPTER 30

Day 3: May 17, 1325 Hours, Daylight Saving Time
Union Station, Washington, DC

KHALIFAH WALKED BENEATH Union Station's barrel ceiling, through the lobby, and out into the afternoon sun. He shifted the tiny video recorder in his breast suitcoat pocket and turned in slow movements to record the entire train station entrance. Then he waited for traffic, nodded to a nearby policeman who watched the crowds, and crossed Columbus Circle toward his SUV parked west of the station entrance.

He moved casually along. He wasn't worried that anyone would approach or question him. His dark skin and businessman-like appearance was easily camouflaged among Washington's cosmopolitan ethnicities. Even in his *taqiyah*, full beard, and dark, expensive Saville Row suit, he did not stand out from the other such men of foreign descent around him. In all the nation's cities, a man such as he was just one of millions going unnoticed.

He was a man of the people on these streets. He was a man who liked to do his own planning and see his targets as they would be seen when he executed his plans.

When he reached the SUV registered to Kazan Limited, he sat behind the steering wheel and appeared to talk on his cell phone—just another commuter checking in with wife or office.

The SUV was parked in a small lot that faced across Columbus circle with a full view of the rail station entrance.

His body equipment continued to record.

Before he left the SUV to hail a cab, he manipulated the car stereo. His combination of digital entries activated a closed-circuit television camera hidden in the vehicle's roof rack. Next, he removed his false eyeglasses and hidden camera and tossed them into the glove box. He scanned the area and, satisfied no one was watching, slid from the SUV and locked the door. He hailed a cab, instructed the driver to bring him to the Galleria Shopping Mall in Tysons Corner, and sat back for the brief trip. There, another transformation would take place and another vehicle awaited him.

Events were in motion. In time, another cool half-million would be in his account.

CHAPTER 31

Day 3: May 17, 1330 Hours, Daylight Saving Time
Winchester, Virginia

VICTORIA'S VISIT LEFT me stewing as I paced my hotel room and tried to make sense of everything. She came for answers. I don't know if she got them, but she left me with more questions. Why had she come "off-the-books"? Sure, she wanted to know who I was. After all, I totally screwed up my initial introduction that first night at the river. But "off-the-books"? For an FBI agent hunting the murderer of one of her own, she didn't ask me any real FBI questions. She just wanted a warm, cozy feeling about me.

She said she got it. Had she?

After the stewing led nowhere but a headache, I decided to work on the Bobby Kruppa problem. Bobby had some explaining to do, and there was no time like the present. Of course, I had to find him. Winchester wasn't that big and Noor told me the general vicinity to look in.

How hard could finding a pudgy, awkward twenty-year-old college kid be?

Easier than I thought, obviously. First, I drove to the University of the Shenandoah Valley on the outskirts of Winchester and looked around a complex of two older hotels. They were the kind with outdoor stairs and room entrances found off any interstate. The buildings had been renovated and turned into campus housing, as Noor had described. Next, around the rear of one unit, I knew exactly which apartment Bobby lived in. It was the first door on the right, atop the stairs, beside the second-floor landing.

How did I know?

Easy. As I pulled into the parking area, Azar and Fariq were pushing their way into a second-floor dorm room. I was sure Bobby Kruppa was inside. This detective stuff isn't all that difficult.

I climbed the outside stairs and slipped around the walkway. I did not see Fariq, Azar, and Bobby when I reached the second floor. As I made my way to the room, I scanned the area looking for any sign of other trouble, like friends of Fariq's and Azar's to be loitering. Nothing. What I did see was Kevin's custom trike motorcycle parked beside a dumpster. Next to it stood a thin, helmeted rider. I watched him climb on board, start the engine, and zoom off.

Sam. Coincidence? I think not.

Bobby's room door was closed and the window blinds drawn. Several shouts and cries reverberated from inside and something slammed hard against the inside door. Bobby cried out again.

I pulled my .45 and stood in front of the door. With my thumb over the peephole so no one could cheat, I knocked on the door. "Housekeeping." I did my best girlie-girl impression. The scuffle inside stopped, but no one came to the door. "Come on or I'll get the manager."

Footsteps reached the door. With a grunt, someone popped the door open four inches.

Just enough.

In one violent movement, I kicked the door and propelled myself through. Azar was on the other side and had his face pressed into the four-inch opening. He got a mouth full of metal door and was knocked into the middle of the room on his back. Inside, I leveled my .45 at Fariq's chest before anyone—especially Fariq—could react. I toed the door closed behind me and contemplated the two thugs across the room.

Fariq had Bobby in a full nelson. Bobby's face was bruised and bloodied. Welts had already formed around his mouth and eyes. His room had been ransacked.

I lazily lowered the pistol toward Fariq's groin. "I'm sure we've seen the same movies."

Fariq, not having missed the nuance of my gesture, released Bobby and stepped back. Bobby crawled onto the couch across the room. Tears streamed down his face. "Thank God," he whimpered. "They're going to kill me. I couldn't find Sam. I called and called. He won't answer me."

"Shut it, Bobby." I kicked Azar in the thigh and kept my gun on Fariq. "Up, Azar. Slow."

Azar complied, and, in broken English, spat, "This is nothing for you here. Walk away or it will surely be bad for you."

We did watch the same movies. I knew all the cool door-kickin' moves and they knew all the cheesy threats. Instead of another movie line, I baited him a bit. "Azar, where are you really from? Baghdad?"

Azar spat at me. "No, pig. I am Iranian."

"Azar!" Fariq yelled. "Be silent. Tell him nothing."

Fariq was shy about his family heritage. Interesting. "Time to go home, boys. If I see you here or at the café or anywhere within a mile of Bobby or Sam and Noor Mallory, I'll forget I'm a peacenik and blow your balls off."

Fariq helped Azar to his feet. "No one will care about this one. No one will care about you, either. Sameh Mallory least of all. Soon you will understand."

That was a funny thing to say.

"Please get them outta here." Bobby's eyes darted from them to me. "I won't call the cops if they promise to leave me alone."

I waved the gun. "Do we have a deal?"

Azar's eye was bloodshot and turning a kaleidoscope of color. His mouth was bleeding and he rubbed his shoulder. Still, he managed to say, "*Baleh.*"

Fariq dragged Azar toward the door. He stopped and turned back to Bobby. "No police. That is our deal. For now. You will not have this protection always."

"No cops. I swear." Bobby left the couch and backed into the corner of the room, like a rat trying to escape. "I told you before I won't talk to the cops. I swear. Leave me alone. You don't have to come back. Please."

Azar aimed a gun-finger at Bobby. "We will be looking at you. We will know if you have lied to us." Then to me, he cocked his gun-finger and pulled the trigger. "You will soon understand."

I walked to the door, shoved them out, then slammed and locked it. When I turned around, my face burned and my muscles wanted to scream. I went to Bobby, grabbed him by the shirt, and pressed him against the wall.

"What, dude?" His eyes bulged and his mouth dropped open. "What's going on?"

"Enough of this, Bobby." I holstered my pistol and jammed an angry finger into his cheek. "Twice now I almost got myself killed for you. There's no third time. What happened at the river?"

His face drained around the blossoming bruises. His eyes darted around and wouldn't settle. His breath came faster and faster as he approached a panic attack.

"Now, Bobby." I ground my finger harder into his cheek. "Or I call Fariq and Azar back for dessert."

"You wouldn't."

I tossed him onto the couch and went to the door. My fingers were closing on the knob when he whimpered jumbled words.

"Pictures. I . . . the body was . . ."

"Spit it out, Bobby. They're still in the parking lot."

"Down at the river." He steadied himself, burning a hole in the carpet with his eyes. "I didn't just find the body."

I folded my arms. "What did you see?"

"It's not what I saw." He shook all over. "It's what I did."

"What did you do?"

He rubbed his eyes and continued to shake. The meltdown lasted two minutes and I didn't intervene. When he finally calmed and looked up, it all made sense.

"Pictures. I took pictures."

CHAPTER 32

Day 3: May 17, 1345 Hours, Daylight Saving Time
Middleburg, Virginia

LaRue raised his glass of white wine and waited for his companion to do the same. "To old friends, Alexei, and new ones."

"New friends? How intriguing." The tall, sturdy Foreigner with dark, sunken eyes cocked his head. His swarthy complexion and gruff, accented voice betrayed his Leningrad roots. "So, you did not invite me here to Middleburg, no matter how beautiful and quaint. What then? To reminisce?"

LaRue allowed a thin smile. "An extraordinary thing has happened, Alexei. I have found myself in possession of information I wish were untrue."

"Oh, what might that be?"

"Terrible things. I am told your people are instigating horrific events on American soil."

Alexei Fedorov sipped his wine with his right hand, keeping his left on his lap below the table in a self-conscious habit, not for the concealment of a weapon. "Preposterous. Do not trust such rumors. There are many who would like to see the old days return and America and Russia at odds again."

"No, no. I have not learned this from outsiders. The source is very credible. Let us say he warmed to me and discussed these matters freely and with candor."

"Warmed?" Fedorov's eyes narrowed. "My dear friend, you play with words."

LaRue continued. "You see, I am told the SVR believes it can keep America focused elsewhere in order to have a freer hand for Russian expansion. Simple misdirection. An old tactic I am familiar with. Divert attention and maneuver quietly."

Fedorov did not like hearing "SVR" spoken anywhere but in his embassy office in Washington, DC, and even then, only in hushed words within his secure SCIF. There, he was *General-Polkovnik*—Colonel General—Alexei Mikhailovich Fedorov, Chief Resident of the Russian Foreign Intelligence Service and senior most officer in the United States. There, he controlled everything. But in Middleburg, he controlled nothing.

"Misdirection?" Fedorov sipped his wine. "I, too, am familiar with such strategy. You, my friend, are a master of this, no? This source of yours, he is perhaps unreliable?"

"My new friend told me his handler was an old master himself, Alexei. You."

"Me? Silliness. I am too old and senior to, how do you say, get my hands dirty."

LaRue smiled again. "Our countries have tried to put the past far behind us. To learn that a Russian operation is unfolding on American soil and costing American lives might set the clock back considerably—to *colder* days."

"Careful, my friend." Fedorov slid forward in his seat. "Are you suggesting we are behind recent atrocities here?"

"I do not suggest anything." LaRue held the old spy's eyes. He didn't move or show any emotion. "I am asking that sensibility return. However, if what I believe is true, I urge you to assist me in correcting this unfortunate matter before I am forced to do so alone. If I am forced to, I will use a wide brush."

"A wide brush?"

"I am fearful." LaRue took a moment to finish his wine. When he set his glass on the table, he folded his hands in front of him. "We teetered on the brink of total destruction in the past. You play with those days again. Putin has flexed his muscle and struts around like a schoolboy seeking admirers—the emperor and his new clothes."

"Be careful." The Russian held up a hand. "America is weak. Even you must admit that. No? Ill-considered wars have exhausted you and poorly executed strategies lessen your credibility. While victory was within your fingers, you failed to grasp it. Now your allies are distrustful. We both know the American flag does not fly so high any longer."

"Your point, Alexei Mikhailovich Fedorov?"

The Russian smiled. "Why not simply allow us to ensure our own security as you have sought to secure yours? Perhaps two world powers can both have what they wish and not interfere with one another."

"Interfere with one another?" LaRue forced a grin. "Have you forgotten our elections?"

"Elections?" The Russian laughed and slapped the table for effect. "Killing one's opponent or removing the voices of opposition by force, now, that is interfering in elections. You speak of e-mails? A ten-year-old's computer tricks. Please, my friend, do not insult me."

LaRue lifted his chin. "I do not hear you speaking of Russia's aggression in Ukraine and the animal you have on a leash, Bashir Assad."

"Now you insult me with words like aggression. Is America's interference in the Middle East not aggression? The goose and gander, my friend. Perhaps America should focus more on its own weaknesses at home than abroad. Russia is simply securing itself against foreign threats as America contends the same in the Middle East. There is no difference."

"No difference?" LaRue's eyes darkened. His grandfatherly smile was replaced by a tight, hard jaw. "You will learn we are not weak in the wake of recent terrorist events, Alexei. You might consider our response should the *Sluzhba Vneshney Razvedki* be caught sponsoring those events."

"No, no, how could you think that? I merely suggest that America has grown fragile and may stand alone very soon."

LaRue didn't speak.

"America should limit its own aggressions and leave Russian affairs to Russia. A mere suggestion."

LaRue removed his eyeglasses for a polishing. "Let me suggest, my dear friend, that Russia may wish to recalculate its perceptions. They are flawed. Don't believe that allies who squabble are not still true allies."

Fedorov stood and bowed his head slightly. "Dangerous times. Perhaps we should all consider the cost of our struggle these last seventy years. You should be careful in suggesting Russian aggression is on your shores."

"Grigori Sokoloff." LaRue's words were served cold and direct. "*Operation Maya.*"

Fedorov took a single step toward the door and stopped. He turned and smiled a warm, nervous smile. "We have been friends for many years, Oscar LaRue. Even during the dark times. Times when our two countries looked for reasons to destroy one another. Even then, you and I found understanding."

"Precisely why I asked you here today, Alexei. Understanding."

The Russian spymaster held his counterpart's eyes in a steady, stern gaze. "Perhaps I will call you late in the week. Surely, friendship will allow me that much?"

"Two days, Alexei." LaRue reached for the half-empty bottle of Sauvignon Blanc. "In three, I cannot be responsible."

General-Polkovnik Alexei Mikhailovich Fedorov nodded warily and looked down, offering a timid wave with his disfigured hand and missing ring finger. "I will do what I can, my friend. No more. No less."

CHAPTER 33

Day 3: May 17, 1415 Hours, Daylight Saving Time
University of the Shenandoah Valley, Winchester, Virginia

"Show me."

Bobby Kruppa inserted a USB drive he'd retrieved from its hiding place above the bathroom ceiling tiles into his notebook computer. Before rescuing him from Azar and Fariq for the second time, I would have called him paranoid.

Not anymore.

"Okay." He tapped on the keyboard. "I encrypted the files so no one could steal them."

After Fariq and Azar left, Bobby and I had been going over what he'd witnessed the night Kevin was killed. We sat at his tiny kitchen table for more than an hour. Stacks of junk, college books, and old pizza boxes surrounded us. Worse, the smell of dirty clothes hung in the air like a gas attack in the Argonne. If this was what I missed by skipping college, I had no regrets.

"This is the first photo." Bobby tapped the screen. "I took this from the boat launch entrance. It's an overall shot and the rest are close-ups."

The digital photograph was dark. I could see the front of Bobby's car in the foreground, and in the distance, a pickup truck was parked with its driver's door open facing the Shenandoah River. A faint image of an arm—at least it looked like an arm—showed over the side of the truck bed. The truck was unscathed at the point he took the photo. The scene flashed before me. Except that when I was there dodging bullets and Kevin was on the ground dying.

"You always go on dates with your camera?" I asked.

"I'm a journalism major. You never know when something crazy will happen. I have to be ready for a story."

Bobby must be an exciting date.

The next image was a closer shot of the lifeless body lying facedown in the bed of the truck. The next was the stainless-steel case beside the front of the pickup. There was something else, too. Something I hadn't seen that night.

"What's that?" I pointed to a dark form on the ground just below the pickup's open door. It was irregularly shaped and about eighteen inches square. It looked as though it had fallen out of the cab when the door opened.

"I don't know," Bobby said. "Let's enhance it."

He clicked on a desktop program and worked the image. After three or four different processes were run over the photo, he guided the image into the center of the screen. "It's a backpack like everyone at school wears."

"Start at the beginning."

Bobby's face scrunched up. "I already told you three times."

"Make it four."

His monotone was slow and unhappy. "Lacey and I were down the road making out. We heard the shots, thought it was thunder, and started to leave. When we reached the boat launch, the truck was there with its doors open. We didn't see anyone around."

"Skip to the photographs."

"You said start at the beginning. I am." Bobby folded his arms. "I got out to see what was up and saw the body."

"You grabbed your camera and took pictures."

Bobby shivered. "Well, first I checked out the guy in the pickup. Lacey locked herself in the car. This could have gotten me a great story in the paper and a guaranteed A for the year. Maybe even a job after school."

It might also get him killed. "Did you search the area?"

"No." He cocked his head. "I'm not stupid."

"Right." I remembered my deal with Victoria and Artie. "After taking the photos, you went for help?"

"Yeah." He hesitated for a moment. "Like I said, the cops took, like, forever. We answered questions for a while, and then they sent us to the station for a statement."

"Bobby, at the scene, you didn't take anything?"

"No. Why?"

"Because that backpack wasn't there afterward."

He stared at the computer screen. "Maybe you missed it."

"No."

"You could have missed it."

"No." I tapped the image on screen. "I would have seen them take it. Everything was in place when the police got there, and I watched their every move."

His face fell. "Someone took it after I left."

"Yes." I watched his face turn to panic. "After you left and before Kevin arrived. There were only minutes between."

Bobby was pale now. His eyes roamed the photograph for another answer. "It was almost an hour before the cops met us at the gas station. A lot can happen in an hour." He clicked through the photographs, one by one. With each image, he shrunk in the chair.

Finally, he understood. "The killer was still there, wasn't he?"

I didn't answer.

"He saw me taking pictures. What do you think was in the backpack?"

"I don't know."

His eyes snapped on something on the screen. "Hey, there's something in the background of this photo. I've never noticed it before."

"What?"

"I'll try to enhance it." His fingers whizzed around the keyboard. "It's a tiny glare of light. Maybe a reflection on the opposite bank of the river. It's too far away. My software can't do much."

I stared at the photograph with the pickup truck in the foreground. Above the hood, across the Shenandoah River, was a faint, ghostly smudge of light.

"It's probably a reflection off the river."

"Maybe." He tried without success to improve the image. His fingers became heavy and demanding on the keys. He held his breath so long he had to gasp for air. "I need better graphics tools to clean this up."

I knew where to get better graphics tools. "Bobby, copy the USB and I'll take it to some friends of mine. They'll work on this."

He went in search of another USB drive in the clutter around the room. I clicked through the images one more time. They told a couple different stories. Only one of them was certain—Bobby had come very close to dying. He knew that now, too. Perhaps Kevin's arrival saved him. Perhaps not.

Time might tell.

I pressed harder. "Tell me about Azar and Fariq. What's with them?"

"God, Mr. Mallory."

"Call me Hunter."

His face screwed up. "Hunter?"

"Hunter." No time for long explanations. "What about your pals earlier?"

He found a spare flash drive in the small refrigerator in the alcove nearby. "Yesterday morning, Fariq and Azar were waiting for me outside in the alley. They roughed me up and told me to forget everything I saw."

"Did they mention your photos?"

"No." He returned to his computer. "Fariq said they were watching me."

"I've got friends. They'll protect you until this is over."

His face lightened as he pushed the thumb drive into the computer. "No one knows about these photographs but Lacey."

"Relax. Maybe Azar and his pals don't know they exist."

"They killed that guy. Maybe even your brother. If someone was still there when I took pictures, then I'm dead, too. Right?"

Maybe. That backpack was missing. The busted stainless-steel case was empty. The body count was already at two. What difference would a scared, pudgy college kid make?

"Where's Lacey?" I asked.

"She went home to see her parents in Maine this morning. Why?"

Good. One less to worry about. "Pack some things. I'm taking you somewhere safe until I get you into witness protection." Artie and I had some negotiating to do before I turned Bobby over to him.

"Okay." His face was blank and staring.

"I'll take care of everything." I scribbled my cell phone number on a piece of paper and slid it across to him. "Put that in your pocket for safekeeping. Do you have more copies of those photographs?"

"Two USB drives and the originals on the computer. I erased the camera's memory."

"Okay, you take the computer. Give me the two drives." I watched his face puzzle up. "No one sees the photos. Not even the cops. Not until I okay it."

"What's going on, Hunter? Why's this happening?"

Without thinking, I said, "It has to do with the terror attack at the mall."

"Terrorists? What are you talking about?" he stuttered. "What's to stop them from killing me?"

"Me."

CHAPTER 34

Day 3: May 17, 1545 Hours, Daylight Saving Time
The George Washington Hotel, Old Town Winchester, Virginia

"Extraordinary."

Here we go again. "Oscar, before you say it, there is no coincidence."

LaRue stood near the windows again across the room. He'd listened to my update since our last meeting in this very hotel. I'd briefed him on Fool's Lake and my discovery of Kevin's stash of money and fake passports. He actually grinned hearing about my arrest and showed no surprise at the appearance of Artie Polo. After a few questions from him, I concluded with my discovery of Bobby Kruppa's photographs.

LaRue folded his arms and looked concerned. "Kruppa is safe? I will send a team."

"He's safe. Right now, any more men running around this town will be noticed."

"Of course," he agreed. "Keep him overnight and get any more you can from him. Shepard will bring a team to you and move him into protective custody in the morning."

"What about Artie?" Artie was gonna be pissed I didn't turn Bobby over to him. "We go way back, Oscar. You know that."

He walked across the room to the small bar and poured us both a drink. I could count the number of times I'd seen LaRue drink this early on one finger. Something was troubling him.

"Oscar?"

After handing me my bourbon, his face twisted a bit. "I am well aware of Polo's involvement. We must take care. If the FBI moves too quickly or incorrectly, we may lose the little edge we now have."

"What edge? What am I missing?"

"Ah, everything, my boy. Everything." He took a long sip of his drink. "Maya is not a person in Baltimore, Hunter. It is a thing. Perhaps the big attack. It is 'Operation Maya.'"

Operation Maya? "How do you know that?"

"Grigori Sokoloff, of course."

Clear as mud again. "Who's he? Can we stop playing 'I've got a secret' and move on?"

Oscar wandered the living room and found an iPad on the coffee table. He tapped a few buttons and the large flat-screen TV powered up. He maneuvered around his iPad like a seventeen-year-old until the TV picture changed. He turned to me and just waited for my reaction.

On screen was a man sitting on a metal chair in a very dark room. Actually, the man was shackled to the chair in the very dark room and he was naked. He was a young man and would have been strong and burly, but his body had been defeated and his shoulders drooped and his head lay down against his chest. When he lifted his chin and looked toward the camera, I recognized him instantly.

"Oscar, that's—"

"Grigori Sokoloff. He is the man who attacked Noor Mallory." Oscar tapped another button and the TV went black. "He is SVR. He is in my care."

"He admitted breaking into Noor's place?"

He shook his head. "We observed him do so."

What? "Care to explain that?"

"That, sir, is irrelevant." Oscar returned to the bar, where I stood still staring at the dark television screen. "What is relevant is that he is SVR."

SVR? Russian intelligence was running around Winchester? What happened to this little town? Terrorists? Russian operatives? The biggest things in town used to be the Apple Blossom Festival and Pancake Day.

My brain ached. "What do the Russians have to do with all this? What did he tell you? What was he doing at Noor's?"

Oscar sat in a straight-back chair near the wall. His face turned a little grim, almost sad. When it did, I knew what he was about to tell me. "Sokoloff was there to clean up."

"Clean up? You mean the money I found at Fool's Lake? The fake Canadian passports Kevin had in bogus names?"

He said nothing. He didn't have to.

Deep down, I knew, and it churned my guts and threatened to come up. "Kevin was bad. He was working for the SVR."

"There is no evidence of that." LaRue's eyes softened. "Sokoloff was dispatched to retrieve any evidence Kevin had that might lead to the SVR. He did not know if Kevin was an asset or not. There is only a peripheral connection."

By peripheral connection, LaRue meant no hard evidence other than too much money, fake passports, and a Russian operative breaking into his house to clean up behind him. You know, nothing "hard" like an SVR Christmas card or a photo of him and Putin having drinks.

I emptied my drink and refilled a very tall, very stiff second one. "What else, Oscar? Give."

He hesitated, cleared his throat, eyed the drink in my hand, and finally he continued. "He told us that Maya was going to take place in Baltimore within the next two weeks. As for the SVR's involvement here, Sokoloff was not privy. He is a foot soldier. A low-level operative."

"Give me five minutes with him and you'll know."

He shook his head. "He has been forthcoming with what he has. For now, you should return to your mission. Leave the SVR and Maya to me. All else is not important."

Wrong. "Kevin's murder is important."

He lifted his chin, began to put me in my place, and thought better of it. "Of course. But they are now one and the same."

Dammit. I started to sip my drink but dumped it into the bar sink instead.

"Look, Oscar, this has been fun. You know, learning about Sokoloff and the SVR playing *Perestroika* in Winchester. I especially love that it's all connected to my brother and a terror cell. Good times, right?"

LaRue just watched me.

"But there's more you're not telling me. I know there is." Another thought hit me. "Hey, you ever heard of a spook named Mo Nassar?"

A dead stare. "Should I?"

"I think he's Agency."

He thought a moment. A moment too long and too contrived. "Ah, yes, of course. I do know of him. Why?"

"Because he's hanging around the FBI task force." I watched him, looking for a lie. Well, in LaRue's case, it wouldn't necessarily be a lie. It might be a clever sleight of hand or a fib. You know, fancy words for a lie. "Do you know him?"

He never batted an eye. "Not directly. Leave him to me either way. It's best you focus on your current task. We both know you don't do well with multitasking."

Ouch. I thought about pursuing Nassar a bit more with LaRue, but all I'd get would be eyeglass polishing and a berating. So, I let it go. "All right, Oscar, I gotta go. I have dinner with Noor and then I have to meet G."

"I will dispatch Shepard to assist with the meeting."

I shook my head. "No. I can't keep you guys out of this if you keep popping up everywhere. You stick out like a sore thumb. It's a meet. I can do this alone."

"Can you? G's value may be more significant than your ego."

Ego? Look who's talking. "No worries, Oscar. I got this." I started for the suite door when his next question turned me around and instantly put me on guard.

"What do you know of Noor Mallory?"

Noor? The way he asked me and the look on his face made me wonder what he knew about her. "She's smart and strong. A former Iranian refugee. She and Kevin adopted a boy."

"Sameh." A scowl darkened his face. "Yes. Sameh was in a boy's home before the adoption. There was some trouble there."

I nodded. "Kevin found him during a homicide investigation."

"Yes, of which Sameh was a suspect. The true murderer was never identified." Oscar looked down for a moment. When he lifted his eyes, they were brighter. "Noor is a very beautiful woman."

Sameh was a teenage murder suspect? Interesting.

He held up a hand to silence any further discussion on Sam and Noor and went into the other room. A moment later, he returned with a black leather wallet. He handed it to me. "You'll require these."

I flipped open the wallet and found a gold badge affixed to one side and an identification card on the other. The badge read "Special Agent" and the ID card declared me a Special Agent for the United States Department of Homeland Security—DHS.

"Woo-hoo." I polished the badge on my shirt. "Do I have to wear a cheap suit and dark sunglasses?"

"Focus, Hunter. Your recent arrest by the authorities and your propensity at similar debacles require strategy."

"Debacles? Hey, I've only been in one or two."

He looked at me with a sour face.

"Okay, maybe more."

He sighed. "There is a card inside the credentials for a Deputy Director at DHS headquarters. He's our man."

I nodded and pocketed the credentials.

"Understand, Hunter," LaRue said with the tone of an angry parent. "The credentials are for complications. They are not for speeding tickets or to impress barroom hussies."

Hussies? Did the most powerful and brilliant man in the intelligence community just use the word "hussies"?

CHAPTER 35

Day 3: May 17, 1610 Hours, Daylight Saving Time
Rural Frederick County, Virginia

CAINE MOVED THROUGH the abandoned building's darkness and emerged in a dimly lit, sterile room facing what had been the outer meat-cutting area of the old Safeway butcher shop. Halfway across the shop, a heavy plastic barrier sealed the back half of the room near the large stainless-steel freezer door. The plastic was opaque, and he could just make out a bulky figure working inside the freezer at a workbench constructed of abandoned butcher's tables. The man's back was to him and his head was down, concentrating on his precarious tasks.

The plastic veil and freezer served as a makeshift laboratory containment vestibule. The freezer had been meticulously modified to provide protection similar to a Level II biohazard lab. The plastic was sealed top to bottom and side to side with additional plastic sheathing overhead to form a sealed cube around the butcher's room. To the right side was an aluminum-framed doorway and a heavy Plexiglas door that led into an inner vestibule and access through the freezer door into the lab work area. The vestibule was the last line of defense against any accidental contamination.

The hiss of air being sucked into the cube prevented any limited escape of the materials the doctor was working on inside.

Simply, the vacuum pulled air in and did not allow air out. The hiss also told Caine the doctor's homemade biocontainment protocols were functioning and he breathed easier.

Several more moments passed when the man inside the freezer—clad in a bulky biohazard suit with an air tank mounted on his back—turned and saw Caine waiting. He momentarily returned to his work. When his task was done and the stainless-steel cylinder he'd been examining was resealed and secured in the pneumatically sealed chest, he exited the freezer, secured the door behind him, and exited into the vestibule. It took him another five minutes to cleanse his protective suit beneath a portable shower and carefully clean himself off before exiting into the basement where Caine waited.

"I was not expecting you, Caine." The man was a tall, clean-shaved Arab pooled in dampness from working in the bio suit. Sweat formed dark pools across his body, stained his shirt, and drained down his face and neck. He was about fifty with dark, intelligent eyes. He wore running shoes, clean blue jeans, and a polo shirt. Everything about the man was professional and neat like a man who belonged in an Ivy League classroom, not an abandoned country meat locker.

He spoke with a thick, Persian accent. "Caine, what of the young man? The one who carried the cylinders?"

"He is not your problem, Doc." Caine measured the man's worry across his face. "It was fast and quiet. He did not suffer."

"Suffer? He was exposed for only a short time. He suffered for hours before they moved him to the farm."

"He did not suffer long after I took over the problem."

Doc, whose real name was Hosni Al-Fayed, professor of bioengineering, shrugged. "Why are you here? Is my family all right?"

"Yes, they are fine, Doc." Caine threw a chin toward the make-shift laboratory. "You made your arrangements with Khalifah, Doc. Not me. But I'm looking after your interests."

"What of my family?"

Caine nodded but said nothing.

Doc walked to the side wall where a small table and chair sat. On the table was a tray with a thermos and cup. He poured a cup of tea and turned back to look at Caine. "Then what?"

Caine ignored the question. "Khalifah doesn't want you wasting time testing the second shipment I brought yesterday. You are to prepare it for use by tomorrow night. The day after at the latest. After it's loaded and prepped, no one is to touch it again. Do you understand?"

"Does he understand that if I do not test it, I cannot be confident of the correct mixture and composition of the shipment to water and air? How will I know if—"

Caine flashed up a hand. "Use the same mixture you have already prepared for the first shipment. It will be fine."

"But what of Saeed?"

Caine held Doc's eyes. "It'll be fine, Doc. Trust me."

"Saeed has my family." Doc's eyes fell. "What choice do I have?"

"None."

CHAPTER 36

Day 3: May 17, 1745 Hours, Daylight Saving Time
Noor Mallory's Residence, Frederick County, Virginia

THANK GOD FOR the Greeks or whoever invented wine. It had to be them. They needed a diversion from Aristotle philosophizing all the time. My diversion was a nice fifty-dollar Cabernet. I hoped it would ease the nerves that twisted my gut during my evening with Noor and Sam. For many years, we'd been family and strangers at the same time. It would take all my wit and charm plus a few glasses of wine to make the night pass. Sometimes, my wit and charm were a little overkill—no, no, it's true, really. The wine was my fallback plan.

I bought two bottles.

Sam toyed with the barbecue grill while Noor and I sat nearby. We tried to cover the missed years, the important ones anyway. She was born in Sāri, Iran. Her father was a university professor in veterinary medicine and her mother a Canadian grade school teacher working at the Canadian mission in Tehran. She and her mother visited Toronto one holiday when she was a child. Noor never left and stayed to attend a private school. It was the only hope for a good education and her escape from the clutches of a grueling society. From Toronto, she came to the States to attend college. Years passed and she became a citizen. She met Kevin in

DC in the nineties at a charity event or something. They married three years later. Unable to have children, they adopted Sam six years ago after he'd lost his parents. He was thirteen. They became a family, and I hadn't known they were even married. Details stayed protected behind a veil of faint smiles and changed topics. Noor was a private person.

More wine, please.

My past was a blur for me. The same places. The same missions. Sand, mountains, bullets . . . blood. Noor wanted to know it all. What countries I'd traveled. What I thought of their people. She still had memories of and a longing to return to Iran. Strangely, our connection was not Kevin. It was her Middle Eastern heritage and my travels. She spoke eloquently about being Iranian in a country where Iranians were the enemy and all things Middle Eastern were suspicious and dangerous. Kevin had always seemed immune to those nuances, even when they adopted Sam. Noor was raised a Westerner, educated in New York, and her mother had wished her Iranian roots would fade. She resisted and still did. She was proud of her heritage. Proud of her people, not their government.

"Noor, how do you like it here?"

"Sometimes it is good." She took a long sip of wine. "Sometimes it is not. Like this morning at the café, people can be . . ."

"Ignorant," I added, lifting my glass. "It's the first stop on the way to bigotry."

She nodded. "Yes. It has always been that way."

"I'm sorry. People get afraid."

"As do I." She flashed a hand in the air. "There is fear enough for us all."

Fear is a terrible thing. Something that didn't need reason or justification. Fear was its own truth. It made good people act badly, and, too often, made bad people act treacherously.

Sometimes, fear was just an excuse for blind hate.

Me, I'm impartial. I lived and worked with Middle Easterners on their home turf. Many were close friends. Often, I shared meals with their families and participated in local traditions. Unfortunately, I also killed some. Bad ones, of course. Those who deserved it. Those who were a stain, a disease, on their own people as much as others. Those who inflicted as much physical pain as emotional. Their people had to endure it all. Like Noor, who had to endure the distrust and hatred for something she had no part in. Those who brought hatred—brought the killing and violence and chaos—deserved what they got.

That was my business. My business paid well.

Noor said little more about her family—and for good reason. Her mother had traveled to Tehran many years ago to bring her sisters and brother back to Toronto. She never returned. Noor was alone. Now, more than ever. For her reminiscence, she brought out her wedding album. It stung that I was neither informed nor invited. My absence from the pictures sent waves of regret churning inside me.

Got any bourbon?

Silence shielded my embarrassment after a few broken, choked words. Sam had been quiet, too. In fact, he hadn't said a word to me since I'd arrived. He'd offered a cursory nod and went about preparing the grill. But, when Noor and I quieted down and scanned the album, he turned and abruptly entered the conversation.

"So, Hunter, you've killed our people? Muslims?"

"Sam!" Noor's eyes exploded. "That is enough."

"No, it's okay." I started to formulate a clever retort. *No, not this time.* "I've killed terrorists. Insurgents. Lots. I didn't ask if they were Muslims. But many were."

He sat very still and silent. I don't know what he thought I'd say, but he wasn't expecting honesty.

I turned to Noor. "You wanted to tell me something at breakfast and wouldn't. How about now?"

"Yes, now." She contemplated her wine glass for the longest time. Just when I thought she would change her mind, she looked up at me with tear-filled eyes. "You hurt Kevin very badly by staying away. He said you would return only in a box. He made excuses about your relationship. He was hiding things. Perhaps that you are CIA."

"I'm sorry, Noor." *Jesus, Hunter, is that all you got?*

"You're sorry?" Sam's face fogged with coldness. "What do you want anyway? I don't trust you."

Time to let the genie out of the bottle. "Trust, Sam? You want to talk about trust? Good." I filled Noor in on what I'd not been able to tell her at breakfast about Sam's reaction to Fariq and Azar at the café. Then, about him being at the college dorm earlier when Bobby was assaulted. She needed to know.

His face was steel and his eyes sent daggers through me.

"Trust goes both ways." I added, "If you're in some kind of trouble, Sam, tell me. I can help."

For a moment, I thought he was going to open the secrets jar. Instead, he did what he'd done before. He retreated into the house.

Noor looked after him with tears trailing down her cheeks. "He has been like this for months. I do not know what to do."

I refilled both of our glasses and slid my chair closer to put a hand on her shoulder. I tried to console her the best I could. "I'm not much good with kids, Noor. Or moms. Dogs, now I'm good with dogs. Oh, and camels. Definitely camels."

She allowed a brief giggle and wiped her cheeks.

"He needs to come to terms with all this."

She shrugged and took my hand in hers. A gentle gesture that sent chills up my arm to every synapse in my body. "All right, Jon Hunter."

"He'll be fine." For a long time we sat there sipping wine and making believe silence was a language. She finally released my hand after forever and that small gesture of compassion changed things somehow. Three days ago, we were strangers. This morning, adversaries. Now, with a touch and soft voice, something else. I glanced at her after what seemed like an hour. Confusion swelled in her eyes and worry softened her face. The air between us was thick with remorse . . . confusion . . . pain. There was no good time to ask the tough questions, so I just did.

"Noor, why did Kevin reach out to me after all these years?"

Her fingers whitened around her wineglass. "I do not know."

"I think you do."

"No." The word was a whisper. She gazed at the house's back door. "I am worried about Sam. Before we adopted him, he was troubled. His mother killed his father in a drunken tirade over another woman. He watched it all. She was imprisoned, of course. Sam went to a facility. Not many adopt Iranian children. He did not do well there. He was ten then, and for two years he did not speak."

"How did you find him?"

"Kevin." Her eyes looked empty. "He was on a case at the children's home. One of the staff was killed. He met Sam there and later we adopted him. He needed someone. We needed someone."

"Kevin did that for me when our folks died." I decided it wasn't the time or the place to ask about Sam being Kevin's murder suspect. "Did Kevin and Sam do well together?"

She nodded. "Kevin got through to him. It took a while. Sam is a good boy. A great boy. He will be a good man in time." The tiniest of smiles touched her lips and then faded abruptly. "I pray this does not start it all again. He hated the medication. I am unsure. Perhaps he needs them now."

"We'll work on it, Noor. You and me."

She looked away for a long time with nothing in her eyes. She was far away, thinking, deciding. Then, something began to rise to the surface. "Kevin and I—we—our marriage—it has been empty for a long time. We stayed together for Sam. I am not sure it was the right decision now. Once, I loved Kevin. I did for a long time."

"It's all right, Noor." No other words would form. "It'll be all right."

Sam returned from inside the house, served steaks and potatoes off the grill, took his plate, and dropped into a chair opposite Noor. We all took a few silent moments to eat. After half the meal and another half bottle of wine, Noor reopened the discussions.

"Jon, the evening he was killed, Kevin spoke with Victoria at about eight. They spoke for a long time, and I think they argued. He left right after."

"What did they argue about?"

She shrugged. "He did not say. He never did. We had not spoken much for months. He came and went at all hours. Most of the time, he worked with *her*, too."

She accented "her" with thick, oozing jealousy.

"They slept in separate rooms," Sam blurted out, unconcerned that he had violated a secret. He caught her glare. "You did."

Their marriage was over. Kevin knew. She knew. I'd pursue that another time. "How was he the night he was killed? I mean, was he okay?"

"I do not know. Kevin was secretive. He was in his den, working. I brought him a beer. He was reading files. He acted strange when I walked in."

"How so?"

Noor took a long swallow of wine. "He scolded me that I should knock. He jumped up and came around the desk like he did not wish me to see what was there. He ordered me from the room."

"What could he have been hiding?"

"I do not know." She shrugged again. "He was so odd the past few months. I did not know him. Ever since he discovered something about your parents' death."

Wait, what? "My parents' death? What was it, Noor?"

"Nearly a year ago, he discovered that the man who killed your parents in the automobile accident was a foreigner. He was an Iraqi refugee. Something in Kevin changed. He brooded about it all the time, and once, when he had too much to drink, he yelled at me that foreigners took his life away. They took you away. I did not understand."

Jesus. "I didn't know any of that, Noor. The guy was a drunk driver and hit our folks late one night. That's all we ever knew. What difference did it make after so many years?"

She shrugged. "None. But, it did to Kevin. He was so worried about money and began hating his job. He said he never finished college because of that man. He began blaming everything on that man. He blamed others, too."

"You and Sam?" I dared a glance at Sam, but he looked away. "You were once . . ."

"Yes, Jon. I was once a refugee. One day we were happy. Problems yes, but happy, I thought. The next, I was one of 'them.'"

Sam started to speak, but Noor's eyes silenced him. He returned to his steak.

She wiped her eyes and changed the subject. "Have you learned about Khalifah or 'G'?"

"Yes, some." I took a chance and told them about the note on my car and my meeting with "G" in a couple hours. I shouldn't have. Good tradecraft meant keeping everything closely held and secret. But right then, with them sitting in front of me, honesty was the only thing that might finally bridge the gaps between us. "I'm meeting him later. I hope it leads to Kevin's killer or at least Khalifah. Artie's people have nothing. Maybe I'll get lucky."

Sam grunted. "You're meeting him alone? Shouldn't the cops be there?"

"No. If he wanted to go to the police, he wouldn't have reached out to me."

He looked away. "You're no cop."

"Enough, Sameh." Noor's words cut. She looked to me and her eyes had a question. "He has a point, Jon. If the police have not learned anything, are you all we have?"

All we have? "Yes. But Artie will come through. He's on our side."

"Great," Sam grunted. "You didn't do so good with Bobby last night, did you?"

I looked at Sameh and the air between us froze. "Actually, Sam, I did just fine. It turns out I was right. Bobby was hiding something. He took photos at the river before the police arrived. Those photos may have evidence about your dad's murder. Maybe even why he was murdered."

"This is true, Jon?" Noor asked, putting a hand to her face. "You may have evidence? What is it?"

I shook my head. "Not sure yet, but it's in the photos. A missing backpack that I'm sure had money in it."

"Why didn't Bobby tell me?" Sam snorted, pushing himself from the table. "I've called him twice this afternoon, and he's not answering."

He better not be. "I have him somewhere safe for the night until I can set up protection. Azar and Fariq seem too interested in getting their hands on him. He's safe for now."

"That is good, Jon." Noor leaned over and took my hand. The gesture drew Sam's ire and his arms snapped closed. She ignored him. "I wish you to stay here."

"Absolutely. At least until this is over. After, we'll see."

Noor's touch was warm and tender. Needful. It all unnerved me. It scared me to death. She scared me to death.

She smiled a warm, comforting smile. "Good. I want you to move in."

Ah, what? "No, no. That won't work."

"Yes, of course. We have a small apartment above the garage. It is not much, but you would be close. You could have meals with us, too."

Sam jumped up and went inside.

I watched him go. "Noor, I shouldn't. Sam would agree."

"He will be fine. Please, Jon. Consider it. For me?"

What the devil was wrong with me? Suddenly, I yearned for a sweltering stone room with a lumpy cot in Goat-Town-Syria. "It wouldn't work."

"I do not care what Sam likes." She stood up and moved around the table behind me. I felt her arms wrapped around my shoulders and her hair fall against my neck. I trembled when she whispered, "I would rather it be you than the deputies nearby. I need you. Sam does, too."

Words wouldn't form. Thoughts wouldn't stop swirling. My breath stopped. It took a moment to settle before taking her hands in mine. "Noor, I have to think about it."

"Yes, of course." She glanced away and then back, holding my eyes. "Drive us to the funeral tomorrow. Please, Jon?"

Steady, Hunter. One, two, three. "Of course."

Gravel crunched out front of the house as a car approached. Thank God.

Noor and I walked around to the front porch as a four-door Chevy rolled to a stop in the driveway beside my rental. Bond climbed out. He leaned against his cruiser and took us in. He looked from Noor to me with the grin of a cat that just picked the canary cage lock.

"Oh, no," Noor whispered and headed for him.

I started to follow when Sam emerged from the house and stood beside me. "Hunter, he wanted Dad out of the way."

"Sam?"

"There's more Mom isn't telling."

No kidding. "Like what?"

"Ask her." When Bond's voice grew louder, Sam added, "I don't trust you, Hunter. I don't like you either. But I like Bond less."

I reached for his shoulder, but he pulled away. "Sam, we need to be friends. We're family."

"No," he said. "Family does not hurt each other. You are not my family. I don't even know who you are. But I know what you are."

Whoa, where was that coming from. "What am I, Sam?"

He grumbled something and went back into the house.

I wanted to follow him, but Bond was animated now. His hands chopped the air. Noor recoiled from him, and I sauntered over.

Tough guys saunter.

"Is everything okay?" I asked.

"What do you want, Hunter?" Bond jutted a square chin at me. "If that's your name today."

"Should I spell it?"

"What are you doing here?"

"I just rented a room here." I looked from Noor to Bond. "What are you doing here?"

Bond turned red. Blood red.

Noor started to speak, but I touched her arm, and she grasped my hand and held it there.

I caught Bond's eyes. "Did you need something, Dave?"

For a long, dangerous moment, his eyes telegraphed my demise appendage by appendage. I braced myself for an attack. Oddly enough, he didn't. Maybe it was the image of me beating down two Middle Eastern thugs. Or maybe he didn't want to stain Noor's driveway with my blood.

"Hunter, I don't know what game you're playing," Bond said. "But I don't like it. You stay clear of Noor and Sam, you hear me?"

I laughed. "It's 'get out of town by sundown'? From now on, call before you stop in. I'd hate to think you were a prowler and shoot you. Or maybe I wouldn't hate it."

Bond's face went dark. His jaw tightened and his teeth ground. Just when I thought he would swing at me, he retreated to his car. "Hunter, I'll be watching. Count on it."

CHAPTER 37

Day 3: May 17, 2115 Hours, Daylight Saving Time
Old Town, Winchester, Virginia

THE HANDLEY REGIONAL Library is located in Winchester's Old Town district a block off the walking mall. Obviously, it's named for John Handley, a Pennsylvania judge who left a bundle in 1895-ish for Winchester to build such a library. Old John had class, thus the Beaux-Arts limestone building that the historians will tell you was built to resemble an open book. I don't see it, but that's what the Internet said. The grand building has an octagonal entrance beneath a central dome that looks very, well, Beaux-Arts, I guess. There are two large wings off the main base with stone relief figures, balustrades, and colonnades—yep, the Internet—those are fancy railings and columns. At night, the library is more impressive than in daylight. The stalwart structure is accented by landscaping lights that gave it a majestic appearance. I love old architecture. That's one of the things I love about Winchester. The turn-of-the-century charm.

Not tonight.

When Bond left Noor's place, I stayed a while longer and exchanged more reminiscence of my travels with her. More to calm her nerves than anything. Sam stayed clear. After another hour, I bade them goodnight and headed for my clandestine rendezvous with the mysterious "G."

The "mysterious" part had my hair up, and I double-checked my .45 twice on my way to Old Town.

"G" could be friend or foe. He could be witness or killer. Because of that, I would observe "G" arrive and be ready for anything. I weaved my way through side streets and alleys in northwest Winchester until I positioned myself on Library Lane, a small street a quarter block northwest of the rear of the library. It was nine twenty when I sat to wait. From the safety of night shadows and a large maple tree, I watched the library and the alley behind it that ran the length of the building and alongside a patio area where picnic tables and benches sat empty. My position allowed me to see whoever approached from three sides.

In Mosul, Iraq, I learned the hard way that when you had such a meeting, you arrive extra early just to watch the other team show. It can save your life. Bad guys like to ambush you or plant IEDs—improvised explosive devices—so when you arrive late, you die a horrible, violent death. LaRue used to say, "The second to arrive dies." I nearly did on my first rendezvous with an Iraqi snitch by ignoring his wisdom. He never let me forget that, either.

My watch showed 10:05 when someone rounded the corner a half a block to my right. The figure crossed the street and headed for the rear of the library. It was about five-four and thin. I couldn't make out his features, but it was a man. He walked slow and uneasy, perhaps worried about a trap.

We already had something in common.

I slipped my .45 out and used the building's shadows to angle behind him as he stopped beside the bushes near the picnic tables. I reached the rear of the bushes, still in total stealth, and lifted my .45. Then, I eased in close.

"Sit at that picnic table, hands on top."

The man jumped and started to turn.

"Easy."

He didn't turn, but his hands slowly rose in surrender. "I sent the note. I am Ghali. I at river. I bring something."

Bingo—"G." I inched forward. "All right. Turn around. Slow. I have a big gun aimed at your head. I don't miss very often."

"*Baleh,* Hunter."

Hunter? I stepped close and patted him down with quick, hasty handfuls of his clothes. "You called this soiree. What do you want?"

"Swar-ray?" Ghali's face twisted and his hands lowered.

"What do you want?"

"Please, you scare me." He smiled, showing a dingy mouthful of teeth. Then he rattled off a download of information that made my head spin. "At river, I there with Saeed and the box. A man bring it to Saeed. I no see him anywhere before that night."

I glanced around. "Who is Saeed?"

Ghali stiffened. "Saeed Mansouri. He is often in Sand Town—Sandy Creek. We are refugees from Afghanistan and Iraq. A few Syrian families arrived now. But Saeed is not one of us. He and his men are terrible men—Iranians. They are outsiders. Saeed Mansouri is a *Raees.*"

I knew what that was. A *"Raees"* was the big boss—the local village gang-boss. Militia chieftain. More succinctly, chief thug.

"Is he a refugee, too?"

Ghali shook his head and looked down. "I will not say. Not here. No. He is not one of us. None of his men are. Do not ask me until you have me safe. But I will tell you Saeed is not the only one. There are others."

Others? Terrorists? I understood why Saeed Mansouri had him scared to death.

"Okay, go on. Tell me about Saeed's box."

Ghali breathed easier. "Saeed tell two of his men to open this box. One man, he afraid, he held the box and would not open it. Saeed mad and shoot. First he hit the box. Then he shoot the man. The box open and fall on him. Very bad. *Alhamdulillah*. He a mad man."

"Whoa, whoa, slow down. Who brought the case? The box, I mean?"

"It come from somewhere I do not know. I was there only to drive. Saeed order me to use my truck."

"Was it Khalifah who sent the box?"

"You know of Khalifah? Caine?"

LaRue was right. Caine was involved. "Was the box a steel case with a funny lock?"

"*Baleh,* funny lock." Ghali shot uneasy glances around the darkness.

I pressed him. "Tell me about Khalifah."

"If you help me. I tell you everything I know. He is a very bad man—he and Caine. But they are outsiders like Saeed Mansouri. They make those in Sand Town do things they not wish to do."

A car made the turn along the street behind the library and Ghali jumped back into the bushes. When it was gone, he stayed put.

"Deal," I said. "I'll help you. Tell me about the case and the killings."

"Everyone fear what in case. Everyone who touched it when it opened is dead." Ghali's head swiveled toward every sound and headlight for a block.

I raised a hand to calm him. "What was in the box?"

Another car passed behind us and slowed.

Ghali backed deeper into the bushes.

The car eased on.

My radar started pinging and now I was jumpy. "What was in the box, G?"

"I want protection." Ghali's voice was hurried, scared. "Saeed, he *divoonei*. You say crazy. Caine, he *alqatil*."

I knew what *alqatil* meant. Killer. Assassin. We knew about the same Caine.

Ghali went on. "Something in the case very bad. Everyone who touched it when the case broke open dead."

Ghali knew more, and I pressed him. "You know more, G. Out with it. What happened after the case broke open?"

"I not know. I run away after he started shooting. I run fast into the woods. I do not want to be near Saeed any longer. I help you find who kill you brother. Saeed and Khalifah have many plans. Big plans. Very bad things."

"Ghali, did you see who shot Kevin Mallory?"

"I know much more. Much." Ghali hesitated; then, "Deal first. Then I give you more."

Well, he might not be the witness I wanted, but he was better than nothing. From my wallet, I pulled out the first bill I could find. A fifty. With the pen I'd swiped from Artie earlier, I jotted my cell phone number on it in bold numbers I could see in the dim light.

"Here's my number." I handed him the fifty. "Call me tomorrow at noon sharp. I'll have everything set up to get you safely to my people."

He stuffed the bill into his jeans. "*Baleh.* I trust you?"

"You trust me."

"Okay, I have message then, 'Why Kevin Mallory not stop the mall? You must help before more happens.'" He thrust his hand into his back pocket.

I lifted my pistol. "Don't be stupid, Ghali."

"No, you no understand. I have something."

Headlights spotlighted us when a car swung sharply around the corner of the library and turned into the alley. Red lights flashed on and a *wooop-wooop* sounded. A voice called out, "Freeze! Don't move!"

Bond.

"Dammit." I turned to Ghali. "Go. Run."

"*Nah, nah.*" Ghali bolted down the alleyway into the darkness. When he did, Bond wrenched his car to the right and hopped the curb to give chase.

Before I knew what had happened, Ghali—the mysterious "G"—and Bond were gone.

So was I.

CHAPTER 38

Day 4: May 18, 0100 Hours, Daylight Saving Time
Fool's Lake, Virginia

ON MY WAY out of Winchester, I took extra precautions to check myself for surveillance. While I dry-cleaned myself, and twice thought I was followed and had to take evasive actions, I called LaRue and filled him in on my meeting and a few tidbits I got from Noor Mallory. He was his charming, curmudgeon self until I brought up the name Saeed Mansouri. I swear I heard his sphincter snap closed.

"Bring Ghali in," Oscar said dryly. "Get him in safely and fast. He could be the key to locating Khalifah and stopping Maya. When he contacts you tomorrow, I will dispatch Shepard to back you up."

"Got it."

"You are sanctioned to take on all risks."

Sanctioned to take on all risks? "Ah, Oscar, is that your way of telling me to take a bullet for him?"

LaRue had hung up.

"Good talk, Oscar," I said to no one. "Oh yeah, I'll be safe. No worries."

That Oscar LaRue—always worried about me.

* * *

It was nearly three hours since leaving Handley Library when darkness swallowed the mountain road beneath me. Even with my high beams on, I nearly veered off into nothingness. Nothingness could have been a brush thicket or a five-hundred-foot crevasse.

When I reached Fool's Lake it was one a.m. The stars flickered through the pine canopy guarding the cabin and gave it a storybook touch. That is, if that story was about murder and terrorists.

At the cabin, I knew Bobby hadn't fared well in my absence. Despite my careful preparations. My directions had been explicit. Rule one—keep the blinds drawn with light and noise at a minimum. Rule two—don't go outside unless it's to run like hell. Rule three—keep my father's double-barreled 12-gauge Ithaca within arm's reach. If anyone showed up with a bad attitude, ventilate them, and institute rule two.

Simple, right?

Beacons of light shined out every window. Rap music penetrated my ears like an artillery barrage. By the time I backed the rental behind the woodshed, my head ached. *Boom-boom-boom, ba-boom, ba-boom.*

Bobby must have thrown a party.

There was no one around the mountain roads, but the music and lights were a beacon for anyone searching for us. What came of my instructions I didn't know. Bobby had been nervous, but after a quick class on how to safely load and shoot the shotgun, he eased up.

The cabin's electricity was out. I hadn't taken the time to crank up the generator. The only light inside should have been the one kerosene lantern I left lit. Except now it looked like Broadway on Saturday night. I did a quick perimeter check and found every one of the half a dozen lanterns and two dozen candles burning inside. But it was the *boom-boom-boom* that irritated me most, and my first act would be the complete and total destruction of Bobby's music collection. With a check through the cabin windows, one thing was clear.

Bobby wasn't there.

My .45 in hand, I returned to the front porch. "Bobby, it's Jon, I'm coming in. Don't shoot."

Boom-boom-boom, ba-boom, ba-boom. Jesus, make it stop.

"Bobby?"

Inside, I flattened myself against the wall and scanned the room in quick, freeze-frame snapshots. No furniture was disturbed. No signs of a struggle or incursion. No shotgun blasts on the walls. No Bobby Kruppa.

"Bobby? Come out!"

Nothing.

All the rooms were the same—empty of the blubbery, pasty-faced college kid with the bull's-eye on his head. When I moved toward the small dinette table in the tiny kitchen, I kicked something across the floor. There was a second something, identical to the first—12-guage shotgun shells. Unspent. Unfired.

Oh crap, kid. What happened?

I scooped up the shells and stuffed them into my pocket. The hair bristled on my neck. The dead bolt on the back door had been opened from the inside but the security chain was pulled out of the door. Someone had forced the door open after the dead bolt was released and ripped it from the wood. I backtracked and slipped out the front door to sneak around back. At the rear corner, secreted by night shadows and murky darkness, I followed my .45 toward the woodshed. Moving low and doing the stalking dance, I scanned for targets. At the shed, my breath finally eased.

No gunshots. No crackle of dried pine needles. No ninja assassins.

The shed door was still locked from the outside. No one could be within.

As I rounded the shed corner toward my rental car, pine branches crackled behind me. I pivoted, swung my pistol around, and tried to intercept whoever approached.

I was half a second too late.

A club collided with my hands and sent my pistol clattering against the woodshed. A bulky figure, wide and ominous, emerged through the night. He was on the backswing and closed on me for a head shot.

Instead of retreating to avoid the impact, I leaped forward and did a jumping-bicycle step and delivered a kick into my attacker's midsection. My instep slammed into flesh and bone. I'd hoped for the solar plexus, but still sent him backward with a loud, guttural *umph*. Before he could rebound, I landed, twisted in a violent arc, and slashed my right leg around. At the apex of the arc, I launched a heel-kick into his middle. The impact exploded an audible burst of wind from him and sent him down hard.

He coughed twice, three times . . . four. He gasped for air.

It would have been easy to finish him. One quick heel-thrust into his windpipe and it would be over. But then all I'd have was a body and no one to interrogate about Bobby's whereabouts. Without that, I might not find him. So I retrieved my .45 and pulled out my cell phone for its flashlight. The assailant didn't know it yet, but he was about to provide me all I wanted to know about the absent Bobby Kruppa.

No, that wasn't necessary. I had all I needed. Bobby was on his back gasping for breath with one hand on his gut and the other waving his surrender.

"Bobby?"

He gasped twice more and struggled to his knees. "Sh . . . sh . . . shit. You almost killed me."

"You attacked me." I helped him to his feet. "I told you to stay inside unless you had to run."

"I . . . know. I know." He bent down and picked up his club— my dad's Ithaca. "I saw car lights go around back. I didn't hear it coming until it was too late."

No kidding. "Maybe your lousy music was too loud."

"Maybe." He handed me the shotgun. "I didn't know it was you. You went around front, and I went out the back. I've been hearing something out here for hours. Someone was out here, I'm sure of it. When you pulled up, I freaked."

A real intruder? Doubtful. "Well, I'm glad you didn't do what I told you to. You might have blown my head off."

"Ah, probably not." He wavered a little and gestured to the shotgun. "I was nervous with the gun so I unloaded it on the kitchen table. I figured I could reload it real fast if someone came. Except I got so scared and dropped the shells. So I ran."

Of course he did. "What happened to my back door?"

"I forgot the chain was hooked."

Well, given the circumstances, it could have been worse. He might have shot me, or himself.

"You know, Bobby," I said, lifting my pistol. "You're lucky."

He stared, and even in the darkness, I could see the fear in his eyes. "Damn, Hunter. Where'd you learn all that martial arts stuff?"

"Let's go inside." Something jabbed me in the brain. I grabbed Bobby by the arm and shoved him sideways against the woodshed. My pistol swept the darkness. "Quiet."

Someone stood fifty feet away in the trees. The figure tried to blend into a large thick of scrub trees. I didn't know how long he'd been there, but it was long enough to have a bead on Bobby and me.

Surprise was his, but I aimed my .45 at his center mass none-theless. "Don't move. I'm armed. Step into the cabin lights and keep your hands away from your body."

When the figure hesitated, I shouted, "Now or I shoot."

Seconds ticked. My pulse raced. Bobby's heavy gasps went si-lent as he tried to press himself through the woodshed wall.

Seconds . . .

CHAPTER 39

Day 4: May 18, 0120 Hours, Daylight Saving Time
Fool's Lake, Virginia

"DON'T SHOOT. IT'S ME." Sam Mallory stepped into the dim cabin light. "What are you two doing here?"

"Sam?" I lowered my pistol and gestured for Bobby to follow me to the cabin. "The question is, what are you doing here?"

Sam was dressed in jeans and a sweatshirt with its sleeves cut off above the elbow. A large sweat stain covered the center of his chest and beneath his arms. His face glistened in the dim light and his hair was disheveled and damp.

"Sam?" I repeated.

He threw a chin at Bobby. "This isn't a hotel, Hunter."

Sam was edgy and had something to share with the class. He wasn't going to be nice about it. But I'd had it. His attitude had worn me thin.

Sam thrust an angry finger at me. "I asked you a question."

Enough. "Yes, you did. I'm just not used to answering to snot-nosed punks. Lose the attitude and tell me what *you're* doing here, Sam."

He ignored me and went inside.

"Hunter?" Bobby's voice was meek. "What's going on?"

Good question. "Go inside. I'll be there in a minute."

He did. I wasn't.

I took a walk—more a stealthy sneak-and-peek—around the perimeter. Sam had emerged from nowhere and there was no car or motorcycle nearby. I walked about a quarter mile down the mountain road and found nothing. It was too dark to try and follow any kind of trail Sam might have left. Back in my early Special Forces days, I'd learned tracking in SERE training—that's Survival, Evasion, Resistance, and Escape. In the Middle East, we had K-9 teams for tracking, and I'd lost what little skills I'd learned. So, other than watching Daniel Boone reruns, I didn't know much about tracking anymore. Out here, I knew enough about these woods to know that bears were behind trees, rattlesnakes under rocks, and sharks in the lake. Well, maybe not sharks.

I jogged back to the cabin, loudly announced my entrance, and went inside. Bobby and Sam stood near the kitchen table arguing about something. The argument abruptly ended when I closed the front door.

Sam said, looking at me like a rattler about to strike, "Okay, Hunter. Just so you know this is my place, and Mom's. You got no right here."

Really? I crossed the room and stepped into him, pressing him back against the wall without so much as touching him. His face contorted and he sucked in air.

"Pay attention, *Sameh*." I leaned in close. "First, this cabin is mine, not yours. My dad willed it to Kevin and me with the provision that one took ownership in the event that the other died or didn't want it. But that's not the issue. It's your attitude. Let's start fresh. No bull. No attitude. Just answers. Quick—fast—*now*."

He stared as though I'd slapped him across the face. His lips started to move, but nothing came out. He locked onto my eyes as long as he could, but his tough-guy credentials weren't up to the job. He broke the stare, glanced at Bobby but found no support, and surrendered with the drop of his shoulders.

"You weren't at the hotel tonight." His voice was weak and timid. "You said you had him somewhere safe, and I thought you might've come here."

"How'd you get up here?"

He looked down at the table. "I got an old truck. I parked it down the mountain a ways where the cutoff trail goes around the other side of the lake. I always parked there when I followed Dad here. It's a hike, but no one sees me coming or going."

The sweaty clothes and hair. "Why sneak around? Why not just drive up and come in?"

He shrugged. "I didn't know what was going on and wanted to find out before you lied to me again and shut me out."

"Lied?"

He shoved away from the table and stood up. "You've been lying to Mom and me since you got here. Truth is, we don't even know if you're Dad's brother. Do we? You're in the CIA or so you say. How do we know?"

Oh yeah, lying is lying.

"The CIA?" Bobby's face exploded. "No kidding? Really? A spy? An assassin?"

"I'm no spy or assassin." I threw up a hand to shut him up. "I'm a consultant."

Bobby grinned. "Have you hunted terrorists? Done secret missions and spy stuff on the enemy?"

"Yes."

"Ever kill anyone?" he added.

"Yes."

"A spy and an assassin. Yup, I nailed it."

Maybe he would make a good reporter. "Forget it. Listen to me, Sam. Kevin was my brother, and yeah, I'm CIA. Was CIA. It's simple." I explained to him, as I had to Noor earlier, about my fun-with-names and who I was, where I've been, and why I'm in Winchester. Sam watched my every word, looking for lies. Bobby took mental notes for his next news story, grinning the whole time.

I was in trouble—quicksand with an anvil tied to my leg.

"That's that." I retrieved the bottle of bourbon and a glass from the cabinet. "Now you know. Your turn, Sam."

His face twisted, and he eyed the bourbon. "Hey, we're over eighteen. How about we—"

"No." I poured one shot into me and two more into the glass. "Why are you friends with Azar and Fariq?"

The air sizzled like fat on a fire.

"What the hell, Sam?" Bobby's eyes darted at him and he stepped close to the table. "Is he right?"

Sam folded his arms and lied. "No."

I eyed him. "Fariq and Azar at the café, remember? You seemed chummy with them. Today, you were outside Bobby's dorm when they were there. Want me to go on?"

Sam's face blanched. He tried to eye me but still couldn't hold it. Instead, he went to his fallback position. He lied. "You're the liar in the family, *Hunter*. You."

Exhaustion. Two fingers of bourbon.

I stepped in close again, grabbed him by the arm, and pushed him up against the wall. I pinned him there with one hand and searched for his cell phone with the other. It was jammed into his front jean pocket. I also found a snub-nosed .38 revolver tucked into his waistband like a gangster.

Bobby neared panic and escaped across the room. "What's with the gun, Sam?"

"Shut up, Bobby. I must protect Mom."

There was angst in Sam's eyes. Maybe because Uncle Hunter had scared the crap out of him. Maybe because I was nearing his secret. Maybe both. Either way, his attitude transformed into fear—momentarily.

I held the gun up. "Okay, Sam, start with the gun and then Azar and Fariq. I warn you, at this minute, I'm not family. I'm a tired, irritated CIA consultant. So talk fast. Tell the truth and don't piss me off."

Sam looked at me for the longest time. Then Bobby. Then his feet. I won.

"Fine." He pulled out a chair and dropped into it. Defeat seeped from every facial muscle he had. "Dad gave me the gun for my eighteenth birthday last year. Whenever I come up here, I carry it. I don't know, just to shoot a box of rounds or something."

"Good story." I manipulated the revolver's cylinder, dumped the rounds into my hand, and dropped the gun on the table. "Why do you have it now?"

"Because I want to." His face was fire and his eyes defiant. He switched personalities like Dr. Jekyll and Mr. Hyde.

"You're only eighteen, Sam," I said in a softer tone. "You can't carry a gun."

"Who cares? Dad was murdered and someone attacked Mom. I'd rather go to jail than be dead."

Not bad logic, crazy as it was. "Who'd you tell about us being here?"

He hesitated a second too long. "No one."

Behind his dark Iranian eyes was a lie. "You're lying."

Sam's eyes told me he was digging in. So I asked, "What about the café and Bobby's dorm?"

He shook his head. "I didn't do anything wrong."

Instead of arguing, I tapped on his cell phone and navigated into his application settings. A couple taps on the screen later and I was looking at a GPS map of Winchester and surrounding Frederick County. On the map were dozens of red dots like pimples on an adolescent. The dots indicated where the phone had checked into the network. Places where Sam had been. With a tap here and there, I displayed the date and time he was at each location. With a few twists and pincers of my fingers, the map enlarged enough to show the location on the streets. I studied it and made a mental note of two addresses that repeatedly reported in. Many of the times of day were late hours, over and over. I stapled the addresses into my brain and tossed Sam the phone.

"Look for yourself."

He caught the phone and glanced at the screen. "What's this?"

"A lie detector."

"What?"

I eyed him. "Your phone tracks you, genius. All you have to do is know how to go back and read the data. I do. That's a map of your movements the past week. Look close, you were at the parking garage by the café last night, Bobby's dorm room earlier, and, oh look, Sand Town." The last one was a guess—more a lie, really—but the look on his face said I'd just hit the mother lode of "I gotchas."

He pincered his fingers and widened the screen over several of the red dots. Each time he did, he cringed. "It's not what you think."

"Then explain."

He started to when Bobby walked over and shoved him hard backward. "You rat. You've been telling them about me. I thought we were friends. I thought you were on my side."

"Easy, Bobby." I grabbed his arm. "Sam's gonna explain." I looked at Sam. "Right, Sam?"

Bobby wasn't having it. "He ratted me out, Hunter. He's telling Fariq and Azar everything. Right? Right?" He shoved Sam again. "That's why they knew everything about me and where to find me, like the café. Sam was like all calm and cool when Fariq and Azar showed. He knew he was safe. Every time they show up, he's there."

I didn't like what one-plus-one was adding up to. "Sam?"

Sam shifted his weight back and forth. He looked from the cell phone to his gun on the table. He lifted his head and snorted fire at me. "You sound like Dad—like Kevin. But you know, he wasn't my dad and you're not my uncle. Neither of you are blood. He thought he could push me around and tell me what to do. But he didn't do the right stuff, either. He was a liar. If you knew all the things he did . . ."

"Easy, Sam. You don't know what you're saying." I reached for his shoulder, but he pulled back. "Come on, settle down. Tell me what's going on."

He thrust a threatening finger at me. "You are nothing to me. You are not family. You're just like him. Go to hell." He snatched up his .38 revolver and bolted out the back door.

"Sam!" I tried but couldn't stop him. He disappeared into the darkness along the lake. I went to the water's edge but couldn't see him along the shore. "Sam!"

He was hiding something. It was tearing him apart. A secret. A lie. Protecting someone. Protecting himself, perhaps? He was on the verge of a meltdown, and his surliness told me the fuse was lit and burning fast. If he melted down at the wrong time, there was no telling the damage he could do. Or to whom.

Had it happened before? Was Sam capable of—*no.*

I stood at the water's edge for the longest time. It was something I'd done when I was a kid to sort out the many insurmountable crises of adolescence—death, an angry brother, math and English. Mostly, over girls. The gentle lapping of the water soothed frayed nerves and eased my anger. Somewhere in the darkness a night bird called. Crickets or frogs or nocturnal birds chirped across the water. All around me seemed at peace, and that unsettled me more than anything.

Was Sam right? Was I nothing to him? Nothing to Noor? Was I just the guy who came home too late?

No. I was the guy who would find Kevin Mallory's killer. I was the guy who would end him. It didn't matter who it was. Friend. Foe. Unknown. The killer ruined too many lives. He'd ruined Noor's and Sam's. He ruined the reconciliation between Kevin and me.

I would slay the dragon who'd laid waste to all of us.

I prayed it wouldn't be someone I knew.

CHAPTER 40

Day 4: May 18, 0535 Hours, Daylight Saving Time
Fool's Lake, Virginia

BY DAWN, EXHAUSTION took me. After Sam's disappearance, I'd patrolled the cabin perimeter every few minutes looking for any sign of intruders or monsters. Last night, Bobby claimed he'd heard someone outside the cabin before I'd arrived. Maybe it was Sam. Maybe it was a bear or a lost lumberjack. Maybe it was Bobby's imagination.

I'd found only darkness.

Bobby was on the couch in an old sleeping bag. Earlier, I'd watched him sneak a few fingers of bourbon and that calmed him. Then, he curled up and went to sleep. I'd breathed a sigh of relief. He'd finally shut up.

I slumped in a chair and caught an hour or so of sleep, but it was restless and lasted just minutes at a time until I gave up. At seven thirty in the morning I found enough old coffee grounds to make a pot. Before I poured my first cup, though, I heard a car—cars—approach.

I rousted Bobby. "Someone's coming. Get into the back bedroom. Stay there until I come for you."

"Huh?" He tried to stand but was twisted in the sleeping bag. His struggle left me wondering. "What?"

Through the front window, I saw the front bumper of a car a hundred yards out at the entrance to the mountain road. "Get a move on, Bobby. Lock the bedroom door."

"Yeah, yeah, okay." He untangled himself and stumbled into the bathroom instead of the bedroom. Instead of locking the door and hiding, he relieved himself into the toilet.

"Sweet Jesus."

The shotgun sat on the kitchen table, loaded, and I scooped it up and headed out the back door. By the time I'd made it to a safe position at the corner of the cabin, three cars waited for me.

Artie Polo stepped out.

Now, how did he find me? Sam? Four more plainclothes cops and Feds stepped out of the other vehicles. Somehow, Artie had found his way up the mountain. No one knew about this place. Sam was the only answer.

I walked into Artie's view. "Good morning."

"Dammit, Hunter." Artie was not a morning person. "Where's Kruppa?" He glared at the shotgun in my hands. "Lose it."

"How'd you know I was here?" I set the shotgun down on the front porch and stepped away from it. I didn't want to give his Wild West pals an excuse to give me a bullet enema. "How'd you know I had Kruppa here?"

"I'm resourceful." He turned and gestured toward his Fedmobile. The front passenger door opened and Victoria stepped out. "Not to mention I have friends."

I thought Kevin kept this place a secret. "Victoria, you pop up in the most interesting places."

She shook her head in more a warning than a disagreement. "You have no idea, Hunter."

Artie gestured for the other cops to hold in place and approached me. He stopped close enough to talk without anyone hearing. "There are developments. I need to ask you some questions. You need to answer them without any BS."

"Sounds serious." His face—tight and cold—worried me. "What's going on?"

Victoria joined us with Bond in her wake. "Hunter, you've got more than that shotgun, so hand it over. Then, get Kruppa out here."

"Slow down." Everyone's knickers had shrunk. Victoria wouldn't look at me. Artie breathed fire. Bond, well, he was Bond. "Somebody tell me what's going on. Is it Sam? Did he do something stupid with the gun?"

"Sam?" Artie eyed me. "What gun?"

"Let's all just relax and get some coffee," I said. But no one blinked.

Victoria glanced toward the cabin. "Hunter, call Kruppa."

The odds against me, I obeyed—something I'm not used to doing. I called Bobby and moments later, he peeked out the front door window, waited for me to nod, and eased outside.

"Hunter?" Bobby said. "What are they doing here?"

I shrugged. "It's out of my hands, Bobby."

With a flip of her chin, Victoria sent two Feds to Bobby. They scooped him up and stuffed him into one of their cars. He argued with them the entire way. They had no idea how long a ride it was going to be back to Winchester.

Boy, was LaRue going to be pissed at me.

Victoria turned back to me. "What do you have to say?"

"Gee, Victoria, ain't we friends anymore?"

"We never were." She folded her arms. "Answer the question."

"I haven't heard a question."

Artie stepped forward. "You met with some informant last night at the library in town. What's that about, Hunter? Withholding information is obstruction."

I looked at Artie and then at Bond. "Wow, you are resourceful."

Artie pointed at me. "What did he tell you, Hunter?"

"I didn't get anything from him, Artie." Okay, a lie. Maybe two. Well, more coming. "Bond showed up and blew the entire meeting. Too bad, too. He has something to share."

Bond jumped forward and snatched my arm. "You're no cop, Hunter."

"Enough, Bond," Victoria barked. "Go with my men and Kruppa to the office."

Bond started to argue but gave up when Artie held up a hand. He stormed off for the car.

Artie ignored him. "Let's hear about your secret rendezvous at the library, Hunter. Before I charge you with obstruction."

I watched Bond climb into the car beside Bobby. "Ask him, Artie. Your attack dog was there. Before I could get anything out of the guy, Bond showed up and chased him down. I left. If you wanted in on it, you should have come alone."

"I didn't send Bond." Artie's eyes dissected me.

"Who was it?" Victoria asked. "When are you meeting him again?"

"I don't know. Like I said, Bond—"

"Chased him off," Artie growled. He motioned to the two FBI agents lingering near the cars. "Search this place. Every nook and cranny."

The men headed into the cabin eager to rearrange my furniture.

To me, Artie said, "You're coming in with us, Hunter. You can help with Kruppa, and then we'll sort out this meeting of yours last night."

That wasn't going to work. I had better things to do. I reached into my pocket and pulled out my spiffy new Department of Homeland Security credentials LaRue gave me for just such emergencies. I handed them to Artie.

I pointed to my creds. "I think I'll pass on the sing-along, Artie. If you have any problems with that, call those folks."

He looked at the badge and credentials and passed them to Victoria. "This is pure fantasy, Hunter. You're no more a DHS agent than I am."

"I am now. Well, as of yesterday."

Victoria looked the creds over. "I think we'll just verify this."

I winked. "Sure. There's a card with a number in there for some deputy director in DC. He'll be happy to help."

Artie glared at me. "My, my, you do have a lot of new friends. I thought you said you haven't heard from Oscar LaRue."

"That was early yesterday. I saw him later, and he said DHS wanted me to be a G-man just like you. So poof, I'm a G-man now. Well, for a while."

Artie let loose a string of expletives that even made me blush.

"Come on, Artie. We're all on the same team."

"Really?" Victoria snapped. "You seem to change teams a lot."

She was warming to me, I could tell.

One of the FBI agents Artie sent to search the house came around the side of the cabin. "Agent Polo, come around back."

That didn't sound good.

I followed Artie and Victoria around the cabin to where the FBI agent and his partner were standing near the woodshed beside my rental car. The first thing I noticed was that the woodpile was strewn about and the place where Kevin's go-bag was hidden was just a freshly dug hole. One of the agents held a shovel and the other held the ballistic-nylon duffel bag—Kevin's go-bag. The bag seemed a little too light to have the ten grand in cash, three passports, and a .380 semiautomatic inside.

The agent holding the shovel said, "We found this mess and the dirt hole." He gestured to what had been the woodpile and the hole where I'd returned the duffel bag for safekeeping. "We found this empty bag in the hole."

Artie went closer and examined the hole, then picked up the name plate from Hunter's grave. He ran his finger around the engraved letters and laughed.

"Really, Hunter? You're named after the dog?"

"Funny." He was born first and he *was* a great dog.

Victoria ignored me. "What was in the bag, Hunter?"

"I don't know." I looked around the rear of the cabin, hoping to find some explanation of who had been there. There wasn't, of course. "I have no idea what happened back here and I've been nothing if not truthful. Well, truthful since you interrogated me last time. Maybe not at the river the first night. But truthful since. Oh, not in my hotel room with Bond either. But later in my hotel with you, yes. And today for sure. Nothing but truthful today."

Artie's eyebrows rose. "Hotel room?"

"She was a wild cat, Artie. Wah-hoo."

Victoria dismissed me with a nasty glance. "It was business. No idea about the bag?"

I shook my head. "Someone was here last night. Ask Bobby. They must have come for whatever was in there. I have no idea what's going on."

Artie said to the agent, "Look around. Check around the other woodpiles and the shed."

One agent kicked apart the remaining woodpile and the other went to the shed door and yanked.

"It's locked," I said. "Key's in the—"

The agent swung the shovel and hacked off the old hasp with one swing. The door popped open and he went inside.

"Agent Polo, Agent Bacarro, there's something here." The agent's voice was hard and brassy. "Inside."

They went to the shed door. But when I got there, things got worse fast.

A body lay wrapped in clear plastic on the dirt floor. It looked like a young Arab, perhaps twenty-five years old. He had been a handsome man, young and slender, with a hard, strong body. Now, his eyes bulged and his face wore a pale, gruesome death mask—the result of the bullet hole in his forehead.

Even through the plastic wrapping I recognized Ghali from the Handley Library.

All eyes fell to me. For once, I was speechless.

CHAPTER 41

Day 4: May 18, 0800 Hours, Daylight Saving Time
Union Station, Washington, DC

THE GRAY DULLES express cab made the long, jerky trek around Columbus Circle through traffic lights and pedestrian traffic to reach the Union Station entrance in Northeast DC. The passenger paid the driver for the fare from Alexandria, tipped him generously, and climbed out. In near panic, he nearly forgot his shoulder bag and had to stop the taxi from leaving to retrieve it.

He was unaccustomed to carrying it. Strangely enough, he had no idea what was in the bag. His instruction had been explicit—do not open the parcel inside, deliver the bag as directed, and his family would be fine. A cash reward awaited him at his destination, too.

Sweating, he crossed the brick street through the steel security bollards and entered the station beneath the grand arch. A moment later, he stood beneath the historic barreled ceiling in the atrium among hundreds of rush-hour passengers scurrying to or from trains.

He checked his watch. He was on time. *Alhamdulillah*—Praise be to Allah.

Sadik Samaan was a tall, lanky Afghanistan refugee. He was clean-shaven with short, tight black hair. He was dressed in a gray suit pressed just that morning, and a white button-down dress shirt. Trying not to draw attention, he moved across the marble floor and headed for the train departure entrance. He tried not to look over his shoulder or make eye contact with anyone. As he approached the center of the atrium, the cell phone he'd been given rang.

"*Salaam?*" He answered too quickly and knew his voice was two octaves too high. "*Baleh.*"

The voice spoke easily and calmly. "Sadik, this is Saeed. Meet me at the center ticket counter on the street level. I have more information for you. I will buy your ticket as well. Go now. Hurry."

"If you please, how will I know you?"

"I know you. Just wait in the center line and I'll meet you shortly."

Saeed Mansouri hung up.

Sadik breathed easier, adjusted the strap of his shoulder bag more securely, and headed for the ticket counter. He walked easier now. He was on time and all would be fine. Saeed would be on time. They would travel to their meeting, and he would make the transfer smoothly. His parents would be freed and even rewarded. All their troubles would be gone. Saeed Mansouri would leave them in pcacc. *Alhamdulillah.*

The ticket lines were long and wound through the lanes of metal stanchions and nylon belts that weaved rivers of people around the floor to guide them to available ticket desks. Security guards posted around the area stood indifferent to the morning commuters and paid Sadik no mind.

He stepped into his place at the center ticket line and waited among the many passengers around him. Ten minutes went by before his cell phone buzzed again. By then, he was deep among the sea of passengers. He slid his cell phone out of his suitcoat pocket and looked at it.

There was no call.

Another buzz.

He was dead before his brain registered that the strange vibration emanated from his shoulder bag.

The explosion ripped through the lines of passengers around Sadik. It vaporized everything in its wake until the blast wave collided with the terminal walls and bounced back, causing a second wave of destruction.

Even before the blast wave began, no one within two hundred yards registered the flash or the ferocious cacophony. They had already perished.

* * *

Eighty miles away in a small, empty office, Khalifah read the text message from Saeed Mansouri. He switched cell phones and watched the pandemonium through the camera mounted in the SUV he'd parked nearby Union Station just yesterday. The crowds ran haphazardly from the station, many directly at the SUV across Columbus Square. Many stumbled out of the station and fell once they reached the street. He waited until a larger crowd formed near the perceived safety of his SUV and dialed a number from memory. The call triggered the second blast within the SUV—turning the heavy automobile into millions of fragment projectiles and deadly shrapnel missiles.

In those few seconds, nearly four hundred people were dead.

CHAPTER 42

Day 4: May 18, 1150 Hours, Daylight Saving Time
FBI Task Force Office, Winchester, Virginia

THE FBI HOLDING cell was more uncomfortable than the cell I'd been in in Amman two years ago. That's in Jordan and they're our ally. That's not to say that the FBI isn't an ally. They're, well, us, and should have better accommodations. The only difference was that here I had a metal chair to sit on, and in Amman I shared a stone bench with eight sweaty, smelly tribesmen. At least now I could put my feet up on the interview table and nap.

Desperate times are exhausting.

I guess having a dead body in your woodshed trumped my DHS credentials. I might have slid past them for hiding Bobby Kruppa for a while, and failing to tell them about meeting with G last night, but the dead guy was a bit much to ask favors over. I'd been there for hours with a bottle of water and the walls for company. Since returning from Fool's Lake—boy, did that name fit now—I'd gotten the cold shoulder from Victoria and no better from Artie. All he said when he walked me into this cell was, "I'd keep quiet if I were you. Things could get a whole lot worse."

I took his advice, uncommon as that was. Needless to say, I failed to mention that the body in the woodshed was Ghali. Kevin's "G." I also couldn't point fingers at Bond for Ghali's murder.

To do so would negate my previous statement that I'd never seen the man in the shed before. Silence was my friend. Sometimes, having a secret was like having two aces up your sleeve.

The metal holding cell door opened. Artie stood in the doorway for a long moment, chewing on some thought in his head. I hoped it wasn't a judge's execution order.

"Hunter, we got hit again." His voice was monotone and bleak. "Terrorists hit Union Station this morning. Real bad. Some kid blew the place to hell and there was a secondary explosion waiting in the parking lot across from the entrance. It's a real mess."

"Any intel?" I asked.

"None. They're still sorting the bodies. It's the worst we've had since 9/11. The President has declared a state of emergency. The military is itching to bomb someone. As soon as they know who's responsible, it's going to start all over again."

"It" was our violent entrance into the Gulf after 9/11.

"Any leads? Anything?"

"Too early to know. DC is in a full-court press. The President is apparently ready to launch a strike. They just don't know at whom yet."

Union Station was one of the busiest train stations in the country. Since it sits in Washington, DC, it's also a symbolic target. *Another* symbolic target. Just like the Pentagon. Just like the Towers. They would start the war all over again. Same tactics, different venue. Union Station and the shopping mall.

"Okay, Hunter. You're out." Artie threw his chin toward the door. "You better keep clean or you'll be back fast enough to make your nose bleed. DHS creds or not."

Well, that's a good start. "Thanks, Artie. I can make Kevin's funeral. I knew you'd come through."

"It wasn't me." He shook his head. "I wanted to hold you

another forty-eight hours. The less you're on the street, the safer Winchester is."

"Then who?"

"Me." Victoria stood in the doorway.

I winked at Artie. "You said she didn't like me."

"It's on her if you screw us again." He rolled his eyes. "Go to your hotel and stay there for a few days. Order room service. Stay out of fights and gun battles."

Good suggestions. "Thanks, Victoria."

"Your contact at DHS vouched for you," she said with a cringe in her eyes. "Even after I told him you had a body in your shed. He didn't seem happy about it. Whoever pulled these strings is gonna have a lot to answer for with him."

I nodded. "I'll send him a fruit basket. Why didn't you just ask your CIA liaison? You know the one. He was slinking around the crime scene and at your offices."

"We did," Artie said. "He didn't confirm or deny you even exist with the Agency any longer. The DHS guy was enough to spring you. For now."

I winked at Victoria. "If the government says it, it must be true. Right?"

"Get out of here." She threw a thumb at the door. "Before I change my mind."

I stood and stretched a bit more. "How about an update? You know, between federal colleagues."

Victoria held up a hand. "We have no comment, okay?"

"Following every lead. Right, blah, blah, blah," I said. "Yeah, I've heard that before."

Artie nodded. "This whole thing is one dead end. We're not getting anywhere on Kevin's killing. A stolen truck that led nowhere. No evidence, no nothing."

Liars. I decided to test the waters a little deeper. "Well, then tell me who Saeed Mansouri is."

Artie looked like I'd just insulted his mother and kicked his dog. Victoria didn't look amused, either, and locked her eyes on me. "Where'd you hear about him, Hunter?"

"What do you have on him?"

Her face was impassive. "No comment."

"Saeed Mansouri is on our radar, Hunter," Artie said, trying to appease me a little. "But everything about him is classified. I'm sure you understand."

"No, I don't." I went to the door and turned around. "How can I understand if you don't tell me anything? How about Caine and Khalifah? Or what about Maya and Baltimore? If you don't share, I can't help."

Nothing.

"All right, I'll drive up to Sand Town and dig around."

Artie and Victoria did the FBI telepathy thing. It lasted several moments before they reached a decision.

Victoria said, "Stay clear of Sandy Creek. We're handling them. We're not at liberty to disclose what we've got, including Khalifah, Caine, and Saeed Mansouri. So, hands off Sandy Creek."

"Hands off?" I frowned. "Well then, being as I'll be getting my intel from DHS and CIA, the FBI won't be in my loop. Too bad, too. Because we're smarter together than alone."

Artie suddenly thought better. "Okay, okay, look, Hunter—"

"Forget it, Artie," I said on my way to the door. "I gotta bury my brother. First, though, I'm gonna pick up my .45 and rental car out front. Unless, of course, you've found a photograph of me and John Wilkes Booth having lunch. But I warn you, I have an alibi for that one, too."

CHAPTER 43

Day 4: May 18, 1500 Hours, Daylight Saving Time
Mount Hebron Cemetery, Winchester, Virginia

WITH DEATH, DYING isn't always the worst thing. It's the funeral. The living must go on. Memories. Sadness. Good-bye. No matter how supportive everyone is, no matter their condolences, nothing helps. There's just emptiness and loss. Someone is gone. Nothing changes that. You must make your way through the well-wishers, prayers, psalms, and the cemetery. Each step is heavy and difficult.

You cannot wait for it to end. Then, you hate when it does.

Finality.

Kevin's service was no different. Except the well-wishers were mostly strangers. When a cop is killed in the line, the ceremony gathers everyone—friends, family, cops, politicians, strangers, and townsfolk. Everyone wanted to show their support. Everyone felt the loss. Yet no one shared it.

Before graveside, my grief had passed. Revenge nestled in its wake. I still felt sadness and loss. But oddly, it didn't consume me. Still, there was emptiness. Pain. Thankfully, I was in control. Perhaps it was our fifteen years of silence. We'd become strangers. Perhaps it was anger and shock. Whatever it was, I was calm and removed.

Outside the funeral hall, ten police motorcycles and thirty cruisers waited. The officers came from all over the state and escorted the black hearse and limousines to the cemetery. At the gravesite, the state police superintendent, Colonel Somebody, delivered a gut-wrenching prayer for all fallen officers. When Kevin's name was chanted, my veneer cracked. I faltered. Noor nearly dropped. Sam and I caught her before she tumbled to her knees. I could barely heft her weight.

Steady. One, two, three ... thirty, thirty-one ... fifty-nine ...

The Honor Guard's rifle salute forged my grief into steel. I found my second wind and tightened my arms around Noor and Sam. Artie touched my shoulder and squeezed. Victoria was beside him and refused my eyes. Hers couldn't rise above the ground. Never had I seen them on Kevin. I knew they saw him now.

My demise was the flag—flags and grieving families—always that. When the flag was crisply folded and laid into Noor's hands—the ceremony for the fallen—it choked my breath and weakened my knees. I cried outright, not swollen eyes and moist cheeks, but a full cascade of grief. The first time since my parents' funeral. The only time. The deafening silence drove a spike into me. Noor trembled against me, and I pulled her closer, trying to draw the pain from her. I took Sam's shoulder in a long crush of support.

Ops-mode failed me.

I couldn't control the pain. Couldn't stay the tears. With closed eyes, my parents' funeral surrounded me. After a moment, the here and now returned. No escape.

I looked into the crowd behind Kevin's headstone. Standing in the rear, just off to one side, I saw LaRue and Shepard. They were in dark suits and both wore a black band around their arms in a symbol of solidarity with a fallen officer.

LaRue's face was stone. He looked up from the grave to me and simply nodded. Shepard caught my eyes and sent me a message. When I looked over at Noor and then back to them, they were gone—vanished as quietly as they had arrived.

Shepard's message needed no deciphering. Revenge is a dish best served cold. Mine would be ice.

* * *

Two hours later, the last mourners left the town hall reception. I drove Noor and Sam home. They sat in the back seat simmering in shock and despair—silent. At home, Noor took a prescribed tranquilizer, and Sam sought refuge in his dad's den. Me, I couldn't relax. I couldn't allow the darkness to consume me. Not now. Not again.

Focus.

I jumped into my rental and returned to the cemetery. There were things to say. Private things. Brother things. Overdue things.

The graveside crew had just left. Only the garden-sized memorial of flowers remained. I strolled through a tree-lined knoll well away from his grave. Even now, Kevin and I were magnets that repelled each other. When finally the right words formed, I crested the knoll and gazed down on him.

Someone was there.

A small woman, who even at a distance was familiar, stood with head bowed and prayed her rosary. She wore dark sunglasses with a scarf pulled tightly around her head. When I moved closer, she looked up and pulled her scarf tighter.

She turned to go.

"Wait," I called, and closed the distance. "No, please don't go."

The closer I got, the more familiar her features became. Of course. It was the young Middle Eastern woman from the Old

Town Café. She had been with her daughter eating ice cream the night I'd met Bobby Kruppa.

I smiled the best I could. "I'm sorry to disturb you. How did you know Kevin?"

She stared and straightened herself with poise and confidence. She held my eyes. There was something strong and proud about her—confident and unapologetic.

"*Motevajeh nemishavam* . . . Ah, I no understand." She nodded politely.

My Arabic wasn't the greatest, but I'm sure she told me she spoke no English.

I gestured toward Kevin's grave. "Please, stay."

For a moment, she looked as though she would speak to me. It lasted only a second before she turned and walked away toward the cemetery gate. I watched her leave and a nagging feeling overtook me. The woman, for whatever reason, waited until everyone was gone before visiting Kevin. Why?

I turned back to Kevin. Unease lingered. Standing there, alone and unsteady, the guilt—born of so many silent years—wrapped its arms around me and squeezed.

I stood with him, whispered a short prayer, and hoped he was in the mood to listen.

CHAPTER 44

Day 4: May 18, 1630 Hours, Daylight Saving Time
One Block from Arlington IFCU Mosque, Arlington, Virginia

CAINE EXECUTED HIS precautionary surveillance-detection maneuvers through Fairfax, DC, and Alexandria. Recent events dictated extra attention, and one mistake could cost him everything. Cost everyone everything. Finally, after his customary changes of cabs, trains, and city blocks, he traveled the final few miles to Arlington by cab for his meeting with Khalifah and the accented man with no ring finger. Two blocks away from Hafez and Fasni, where his colleagues waited, the cabbie slowed and pulled to the curb.

"No closer, buddy. Cops have the road blocked. What you wanna do?"

Half a block ahead, a row of flashing police lights blocked traffic and uniformed officers milled around. Caine climbed out of the cab and handed the cabbie a twenty. "Stay right here. I'll be back."

"You got five minutes. I keep it if the cops chase me out."

Caine walked toward the police but found the reason for the barricade before he even reached them. His plans then changed. He took out his phone and tapped in a phone number from memory.

Khalifah answered on the first ring. "Where are you? You're late."

"Look out your window. I'm not getting through that." He tapped the call off and pocketed his phone.

Down the boulevard, a block west of Hafez and Fasni, a crowd of protestors was swelling in front of the Arlington IFCU Mosque. A second line of Arlington County police were positioned to protect the mosque entrance and separate the protestors from an equally growing crowd of Muslims attempting to enter for afternoon prayer. Angry words volleyed between the crowds. One of the protestors chanted angry slogans using a megaphone, agitating the followers even more.

More protestors arrived. This group was armed with signs and hastily prepared banners demanding justice for the Fair Oaks and Union Station victims. Some of them wore old clothes bathed in red paint. Banners displayed huge photographs of the attack's carnage.

The crowd was morphing into a mob, and it began moving toward the police as signs stabbed the air and were readied as clubs. Chants turned to shrill threats. Protestors, spurred by anger and the fever pitch of the crowd's emotional swell, edged toward thuggery.

From somewhere inside the Muslim lines, its own anger swelled as the worshippers were pushed away from the mosque by the police. Pushing and shoving began as they attempted in vain to breach the police line and engage the protestors.

Flashpoint.

As Caine reached his waiting cab, a gunshot cracked the air from somewhere beyond the mosque. The police near the cab drew their weapons and rushed in. The chanting turned to panicked screams as fear erupted. Someone cried out for an ambulance. Police commands to disperse echoed up the boulevard.

Another gunshot.

"Get me out of here," Caine barked at the cabbie as he jumped into the cab. "Dulles Airport. Now."

As the cab made a hasty U-turn, Caine turned and looked back as the crowd churned out of control. He understood Operation Maya now. At least part of it. The Foreigner had lit a fuse of molten terror, and with each new attack, fear would explode over and over across the country.

From there, the country was on its way back to war.

CHAPTER 45

Day 4: May 18, 1830 Hours, Daylight Saving Time
Noor Mallory's Residence, Frederick County, Virginia

THE MOVE INTO Noor's garage loft was both a distraction and a curse. It gave me something else to think about other than the funeral. A curse because this was Kevin's home. I didn't belong. I lugged my oversized duffel and a backpack full of dirty clothes up the outside staircase and stumbled through the doorway. The duffel went on the bed. The backpack on the floor.

Voila, all moved in.

The loft was not a four-star suite, but it had the basics and beat my hotel. Actually, it beat most hotels I'd been in in recent years. A five-star suite in those places meant the bathroom was *inside* the building. This was heaven. It was close to Noor and Sam, and I wouldn't hear TV blaring through the walls or some trucker's torrid misadventure.

"Jon?" Noor stood in the doorway with two steaming mugs. "Are you settled?"

I glanced at my duffel on the bed. "Sure. Noor, I can't thank you enough. This is great."

"Coffee?" She handed me a mug, sipped hers, and glanced around. After several moments, she'd run out of ways to avoid eye contact and still she hadn't moved from the door.

"What is it, Noor? What's wrong?" What a stupid question considering today.

"Well...there is something I need to show you." She bent down outside the doorway and retrieved a package. "This was hidden in the barn." She handed me a plastic shopping bag wrapped around a bundle. The bundle had the remnants of duct tape used to seal it. She'd yanked at the tape and exposed the contents.

Money. Cash. Lots of it. Twenty dollar bills still wrapped in the original banking bands.

I pulled out several stacks of crisp twenties and tried to do the math in my head. I was never good at arithmetic.

"Five thousand. There are nineteen more in the barn."

That math was easy. A hundred thousand dollars. Add that to the ten grand that I found at the cabin and things looked bad for Kevin. What had happened to him over the years?

"Noor? Kevin had this? It looks like he—"

"Do not say that. Not Kevin. No." Her face flushed and she grabbed a bundle of cash. "It cannot be. Please tell me there is another reason for this. Please, Jon."

"Noor, I need to tell you some things." Fair was fair. I'd been the filling in a shit sandwich since I arrived in town. Now, I was living a hundred feet from her front door. She deserved to know the details. She deserved to know it all.

"More despair." It wasn't a question and her eyes lowered. She walked to the dinette table and sat. "All right, Jon Hunter. Tell me."

I swallowed hard. "Kevin never sold the cabin. He kept it secret, and I don't know why."

"But...we needed money. He said we were in trouble."

I shrugged. "The cabin wasn't sold and still there's this cash."

She slowly shook her head. "I do not understand. He did not sell and he has this money. What does this all mean?"

"There's more." I told her about Bobby Kruppa and hiding him at the cabin. I told her everything including the FEMA and FBI shenanigans at the river and meeting Ghali last night. Even harder, I explained about finding him dead this morning. When her eyes closed and she started to rise for a retreat from the loft, I blurted my innocence and my release by the FBI. I didn't want her thinking I was a mass murderer and couldn't get the proof out fast enough. If I was going to gain her trust, I had to be honest. I poured it all out, and every syllable was bitter and hard to pronounce.

By the time I'd reached a safe place to breathe, she stood by the door with a confused, anxious look in her eyes. She stared at the floor and tried to absorb it all. She tried to make sense of a dead husband and a brother-in-law bathed in trouble.

"What does this all mean, Jon? Kevin was in some kind of trouble. That is clear to me now. You have not been here for years and now you are caught up in it, too." She folded her arms, leaned against the door, and looked at me with soft, painful eyes. "Did the man who broke in here come for this money? Please—tell me you do not think Kevin and that man were . . ."

"Partners? No." Deep down, though, it was possible. Regardless of what LaRue thought. The best I could do for Noor right then was lie. "It'll be okay, Noor."

She shook her head and wept.

Without thinking, I stood and went to her, pulling her to me and gently kissing her on the forehead. "Whatever this is, I'll take care of it. I promise."

She pulled away and looked up into my eyes, searching for something hidden from both of us. She leaned close and pressed her cheek into my chest. Her body trembled, and for a long time, she clung to me with familiarity I hadn't felt, well, ever.

Fingers of fear seized me. I had no idea what to say or do. I did nothing. Said nothing. Moments were hours and the nothing I did became heavy and daunting. Everything I knew about women—any woman—I'd already played with cheap one-liners on Victoria. I was out of ammo. Spent.

After a long time, she leaned back and faced me again. "You are nothing like Kevin. Nothing any longer, at least. Just then, if I closed my eyes, the man I once knew had returned."

My heart stopped. I struggled for words. If there was one good reason I spent most of my life alone, it was moments like these.

"Noor, I'm sorry. I'm being too—"

"No, you are not." A faint smile etched through falling tears. "You are all I have now. You and Sameh. Please, be my family. Do not be afraid."

Afraid? Afraid to join Kevin's family or afraid of her? Perhaps the sudden warmth of affection that shouldn't be there? Neither? Both.

Time to change the subject. "Noor, did you know Kevin had passports for you and Sameh, and himself, with false names?"

"False names?" Her beautiful dark eyes exploded. "Was Kevin so bad we had to run?"

My cell phone rang. *Thank God*.

It was Artie. "Hunter, we need to meet."

"Sure, Artie."

"I'm at the Valley Road House."

"When?"

"Nine thirty. Hunter, come to listen."

Noor had said about the same to me. "Sure, Artie. I always have an open mind."

"Of course you do. Nine thirty, Jon."

Click.

What was this about? A thought popped into my brain. "Noor, you told me Kevin started acting odd a few months ago."

"Yes, and he scared me very often, too. He became moody. Angry. We hadn't talked much for two years, but it became worse. Sometimes, he would go out at night and not come home for a day or more. No explanation. Never."

"When did it start? Exactly?"

She thought a moment. A tear landed on her cheek. Another. "He forgot Valentine's Day. I never cared for the custom, but he loved it. He never forgot. It was then I knew our marriage was truly over. It had been for a long time. But then I knew."

"Valentine's Day," I repeated, more for my benefit than hers. "Did anything else happen around that time?"

She thought a long time, looking down. When she looked up, there were tears in her eyes. "Yes. He told me just before that someone gave him a file, a secret file, about your parents' death. This file said the man who killed them was a refugee here. Someone who was supposed to be sent home to Iraq. Instead, even after killing your parents, this man was allowed to stay in this country. Kevin was angry. He was in a rage as he told me this thing."

Who was the someone who gave him the secret file? If there was information on the drunk driver, it was never released to us before. Kevin and I never sued. Mom and Dad's life insurance was more than what we needed and all we wanted to do was move on. The faster we moved beyond the accident, the better. So why, after all these years, would someone think it important that he know those details?

"It's all confusing, Noor. I just don't know what it means."

"He was never the same." She leaned against me again, sending a shiver through me like a heat wave. "He had a terrible fight with Polo and Dave. Dave and Kevin were close, but the past few months they were not. My husband was not the man I married. This man was not Sameh's father any longer. It made me very sad."

A month after he changed, he began searching for me. If he wanted me to handle it—whatever *it* was—then *it* had to be bad. Calling for me cost his pride. That was an expensive price to pay after all these years. Breaking the silence was the down payment. Admitting he needed my skills was the vig on a twenty-year debt.

I said as much to Noor. Then added, "Do you have a gun?"

She nodded.

"Can you use it?"

Her smile was as surprising as it was devilish. Neither had I seen before. "I am Iranian. Of course I can use a gun."

"Good. Get it and keep it with you."

"And, Jon Hunter," she said and kissed my cheek, "I am not afraid to kill."

CHAPTER 46

Day 4: May 18, 1830 Hours, Daylight Saving Time
Alexandria, Virginia

LaRue sat in silence as Shepard pulled the Mercedes into the Alexandria office complex's underground parking garage and backed into a space near the elevators. When LaRue climbed out of the back seat, he waited for Shepard to slip on leather driving gloves and double-check the weight beneath the overcoat draped over his arm.

LaRue asked, "How much time do we have?"

"No more than two more hours, sir," Shepard said, glancing at his watch. "The FBI found enough of the bomb car outside Union Station to trace back to here. Our asset is slowing the progress until we're through."

"Very well. Proceed."

They moved together to the elevators and took the car up to the fifth floor. There, they made a left and followed the corridor down to the first suite on the left—Number 509, belonging to Kazan Limited, Importers of Fine Middle Eastern Furnishings. They knew the suite number from the registration for a dark SUV that had been parked outside Union Station that morning. Just before, of course, it exploded and killed hundreds fleeing Union Station.

The suite door sign requested visitors to ring the bell. Instead, LaRue nodded to Shepard, who lifted his right hand from beneath the raincoat.

Shepard tapped the earbud in his left ear and whispered, "Ready. Eyes on?"

The voice responded, "One target inside to your . . . right. One signature in the rear office on left. No other signatures. Looks like they're cleaning up."

"Confirmed. Go on three." Shepard stepped in front of the door and removed an electronic lock pick tool the shape of an electric toothbrush from his jacket. He quietly inserted the pick just as the telephone inside rang. He began the countdown. "One, two—" The phone stopped ringing. Three seconds of silence. It began to ring again. Timed to the third ring, Shepard turned the knob and slowly eased the door open, keeping his right hand at his waist with the silenced .22 pistol.

LaRue followed him through the door and silently closed it behind them.

They stood in a small reception area adjacent to a hallway that traversed the entire front of the suite. Shepard dropped the raincoat on a chair, lifted the .22 into a two-hand shooting position at eye level, and moved through the hall to the offices in the rear.

The man standing near the rear window looked up. He panicked and made a dive for a submachine gun lying on the rickety wood table near the office couch.

He never made it.

Shepard had readied for a wounding shot—an arm, shoulder, or perhaps a knee. The man's jerky dive over for the subgun disrupted the shot and the .22 hit him on the left side of his neck and exited through the right. The round shredded the carotid artery and shattered his windpipe. A gush of blood erupted over the floor. The man grasped his throat in a mute spasm for survival, but the end was mere moments away.

"Dammit." Shepard kept his weapon poised, but the man made no further attempt to reach the subgun. "Sorry, sir."

"Regrettable." LaRue turned to secure the remaining offices. Before he took one step, the second man emerged from behind them, holding a shotgun. LaRue raised a hand. "No."

The crisp crack of the office window did not startle either Shepard or LaRue when it killed the man holding the shotgun. From across the street, the sniper's bullet struck the man in the left eye and ended his life before his brain perceived the sound of breaking glass.

Shepard tapped his communication earbud. "Targets down. No joy."

"Copy. Standing by."

LaRue surveyed the offices. He knew what they would find, but the sight disturbed him nonetheless. He'd anticipated everything, but did not yet understand the implications. That would come in time. But to do so, they needed another prisoner. Another interviewee. Someone higher in the food chain than Grigori Sokoloff. With each rung up the ladder, more information could be gleaned. Each step brought them closer to Khalifah. Closer to the source. Looking at the dead assailant lying in the middle of the living room, he knew they needed to climb the ladder much faster. Each step took time. Time he did not have.

There were two other bodies in the room besides the two dead assailants. Both were bound and gagged. Each was dressed casually, taken that morning before their workday began. The older of them, a woman of perhaps fifty, lay on her side on the couch. Her eyes were wide saucers at having witnessed her fate unfold. The second body was a young woman whose resemblance to the older woman was unquestionable. She was twenty-five at best and she sat at the desk facing the older woman. LaRue knew they were mother and daughter. Not simply from the maternal resemblance, but from the file Shepard provided him on the drive there. Kazan Limited was owned by Sahar and Sadik Samaan—refugees who built a business of foreign imports even before fleeing Afghanistan and seeking refuge in the United States during the worst years of that war. Sahar's mother, Amtullah Nasry, was also a Syrian refugee. Hours earlier, Sadik murdered hundreds at Union Station. Now, Sahar and Amtullah stared blindly at their office ceiling. Both women's throats were severed almost in two. The knife had been large and the killer strong, succinct, and skilled. Blood soaked their clothes and pooled on their laps—after the strike, their hearts continued to pump blood for life-draining seconds before their brains bade them stop and succumb to death.

"I don't understand, sir," Shepard said. "Sadik carried out the Union Station attack for them. Why would they still kill the family? This is just like the mall."

"Why indeed?"

Shepard moved to the dead man. He examined his pockets and found nothing. But when he rolled him over, he studied his Persian features. "Iranian, I believe."

LaRue went to the desk and closed Sahar's eyes in a slow, reverent gesture. "Yes. Illegally here, no doubt."

Shepard checked the second assailant. "Him, too, sir. A few minutes alone with one of them might have helped."

"No, I think not." LaRue took a long breath. "We need another. Not a soldier. We need a captain. We must reach the top more quickly."

"How about a general, sir?"

LaRue walked to the large office windows, pulled shards of broken glass from the frame, and gave a wave to the sniper across the street. He walked around the room to a credenza with photographs of the young Sahar Samaan and her husband, Sadik. He picked up the photo, removed it from the frame, and tucked it into his jacket pocket.

"If you can bring me a general," LaRue said, "our task might be done. But I think not."

"No, sir, I don't suppose so."

"We must stay the course. We will work up their chain of command until we have the right one. When we do, it will all fall into place. But we must advance soon."

"That will take time, sir," Shepard said, snapping cell phone photographs of the assailants. "There could be more like this."

LaRue removed his eyeglasses for a polishing. "Ah, there will be, Shepard. There will be."

CHAPTER 47

Day 4: May 18, 2055 Hours, Daylight Saving Time
Noor Mallory's Residence, Winchester, Virginia

IT WAS JUST before nine p.m. when Noor walked me to her front door. I bade her lock up and keep her gun close. As I reached for the door, she took my arm and moved in close. For a moment, I thought she would kiss me, but instead she dropped her eyes to the floor.

"I wish you to understand. Kevin and I, well, he ended our marriage very long ago. We stayed for Sam. There was nothing else. There hasn't been anything else."

I said nothing.

"I hear him in your voice. I see his eyes in yours." She turned away. "But that is all. You and he are so different. You have talked to me more since you have returned than he has in a year. You are daring and adventurous. He was not. Yes, he was a brave man to do what he did. But his heart was not yours."

"Noor, why are you telling me this?"

She opened the door and refused to look at me. "I do not wish you to think me a bad wife."

"I don't think that." I checked my watch. Time to go. *Thank God.* "We'll talk more when I get back. Lock up."

I couldn't get Noor's parting words out of my head on the drive into town. What had she done? Something with Bond? Was she warming too much to me? That couldn't be. No, she was family and any thought of that was just—*uncomfortable*. She had something else on her mind. Something that evaded me.

Twenty-five minutes later, I pulled into the Valley Road House parking lot along Interstate 81 just south of town where it shared the lot with my hotel. When I ambled in—tough guys amble—I was at home. The aroma of sizzling beef and spilled beer hung in the air. Laughter. Clinking glasses. Loud jukebox music. My anguish disappeared when the bosomy waitress winked at me and asked me to meet her after closing.

No, that didn't really happen, but it could have. Really.

Artie was nowhere to be found, so I went back outside to my car to check in with LaRue when I saw Artie park and walk across the lot toward the bar. I was just climbing out of my car to hail him when an old beat-up Nissan rolled in and parked near Artie's car. The dome light came on and I spotted my old pal Fariq, the knife-wielding, bad-attitude thug who'd stalked Bobby Kruppa. There was at least one other person in the car, and I was betting that was Azar.

Now, what were they doing on Artie's heals?

From the distance, it was hard to tell what they were up to, but a moment later, the car started and they began trolling the lot. I ducked down just in time when they passed me. A few seconds later, they made another pass.

This was an opportunity to follow him. Maybe I'd get lucky and he'd lead me to Khalifah or Caine. How fun would that be?

For a second I considered grabbing Artie, but there was no time. Instead, I sent him a fast text, updated him, and promised to call as soon as I found out where they were going. A moment before the Nissan left the lot for the highway, he replied, "Hunter, I'm bringing Victoria in on this. We'll be ready in ten minutes. Send your location. No action without us."

The Nissan was already at the light out in front of the bar, and I would lose them if I didn't move fast. In a second I'd started the rental, pulled across the lot with my lights off to not draw attention, and fell into place three cars behind the Nissan.

Traffic was light and I had to give the Nissan extra space so as not to tip my hand. The Nissan jumped the traffic light and accelerated onto the ramp for Interstate 81 south out of Winchester. As I reached the last Winchester exit, I grabbed my cell phone and called LaRue. If there was anyone who could send the cavalry in time, it was him. He answered on the second ring. In a minute, I'd explained what I was doing and he didn't disappoint.

"All right, Hunter. Keep him in your sights. I've locked the UAV onto your GPS. It'll be on station in ten. Shepard in fifteen."

"You have your own UAV?"

"I want him alive, Jon. No gunfights."

He sounded more and more like Artie Polo all the time. "Sure, sure. I gotta call Artie."

"No, you will not." It was not a suggestion. "You are to take Fariq alone. No outsiders."

Dammit, Artie and Victoria were only moments behind me. "Okay, Oscar. Then Shepard better be here faster. I'm not waiting." I tapped off the call.

The Nissan slowed a bit and kept its speed at sixty-five. After another two miles, they took the next exit and headed north toward the mountains.

I checked my watch. Ten minutes had passed. LaRue's eye-in-the-sky should be on station—that is, overhead.

My cell phone rang. It was Victoria, and I ignored it and put it on vibrate. Better silence than a lie. If I lied, she'd see through it in no time. Explaining how I was about to kidnap a possible federal suspect would be touchy with all that procedure and rights and complications. Hell, they stole my $879,928.66 under the Patriot Act, so I can snatch one or two terrorists without reading them their rights.

I shortened the distance to the Nissan just as they rolled off the road into an abandoned gas station that was dark and empty. Hoping Shepard was close by and the UAV was overhead tracking me, I passed the Nissan sitting idle in the lot and continued another quarter mile down the road until I found a place to pull off and hide my car.

After checking my .45 twice, I headed toward the gas station on foot.

The area around the abandoned gas station was wooded, and I managed to jog to within a few hundred yards without worry. Closing the distance, my breath came a little faster and my heart started to rumba with anticipation. Somewhere ahead were at least two men. One was Fariq and the other probably Azar. Both were assuredly killers. There were two reasons the Nissan stopped at the empty gas station. One, they were checking for a tail and might be on to me. And two, they were already on to me and were setting a trap.

Both scenarios ended badly for someone. The key now was not to be that someone.

I knelt behind a stand of scrub trees and surveyed the gas station lot. The Nissan was still parked in the front lot near the ancient gas pumps, motor running. The interior was dark and I couldn't see inside. I had no idea if Fariq and his pal were still there. My eyes were adjusted to the darkness and I carefully scanned the area looking for any telltale movement or hidden dangers.

Nothing.

Although I knew I'd probably never see it, I glanced skyward, hoping LaRue's UAV was somewhere above. Hope is never a strategy, so with my .45 out, I inched from the trees to the rear of the garage lot. The back area was a junkyard. There were skeletons of old cars and stacks of rusted engine parts, acetylene cylinders, and machine junk. There was a back door to the shop at the rear of the garage. Near the side of the door, about three feet from the rear wall, was a large, steel-framed tank that stood five feet tall and as wide, once used for kerosene or discarded engine oil.

There were dozens of places to ambush someone from all directions. Any one of them would allow an assailant to hide and wait for his prey before easily gunning him down.

Fariq and his pal were, of course, the assailants. I was the prey. No choice.

Keeping low, I jogged to the side of the lot and found a spot behind a hefty stack of metal junk and took cover. Once there, I crawled to an old Ford sedan that had no doors or engine but provided me some concealment from the yard.

So far so good.

Peering around the sides of the Ford gave me a good view of the side of the garage. Unfortunately, I had no view beyond the piles of junk and debris surrounding me.

Time to move.

I slipped around the rear of the Ford and crawled to an old station wagon skeleton in worse shape than the Ford. From there, I continued to a stack of rusted engine blocks ten feet closer to the garage.

Creaking metal ahead sent me diving onto my face for cover. No bullets flew.

Just as I rose to one knee to move again, my cell phone vibrated in my jeans pocket and scared me to death. LaRue. I knelt behind some junk and read his text. "Tweety has no heat signatures on the perimeter. Two at the sedan. Many blind spots. Proceed."

The UAV was on station.

My breath eased a bit and I stood. A few deep breaths and my heart rate hummed along as I readied myself to move around the building and take Fariq and his pal at their car. I sprinted to the corner of the garage, slipped along the rear wall, and approached the front corner.

A low murmur of voices grew louder with each step.

Ice seized my spine. LaRue was wrong. There should have been three heat signatures.

The air exploded with automatic weapons fire behind me. The bullets riddled the wall chest high, chattering toward me. Had I not heard the creek of metal behind me and turned in time to see the muzzle flash, I'd be dead.

With the first flash, I dropped facedown, rolled sideways, and snapped off three shots at the shooter. He'd obviously been concealed somewhere in the junk pile secreted from LaRue's UAV.

Concrete fragments peppered me and one stung deep into my neck. The perp's subgun chewed up concrete and earth and headed directly for me. I rolled away from the garage wall just in time before the spray of bullets chattered the ground where I'd been.

Running feet.

The two men at the Nissan were joining the ambush. The shooter angled behind me.

I was caught in a lead trap and the trap was closing fast.

Pulling my cell phone from my jeans, I tapped the speed button for LaRue, hit speaker, and tossed the phone a dozen feet away near a stack of old tires. The screen lit up just as it began to ring.

I rolled onto my back with my feet toward the front of the garage and tried to calm the adrenaline gurgling in my veins.

LaRue answered the second the two men appeared around the front corner of the garage.

"Hunter?" LaRue's voice boomed. "Hunter?"

Both men opened up with subguns at my phone and pressed forward, closing the distance to what they thought was me. They fired rapidly and dead on target.

Wrong target.

I fired four shots the moment they cleared the edge of the garage.

Both went down and cried out. One tried to fire again, this time at my position, and I sent two more rounds into them.

Silence.

My arms thrust my .45 backward over my head toward the rear yard. The first assailant ran toward me, cleared the corner of the building, and fired at the tires, too.

Rule three of mortal combat, pal—never leave cover unless you have to. Never.

I waited for him to get within a dozen feet of me and fired, aiming low and trying to take him alive. All would be for naught if I handed LaRue three corpses.

My second and third shots hit home.

The assailant screamed in agony, faltered, fired another short burst from the subgun, and fell.

I was on my feet and angled toward him. "*Sheleek mekonam!* I'll shoot!" I closed on him, kicked away a Styer subgun, and stood over him—my .45 aimed at his face.

It was Fariq, and he had a nice bullet hole in his left leg just above the knee.

"Surrender. We surrender," he coughed between the agony. "Lawyer. Doctor. This is America. We have rights."

Movement behind me. I spun.

"Hold." Shepard eased out from the garage corner behind me and moved to Fariq's men. "One dead. One wounded in the shoulder."

Fariq squealed again, "This is America. We have rights. I want a doctor. I want a lawyer."

"Sorry, Fariq, I'm all out of doctors and lawyers. How about an old, crusty dude with a bad sense of humor and lots of questions? He'll give you a Band-Aid."

Shepard knelt beside the wounded assailant and tended to his shoulder. "Christ, Hunter, the old man said no gunfights."

"They started it." I kicked Fariq's wounded leg. "Tell him, Fariq. Tell him you started it."

Fariq said nothing.

I turned to Shepard. "What did he expect?"

"The UAV's been recording. He saw it all."

He didn't see the third assailant. "Does this mean I'll get some of my $879,928.66 back now?"

CHAPTER 48

Day 5: May 19, 0630 Hours, Daylight Saving Time
Western Loudoun County, Virginia

MILES OFF THE secondary country road, tucked away in rural farmland and surrounded by dense woods and countryside, I sat in the basement of a two-story nineteenth-century farmhouse. Shepard had led me here after we bumped and jumbled along the country roads hours ago.

This was another of LaRue's safe houses. He was a real boon for the local real estate market.

It was a good place to do what we were doing—interrogating prisoners and hiding a body. We were miles from the nearest neighbor, and no one could hear or see what we were up to.

Not that we were up to anything *really* bad, mind you. But time was ticking, and we weren't getting anywhere on Khalifah and Operation Maya. We separated the two men, who were as I'd suspected, Fariq and Azar. The third man, the dead one, had no ID and no one was offering any information. Shepard patched them up better than most combat medics I'd seen in action. After hours of questions, we were no further along than we had been last night.

Fariq sat on a metal folding chair in front of me in the main basement, and Azar sat on an equally rickety chair in another room behind us. What we got from them was nothing. Azar refused to give up his name. That was really stupid since he knew I knew it. Fariq refused to look at us when we spoke.

One little thing changed the dynamics a bit.

Shepard leaned down into his ear and spoke in Persian. "We know about Maya. We know about the next attack. If you help us, we will give you immunity."

Fariq grinned and stole a glance at Shepard's watch. "I think you do not know."

I moved to Oscar standing in the rear of the room observing us. "It's soon, Oscar. He got all giggly when he saw Shepard's watch. We're out of time."

"I agree." LaRue raised his chin and looked at me but called to Shepard, "Please begin with the ADS."

Shepard slapped Fariq on the back. "Oh good, pal. It's time for the death ray. Last chance, talk to me."

Fariq spit into his face.

"I'm going to enjoy this, asshole," Shepard said. He went to a table on the side of the room and pulled a dustcover off a large suitcase. From inside the case he took out a strange gadget that reminded me of a toaster oven.

I said as much to Shepard.

"You win the prize." Shepard looked at Fariq. "See this, Fariq? It's like a microwave oven, but without doors. It cooks things that turn until we get answers. I turn it on, microwave you until you're done, and you'll give me answers."

The Iranian gritted his teeth. "If I do not?"

"Then you'll fry. Literally."

I looked over the device and recognized it from its testing in Kabul several years ago. It was an Active Denial System and it was mean.

Shepard aimed the device at Fariq. "I'd move, Hunter. Unless you want to sauté, too."

He turned on the device.

Seconds later, Fariq vibrated in his chair—twisting and thrusting and trying to escape some unseen pain. He broke into a sweat, gritted his teeth, and thrashed around, trying to break the bonds. After several seconds, Shepard turned the device off.

"Now, have anything to say, Fariq?" Shepard asked.

The Iranian spat again. "Kill me, pig. I am ready. *Allahu Akbar*."

Shepard repeated the episode and received the same resistance—spit, denial, resistance.

Enough. I went to Fariq and leaned in close, pulled my .45 out, and stuck it into his chest. "I'm done with these games, pal. How about you?"

He tried to grin, but the tension on his sweaty face stopped him. "Pig. My brother and I will not talk."

"Brother?" I winked. "Azar is your brother? Say good-bye."

LaRue came forward. "Hunter? What are you doing?"

"Saving time." I walked across the basement to one of the two doors there. One remained locked, and behind the other was Azar. I swung the door open, went inside, and slammed the door behind me.

Azar was strapped to a chair that was bolted to the floor in the rear of the room. He was stripped down to his shorts and nothing else. His head was covered with a black hood and his ears deafened with a pair of large noise-cancelling headphones.

"Alright, asshole, where's the next hit? Today?" I yelled loud enough to be heard in the next county. "Talk, now."

Nothing.

"Talk." I lifted the .45 and fired.

The man bounced in the chair and screamed. Even .45s can get through noise-cancelling headphones.

"Where is it? Tell me."

Nothing.

I fired again.

Another outburst of fear and pain.

"Where?"

Nothing.

My last shot ended the debate, and I returned to Fariq with blood dripping from my cheek. "Too bad. He wasn't cooperative."

Fariq couldn't take his eyes off the blood splatters on my cheek and hands.

"What . . . what . . . what have you done?" His eyes were big and scared, and his pulse pounded in his neck. "This is America. We have rights. What have you done to Azar?"

Shepard's face was raw, but he didn't speak. LaRue lowered his head and cursed at me, turned his back, and retreated to the stairs.

"Screw your rights." I touched my .45 to Fariq's groin and held his eyes in mine. "Same deal, asshole. Where is the hit and when?"

For a long moment, he stared at the blood splatter on my cheek.

"Hunter, no," Shepard said, reaching for my arm. "Not this way. Not again."

"Well, tough guy?" I whispered to Fariq. "Three, two, one—"

"Eight a.m. Leesburg. I will tell you. Stop. Stop this now!"

I stepped back and lowered my gun. "Now, that wasn't so hard, was it?"

Between sips of water from a bottle Shepard gave him, Fariq Wassef Azmeh, first son of Haroun and a fellow guardian soldier, told us everything he knew. He was a *Pāsdār* in the Iranian Revolutionary Guard Corp. Unfortunately, he was a low-level *Pāsdār*, but he confirmed some important details, like Saeed

Mansouri was the IRGC commander orchestrating the recent attacks, and that Caine was aiding Khalifah. Who Khalifah was and what organization he was tied to was unknown. To ask meant death.

The mere mention of Khalifah's name caused Fariq to beg for asylum—or execution.

When we were sure he'd emptied his brain, I beckoned LaRue and Shepard to the rear of the basement. "Shepard, you better check Azar. I think he shit himself when I shot up the wall beside his head."

CHAPTER 49

Day 5: May 19, 0815 Hours, Daylight Saving Time
North and South Middle School, Outside Leesburg, Virginia

THE ATTACK AT the North and South Middle School began before we were ready.

Traffic had stopped halfway down the boulevard in front of the school as buses and parents lined up to drop off children for classes—the calm before the storm. If not for the sheriff's deputy at the bus entrance, the lethality would have been staggering. Luck and some higher power—higher than Oscar LaRue—caused the deputy to be out of his car holding oncoming traffic. One of the school buses got stuck halfway across the boulevard while trying to enter the school. Angry drivers brought the deputy out to ensure cooler heads prevailed.

The terrorists hadn't expected this.

We were three cars behind the blue sedan when it broke from traffic and attempted to veer around the deputy into the school lot. When it accelerated toward him with tires squealing, the deputy instinctively drew his sidearm. The sedan's passenger leaned out the window and opened up with a machine gun that strafed the deputy's midsection. He still managed to fire several shots into the sedan's windshield before falling.

The vehicle skidded out of control and slammed broadside into the school bus blocking the lanes. The passenger, perhaps injured, fumbled to escape the vehicle with assault rifle in hand. His door was jammed.

"Go! Go! Go!" I yelled, but Shepard was already accelerating.

He stomped the gas and careened around the line of cars. I hung out the window with an MP5 9-millimeter subgun—courtesy of Oscar LaRue's farmhouse pantry—and readied. "Barricade!"

We smashed through the rear of a small coupe that was trying to turn around and avoid the vehicle backup. We plowed across the lane to the school entrance. Five feet before the entrance, Shepard yanked the emergency brake, put the vehicle into a slide, and wrenched the wheel to the left. He bootlegged us to a stop, blocking the school entrance.

My body was reacting faster than my brain could formulate commands. I was out and shooting on the run. Shepard was moving now, too.

My first three-round burst strafed the sedan but missed the passenger. My second hit him across the shoulders as he lifted an AK-74 above the sedan's roof to assault the bus. He got off one short burst before my third volley hit center mass and obliterated his heart. I closed on the car and put a burst into the driver.

Two down.

Subgun fire from behind me spun me around. I followed my front sight, searching for a target, and saw Shepard tracking a new threat. A green four-door had hopped the sidewalk farther behind us in traffic and had made a run across the lawn toward the school buses offloading children. Shepard went for the tires first. On his third burst, the driver's front tires succumbed and the vehicle shuttered but still lumbered forward. He adjusted fire and his rounds obliterated the vehicle's windshield.

At a dead run, I angled between two buses and put myself between them and the four-door. My MP5 was up tracking the injured vehicle.

The four-door stutter rolled forward as two men jumped out with AKs firing. One of them rained 7.62 rounds along a bus's side row of windows rear-to-front. His second burst reversed direction front-to-rear at seat level.

Crouching, I advanced on the shooter, firing three-round bursts. I put him down with the second. As I did, something punched me hard in my shoulder and chest and knocked the wind out of me. I went down. A terrorist had hit my body armor with two rounds that could have killed me—*luck*. All they succeeded in doing was knocking me down and stealing some wind.

Movement was survival.

I gasped for breath, staggered to my feet, and let fly a burst that put him down hard. I dropped the magazine, slapped a fresh one into the MP5's receiver, and put two more rounds into each of the attackers as they lay in the grass.

Rule four of mortal combat—victory is not for the squeamish.
Four down.

Subgun fire and a vehicle crash spun me around again. The four-door had fumbled along its path and crashed into the sheriff's cruiser near the school entrance.

Shepard advanced on the four-door, shooting high into the passenger's compartment in tight, controlled bursts. He paused, moved in close, and yelled something in Arabic I couldn't make out. A second later, someone crawled from the front seat with his hands in surrender.

"*Deraz bekesh, hamoonjah bemoon.*"—Down, stay down—
Shepard yelled.

Children's screams broke through my concentration.

Ops-mode had engaged when the first terrorist fired. It controlled me still, pivoting me in slow semicircles, searching for threats, hunting targets. Another breath. Three. Four. My pulse steadied. My muscles readied. *Focus.*

No other cars broke traffic. No AKs cracked the air. There was chaos. Screams. Cries. Running feet. Chaos.

Seconds turned into minutes before I dared leave my vigil and join Shepard. He'd hog-tied his captive with zip ties and knelt beside the deputy to check his wounds.

"He's got two in him but he's alive," Shepard yelled. "Stay here. Cops are one mike out." Then he hoisted the terrorist by the belt, dragged him to our car, and stuffed him in the trunk. "Get me thirty minutes at least."

"Right. Tell Oscar they started it."

He threw a thumbs-up, climbed in, and roared around the carnage into the open boulevard lane.

Gone.

Teachers ran from the school and rendered aid to the students. I kept my MP5 in hand and willed the remaining adrenaline to retreat and ops-mode to return to quarters. Carefully, watching for any telltale sign of a second wave, I moved to the front of the school.

I'd taken ten steps when the explosion half a block away knocked me across the grass.

CHAPTER 50

Day 5: May 19, 0945 Hours, Daylight Saving Time
North and South Middle School, Outside Leesburg, Virginia

IT COULD HAVE been worse. Much worse. Unthinkably worse.

Dozens of ambulances, as many fire trucks, and three times that in police and federal cop cars were strewn across the boulevard and school grounds. Tactical teams were just emerging from the school after two sweeps with explosive detection dogs and remote robots. A helicopter circled overhead with snipers hanging out their doors, tethered securely, ready to eliminate anything that might emerge for another wave. There were gurneys and doctors and parents and teachers everywhere. Schoolchildren corralled into a fenced playground were being examined by nurses and EMTs. Dozens of tactical cops formed a perimeter around them. Children cried for parents. Adults not consumed with the injured tried to console them.

Terror.

How to explain the unexplainable? How do you say "it'll be all right" when it's a lie a thousand times over? How do you fade the sight of their friends and bus drivers lying on the sidewalk, some draped with white cloths while others were frantically treated for life?

How indeed.

It could have been worse. Four gunmen with AK-74 assault rifles could have killed a hundred or more. But they hadn't. A smart deputy with a fast draw and two lucky consultants in the right place at the right time. Tons of luck.

Even more lead.

"It's like Union Station," a burly FBI man said, gesturing toward the billowing smoke half a block from the school. "Except they tried a direct assault instead of bombs. The vehicle in the park was meant for victims moving for cover."

"I don't think so," I said without thinking. What was it LaRue had said? Oh yeah, keep my mouth shut. Too late.

The FBI man, Agent Linley, looked over at me. "You have another opinion, Agent Hunter?"

Agent Hunter? Oh, right, I'd flashed my new DHS creds at the cops the moment they arrived. It was an act of self-defense so they wouldn't shoot the only standing guy with an MP5.

"That explosion went off minutes after the initial assault. Had these guys been successful, they'd still be shooting. There wouldn't have been anyone escaping and no cops on scene yet. The bomb wasn't meant for that."

Linley considered that for a long time. Instead of commenting, he grunted something and walked off toward the rising smoke.

Another FBI agent approached me. She had been speaking with teachers and EMTs. As she walked over, she spoke on her cell phone, updating the WFO. Her face was pale and sunken—blood and schoolkids. The nightmare scenario.

"Agent Hunter, I don't get your story," Agent Combs said, rubbing tension from her eyes. "But thank God. One of the drivers was life-flighted out. It's touch and go. We have ten gunshot injuries—a bus attendant and nine kids. Two are life-threatening and on the life flight. The EMTs are working their asses off. Forty-three kids suffered various injuries from broken arms when they ducked for cover, to cuts and abrasions from glass and metal fragments. There are only two fatalities not counting the bad guys."

I looked at the first bus at the school entrance. The blue sedan was wedged into its side right at the rear wheel well. The car had been shredded by Shepard's MP5.

The bus driver took the worst hit. When the shooting started, Willy Strauss, a former Army grunt driving school buses to supplement retirement pay, jumped up and began herding the children onto the floor for cover. His bus was stranded between lanes and had nowhere to go. The first terrorist's initial assault struck Strauss as he ran down the aisle protecting the children. Saving his kids cost him his life.

"It could have been better." I spit bile into the grass nearby. "All the kids going to make it?"

Agent Combs shrugged. "We don't know. We hope and pray. Now, I need you to run it all by me one more time."

Here we go, déjà vu. She was reading from Bond's playbook.

"It'll be in my report, Agent, but fine." A deep breath and I tried to remember what I'd told her an hour ago. "My partner and I, Agent, *er*, Biggs, were surveilling this perp's house." I gave her the address Fariq had spilled earlier. "Two men left that house and we followed them here. Before we could call in for backup, this started. You know the rest."

"Your partner returned to recheck that address?"

I nodded.

"Alone?" Agent Combs stopped nodding. "What brought you to the perp's house to begin with?"

Good question. A better lie. "An anonymous tip. Probably a neighbor. We weren't sure of the veracity, so we were checking it alone. That's why we didn't have backup handy."

"Right. You said that." She shook her head. "You just happened to have a couple H&K MP5s in the front seat with you? Most of us have our tactical gear in the trunk."

Oops. "Look, I keep my go-bag in arm's reach. It's a habit from the Gulf."

"Iraq or Afghanistan? I was in Afghanistan."

Uh-oh. "That's classified."

She smiled and nodded again. "You're not really DHS, are you?"

I winked.

Agent Combs gave me an odd sideways look. Sort of like a parent when I picked up their daughter on our first date. She knew I was up to something but didn't want to come right out and castrate me without proof.

"The WFO has never heard of you and never heard of this supposed operation of yours. DHS has a record of you, but no one knows anything. Isn't that odd?"

"It's classified. I told you."

"You did. Just don't move right now, okay? I'm going to check." Her cell phone rang and when she took the call, her eyes went from "who cares" to "oh crap." She listened, saying nothing more than "yes, sir" and "no, sir" for a long time. Then she tapped the call off and slid it back into her pocket. She glared at me.

"What?" I tried to decide if I were going to jail again. "Something I said?"

"That was Special Assistant Director McNamara at headquarters. I've never spoken to the Special Assistant Director before. In fact, the Assistant Director is about ten bosses over my head. Normally, my boss would call and chew my ass, but no, Special Assistant Director McNamara, the Special Assistant to the Director himself, did. *Personally.*"

Uh-oh. "And?"

"I'm to accept your statement and provide you every courtesy until your ride gets here."

"My ride?"

Agent Combs nodded. "Yes, since your partner left, you'll need a ride."

"Yes, thanks."

"Strange about Biggs, though." Her eyes said she wasn't sure about me. "He hasn't shown up at the subject's house yet. So we'll take you to wherever you disappear to."

"Thanks."

A voice called from behind us. "I've got it from here, Agent Combs."

Victoria Bacarro walked through the crowd of parents and teachers milling about the students.

"Hello, Hunter." Victoria's words had icicles hanging off. "I'm sorry, it's Special Agent Hunter, right?"

She was a bit upset with me. "Victoria, good morning."

"No, it's not." She gave Agent Combs a flip of her head and sent her off. When we were alone, she stepped in close and bore ice through my eyes. "Some big-shot DC suit from the WFO called."

"Special Assistant Director McNamara."

"Yes, actually." She poked me in the chest. "Your assignment is real hush-hush. Before he hung up, he told me to get my ass down here because you just stopped a terror attack against these kids."

"It was luck."

"Luck my ass."

I said nothing.

"Get in my car, Hunter. We have a lot to talk about."

CHAPTER 51

Day 5: May 19, 1040 Hours, Daylight Saving Time
Western Virginia

THE RIDE TO Winchester was great. Just me and my gal Victoria. We laughed, played music, and told jokes. Wait, no. None of that happened. The moment I shut the car door she began grilling me. Minus the hot lights, it was an interrogation.

After answering most of her questions truthfully, I held up a hand. "Enough. We're on the same side. I'm a G-man. You're a G-girl."

She wasn't impressed. "You've got some very powerful friends, Hunter. All of a sudden, too."

"To know mc is to love me."

She drove for another mile without a word. Then she started again. "Tell me again how you fell into this attack?"

I gave her the story verbatim as Shepard and I had rehearsed and as I'd told Agent Combs. "Dumb luck, Victoria. If we'd been five minutes later, it would have been over."

"Where's this mysterious partner of yours? What was his name?"

"I cannot comment further." Payback. "We're following every lead."

She shook her head and pulled the car off to the roadside.

Strangely, she reached across the seat and put a hand on my cheek with odd familiarity. For a moment, she looked into my eyes with a softness and understanding that I'd not seen in her. Just when I thought she'd lean over and kiss me—yeah, okay, my mind was playing tricks on me—she slapped me hard on the cheek.

"You're lying, Hunter. Who's your informant inside Saeed's group?"

Time for the CIA two-step. "It was an anonymous."

"Really? How does someone living in a garage loft get an anonymous anything?"

She had me there.

"LaRue again. You guys have an operation going. Don't you?" She gripped the steering wheel so tight her fingers went pale. "You and Polo. You're cut from the same cloth. You play the 'need to know' game and I get nothing. That's exactly what drove Kev away. Why would he want you back for this?"

The way she accentuated "Kev" rang a bell in my brain under the category of *Married men involved with unmarried ladies for 100 dollars.*

Her voice was tiny and tears welled in her eyes. "Just once, how about a little honesty?"

Damn. Damn. Double damn.

She reached for the gearshift, and I took her hand. "You loved Kevin."

The kewpie doll was mine.

Victoria dropped her head and let it rain. Her hands went to her face and tried to cover the anguish, but the sobs shook her. The more she tried to contain them, the more they came.

I let her go.

After a long time, she wiped her eyes. "Yes, goddammit, yes. We were involved. I'm sorry. Sorry for Noor. But it happened, and I couldn't help it. Neither could he. His marriage was over except for the paperwork. Now he's dead. Gone. All I have are lies and *you*."

Damn. "Do you know who killed him?"

"What? No. I would have told you."

"Maybe, maybe not." I reached over and took her hand again. Why, I had no idea, but I think that's what guys are supposed to do in times like this. "Here it is. The truth. I'm really a rogue CIA consultant. Oscar LaRue got me the DHS creds so I could stop Khalifah and thwart his next evil attack without me getting arrested."

She forced a smile. "Tell me what I don't know."

"Oh, yeah." I told her the truth behind my role in the North and South School *and* witnessing the mall attack days before. She couldn't believe the story, especially about having two Iranians captive in Oscar's safe house. "I think Oscar has someone inside, but he's not sharing. I got lucky is all."

"Lucky? You got into a shoot-out with three Iranian terrorists last night and now have them hostage."

"Detained." I put a finger to my lips. "Shssh. We don't take hostages, Victoria. We detained them for further questioning."

She shook her head. "Right. Whatever. I don't get it. We have been monitoring chatter, and there's nothing that indicates all this should be happening. These terrorists are operating a lot smarter."

Chatter was an interesting concept with intelligence folks. In layman's terms, those that I understand, NSA sucks up most of the communications from cells, the Internet, and whatever in key parts of the world. Well, most of the world. They slice and dice and look for patterns, keywords, and people. Chatter is the by-product of the volume, tone, and content of communications in certain targeted areas—known bad guys and bad guy locations.

Too much chatter means something is brewing. When the chatter goes quiet, hold on to your socks, because the shit is about to hit the fan.

According to Victoria, nothing in the chatter surrounding the recent events seemed to suggest the bad guys weren't tipping their hand. Or we'd missed it. It's possible, even with modern intelligence wizardry. If you grab two trillion gazillion intercepts from the airways around the world, you might miss the mention of "bomb" now and then. It can happen. Not often, but it can still happen.

"Do you guys have anyone inside, Victoria?"

"Yes." She shook her head. "The night Kevin was killed, my asset warned me that Saeed was picking something important up at the river. He didn't know what it was but was going to find out. It was our first big break. We think Saeed is IRGC and they're behind the mall and Union Station attacks, and now the school."

"Where's your asset now?"

She frowned. "He was burned up in that pickup truck at the river."

"Damn." I thought about Kevin going to the river. "Follow the money."

"The money?"

"From the missing backpack in Kruppa's photographs."

"What makes you think there was money in it?" Victoria asked.

"What else would it be?" I snorted. "Laundry? A picnic lunch?" Something struck me and I changed tack. "Victoria, you called Kevin that night. What about?"

"No, I didn't." Her face saddened. "Noor told you that. She told Artie, too. I did not call him. We weren't talking for a few days."

"Lover's quarrel?" I regretted the words as they passed my lips. "Sorry."

She shrugged. "Kevin shouldn't have been at the river. We didn't send him, and he didn't tell anyone he was going."

One hundred grand in cash. I knew the answer. "He was there because he was being paid off for something."

She didn't answer and looked out the window.

"I know, Victoria. Or at least, I think I do." I told her about the money hidden at Noor's house. She wasn't surprised and I said as much. "You were on to him?"

She shook her head. "Not really. But I knew something odd was going on for months. He wasn't himself. He was always angry and distant. Often secretive. Even from me, and yes, that was unusual."

It sucks, but it made sense. Kevin had gone bad—a rogue cop taking bribes and doing God only knows what for all that cash. But it didn't explain the passports with fake names. None of that made sense.

Victoria reached over and squeezed my arm. "Kevin wasn't supposed to be at the river, Jon. It looks bad."

"What, he shot your asset and tossed the gun? Then he shot himself and tossed that gun? Who shot at me?"

"No one said he worked alone." She held my eyes.

"Okay, I'm listening."

Victoria looked down. "There's more." She gathered her thoughts as she closed her eyes. "Artie found something on the hillside hidden beneath an old tree, too."

"What?"

She opened her eyes and studied me. "The missing backpack. Before Kruppa's photos showed us it was missing."

Oh, no.

"Another fifty grand, Hunter."

My heart almost stopped. "I thought you didn't find any evidence, Victoria."

"We're protecting Kevin." Her eyes softened. "No one knows this but Artie and me. We found it ourselves. None of it has been entered into evidence. Nor will it be."

I said nothing.

Her eyes filled with pity. "A dirty cop won't get any survivor benefits, Hunter. He wouldn't have gotten that police funeral with honors, either. Noor deserves better."

She and Artie were protecting Noor. Protecting Kevin's reputation.

I swallowed hard. "Thank you."

She reached into her pocket and produced my fifty-dollar bill I'd given "G" at the library. "Ghali had this. There's a phone number on it."

Oops.

"Your phone, Hunter."

Well, not my phone any longer. Fariq and his pals shot the crap out of it last night.

"You knew all this time, Victoria? Even before you released me yesterday?"

She grinned a self-satisfying grin. We sat there eyeing each other—the fox and the hound. "You owe Artie. He wanted you out. I wanted to slap you in jail for obstruction."

She'd been pretty honest with me, and while I knew she wasn't telling me everything, I decided to throw her some help. "Victoria, my people think that Kevin was trying to warn me about the attacks. First, the mall bomber lived at the Christian Run address. His family was held hostage to force him to carry out the attack."

"We think the same things. How did you know about the family at Christian Run?"

I shrugged. "It's a secret."

"LaRue." She shook her head. "What about what Kevin said, 'Maya in Baltimore'?"

I gave her a taste of what LaRue had told me. "Maya is not a person. It's the code name of some pending attack. Maya will be the attack in Baltimore. Somewhere, sometime soon."

Her eyes got big and she looked down, contemplating everything I'd told her. "Is LaRue sure?"

"As sure as we can be. It all makes sense. Khalifah is calling the shots. Caine is his intelligence man, and Saeed runs the terror cells. We just don't know how many there are."

After a long time, she started the car and pulled back into traffic heading for Winchester. "Okay, Hunter, from now on, you and me, we're on the same team?"

"Of course. What about Artie?"

She frowned. "What about him?"

Reluctance? "He and I go way back. I trust him and he never slaps me."

She giggled a little, relieving some tension. "I don't think he trusts me at all."

Wow, two FBI agents and no one trusts anyone. "Well, leave Artie to me. He owes me from Riyadh."

"Let me guess, you got into a gunfight or two?"

I winked. Oh boy, she really had my number.

CHAPTER 52

Day 5: May 19, 1200 Hours, Daylight Saving Time
Old Town, Winchester, Virginia

"Yes, Director, I understand." Oscar LaRue sat at the small dinette table in his George Washington Hotel suite and contemplated the secure speakerphone where the voice of the DCI—Deputy Director of Intelligence—emanated from. "For the record, Director, I do not share the DO's assessment. The facts on the ground are simply not what they appear."

The DCI's thoughts were calm and succinct, no matter the crisis, and always indifferent to Washington politics. It was a trait that held the President's ear for many years. "LaRue, all roads point to the IRGC. It is unprecedented that the Iranians are operating so overtly here. Are you telling me there is another explanation? Other facts I don't have?"

"Yes, Director." LaRue closed his eyes and inventoried his data. "I confess that the attacks on Fair Oaks and Union Station were carried out by Afghan and Iraqi refugees. Their families were subsequently killed. Two separate nationalities of refugees participated in the attack at the Leesburg school. However, all those involved, all of the families at least, were dedicated to becoming American citizens and rebuilding their lives *here*. None were connected to extremists or radical groups or showed any indication of threat. Above all, we were caught off guard. No chatter. No intelligence. No reason to even consider them potential risks. That fact is my key concern."

"We were not watching them? These families were not subject to FISA operations?"

"Correct." LaRue raised a finger in the air to make a point, knowing the DCI was some sixty-five miles away at Langley. "Forensic results from the secondary car bombs at each target led us to Kazan Limited, a Middle Eastern importer. Most interesting were results from the school assault."

"Yes, I read the reports." The DCI's voice was uncharacteristically sharp. "The driver's family was also held hostage, as were those in the previous attacks. But the men delivering the ground assault were suspected IRGC."

LaRue raised a hand even though the motion was moot. "Sir, the IRGC *Pāsdārān* had taken the identities of refugees already cleared to be in the States. These operations are being run with far more clarity and organization than any ISIS or other group has done since 9/11. I do not believe the IRGC is solely behind this wave of threats."

The Director was silent.

"There is more than we can see here." LaRue stood and began pacing. "My analysis is too raw and untested. I need more time."

"Time? We don't have much time, LaRue. Have you seen the news? There's chaos brewing all across the country. Things are getting out of hand. Completely out of control. There aren't enough police to protect the mosques. The Muslim community is threatening to protect themselves. Do you know what that means?"

"I do."

"Dammit, do we have potential targets yet? Do we know what is next?"

LaRue hesitated. To reveal too much to the Director might cause a reaction in Washington that might tip their hand. To reveal too little could cause a cataclysm. "Many, sir. Clearly, Washington is always a target of opportunity. There are many soft targets as well—schools, shopping centers, more transportation terminals. But my concern, sir, is for the Baltimore Harbor."

A pause. Finally, the DCI said in hushed tones as though concerned someone else might hear, "The Israeli delegation meets with the President at the Baltimore Harbor."

"Yes, at the National Aquarium, sir. A substantial endowment from the Leviev-Blumenthal Trust is being presented to the facility in two days. It's a show of goodwill to heal wounds inflicted these past years."

The DCI grumbled something and his tone hardened. "Right, of course. Nonetheless, the Joint Chiefs are readying a response. Special Operations are already increasing their footprint in the Gulf. Naval resources are moving."

"I understand, Director."

"The Attorney General is drafting a plan to round up Middle Eastern refugees for interrogation and a complete reverification of their status. I do not have to tell you that action will effectively set us back seventy-five years."

"Internment. Yes, Director. I understand. You must intercede. I need more time."

The DCI was silent. When he spoke, his tone was stressed and dark. "The President is prepared to authorize strikes within the week. LaRue, it's 9/11 all over again. Perhaps worse. We're going back to war."

LaRue said nothing.

"You have twenty-four hours, LaRue. Get me an answer I can brief the President. If there's one that keeps us from a war, bring it fast. If not, God help us all."

CHAPTER 53

Day 5: May 19, 1200 Hours, Daylight Saving Time
Winchester, Virginia

VICTORIA DROPPED ME at my hotel where LaRue had my rental car returned. I hopped out and walked around to her window.

"What now, Victoria?"

She looked at her watch. "Let's meet for lunch in an hour. We can talk more then."

"Good plan," I said, "and bring Artie. Maybe the three of us should talk. You know, compare notes."

"All right, I'll call him." She reached for her cell phone just as it rang. She took the call and her demeanor evaporated instantly into uneasiness.

"What's wrong, Victoria?"

"All right, I'm on my way." She listened for a few more moments. "Keep a lid on this until I get there. No outsiders. Bureau only."

"What, for Christ's sake?"

She stuffed her phone into her pocket. "Our safe house outside town was hit an hour ago. Two agents are dead."

"Oh, no. What about—"

"Kruppa." Her voice was ice. "Bobby is gone."

CHAPTER 54

Day 5: May 19, 1215 Hours, Daylight Saving Time
Winchester, Virginia

BOBBY GONE? IF Khalifah had Bobby, he was as good as dead.

As much as I begged, Victoria refused to allow me to tag along. Instead, I needed to get to Noor's house. I hadn't checked back in, and that was as good a place as any to wait on news of Bobby. Besides, there was no telling how many messages she'd left me last night through the wee hours of the morning. My phone had died a violent death last night, and LaRue gave me another burner phone so no one could trace me. She didn't have my new number.

I reached my rental when a dark blue Mercedes drove into the lot, around the last row of cars, and made a beeline for me. I gripped my .45 in the small of my back.

Gunfights were becoming way too commonplace around here, even for me.

When the Mercedes rolled to a stop and the driver's window rolled down, I was shocked.

Edik Yurievich Petrov.

"Hello, Edik," I said, releasing my pistol and walking to the side of the car. "What are you doing here?"

"Looking for you, my friend." His face was sweaty and pale. "Before it is too late."

Now, that was an ominous thing to say. Even given the last seventy-two hours.

"Maybe you should explain that. Quick."

He sighed and kept his eyes moving outside the Mercedes. "I will try, Jon Mallory. Oh, forgive me. You are really Jon Hunter, CIA consultant and terrorist hunter."

My hand returned to my .45 and it made me calmer to keep it there. "What can I do for you?"

Edik's eyes caught something in his rearview mirror that made him pause. After the car he'd been watching stopped at the entrance of the hotel and an old woman with blue hair climbed out, he breathed a bit easier.

He leaned out the window a bit. "Business is business, my friend. I told you, I invest. I invested in some land and a restaurant last year. I own some property in Sandy Creek."

"Sand Town," I said. "Also very interesting."

He shrugged. "Yes, Sand Town. An ugly name, no? It was too late. These thugs, those barbarians, moved in and took over many of the families there. They were good families, too. Hardworking refugees who only wanted peace and safety. Then the outsiders came."

I thought about the families of the bombers at the mall and Union Station. All they wanted was their loved ones home. I told him exactly that and my words caused him to look away.

I added, "Who were these outsiders, Edik?"

His eyes, and his voice, hardened. "Iranian animals. They are not who they say they are. I fear the worst. I believe they are—"

"IRGC. Iranian special operations."

"You know?" He eyed me, stopping his vigil around the parking lot. "Did Kevin inform you of these things?"

Familiarity betrayed him. "You more than knew my brother well, didn't you?"

For a long time, I readied for his denial. When he spoke, his voice was just above a whisper. Was it embarrassment or caution? "Yes. I knew your brother well."

"Tell me."

Edik got a faraway look in his eyes, and for a moment, he sat looking through me as though I weren't there. "Many things I know."

"What things?"

He focused on my eyes then. "You are still CIA?"

I shrugged. "Not really. Yeah. No."

His brow wrinkled and somewhere in his thoughts he must have decided it didn't matter. "Tell me what Kevin told you. I will fill in the missing pieces."

"How do you know there are missing pieces?"

He looked hard at me. "Because if there were not, then many bad things would not now be about to happen."

Time to reel him in. "Before he died, Kevin told me something about Maya in Baltimore and Khalifah. I need to know more about both. Much more. I need to find Khalifah and stop Operation Maya."

Edik's face went pale, and he instantly began to sweat. His eyes darted from the rearview mirror out the windows. When he spoke, his voice was shaken and hallow.

"You know much but still not enough," he said. "I have put everything into my small businesses. Kevin and I, we had an arrangement."

Petrov was one of Kevin's informants.

"Okay, whatever it was, I'll match it. Now, what don't I know?"

"I tell you and then it is over." His eyes softened and he looked down. "Please? These are dangerous men. Saeed Mansouri is a puppet. He is not the real threat."

"I know. It's Khalifah."

His eyes closed. "No."

I let go of my pistol and knelt next to his door to lean in close and catch his eyes. "Look, Edik, I have to move fast. Tell me what you know."

Without warning, Edik Yurievich Petrov reached up and put his fleshy hand on my cheek. Russians, whether they grew up in New York or Leningrad, knew the art of communication with just a touch. They saw no weakness in this, no embarrassment, no risk.

"I want out of this. I swear to you, I did not know anything before . . . Give me your number."

I rattled it off.

He let go of my cheek and put the Mercedes into drive. A second before he drove away, his words were a whisper, but they chilled me all the same.

"I will call you soon. Trust no one, Jon Hunter. They will kill you, too."

CHAPTER 55

Day 5: May 19, 1215 Hours, Daylight Saving Time
Western Loudoun County, Virginia

GRIGORI SOKOLOFF LAY on the makeshift bed in the corner of the barren cellar room. Beside him, sitting on a small cardboard box, was a plastic pitcher of water and paper cup. The box was within reach of his left hand. His right was handcuffed to the metal bed frame, keeping him from venturing off the bed.

Grigori had lost time. His isolation left him disoriented and weak. Except for the occasional sip of water, he lay back and tried to gain control of his emotions and body. His training had prepared him for much, but his masters had relied heavily on his tough upbringing for the rest. The SVR envisioned arduous interrogations, not isolation and sensory deprivation. How does one prepare for *no* interrogation—something that is nothing? No questions, no repeated abuse or even physical contact, no sound, no scents or stimulus or connection. Simply nothing. They believed they knew the limits the Americans would go, and they prepared their operatives well within those tolerances.

But Grigori had never expected the heat ray.

He'd never believed such a device existed nor had his masters believed the Americans capable, or willing, to use such a thing. After all, after simply using water and fear to interrogate terrorists taken from the battlefield, the Americans had grown meek and squeamish about such methods. In Russia, such things were child's play to elicit the simplest of confessions. But with this new device, there was no preparation. No comprehension of such a device. When it was used, his skin felt as though it was melting. Yet afterward, no scars or burns resulted. What had this ray done to him? How macabre had the Americans become? He had trained on waterboarding and physical abuse. He could endure three times what most men could. But when the heat bubbled over his body, his training was no match. It was medieval. Simplistic. A penetrating torture that left no footprint. No mark. No evidence. No damage.

The Americans were worse than he feared. Worse than even Moscow understood.

The basement around him was dimly lit by covered casement windows that allowed faint, opaque light to filter in from above. There was no sound. When the upstairs door had opened before and the dim light shined in, he noticed the panels installed on the ceiling to deaden any noise. The floor was cold and hard. The cement walls were barren. There was just him and his metal cot, the cardboard-box table, pitcher of water, and cup. Nothing else.

Briefly, he recalled his favorite boyhood book and let his mind hide in its chapters—a technique that he'd trained himself to use when resisting interrogations. He loved Dumas' *The Count of Monte Cristo* and his struggle at Château d'If. He laughed to himself. Could he be Dantès?

There was nothing to know but him and the silence.

No, that was wrong. Across the basement on the far wall were two doors he'd noticed before the American assassin hooded him. How many days ago? One of the doors had been open and the interior dark. Now it was closed and a heavy dead bolt secured it. Men had been moved into the rooms. Silent men. When the man, Shepard, had placed the headphones and hood on him again, there was no telling what treachery they had conducted in those rooms.

He was no longer alone. Was there an Abbé Faria? Others?

The upstairs door suddenly banged open and shook him from his thoughts. Voices grew loud for the first time. Light danced and fluttered down the stairs, casting shadows from the upper landing.

Grigori sat upright against the cold concrete wall and waited. Something had changed. Something was about to happen that the Americans hadn't done before.

Fear. Was the heat ray not enough?

Something heavy tumbled down the stairs and crashed into a pile at the bottom not thirty feet from him. The form rolled over and faced him. It was the man that had questioned him over and over. Shepard. Another man descended the stairs. At the bottom, he fired two shots into Shepard's still form. The shots, muffled by an extraordinarily thick silencer, were still startling and sent shockwaves through him. His isolation had dulled his senses and the muffled gunshots shattered the air around him.

Grigori moved to the edge of the bed and sat upright, trying to project strength and fearlessness. If he was to die, he would die with dignity. Death was death. Pride was all he had left. He would soon have both.

"I am ready," he said to the man dressed in dark clothing. "Do as you must. I am not afraid."

The man had hard features and dark eyes. His hair pulled back tightly into a stubby ponytail. He stood watching Grigori and tucked his pistol into a holster beneath his jacket. He surveyed the room and moved to the bed, stooped, and unlocked Grigori's handcuff without a word.

"What is this?" Grigori asked rubbing his wrist and remaining ready for some kind of trick. "Who are you?"

"Caine," the dark-clothed man said. "Khalifah sent me. Your situation has caused concern. He dares not contact *General-Polkovnik Fedorov* directly until *Operatsiya Maya* is concluded."

Grigori nodded and stood on wobbly legs. He reverted to Russian. "*Da. Ya nichevo ne govoril.*—I said nothing."

"*Ja ponimaju*—I understand." Caine continued in English, "He knew you wouldn't. Make your way to his safe house. Tell him this—*exactly this*—'Wine grows best in the warm summer breeze.' He will know it came from me and that you are secure."

Grigori tried to calm his nerves and memorize the code phrase.

"Repeat it to me. Now."

"Wine grows best in the summer breeze."

"*Nyet.*" Caine grabbed Grigori's arm, jerked him to his feet, and shook him. "Again. Wine grows best in the warm summer breeze."

"*Da, da.*" Grigori steadied himself. "Wine grows best in the warm summer breeze."

Caine looked at a small table near the stairs. Grigori's cowboy boots, wallet, and old green military field jacket were there. "*Da*, you have it. Get your things and go. I'll clean this mess up. The others will return soon. Go now."

"I know there are others here." Grigori slipped on his boots and jacket and regarded Caine. Without another word, he went to the locked doors, levered the first dead bolt open, and pushed the door in. Inside was a hooded figure wearing headphones. The figure was strapped to a steel chair as Grigori had been days before. The figure was still.

Grigori turned back to Caine. "One of mine?"

"*Da*. They caught him at the school. He's close to talking."

"The others?"

Caine cocked his head. "Fariq and his brother, Azar. Hunter took him last night. I have a car outside, you go. I'll clean up here."

"*Nyet*." Grigori moved behind the figure. In one violent movement, he grasped the figure's head, wrenched it to the right, and snapped his neck.

The figure's head bobbed forward. Then he went to the second room, went inside, and repeated the actions to two men lying on cots and bandaged from injuries.

In a few seconds, all three men were dead.

Caine watched Grigori emerge from the second holding cell. "You could have taken them with you."

"*Nyet*. The pissy camel lovers. *Pawns*. They need not live." Grigori turned and went to the foot of the stairs. He stopped over his captor's motionless body, reared back, and kicked him violently in the ribs. "I would like to kill you myself."

CHAPTER 56

Day 5: May 19, 1240 Hours, Daylight Saving Time
Noor Mallory's Residence, Frederick County, Virginia

PETROV HAD A key to Operation Maya.

Following Petrov was not practical. If he caught me, I might spook him and he could change his mind about helping me and simply run. No, I needed to give him space. He came to me on his own. He would call me, and as fast as I could convince him, he'd tell me what he knew. I doubted Edik was a threat, either. If he'd wanted to harm me or help Saeed to kill me, he just missed his best chance.

No, Petrov was a good guy. He just needed a little more time. It might cut it close, but I had confidence he'd come through. So, after Petrov left, I drove like a madman to Noor's house. As I approached her driveway, I didn't see the sheriff's patrol standing watch. A tingle tiptoed up my spine. Maybe the events at the safe house, the missing Bobby Kruppa, and the other turmoil caused manpower shortages.

Maybe.

I found Noor and Sam at the garage. They were arguing. Sam's defiant, condescending arms were folded in front of him as he looked everywhere but at her. Noor's face was tight and her eyes aflame. Her hands flew, her head shook, and twice she reached out and grabbed Sam by the shoulder and shook him.

As I walked to them, Noor spun toward me. "Jon? What happened to you? I waited for you all night."

"I was working." I stopped close to her and softened my voice. "Sorry, I should have called. What's wrong?"

"Tell him." Noor thrust a finger toward Sam. "Tell Sam he should not go out without telling me where and when he will return. Tell him I need him to stay close."

"Sam, your mom has a point." There, I told him. Now, a little diplomacy. "Noor, he is nineteen. Maybe a little halfway would work."

"No." Her hand sliced the air. "This is my home. My rules. There is no halfway."

Sam reeled back. "Of course not. That's what you told Dad, too."

Noor lowered her head and turned away. Sam looked at me with contempt dripping from his glare.

I needed Sam's help. "Sam, I need to talk to you about Bobby."

He suddenly blurted, "He wants to meet you in an hour at the old Darby Farm on Route 50."

"Oh, yes." Noor's voice boomed again. "The Darby Farm, Sameh? You would drink and smoke and do whatever boys do there that is wrong."

I held up a hand. "When did you hear from Bobby?"

"He ran away from the FBI," he said. "That's what he wants to see you about, I guess."

"What did he tell you?" My thoughts were spinning. "Come on, Sam, it's important."

"How should I know?" He flashed angry eyes. "He wants you, not me. That's it. Go find out yourself. You two deserve each other."

"Is he all right?"

"I guess. He didn't say."

"When did you speak with him?"

Sam shrugged. "About a half hour ago."

"I need to go to him, now." I turned to Noor. "The deputy's gone from the road. Call Bond and let him know."

She gazed down the drive. "Gone?"

"It's probably nothing. But let's check."

She nodded.

I put a hand on Sam's shoulder. "You know where this farm is. Can you show me? It'll be faster."

"No. You're the CIA man. You're the liar and a killer."

I thrust up a hand. "Whoa, there, Sam. I'm no killer. Not the way you mean it."

"Whatever." He looked at me, then Noor. "I'm not going anywhere with you." He rattled off the directions to an old farm property about ten miles outside Winchester heading west into the mountains. He described an old country dirt road just a mile from us that would cut several miles off of the trip. "You're on your own."

I made mental notes and turned to Noor. "Okay. But listen to me. Until that deputy returns, get your revolver and keep it handy."

She lifted the hem of her shirt and showed me her pistol. "Yes. I think that is a good idea."

CHAPTER 57

Day 5: May 19, 1315 Hours, Daylight Saving Time
Noor Mallory's Residence, Frederick County, Virginia

AFTER A FAST change of clothes, I headed out to meet Bobby. I wanted to reach him early in case Victoria's agents were on his trail. Whatever Bobby knew that caused him to run from the FBI needed to reach my ears before anyone else's. Once I had him, I'd turn him over to LaRue and Shepard.

If Khalifah had found him in the FBI's safe house, he could find him again.

Two miles back toward Winchester, I found the shortcut Sam told me of. It was concealed beside a row of mailboxes that could have easily been mistaken for a private driveway. Once on it, I hit the gas and headed toward Route 50 and the old Darby Farm. Two miles farther on, amidst a swirl of dust, a sheriff's cruiser came around the turn ahead of me. He'd come from the Route 50 end of the road, passed me, did a fast U-turn, and whelped his siren as he caught back up to me.

"What the hell?"

The cruiser's siren whelped again. Its grill lights flashed and he clung to my bumper, laying on his horn.

"You gotta be kidding me."

I braked hard and pulled the rental off onto a narrow edge of tall grass. When I released my seat belt and looked into the side mirror, a pistol barrel touched the side of my cheek.

I froze.

"Okay," a familiar voice said, "hands on the steering wheel real slow." Bond's voice was chilling. His demeanor was calm and steely. "Or not, your choice."

"Or not" meant he hoped for a reason to shoot. I obeyed, of course. Not just because he was the law, but because I didn't want my brains mixing with the dust and bugs on my windshield. Truth be told, Bond scared the hell out of me.

"Okay, Dave, relax."

"Shut up, Hunter. Keep your hands on the steering wheel." His voice was calm and icy. "With your left hand, reach through the steering wheel and turn off the ignition. Then slowly drop the keys out this window."

I did. In fact, I was happy to comply.

"Now, come out of the vehicle. Slow." He stepped back from the door. "Open the door from the outside. Hands where I can see them. Move."

I did that, too.

Once on my feet, Bond grabbed my right arm with one hand and kept his pistol on me with his other. He spun me around and slammed me against the car. Twice he kicked at the insides of my legs to spread them wider and wider apart. Any wider and he could make a wish.

"Freeze."

"I got it, Dave." My groin muscles cried in agony. "Take it easy, will ya? We're on the same side."

"Shut up. Interlace your fingers over your head. Do it."

I complied, and he grasped my entwined hands and dragged me back toward the trunk of my car. Once there, he drove two palm-heel thrusts into my back and sent me sprawling over the trunk. "Stay down."

I gasped, "Will you relax? What's this about?"

Two hard fists slammed into my kidneys and dropped me to my knees. I coughed and gagged for breath. A kick pounded into my side. I gasped again and he grabbed my collar, dragged me back to my feet, and pushed me over the car trunk again. This time, instead of pummeling me, he spun me around and thrust a finger into my chest.

"I'm taking you in for reckless driving, resisting arrest, and whatever else I can think of on the way."

I watched the hate in his eyes boil and decided to mind my manners.

"You gotta let me go. Dammit, listen to me, Dave. In my right breast pocket, I've got DHS creds."

"I don't care." Bond stepped back and raised his pistol with an icy, dark smile. A Hannibal Lector smile. "Turn around."

Time was ticking. I had to get to Bobby but I wouldn't if I went to jail or if Bond just shot me. My options were zero.

"Will you listen?" I eased around and lowered my hands behind my back. "Bobby Kruppa is missing from the FBI safe house. I'm headed to meet him now."

"Bull."

While I expected another beating, Bond snapped the cuffs on me and ratcheted them so tight I winced. He found my .45 holstered behind my back and tugged it out. He dropped the magazine and the chambered round into his hand and laid all of it on the trunk above my head. Next, he grabbed my arms, pulled me off the car, and spun me around again to face him. His transformation from Mr. Hyde to Dr. Jekyll was complete.

"What about Kruppa?" He pressed into me again and dug around my jacket pocket. When he found my DHS credentials, he read them briefly, laughed, and tossed them onto the trunk beside my pistol. "I'll add impersonating a federal agent to the charges."

"It's legit. Call Artie or Victoria."

He tensed. "What about Kruppa?"

Thank God, reason was returning. "He called Sam. I'm going to meet him up the road. He's scared to death. Come with me if you want, but dammit, let's go."

He didn't respond.

"Come on, Bond. Something's going on. Your deputy is gone from Noor's house, too. Call her. Dammit, call Victoria and Artie or Noor. Do something, but get on with it."

He watched me and holstered his pistol, leaving his hand resting on it. Without a word, he grabbed me, spun me around, and slammed me over the trunk again. He held the handcuff chain and lifted my arms so high my shoulders threatened to pop off.

"Stay put. Move and I'll shoot your sorry ass."

He let go and I heard him move to his cruiser. His voice was muffled, but I could tell he was talking to Noor. I did make out, "Call if you need anything. I'll find Sam." A second later, he pulled my arms back into the air and the pain shot up through my shoulders. He twisted the handcuffs back and forth and finally removed them. He sent a knee into my thigh that dropped me onto one knee.

He stepped back.

"You're a real bastard." I rolled my shoulders and straightened myself as I rubbed my wrists and arms. "What did Noor say?"

"Enough. Sam's run off again. I'm going over there. You stay clear."

"Come with me to find Bobby first." My voice had a touch of not-so-hidden anger.

"I'll do my job. You do whatever you do."

He climbed into his cruiser, pulled around my car almost on top of me, and rolled his passenger window down. "You might have been some kind of CIA hotshot, but out here, you're nothing. You and me are gonna collide real soon, Hunter."

He was gone in a cloud of dust and flying gravel.

CHAPTER 58

Day 5: May 19, 1315 Hours, Daylight Saving Time
The George Washington Hotel, Winchester, Virginia

OSCAR LARUE SIPPED his lunchtime Earl Grey and watched the closed-circuit television picture across the room. He'd watched the recording three times since he'd returned to the suite. The large 52-inch TV screen was normally enjoyed by other guests for sports and late-night pornography. Today, however, he was watching reruns of Grigori Sokoloff executing his comrades in his Loudoun countryside safe house. A moment later, the enigmatic Caine dragged Shepard's body into one of the holding cells. He returned to the basement and tossed Sokoloff something as Sokoloff dressed in his own clothes—stripped of them by his captors and left piled on a chair in the basement. When he was finished, Sokoloff disappeared from the camera's view up the basement steps.

LaRue tapped a button on the surveillance system remote and changed the picture to an exterior camera mounted clandestinely across from the farmhouse. The videotape picked Sokoloff up as he emerged from the farmhouse. A few seconds later, Sokoloff sprinted off the porch to a small two-door sedan parked beside the farmhouse, dug in his pocket, and extracted the keys Caine had given him.

Dirt and gravel flew as Sokoloff made his escape.

LaRue frowned and picked up his secure satellite phone, dialed a coded number, and waited for it to connect.

"Sokoloff has escaped our Loudoun facility. He's left a mess behind. Caine is there now but won't be for long. Get a team there ASAP. Chopper them in to clean up and secure the facility."

The voice on the phone lasted but a few sentences.

LaRue stood and began to pace. "I have Tweety in the air already. You secure the facility, I'll worry about Sokoloff."

LaRue hung up.

Seconds later, the aerial feed from Tweety's UAV camera connected to the GPS mapping software and tracked Sokoloff out of Middleburg.

Not wanting to let an excellent grilled salmon salad go to waste, LaRue poured a fresh cup of Earl Grey, sat back down, and finished his lunch.

CHAPTER 59

Day 5: May 19, 1400 Hours, Daylight Saving Time
Darby Farm Road, Frederick County, Virginia

BOBBY WAS WAITING for me inside the old barn at the Darby Farm.

He'd been there only a little while. I didn't recognize him at first. The bullet had entered the rear of his head and had blown a chunk of his face away on exit. Unfortunately, I didn't need his entire face to know who had occupied that dumpy, disheveled body in its living days.

"Bobby, who did this?"

My words fell on ears dead less than an hour. His blood had begun to settle in the lower parts of his body leaving the exposed skin pale and meek. His flesh was cool to the touch. I doubted if young Bobby Kruppa, aspiring journalist and chess grandmaster, had been executed more than thirty minutes before.

Emotions tried to seize me. I fought back. If they took over, I was finished. I had caused Bobby's killing as much as if I'd pulled the trigger myself. Someone powerful and connected had located the FBI safe house. Someone had penetrated either the FBI or the local sheriff. Perhaps both.

That person—Khalifah, I was sure—was going to die very badly. He'd taken my brother and now the innocent kid who lay dead before me.

I was going to enjoy killing him.

* * *

Caine stood behind some overgrown apple trees two hundred yards from the barn's open door. He and one of Saeed Mansouri's most trusted operatives, his senior IRGC lieutenant, had been waiting for Hunter to arrive since Khalifah had killed the young student. Caine had objected. There was more value in his living than his death.

Khalifah, however, saw the pudgy-faced boy only as bait.

Now, the lieutenant raised the AK-74 Kalashnikov and started toward the barn.

"No." Caine grabbed his arm and restrained him. "We wait."

"Wait?" the lieutenant snapped in Persian. "For what? He is our target. We kill him now."

"We wait."

The lieutenant pulled his arm free, growled some slur Caine did not understand, and started for the barn again. He made it three steps before Caine caught him, swung him around, and dropped him with a violent punch that rocked his head back and took teeth and blood from him.

It took the lieutenant several moments to recover and stagger to one leg. He glanced down at the Kalashnikov at his feet. "What is this, Caine? What do you do?"

Caine held a silenced .22 pistol in his hand. "You and that animal, Saeed, are in such a hurry for blood. All of you. You know nothing of tactics. Nothing of quiet progress. You only know blood."

The lieutenant spat at Caine and reached for the Kalashnikov. "You are no assassin. You are no soldier. Wait until Saeed and Khalifah hear of this." He swung the rifle up at Caine's chest. "You are finished. Many times you have failed the kill. You are no—"

A nearly inaudible *thwack* stopped his rant.

The .22 is a small, delicate round. Its ballistics are easier to silence than most other handgun ammunition. The Israelis mastered it as a perfect close-quarter assassin's tool. What was good for Mossad was good for Caine.

Caine's .22 hit the lieutenant dead center into his heart. The sound might have carried halfway to the barn at best. The lieutenant was stunned and looked down at the gurgle of blood escaping his chest before he realized he was dead.

When he did, his last words were, "You are no assassin. *Allah...*"

"Yes, I am." Caine put another round into the Iranian's left eye. "After all, I killed you."

CHAPTER 60

Day 5: May 19, 1545 Hours, Daylight Saving Time
Darby Farm Road, Frederick County, Virginia

"ANOTHER BODY." BOND shot me a sideways glance. "Not surprising that you're standing over it."

"I didn't kill Bobby." I jumped off the FBI sedan's hood and headed for him, stopping within a good right hook's range. "You think I broke him away from your protective detail, sneaked him up to this secluded barn, and killed him? Then I called you guys?"

Bond jammed a finger at me. An angry, hate-filled finger. "Sounds right to me."

"When did I do all this, Bond? When I was in Leesburg stopping a terror attack on the school or when I was with Victoria Bacarro afterward?"

Bond stared as his face reddened.

"Got any other stupid ideas?"

Victoria walked out of the barn just as Bond sneered and walked away. I watched, wondering if she'd mind if I put a bullet in the back of his skull and claim temporary insanity.

Victoria read my mind. "Forget him, Hunter. He's not worth it."

"Just one shot. I'll do the paperwork."

"We found another body nearby." She turned toward a group of FBI agents moving through the overgrown orchard across the road. "No ID yet, but I'm thinking it's one of Saeed's men."

"One of his men?" I looked after the FBI team searching the orchard. "I didn't kill him. So who did?"

"No guesses. Maybe some kind of internal fight. Who knows? None of this is making any sense."

I knew people who could help. "I'm going to call some people at Langley."

"No, you're not," a husky voice said behind us.

I turned and saw Mo Nassar standing behind us with Artie Polo. The two came closer, and Nassar aimed a bony finger at me. "You're a lying son of a bitch, Hunter."

Nope, we weren't going to be best buddies. "I don't think we've been properly introduced. That is, one son of a bitch to another."

Artie held up his hand. "This is Special Agent Mo Nassar."

"FBI," Mo added.

"I'm Homeland Security." I grinned. "We're both liars, Mo."

"Officially, Hunter," Artie said, "Agent Nassar is part of the FBI. He's our liaison with the Agency and on our task force under FBI operational control."

I snapped a glance at Victoria. "Mo's your CIA liaison?"

"He is," she said. "He's been with us for several months now."

Something tickled my brain. "Before Kevin joined?"

Artie shook his head. "No, since this winter. Why?"

The snippets of Kevin's moods and behavior struck me. Months ago, he suddenly disliked and distrusted everyone at the task force. That coincidence drew like a magnet to Nassar. It all seemed to congeal around "several months ago" in time for Nassar's arrival.

"Why's the CIA involved in a domestic task force, Mo? I can call you Mo, right?"

Mo snapped, "Where were you when our safe house was hit and Kruppa disappeared?"

"*Our* safe house?" I asked.

Victoria held up a hand. "He was with me, Mo. After the school attack this morning, I brought him back. His alibi is solid. We were heading for lunch when—"

"Lunch?" Mo snapped at Victoria. "Who authorized you to go to lunch with him?"

"Whoa, pal," I said, stepping toward him. "I've been out of the country for a long time, but I'm pretty sure there's no law prohibiting lunch."

Nassar jumped forward and grabbed for my collar, but I shoved him back and off-balance. "Easy, pal. I'm not in the mood."

Artie patted the air. "Relax, Mo. I'll handle Hunter."

"Damn right you will." Mo wagged his finger at me. "You'd better rein him in. There's too much at stake."

"Mo, he's got Homeland's backing. How, I have no idea. But it's legit, more or less."

"Less," Mo snorted. "Langley says he's out. He's finished. They ripped up every contract he ever had. He walked off the job."

Enough. I stepped forward again and eyeballed Mo like the worm he was. "I didn't walk off anywhere. In fact, you don't walk off to anywhere in the desert. A little misunderstanding and everything is just fine now. I'm staying right here."

"Screw you, Hunter."

"Enough," Artie yelled and drew stares from the agents working the scene. "Back off, Mo. Now."

I shrugged. "Okay, Artie, truce."

"Look, Hunter, you screwed up. Face it."

"Hold on a minute, Artie." I looked at him with an edge. "I didn't screw up anything. Kruppa got word to me, and I came here to find him. I found him dead."

"Why didn't he call us?" Mo said. "Or just 911?"

"Maybe he didn't trust you? You were supposed to protect him before, right? How'd that work out?"

Mo looked at me, then Artie, and back to me. I thought he was going to charge, but he surprised me. "Okay, okay, yes. You're right."

"Let's all play nice now, boys." Victoria stepped forward now and grabbed my arm. "I'm taking Hunter to interview Sam Mallory again."

"It is Sameh," Mo snorted. "Not Sam. Heritage is important."

I cocked my head. "Funny, everyone calls you Mo, right? What about heritage? Or are you one of the Three Stooges?"

That was probably the wrong thing to say.

Mo's mouth twisted, and he stewed for a moment. Then he gave me the once-over. "Did anyone check his gun?"

Artie shook his head. "The body was hit with a .22 cal. Hunter has a .45. We're still working the scene."

"It's Caine," I said. "He was trained by Mossad and they're known for using a twenty-two in close. Even you should know that, Mo."

Mo looked at me with a sour face. "You should know."

"I do."

Artie asked, "Why would Caine kill his own man?"

"He's here working with Khalifah and has to babysit the IRGC goons. Maybe he doesn't like company. Maybe this goon tried something stupid."

"That's the stupidest thing I've ever heard," Mo snorted.

I snorted back. "I heard Khalifah isn't the real threat. There's someone else. Someone pulling his strings."

"Where'd you get that, Hunter?" Artie asked.

"Edik Petrov." The name came out before I could stop myself. "He's a local businessman."

"Petrov?" Mo almost came out of his skin. "What are you doing talking to him?"

"I don't need permission to talk to him." Dammit, I never should have given them his name. "Look, he came to me confidentially. Let's keep it that way."

Artie looked at me with sullen eyes. "What did he give you?"

"Nothing yet. But he will. Soon."

Mo wasn't having that. "Give us everything from him. We've tried to get to him for months. He went to you? Bull."

"I told you," I said, grinning to piss him off. "He said Khalifah wasn't the big boss and then said he'd get back to me. That's it. No more."

Mo drove an angry finger toward me. "You're lying."

I laughed. "Prove it."

He growled something I didn't hear, and I laughed again, turning his dark Arab face red.

"Get him out of here," Artie grunted at Victoria. "Call me as soon as you finish with Sam. I want to know exactly what Kruppa said to him and how he managed to call him if he was with Caine."

Mo grunted. "*If* he was with Caine. Right, Hunter?"

One shot. That's all I wanted. One shot.

CHAPTER 61

Day 5: May 19, 1600 Hours, Daylight Saving Time
Western Frederick County, Virginia

"Mo Nassar is CIA and he's been up to his eyeballs in this all along," I said, as Victoria drove toward Noor's house. "Why is everyone keeping this a secret?"

"You're the one keeping secrets."

"Not about him."

"No, about everything else." She made the turn off Route 50 onto the dirt shortcut I'd taken earlier and headed for Noor's. "Like I said, he showed up a few months ago with Artie. He comes and goes and never tells us anything. Today is the first time I've actually heard him in conversation. Interesting, considering it was with you."

I bring out the best in people. "He should have known about me since I arrived. He didn't tell you guys anything?"

"No. Odd."

Swell guy. Now, I had two assholes I wanted to shoot. Bond and him. Which one to shoot first? Did it matter?

"Victoria, you told me that Kevin changed a lot a few months ago, right?"

"Yes, around February. Why?"

"That's also when Nassar showed up, right?"

She thought for a long time. "Sure, he showed around then. What are you suggesting?"

"I don't believe in coincidence."

"Neither do I." She looked away at nothing. "Is that why Kevin wanted you home? Nassar? He thought you could help him since both of you are CIA?"

Maybe. "If I learned anything about the Agency, it's that it's like an onion. There are too many layers to count. Not all the layers are nice guys like me. Some are rotten."

"What about your friend LaRue? Do you trust him?"

"Always have."

"Were you telling the truth about Edik Petrov? He hasn't given you anything yet?"

"I gave it to you guys straight. He approached me outside the hotel earlier when you dropped me off." I told her about the deal he had with Kevin. Protection for information.

"Kev never told me. I don't think he ever declared Petrov as an informant, either. There is no paperwork on any of that. That's not procedure."

Neither was having a hundred grand hidden at your house, but I didn't bring that up.

Instead, I summarized the situation. "Mo Nassar and Oscar LaRue. Caine and Khalifah. Stir in the Iranians. They're all playing together in our backyard. Too many coincidences."

She glanced at me with a funny, sideways sneer. "Funny how coincidences follow you CIA guys around."

There was nothing funny about it.

* * *

"I already told you, Bobby didn't say anything else." Sam stood beside Noor in their kitchen, facing Victoria and me. His face was red and his eyes darting. "Why are you asking me all these questions?"

Victoria stood beside the kitchen table. "I'm sorry, but Bobby's dead. Someone found our safe house and killed our agents. Bobby was taken. Hunter found him at the Darby Farm."

"Dead?" Sam's face paled and his eyes burst wide, first glaring at Victoria and then me. "Bobby? Bobby's dead?"

Noor put an arm around him.

"I'm afraid so." I stepped forward. "Sam—"

Sam pulled from Noor and lunged at me, hammering a fist into my chest and trying a right hook at my face. "You did this. You killed him, too!"

I blocked the punches, grabbed his arms, and pushed him back to pin him against the kitchen wall. "No, Sam. I didn't kill him or your dad. You know that."

Victoria took my arm and gently pulled me away. "Sam, Hunter had nothing to do with this. I swear to you. You need to be honest with us."

"Does she need to be here?" Noor's hand sliced the air and she pulled Sam away from me. "I do not want her here, Jon. Please. This is difficult enough."

Victoria's face reddened. She walked into the hall and disappeared.

Sam retreated across the kitchen. He stared out the open door for a long time, struggling with something. He began to cry and refused to turn around.

Was it fear? Loss? Perhaps shame?

Noor looked right at me. "I am sorry. I am sorry for Bobby Kruppa. Sameh knows nothing else. Please—"

"He texted me." Sam spun back around. His face was streaked with tears. "I didn't talk to him. I got a text right before you got here earlier. He told me he got away from the safe house and needed to meet you at the Darby Farm. That's it. I asked him what was going on, but he didn't answer."

"Show me." I extended my open hand. "Let me see your phone."

He straightened. "You don't believe me?"

"Of course I do, Sam. Victoria can trace it, that's all."

"I am lying?" Sam came at me and shoved me hard backward. "The hell with you, Hunter. Whoever you are. The hell with you. You did all this. You."

"Sam, I just want to help."

"Go to hell." He shoved me back again and ran out the rear kitchen door.

Noor grabbed my arm when I started after him. "Let him go, Jon. He hurts. He's confused. He needs time."

I didn't have time. I had to have that phone. I had to know what was spinning Sam out of control, and I didn't think it was just the revelation that Bobby Kruppa was dead. There was something else, something he seemed to just now grasp. Had he known something was wrong and failed to tell me? Why was all this guilt aimed at me?

The roar of Sam's motorcycle pulled me out of the kitchen. But by the time I reached the yard, he was gone. I turned to go back inside, but Noor was standing right behind me. Her face was a mixture of sadness and concern, and she stared at me as though some deep secret was about to percolate out.

"Noor? What is it?"

"There is something you must know. It cannot wait." She moved close to me and held my eyes. "Kevin did not send for you."

What?

"I sent the letter." She reached out and took my hand, squeezed it, and held it in both of hers. "I did not know what to do. Our marriage was finished, and he began to frighten me. I knew it was that one, Bacarro, who was taking him over. His moods were dangerous, and I did not know what to do. I have no family to turn to."

Where was this going? "Noor, you?"

"Yes." She nodded. "Kevin told me about you, and I found the address for your mail. I wrote the note carefully. I tried to sound like Kevin and write like him in case you remembered."

I wouldn't have.

"But I did not mail it right away. I called Dave and told him of my worries. He said he would take care of it. Days later, a strange FBI man, a Muslim, came to my house and tried to force me to speak to him. I would not. I was afraid."

"Mo Nassar?"

She nodded.

"He's CIA, Noor. He worked with Artie and Victoria. Bond must have told him."

Her faced blanched. "Dave? He betrayed me?"

"Maybe. Yes."

She looked to the ground and squeezed my hand again. "I had nowhere to turn. I mailed the letter and hoped you would come home. I thought if anyone could help Kevin, it would be you. If you could not help him, perhaps you could help me."

Help her? "Why do you need help, Noor? Help for what?"

She crushed herself into me and pulled my arms around her, somehow knowing I wouldn't do it on my own. "I cannot do this alone, Jon. I cannot. Sameh will be all right. I am not sure of me. Please, come back to me tonight. Send Victoria away and come back. I need to be with someone. I need to be with family."

Words would not form. My arms tightened around her. I didn't know why or whether this was a response to her pleas or my emotions. I wasn't good at emotions. Oh, sure, anger and fear I was a pro at but the rest? Affection? *Love?* What I knew about those was somewhere in my distant past. Except, maybe, for Sadie, my girl waiting in Riyadh.

"Noor, I . . . I don't know what to say."

She stood on her tiptoes to whisper in my ear. "Say yes."

CHAPTER 62

Day 5: May 19, 1715 Hours, Daylight Saving Time
Catonsville, Maryland

SAEED MANSOURI SAT at the head of the family dining table with his hands folded in front of him. Across the table sat a young couple. They were first-generation Afghanis who made a life for themselves working multiple jobs. They were months from buying their first home in Catonsville, where a large Muslim population offered them community and security.

This day, however, the young couple realized that security was a thing of the past and if they were to survive the night, Allah would truly have to bless them.

Standing behind the couple were two other IRGC *Pāsdārān* dressed in Western clothing in contrast to the Muslim garb the couple wore. The commandos carried Styr submachine pistols and stared impassively at the couple.

Saeed broke the silence that had hovered over the room since he and his men had forced their way into the home and taken the couple hostage. "You will do what I ask of you?"

The husband, a young twenty-five-year-old shop owner selling sweets and exotic teas, could hardly contain the terror in his voice. "*Baleh*, of course. But I do not understand."

"Understand? I do not care if you understand," Saeed said dryly. "You simply must do. You will provide my men access to your shop for the next two days. You will tell anyone concerned they are family. They are with you to learn."

The husband nodded. "Yes. I understand."

"Then what?" Saeed demanded.

"Why? What will they do in my shop? It is a small shop overlooking the Inner Harbor. Surely there cannot be any value in my shop?"

One of Saeed's men stepped forward and struck his wife, a pretty, pregnant girl barely nineteen, behind the head and sent her crashing to the floor from her chair. When the husband jumped up, the commando struck him in the cheek with the butt of the machine pistol.

"Enough," Saeed said. "You will do as I command." He nodded to the commando, and the commando allowed the husband to sit his wife back on the dining room chair. "Do you understand now?"

The husband's cheek was bleeding, but he nodded and pulled his wife to his side. "*Baleh.*"

"Good. That is very good." Saeed stood and went closer to the couple. He stroked the wife's long, dark hair and gently caressed her shoulder with one hand. "If you do this without fail, without difficulty, you will be rewarded."

"We do not need reward," the husband said, surprised. "Just leave us in peace when you are done."

Saeed shook his head and caressed the wife's shoulder again. "No, no. First, you will be given twenty thousand American dollars. Think of what you can do for your new family with such money."

The husband's eyes exploded and he looked to his wife. "Thank you. But, we do not need the money. Just leave us in peace."

"Ah, we will, we will." Saeed leaned down and kissed the young wife on the cheek. "We will leave you in peace, with much money. Your true reward will be Allah's blessing."

The couple sat very still and watched Saeed leave the dining room with the thin, bearded Iranian who'd struck them.

In the front room, Saeed spoke quietly to his junior lieutenant. "You will take him to his office later this evening. Become familiar with the area. Return here with him and secure this house."

The IRGC lieutenant nodded. "Yes, of course. What of the woman? Should we kill them together or shall I—"

"No. Neither is to die yet." Saeed clutched the lieutenant's throat in his hand and squeezed. "Be very careful with this instruction. I wish them to live. I have other plans. Do nothing that threatens their lives. This is very important. If you kill them, I will return that upon you."

The lieutenant nodded and managed, "Yes, sir. As you command."

Saeed released the commando. "You will use two of your best men, but none Iranian. I want two of the Afghani recruits to guard her. No need for our men to waste time here. They will stay here and ensure the two are unharmed until I give the order. Afterwards, they can do with them what they wish."

"What for me, sir?"

Saeed took his lieutenant's shoulders in his hands. "You will return to Virginia and ready your men. Be ready on a moment's order from me. Maya is close. Very, very close."

The lieutenant straightened in respect. "Yes, sir. Allah be praised."

"*Baleh, Alhamdulillah.*" Saeed looked into the dining room at his hostages. "This time, however, Allah will not be so merciful."

* * *

Khalifah and the Foreigner selected Catonsville for its Muslim population and proximity to Baltimore's Inner Harbor. Neither of them understood how well lit the fuse in this Baltimore suburb already was.

Five blocks from the small apartment, a Somali cab driver was illegally parked near the crosswalk. He waited across from a coffee shop in a local strip mall, sipping tea and reading a newspaper. He parked there each afternoon waiting for a young, local grocery clerk to purchase a last cup of coffee and pastries for his morning breakfast before taking the cab home across town. His passenger was another Somali that the cabbie met months before at that very spot. They lived two blocks apart, and the cabbie gave him a free ride home each evening when they were both done from the day's work.

This night, they would be late arriving home.

The grocery clerk, a thin man with dark gaunt, Somali features, left the coffee shop balancing a bag of pastries and a cup of tea in one hand while he held the door for two young women going inside. Three workmen from a nearby store under renovation ambled down the sidewalk behind the women. When the clerk held open the door, one of the workmen, a short, scruffy-faced, round man, slapped the tea from his hand and tore the bag of pastries away, threw it onto the sidewalk, and crushed it with his boot.

"Friggin' towelhead. Go home where you belong," another of the workmen growled. "Go kill your own friggin' people."

"Please," the clerk said meekly, trying to force a smile. "This is my home. I work in the grocery here. I am an American. Leave me, I beg you."

The scruffy-faced workman lashed out and punched the clerk in the face, knocking him backward into the corner of the open door. He followed it with another punch that dropped the clerk to the pavement.

The other two men began kicking him over and over. They cursed and laughed in unison.

"Stop this!" the cabbie yelled and ran from his cab across the street. "Do not do this. Stop. He has done nothing."

Two more local workmen emerged from the coffee shop and saw the cabbie charging the scene. One of them glanced down at the fallen clerk still being pummeled and met the cabbie in midstride. He grabbed him by the shirt, lifted him in the air, and shook him.

"What are you gonna do, pal? You foreigners should get the hell out of here." He spun the cabbie around and threw him toward the coffee shop window.

The cabbie crashed through the window and landed inside atop a table. His face and arms were shredded with cuts and more glass rained down on him. He cried out and raised bloodied hands, but no one came to his aide.

"You bastards attack us? How does that feel?" the scruffy workman yelled. Then he and another grabbed the clerk up from the sidewalk and tossed him into the street, forcing an oncoming car to skid and swerve to avoid hitting him.

A small crowd from several of the adjacent shops formed—young, old, white, black, Latino—no one rushed forward to help the injured Somali. Instead, they stood and watched with numb and dispassionate faces.

One of the other workmen, a thin, balding man with a hook nose and darting, bug-like eyes, jogged across the street to the illegally parked cab.

"Look at this, guys. He's so much better than us he can park here. Maybe he was going to bomb us." The workman leaned in the cab window and pulled the cabbie's newspaper out. He shredded parts of it, opened the cab's gas tank, and stuffed the newspaper partially inside.

"See how he likes it." The workman dug into his pocket, produced a cigarette lighter, and lit the newspaper. He ran to the sidewalk.

Moments later, with a crowd of indifferent onlookers gathering, the cab exploded.

People began to cheer.

CHAPTER 63

Day 5: May 19, 1730 Hours, Daylight Saving Time
FBI Task Force Offices, Winchester, Virginia

VICTORIA AND I split up to look for Sam.

She headed for the haunts Noor knew of, and I went in a totally different direction. I sort of failed to tell her where I was headed. It bothered me that Sam seemed chummy with Azar and Fariq. So after Victoria left, I looked up several of the addresses I'd found on Sam's cell phone the other night at the cabin. What I found sent me to Sand Town. Sam had been there several times in the past couple weeks. I wanted to know why.

I made the drive in twenty minutes and only got lost once. Embarrassing, too, since I was following my cell phone map program. When I drove down the county road and into town, at first, I thought I'd stumbled into some old ghost town. Most of the houses along the road were old and in bad need of repair. None had mowed lawns or recent paint and seemed not to have any residents, either. There was no one on the street or sitting on porches. There was no one around at all. The entire town seemed empty.

After two turns cruising the only three side streets, I double backed to make sure I hadn't missed some hidden metropolis. I found what had to be the center of town. It wasn't on the main county road but one street south, where two of the three side streets intersected in front of an abandoned Safeway on one corner, and a two-story cement block garage whose sign still dangled from above one garage bay and read "Sandy Creek Repairs, Est. 1953." Inside the garage were two yellow school buses in various states of repair. All around the buses were chests of tools and parts lying about. So far, these were the only signs of life I'd seen.

As I drove past the garage, a dark-skinned man walked around the rear of one of the buses and froze when he saw me. I only saw him for a second, but when he saw me, he disappeared immediately. By the time I turned around and looked back, he was already gone.

Now, now, don't be shy.

My tires complained all the way around a quick U-turn, and I parked just outside the garage. But as I climbed out of the rental, another car made the turn at the intersection and pulled up beside me.

Artie Polo. What a coincidence.

Artie whipped his car in front of mine and jumped out. "Hunter, what are you doing here?"

"Looking for Sam." I slid onto the hood of my rental. "What are you doing here? I thought you guys weren't interested in this place without all that legal mumbo-jumbo."

"Oh, you mean evidence and warrants and probable cause? That legal mumbo-jumbo?"

I nodded. "Exactly. So, what *are* you doing here?"

"My job." Artie walked over and folded his arms, looking me over. "Now, your turn."

I threw a chin toward the garage. "Looking for Sam. This place is a ghost town, Artie, but there's a mechanic inside. Maybe he's seen Sam."

"What makes you think Sam hangs around here?" Artie set his jaw with that FBI-in-charge look. "A little far out of town, isn't it?"

I told him about Sam running off from Noor's and I explained what I'd discovered on Sam's cell phone at Fool's Lake the night before last. He was nodding the moment I explained about using the phone's check-in details from its settings.

"Smooth, Hunter. Here I thought you had some kind of spook intel I didn't."

"Just common sense." I gestured to the garage again. "Victoria and I are looking for Sam, and I figured I'd come visit here. Want to help me roust the locals? I'll call Victoria, and we can start with the mechanic."

"We better talk." Artie's face got tense and he lowered his eyes. "Victoria's a problem, Jon."

Uh-oh. That didn't sound good at all. Artie wanted to share without any quid pro quo, and about Victoria, too. "What? She didn't file a sexual harassment suit against me, did she?"

"No, get serious, Hunter." He took out a folded piece of paper from his jacket pocket and handed it to me. "I was going to talk to you later but maybe now's better. You know, away from the office."

"What? You're acting a little spooky, even for me, Artie."

"Victoria's lying to us."

"About what?" I unfolded the paper and looked it over. It was a copy of a cell phone printout with several calls highlighted. Many of them were Kevin's cell phone and a few back to the FBI task force. I knew because Artie had labeled the calls in his chicken-scratch handwriting.

"It's from a burner phone." Artie's eyes grew darker. "The phone comes from a shop outside Leesburg. There are two calls the night Kevin was murdered at the river. One about an hour before and one just about when it was going down. We never recovered his phone."

"Okay, let's make believe I don't know what this tells us." I didn't, but suddenly there was a nagging tap on my brain. "This is—"

"Victoria's. We got into Kevin's phone records and found this burner number. It took them a couple days, but they traced it. Victoria bought it several months ago."

It couldn't be. "You can trace burner phones?"

"You'd be surprised what we can do when we know what we're looking for."

"You were looking for her?"

He said nothing.

Dammit. "What else do you have?"

"Hunter." He looked away a moment. "There are calls to another burner phone, too. The number's come up before, and we're sure it belongs to Saeed Mansouri. We can't prove it yet, but we're working on it."

"What? Are you sure?" The look on his face was sure. "What's her motive?"

"The oldest motive in the world. Money. She was in Saudi and Kabul with an FBI team for a couple months a year or more ago. Before she left, her father had been gravely ill, and she almost went under paying his medical bills."

"And?"

"When she returned, her problems went away. Suddenly. No more money troubles." Artie hesitated before delivering another hard blow. "She came back to DC and all but begged for this assignment on the task force."

"She asked to get here? Why?" When the questions left my lips, the answer reached my brain. "You're saying she made some kind of connection in the Middle East and they paid her off? Then she came here to be a double agent?"

"Yes." Artie looked down and his face got tight and angry. "There's a reason we haven't been able to get a foothold in this town, Hunter, or with Saeed Mansouri specifically. Victoria's the reason. Maybe that's what got Kevin murdered, too. Maybe Kevin was part of it and maybe not. Maybe it's been Victoria all along and she framed him."

Was it possible? Had she betrayed everyone? Betrayed Kevin?

I started to question him when he held up a hand. "I know about the hundred grand at Noor's place. Victoria was very quick to tell me about it earlier. Too quick. It's like she was adding a nail to his coffin or something."

"I know I should have told you. I've been working my own angles, Artie. Sorry." When he shrugged, I pressed him some more. "You think she's actually working with Khalifah?"

He nodded. "It's very possible. I haven't any other explanation. This proves she's been lying."

"I don't hear any hard evidence, Artie. Just speculation. These calls could be anything."

He nodded. "Unfortunately, you're right. But why do you think I spend so much time out here instead of my cushy office in DC? I'm responsible for this mess. I have to untangle it."

Dammit, Artie was making some sense. Could it be true?

"Hunter, keep this to yourself. I don't want to spook her until I have the rest of the proof."

All I could do was nod and curse.

"Good." He took the phone printout from me and pocketed it. "Now, you need to leave, Hunter. I've got agents coming in a few minutes to help me and I don't want you mucking this up. If Sam's here, I'll find him. If he's been here, I'll let you know pronto."

Well, it wasn't going to take more than one more agent to cover this place, so my time was best spent elsewhere looking for Sam. I told him as much and reluctantly climbed back into my car. "Call me with anything on him, Artie. As soon as you get it. He's scared and upset about Bobby. Let me talk to him first. Deal?"

"Deal. But I get what you get. All of it."

* * *

As I headed back to Winchester, Victoria was stuck in my thoughts. It was bad enough Kevin had an affair with her, but for her to be a double agent for Khalifah turned my stomach. *If,* I should say. Artie seemed a bit too positive about her with just a cell phone bill. He had something else. Something more damning that he wasn't sharing. I'd known him a long time, and he wasn't a guy to make accusations without hard evidence.

Could it be as simple as he said?

I decided to find Bond just in case he'd seen Sam around town. Maybe he could put the word out and the deputies could be looking for him. So I returned to the task force and, just as I was about to jump out of my car in the rear lot, I noticed Bond sitting in his car alongside the task force's building. He hadn't noticed me, so I stayed put and watched him. Maybe I'd have a few motivational words with him about his rabid assault on me earlier.

I was about to walk over to ask him about Sam when another car pulled up and parked driver's side to driver's side with him. The newcomer spoke with Bond through the open window. After several moments, the newcomer handed a large manila package out the window to Bond. The car backed up and headed out of the parking lot. He passed near enough for me to see him.

Mo Nassar.

What were these two up to?

There was only one way to know. I followed him.

Surveilling someone who doesn't want to be followed is tricky. Especially alone. You have to give the suspect lots of room. But not too much room. Then, let them run their own surveillance detection without you getting caught. That includes lane changes, U-turns, and other tricks without being pulled in too close. Sometimes, you have to let them make the turn and pass by, then recover and double back to find them again—hopefully. Sometimes it works. Sometimes it doesn't.

It didn't for me, and twice I lost Nassar, who was heading east out of town. I missed a traffic light and got stuck behind two mopeds. But he was careless. Fueled by CIA hubris, I'm sure. He never checked for a tail. He easily could have pulled to the roadside to watch for anyone fading back or pulling over, too, or gone completely around the block to see who followed him through. He simply crossed Winchester and picked up Route 7 East. No deviations.

Still, to be safe, I stayed way back.

Luckily, I never lost sight of him for more than a few moments. Each time, he was still heading east, and I was able to keep him in my sights about a half a mile ahead of me while we made the trip to nearby Berryville. There, he wormed his way along some side streets to a condominium development south of town. I pulled into a shopping center and parked with a good view of the condo entrance. There were two condo buildings, and they both faced a small courtyard in front of the parking lot. All of that was in my sights.

A good thing, too.

Thirty minutes later, Nassar reappeared out of one of the buildings and jumped in his car. Tempted as I was to follow him out, I waited. Why, I had no idea, but my gut wasn't just grumbling from hunger, it was telling me I was about to score.

Oh, yeah.

Fifteen minutes after Nassar left, a familiar face left the same condo entrance and walked to the far end of the parking lot. He climbed into an old, beat-up pickup truck and drove quickly out of the lot. He passed my position twice. When he did, I got a good look at him between a dozen other cars and again when he drove off.

Caine.

Bond. Nassar. Caine.

Happy birthday to me.

* * *

I considered tailing Caine but doubted he'd be as careless as Nassar. I didn't have the help to properly tail him, and if he caught me, he could ambush and kill me before I realized it was too late.

Bond, Nassar, and Caine? What was going on in sleepy Winchester that had a rogue lovesick cop, a duplicitous CIA spook, and an international assassin all holding hands?

On my way back to town, I called LaRue.

"Pour me a very tall bourbon, Oscar. We have to talk."

His voice was gruffer than usual. "I'm at the hotel. Has something changed?"

"Oh, yeah." I stomped on the gas. "Mo Nassar."

CHAPTER 64

Day 5: May 19, 1915 Hours, Daylight Saving Time
Rural Frederick County, Virginia

"SAEED WILL KILL us both." Doc shoved Caine back from his laboratory table outside the makeshift bio lab. He tried to strike Caine across the face, but Caine blocked the assault without effort. "You pig. Saeed already asked about the sarin supply. He wanted the test results."

"On which sample?"

Doc raised his chin. "The sample you have. If he finds out what you've done, he'll kill us both."

Caine lashed out a right hand and grabbed Doc by the throat. He pushed him backward over the lab table with ferocious force and pinned him there. "Then he shouldn't find out, Doc. That would be bad for both of us."

"I must tell him," Doc croaked, gasping for breath. "He will kill me and my family if I do not."

"Only you and I know this batch of sarin is inert, right?"

Doc managed a meek nod. "You switched the cylinders."

"Listen, Doc." Caine relaxed his grip but didn't release him. "You and I are the only ones who could know I swapped them. Saeed's a thug. He wouldn't know the difference between sarin and *Shamshiri* tea."

Doc's eyes got big. "What have you done with the other cylinders?"

"I found a higher bidder. A much better price. Do you know how much money this stuff is worth?"

"You're selling it?"

Caine said nothing.

"It is so lethal. Only someone who wishes to use it as Khalifah does would pay you."

Caine still said nothing.

"I see." Doc closed his eyes. "Saeed has taken the remaining cylinders away."

"What?" Caine looked around the lab furiously. "Taken where?"

Doc shook his head. "I do not know. He had me prepare three cylinders earlier and place them in the protective case. His men took them."

"You're lying." Caine tightened his grip on the scientist. "Where were they taken?"

"I do not know." Doc's face twisted and fear filled his eyes. "But I can find out. I want money. Half of what you receive. But first, you must save my family before Saeed kills them. Please."

Caine studied him for a long time without allowing him to move from the table. "What makes you think I can save your family?"

"Saeed's men call you an *alqatil*. The assassin." Doc's eyes bore into him. "Saeed holds my family. If I do not do these things, they will kill them. Save them, Caine, and pay me so I may escape with my family. Only then will I help you."

"Ten percent," Caine said, releasing his grip on him.

"No." Doc struck quickly and caught Caine unsuspecting with a heavy glass container across the temple. As Caine fell back, Doc grabbed a glass vial from the table and hurled it at him. "Mercenary, do you believe I will help you? Saeed will trade my family for you now. He will pay."

The vial crashed on the floor at Caine's feet and splattered his legs, instantly burning holes in his pants and leather boots. Acid. As the vile struck, he pulled his switchblade out, launched himself on top of the scientist, and plunged the knife into his solar plexus. Grasping the man's throat with one hand for control, he twisted side to side and up in violent, staccato movements.

It was over. Doctor Hosni Al-Fayed was dead before Caine realized he'd reacted.

"Fool. Your family's already dead."

CHAPTER 65

Day 5: May 19, 1915 Hours, Daylight Saving Time
The George Washington Hotel, Winchester, Virginia

"SARIN NERVE AGENT?" I couldn't believe what LaRue had just told me.

We were sitting in his suite's living room. I had my legs propped up on a glass coffee table, much to his ire, and LaRue was sipping a fresh cup of tea across from me in a large leather chair. He dropped "sarin nerve agent" on me like he was offering me tea—"This chamomile is divine. Oh, and the Iranians have smuggled sarin nerve agent into the country. Have a cookie?"

I stared at him. "I'm chasing sarin?"

"Yes." LaRue was, as always, polishing his eyeglasses while he contemplated his next response. "That is what was spilled at the river and why the truck was torched that night. Whoever was there—Caine, I believe—was ensuring any spillage was destroyed."

Sarin is a lethal nerve agent. A chemical weapon of mass destruction. There are many such nerve agents, but sarin is a favorite of the former Soviet Union and some in the Middle East—like Iran, Libya, and Syria. You know, club whacko. Sarin is nasty stuff, too. It can be deployed in many ways, including air-dropped bombs, weaponized aerosols, and ground-level releases. If you are unlucky enough to be there when it's used, you won't be able to breathe, you'll be nauseated and drool, and then the bad stuff happens. You'll lose control of your bodily functions. All of them. Eventually, you'll twitch and jerk about until you fall into a coma and suffocate. Death is not fast or fun. No fun at all.

"You're just telling me this now?"

He just looked at me and replaced his eyeglasses.

"Anything else I need to know?"

"We believe it came in from Syria or perhaps direct from Iran." He slipped his glasses on and adjusted the fit. "Khalifah's delivery method is unclear. He and Caine have enough to kill thousands. If Baltimore is indeed the target, it could be horrific."

I got up and paced the living room. As I watched LaRue, he was calm and cool. No sign that Armageddon loomed in the room.

I felt a chill even thinking about sarin gas. "How do you know how much they have?"

He said nothing.

The CIA stall. "I'm supposed to find it and the remaining targets, right?"

He nodded slowly. "Shepard and I were working another component. Unfortunately, there was a major setback."

"How major?"

He stood and walked to the window. This was not a melodramatic gesture. "Sokoloff escaped. We were on the verge of learning everything. Shepard was killed."

Shepard was dead? "Why didn't you call me? Is Noor in danger?"

"No. We know where he's going. It is not to Winchester."

"Shepard? What happened?"

He didn't turn around. "It is a cost of our business, Hunter. We will address that failure another time."

"No, now."

He thrust up a hand for silence as he looked at nothing outside the window. "Please. Another time."

I said nothing.

He went to the small kitchenette, returned with a small ballistic nylon pouch, and handed it to me. "You will go nowhere without this."

The pouch was about eight inches long and a couple inches in circumference. It had a snazzy belt clip affixed like a case for eyeglasses.

He aimed his omnipotent finger at me. "Nowhere, Hunter. Do not fail in that."

Inside the pouch were two narrow, plastic pen-like devices the size of a heavy, thick magic marker. I'd carried these kits many times on the battlefield and during other sensitive operations. It was a Mark 1 nerve agent kit. The kit contained atropine and pralidoxime chloride—or 2-PAM—auto-injectors. One of only a couple defenses against nerve agents. If exposed to, say, *sarin*, you plunged the atropine injector into your thigh and a long, painful needle plunged into your leg and injected the antidote. Repeat with the 2-PAM injector. Then hope and pray the antidote worked. Survival depended on the nerve agent, timing, and, above all, luck.

"Okay, Oscar. I understand." I clipped the Mark 1 kit to my belt. "What about Mo Nassar?"

Before he'd dropped the sarin bombshell on me, I'd told him about Nassar and his connection at Kevin's crime scene and the sheriff's office. He'd avoided comment and immediately offered me tea, cookies, and sarin gas.

"Leave Nassar to me."

"That's what you told me the other night. What are you going to do with him?"

"Immaterial. He is a small fish seeking promotion. He's an irritant and nothing more. Focus on your mission."

That was about as nice a "mind your own business" as LaRue ever offered.

Something tickled my brain. "Oscar, one of Kevin's informants, a Russian immigrant named Edik Petrov, reached out to me. He told me that Khalifah isn't the real threat."

"He is correct." LaRue lifted his chin. "Tell me all he's told you."

I did and it wasn't much. "He's going to call me with more if we will protect him."

"Make the deal. Then complete your mission. Quickly."

"Oh, you mean my mission to find Khalifah and figure out what he's up to? Or the mission to hunt down Caine and Saeed and his band of Iranian IRGC goons? Or the mission to locate the sarin nerve agent before they attack and stop it?"

LaRue smiled. "Yes, it is really that simple."

CHAPTER 66

Day 5: May 19, 2245 Hours, Daylight Saving Time
Fool's Lake, Virginia

SAM MALLORY WAS nowhere. Nowhere I could find, anyway. It was late when I finished with LaRue, and after another hour hunting for Sam, I decided to check the cabin. Noor hadn't heard from him yet and she was terrified. With some luck, he'd gone to Fool's Lake for the same solace I'd found at his age.

Unfortunately, I was wrong. The cabin was empty. I was just about to call Noor again when a key turned in the front door. I was on my feet with my pistol ready before the door clicked. It's a good thing I didn't shoot first and ask questions later.

Victoria Bacarro slinked in the door. "I knew I'd find you here. Just like Kev. Always running away to sulk."

"You have a key?"

She held it up. "Yep. But then, you figured that out a while ago."

I nodded.

"Got any bourbon?"

I shook my head in a lie. "Victoria, unless you've found Sam, I have to go."

Her face flushed instantly, and she stared at me as though I'd thrust a spear through her heart. "Sam will turn up. He's a kid. He'll be fine."

"You're right, Victoria," I said, gesturing toward the door. "He is a kid, and he's scared and angry and hurting. What's wrong with you?"

She looked down for a long moment before she turned and locked the door, tossed the key on the fireplace mantel, and dropped into the couch across from me. When she did, I noticed two very unusual things about her. First, her face was red and tear-streaked in the dim light. Second, her eyes held more than sadness—they held need.

Crap, and me without a conscience.

CHAPTER 67

Day 6: May 20, 0015 Hours, Daylight Saving Time
Fool's Lake, Virginia

MY LUCK WITH women could be summarized with one word. None.

On one trip to Germany, I fell in love with a beautiful Bulgarian maiden. She turned out to be married to a very jealous diplomat with two bodyguards. What the bodyguards lacked in humor, they made up for with muscle. Thankfully, those bones have healed. Three years ago, it was Amira. She was a lovely girl from Qatar. She once told me that she thought about me day and night. Much to my regret, she was also a Syrian agent who tried to kill me—*twice*. So much for being on someone's mind.

Like the IRGC being in Winchester, women mystify me.

"I don't know what to tell you, Jon," Victoria shouted. "It's not my phone!"

Wow, if this was foreplay, I'd been in the desert too long.

After locking me into my own cabin, Victoria ended up on the couch with a glass of bourbon. After a long few minutes of silence and half her drink, I stupidly asked about her calling Kevin the night he was murdered. She denied it again. Then I hit her with burner phone discovery. That's when lightning struck.

The rant began.

"Polo asked me the same thing."

Polo? Not Artie or Agent Polo? Just Polo. "I saw the phone printouts, Victoria. What are you hiding?"

She slammed back a full mouthful of bourbon and refilled the glass. She wandered the living room and the sizzle in her eyes told me she was trying to calm down. Then she downed the new bourbon and threw the empty glass into the fireplace.

"Damn you, Hunter."

What did I do?

She crossed the room and grabbed me by the shirt. She was crying and looking down at nothing. "Damn you. You're so much like Kev but so damn different, too. We were in love. At least, I thought we were. I was. You and Noor and Polo think I killed him? I set him up? Why would I do that?"

As always, I fumbled. I just stood there and finally slipped my hand onto her arm and gave her a reassuring squeeze. "Tell me about the burner phone, Victoria, and the call."

"There was no goddamn call. No phone." She pulled her arm away but didn't retreat. "Why won't you believe me?"

Oh, I don't know. Evidence?

She burst into tears and went to the front door. She stood there with one hand on the handle and the other over her eyes. Her body shook as the tears rained down.

"Victoria? What's wrong? What aren't you telling me?"

She turned, dropped her face into her hands, and wept openly. "What's wrong? My career is over, Hunter. Get that? Over."

Yeah, it probably was. "I'm sorry, Victoria."

"I don't care," she cried and lifted her face to me. Her eyes were sad and swelled and her voice quivered. "The only man I've gotten close to in years was a bad cop and now he's dead. Now you're here and you remind me of him with every word. I know I have to let go. Dammit."

"It's all right." I moved beside her and put a hand on her shoulder. "Forget Artie and this mess. I understand about Kevin. I do. It takes time."

She fell against me with her cheek on my shoulder. "No. There is no time, Jon. I'm all out of time. I just need to forget. Just for a little while. I hurt so bad."

"I know." No, I didn't. I didn't know anything, and I stepped away from her when the warning bells went off. "Victoria, I don't think—"

"Jon, I just want to forget. Just for a while."

Victoria looked at me as she undid her blouse buttons, showing a taut, tanned belly. Her bosom was full and round and had pushed the silk away in the dim cabin light. Her chest heaved and her eyes locked on me. With slow, almost unperceivable movements, she came to me and crushed herself tight, forcing my hand to slip her blouse away.

I say forced because I don't want any misunderstandings. The next few hours I might be a captive of a beautiful, alluring FBI agent who used her wiles and superior training to their fullest. I was powerless to resist. I tried. Dear God, I tried.

Truly.

CHAPTER 68

Day 6: May 20, 0600 Hours, Daylight Saving Time
Washington Capital Beltway, Virginia

KHALIFAH LEFT THE Washington Capital Beltway, Interstate 495, onto the ramp to the George Washington Parkway heading southeast toward DC. He changed lanes several times, slowed, sped up, and constantly watched for any possible surveillance in the few headlights behind him. Halfway to the Chain Bridge that spanned the Potomac into the Capital, he pulled to the roadside and let all visible traffic pass him before continuing on his way. Along the route he made mental notes of his surroundings, turns, and exits, and he continued to seek out any threats following him.

Satisfied he'd had no surveillance, he maneuvered through the turns for Chain Bridge and reversed direction, returning to I-495 and continuing his dance the remaining forty miles to Baltimore.

There, he repeated his surveillance detection tactics, reversed direction twice, and wound his way to the Inner Harbor.

Before beginning the long trip home, he parked in an alley just off restaurant row and strolled through the lit streets and walkways, taking careful note of the security cameras and vehicle barriers protecting the pedestrian streets around the Inner Harbor.

As he passed a *Baltimore Sun* vending machine, the front page caught his eye. A collage of photographs filled the top fold. Each had a horrific scene—bodies in the street, burning cars, a mosque in flames. The caption above the photographs read, "President Calls for Calm." He inserted several coins and withdrew a newspaper.

The story below the fold said it all. Across the country, mobs had taken to the streets to protest the string of terrorist bombings. Smaller, lesser-known copycat events had begun around the country. In St. Paul, Minnesota, a sniper had killed three Muslims walking to morning prayer. A car rammed the front door of a small, remote mosque in Canton, Ohio, and burst into flames. In Tempe, Arizona, a series of mail bombs were caught on their way to Middle Eastern neighborhoods.

Fear had turned to anger. Anger had turned to revenge. Revenge had vanquished reason.

Khalifah tucked the paper under his arm. Even he had not considered these consequences. Perhaps there was another million in his future.

Operation Maya was ahead of schedule.

His reconnoitering concluded, Khalifah returned to his SUV to make the long, circuitous drive back to Winchester.

The Inner Harbor was beautiful and full of tourists this time of year. It was perfect for his surprise.

CHAPTER 69

Day 6: May 20, 0600 Hours, Daylight Saving Time
Fool's Lake, Virginia

MY PHONE RANG and I nearly tumbled from the couch onto the carpet. I shook myself awake and sat upright. The cabin was silent. Light was just flickering through the window and the air was chilly in the early morning hours. I was knotted in my clothes from a rough sleep on the ancient, narrow couch, and my .45, extra mags, and my Mark 1 anti-nerve agent kit were piled on the floor beside me.

Despite a life with fewer women than I'd care to admit, even Victoria's full-court press hadn't breached my sanity. I had to admit it—I was crazy about Noor but not insane about anyone. Noor was Kevin's, *er*, widow. She was out of reach. Maybe forever. Victoria, on the other hand, had made it very clear to me that she was on the menu. Except I couldn't bring myself to her table. Somehow, ridiculous as it sounded, I had felt an instant pang of guilt and couldn't get Noor's sorrow off my mind.

So, after struggling to escape her net, I banished Victoria to my bed and retreated to the couch—*alone*.

"Victoria?"

Sleepily, I checked the cabin and looked around outside.

She was gone.

I grabbed by cell phone and read the screen. It was barely six a.m.

My phone had a dozen text messages this morning. The latest one was ominous. *"Hunter. Urgent. Call Now. Artie."*

There were also half a dozen texts and missed calls from Noor. They all said essentially the same thing—*Where are you? Please, call me.* But it was the last text that had my attention—*Jon, an Edik Petrov e-mailed you on Kevin's e-mail. You need to see this. Please call.*

First things first. I dialed Artie's cell phone, and he picked up on the first ring.

"Where have you been, Jon?"

"My cabin. What's going on?"

"Victoria's missing."

"Missing? She and I were . . ."

Awkward silence; then, "Oh, shit, Hunter. You didn't sleep with her? Put her on."

"She's not here." I walked to the kitchen, hunting the makings of coffee. "She left." Well, that wasn't a lie. She was gone.

"What time did she leave?" His voice was cranky. "Exactly?"

"I don't know. We were up talking very late. Very late. I went to sleep, and when I woke up a few minutes ago, she was already gone."

Artie's voice was steel. "Come to the office, Jon. If she's not there, then Victoria is missing and what little evidence we had on Kevin's case is gone, too."

"What are you talking about?" I thought about the unholy trio yesterday of Bond, Nassar, and Caine. "What makes you think it was her?"

"Get in here." His voice was low. "Victoria isn't answering calls and her FBI car tracker is dead. Someone got into the evidence locker at the task force and took everything we had on Kevin's case. I know it's not much. That includes the backups of Kruppa's photos."

Victoria? "It's not her, Artie. I have a lot to tell you. Not on this cell, though. I'll be there in an hour."

He clicked off the phone.

Dammit.

I tried Victoria's cell phone and got no answer. I tried again five times. I dialed Noor's and got the same. Last, Sam's. Nothing. Every call went to voice mail. After a shower and cleaning up, my phone pinged again with another text.

Things are so complicated, Jon. More so now. I wish you had come home sooner—Victoria.

So do I, Victoria. So do I.

CHAPTER 70

Day 6: May 20, 0730 Hours, Daylight Saving Time
Winchester, Virginia

I HIT NINETY miles an hour once I left the mountain roads. All the while hitting redial on my cell phone trying to reach Noor and Sam. Voice mail. Voice mail. Closing on a hundred, I dialed Victoria's number and got nothing. Not even voice mail.

What did that mean?

The miles flashed by until I slid off the county road into Noor's driveway. As I did, the first thing I saw, or didn't see, was the deputy at the driveway again. I floored the rental, fishtailed down the drive, and skidded through the gravel to a stop almost on the porch. I ran for the front door with my .45 out and ready.

"Noor? Sam?"

Nothing.

A tingle started in my spine and spread through me like wildfire. Noor and Sam were in danger. They were in the middle of whatever hornet's nest I'd kicked over, and the killers were swarming.

The front door was unlocked and I eased inside.

No sounds. No movement. Nothing but my breath and heart rising in tempo.

Easy, Hunter, easy. One, two, three.

One slow step at a time, I maneuvered room to room, pivoting through the hallway, covering every dark corner and every opening. I moved through the first floor, ready to take unfriendly targets and worry about questions later. I focused my thoughts, steadied my breathing, and concentrated on my next step. Every one took a year off my life.

One wrong step and it would take all of them.

At the entrance to Kevin's den, I froze. There was someone inside sitting behind the desk, staring out into the hall at me.

I raised my .45 and eased halfway into the doorway.

Oh, no, not again.

Edik Yurievich Petrov sat upright in Kevin's leather office chair staring through dead, bulging eyes. Duct tape covered his mouth and bound his arms to the chair. His face was a mass of dark, black bruises and oozing contusions. His arms showed the signs of a violent interrogation gone badly—broken fingers, disfigured elbows, and slices up and down his skin that gave only dark, matted blood now.

Edik Petrov had undergone brutal, horrifying torture. Had his secrets destined for me been revealed to someone else?

I slid into the room and pivoted in a circle searching for a target.

"Noor?" I called out. "Noor?"

I heard, no, I *felt* something moving. A foot touched hardwood behind me.

I spun but the synapses in my brain never registered the face.

Pain. Stabbing, spreading, pulsating pain. Every nerve in my body screamed in unison. My breath stopped. Lightning erupted in my eyes. I flailed and convulsed toward the floor. Sometime before I hit the hardwood, the desk rose up and found my head.

Darkness.

CHAPTER 71

Day 6: May 20, 1115 Hours, Daylight Saving Time
Leesburg, Virginia

"WHAT ARE YOU doing here?" Alexei Fedorov asked the man holding a gun across his safe house room. "How did you find this place of mine?"

Caine stepped out of the narrow hallway and kept his silenced Beretta level with Alexei-the-Foreigner's midsection. Caine spoke in Russian. "Where is Grigori?"

"You are too impudent. You know my orders. You were never to meet me without my direction. You come here why?"

"Comrade, where is Grigori?"

Fedorov's eyes betrayed him with a glance toward the small kitchen alcove. "Come out, Grigori. You fool. You led him to me."

The pale, weakened Grigori Sokoloff stepped around the corner and into Fedorov's small living room.

Caine was matter-of-fact. "I've watched LaRue's safe house. When I felt it was safe, I retrieved your man. Yes, I followed him."

"But . . . but . . . I took all the precautions," Grigori snapped. "You could not have followed me."

"Yet here I am." Caine waved the gun to herd Grigori closer to Fedorov. "I came to renegotiate our deal, Colonel General. Without Khalifah."

Fedorov's eyes widened and a wry smile cut the corners of his mouth. "I see. When I retained your services in Damascus, I made it very clear they were nonnegotiable. Was this not the case?"

Caine nodded. "It was. But your contract was not in good faith, Colonel General. You failed to tell me you were planning to attack this country with sarin from the animals in the IRGC. This changes things significantly."

"Really? Then why is it just now you raise this question?" Fedorov waved dismissively. "Since when does a man of your talents care about sarin gas or other means? You were paid a significant amount. You were told what you needed to know. I engaged you to assist Khalifah and control Saeed. You were to use your considerable talents when needed. So, if we are to renegotiate, perhaps you should return some of the many US dollars I have paid you, no?"

"No?" Caine angled across the room to a straight-backed chair where he allowed himself to sit and rest his Beretta on his knee. "You've made it very difficult for me to find future work for quite some time, Alexei. Grigori has told LaRue everything. Now, he and the FBI know my name and my face. It will be some time before I can openly be engaged."

Grigori spun toward Fedorov. "That is a lie, Colonel General. I told them only small details to avoid their torture and have them believe I was being truthful. I had no choice. I spoke nothing of Caine. How could I? I knew nothing."

"Operation Maya," Caine said dryly. "Your plan to inspire the Americans to redouble their attentions in Afghanistan and Iraq, and to close the gates against any future refugees. Operation Maya was to engage the Americans elsewhere so Russia could move westward again over its prior empire."

Fedorov looked at Grigori. His eyes were cold and empty—condemning eyes. "He is well informed, is he not, Grigori?"

Grigori shook his head. "No."

Fedorov turned back to Caine. "How did you come to these conclusions, Caine?"

"I found Grigori's file in the safe house. I have that file and the videotapes of Grigori's confessions. It was simple."

Fedorov closed his eyes and lowered his head for a long moment. "No. I think not, Caine. Grigori did not know those details. Yes, he knew some, as the Americans would say, big-picture things. But not those details."

"Are you sure? Then how else would I have known?"

Grigori reached out and grabbed Fedorov's arm. "Sir, no, *please*. I told them no such things. Perhaps it is Caine who—"

The shot from Caine's silenced Beretta struck Grigori in the forehead just above his nose. The sound, silenced only to a small degree, reverberated around the small apartment with little furnishings to absorb it. Grigori staggered backward, tripped over nothing, and collapsed onto the floor behind Fedorov's chair.

"Now, Alexei, there is another problem," Caine said, turning the gun toward him. "Your plans are in LaRue's hands. Did Sokoloff know of the other targets after Baltimore?"

Fedorov, a man not unaccustomed to violence, was startled by Grigori's execution. "Other targets?"

"Yes. They must be warned. LaRue could already be moving on them."

Fedorov's brow furrowed in confusion "It is only you and Saeed's cell. He has secured a home in Catonsville for the final push to the harbor."

"Give me the address. They must be moved or Maya will fail."

Fedorov's eyes narrowed on Caine, and he stayed immobile. He contemplated his hands for the longest time and then gave him the address within the Arab neighborhood outside Baltimore. "LaRue was to find them, Caine. It will ensure the Americans believe this was an Arab attack, not one so coyly orchestrated by us. But, perhaps you should ensure LaRue and his people do find the Catonsville clues. After all, Grigori did not have that information."

Caine nodded. "I'll see to it myself. There will be no question of their involvement when I finish."

"Good." Fedorov raised his chin. "You should know, however, that, for now, Maya is all I have. When it is successful, Moscow will surely authorize me another. You will be rewarded for seeing me through this."

Caine smiled. "No other?"

"No, no. There is another. A surprise, my friend. A special surprise."

"What is this surprise?"

Fedorov grinned. "If I told you, it would not be a surprise."

"This surprise is the last cell?"

"Yes, but only later. After." Fedorov smiled. "Go now, Caine. Khalifah has the final plans ready. He will execute Maya within hours."

"Tell me now."

Fedorov shook his head. "Khalifah will brief you on what you need to know. Return to Winchester. Time is short."

"One target? You lied to me, Fedorov. You promised me much more work than this."

"*Nyet, nyet.*" Fedorov folded his hands in earnest. "Operation Maya is a beginning. A simple plan. A plan of my own making, too. Moscow knows nothing of it. They don't wish to know. That is why I have not planned for more cells. When it is successful, they will support me and we will move elsewhere. New York, Chicago, perhaps California. Moscow only wants the Americans out of our path to restrengthen our country. Regaining some of our lost territories is the first step. From there, we will rebuild our former union."

Caine went across the room to the windows. He moved a corner of the closed blinds and took a long time checking the area outside. "Launching these attacks will distract the Americans that much?"

"*Da*," Fedorov said smiling. "They are easily distracted these past years. They have withdrawn from the world. Their invasion of the Middle East was behind claims of national security. Yet, when we do the same in Crimea and Syria, they rattle sabers and cause the world to look at us with old, Cold War eyes."

Caine said nothing.

Fedorov continued. "But, give them a reason to worry again about their own national security and they will leave us alone and keep their prying to rhetoric and saber rattling. They will take no actions. Their voice is not the same as it once was in NATO. The more they are focused on the Arabs, the less they are focused on us. America's will is broken. Russia will rise again soon, Caine. Very, very soon."

"There is no connection to your SVR?" Caine said. "You are sure?"

Fedorov stood, walked to the alcove, and opened the small refrigerator as Caine tracked him with the Beretta. He retrieved a bottle of Russian vodka and two chilled glasses, poured two tall drinks, and returned. He offered one to Caine and raised his glass. "My mercenary friend, there is no connection to me. Not after Grigori. There is no SVR connection left for them to chase."

Caine moved away from Fedorov and sipped his vodka. "You directed Khalifah and Saeed to use refugees to make the attacks look like they came from ISIS or another brand. It's all a ruse to distract the Americans."

"*Da*. They were easy recruits." Fedorov shrugged. "After the breadcrumbs we have left, who is to say it was not ISIS? Make this an Arab problem and America will not worry so much about Russia."

Caine said nothing. He set his glass down on a small coffee table near the windows and checked outside again.

"Caine," Fedorov said in a strong, husky voice, "you have proven yourself. I have many new endeavors for you. But time is short. America is about to believe that Armageddon has landed on its shores."

"Now, Alexei, first things first." Caine turned the gun on him again. "Let's you and I agree on what Grigori's file and three cylinders of sarin are worth in today's marketplace. Shall we?"

Fedorov threw his head back and laughed again. "*Da, da*. Of course. What is it you wish?"

"I wish more money. I have half the sarin Saeed Mansouri is supposed to use." Caine eyed the Russian SVR man. "Do you have enough sarin for this new target?"

"What is your price?"

Twenty minutes later, Caine shook Colonel General Alexei Mikhailovich Fedorov's hand and slipped out the rear door.

CHAPTER 72

Day 6: May 20, 1330 Hours, Daylight Saving Time
Leesburg, Virginia

OSCAR LARUE WALKED through Fedorov's front door just after one of the three heavily armed men silently picked the lock and preceded the spymaster through.

Fedorov stood from his chair. "What is the meaning of this? You?"

"Good afternoon, Alexei." LaRue waved at his men to search the apartment. "How fortuitous you're still here. Grigori, too. Ah, I see he's already dead. No matter. You will do just fine."

Fedorov looked amused and picked up his glass of vodka. "You think you know something? Tell me."

"I know everything, Alexei. Everything."

Fedorov watched the armed commandos move through the small apartment, checking every door and cabinet. "Ah, more lies from a disgruntled colleague?" He motioned to Grigori's body across the room.

LaRue said nothing.

"Then what is it that you seek here?"

LaRue stepped forward and handed Fedorov a folder. Inside were transcripts of Grigori, Fariq, and Azar's confessions. He waited until Fedorov had read snippets of several of the pages.

"This is just a taste, Alexei. We have the details as well. Your movement of men, payments, communications. Everything."

"I have never known you to be this foolish, my friend." Fedorov closed the folder. "You are getting excitable in your old age, no?"

LaRue said nothing.

"Ah, I see. No matter. You are forgetting the golden rule."

"The golden rule?"

"Diplomatic immunity." Fedorov returned to the refrigerator and refilled his vodka glass, stepping over Grigori's body like it was a dog sleeping at his feet. "You see, this is pointless."

"Unfortunately, no." LaRue lifted his chin. "You and your Iranian surrogates have executed attacks on our soil. Hundreds are dead. All by your hand. By your direction."

"I have no connection to those savages. The rantings of a rogue Persian tortured into false confession is no proof."

"It is over, Alexei. Your actions are an act of war."

Fedorov threw back his head and laughed. "War? America is too weary. Your history will not allow you to shed blood without facts. Iraq still haunts you. You have no facts, but still I have immunity. This theater of yours is over."

LaRue walked casually to Fedorov and took his vodka glass. He downed it before the SVR man's eyes. "You have turned our streets into battlegrounds. Our people are fighting each other over faith and fear. All because of you."

"Nonsense. Your people are simply releasing what has been pent up for a decade. What is your offer?"

"You misunderstand, Fedorov. There is no offer. You and the Iranians are accountable."

"Accountable?" Colonel General Fedorov let slip a nervous grin. "You will never go to war with Iran. That would mean the destruction of Israel. You would never consider war with Russia, either. You prefer helpless, insignificant countries to battle."

"Accountable, Alexei."

"Impossible." Fedorov was failing to show his confidence as sweat formed on his brow and began to trickle downward. "Your debt strangles you. Your politics cripple you. There is no American will remaining."

"Unfortunately, Alexei, you miscalculated. You used the IRGC to exploit innocent refugees to carry out Operation Maya. You hope to destabilize us to allow Moscow to move on its old territories in Europe."

"You can prove nothing," Fedorov said hesitantly. "Now, to allow you to keep some face, Oscar LaRue, what are your terms?"

"There are no terms." LaRue nodded to the masked commando nearest Fedorov. The man removed his balaclava and stepped forward. LaRue continued. "It seems Operation Maya concerns Moscow greatly. They don't wish to be embarrassed, as we don't wish to report to Congress our own failures to protect the homeland."

"Your failures are far more than that."

LaRue regarded the Russian colonel general. "I am confused by one fact, Alexei. I understand what you wished to gain from Operation Maya. I do not understand, however, what your Iranian friends wished to gain."

"It should be obvious." Fedorov forced a laugh again. "They have grown tired of embarrassing you abroad. They merely wished to taunt you on your own soil."

LaRue nodded. "Another grave miscalculation. I am afraid it is over now."

"I do not understand." Fedorov paled. "Moscow will never allow you—"

"Alexei Mikhailovich Fedorov," said the unmasked commando in a thick, coarse Russian accent, "Moscow has sent me and I have heard enough."

Fedorov turned to the man. "Who are you? What is this about?"

"Names are not important, Colonel General. But if you wish, you may know me as Boris." Boris turned to LaRue. "Does this arrangement satisfy you that we are not responsible for Operation Maya?"

LaRue studied Fedorov for a long moment. "It is a beginning."

"No." Fedorov stepped in front of Boris and turned toward LaRue. "Wait, I can give you Khalifah. You have been hunting him for years."

"*Dasvidanya*, my old friend." LaRue turned his back on the two Russian *Sluzhba Vneshney Razvedki* men. "I am sorry."

Boris moved quickly and looped a wire garrote around Fedorov's throat. It took only seconds.

CHAPTER 73

Day 6: May 20, 1430 Hours, Daylight Saving Time
Catonsville, Maryland

"WHAT IS IT you do with us?" the young tea merchant asked Caine. "Please, tell me. My wife and I do nothing for those men."

Caine opened the front door and gestured toward his car. "Get into my car and wait. Don't do anything stupid like running. If you do, I'll kill you before you get off your sidewalk."

The tea merchant bundled up his pregnant wife and guided her to the door. "As you wish."

"Thank you," the merchant's wife said in a mere whisper. She glanced back at the two Afghani mercenaries lying dead in the hallway behind them. "They were very bad men."

Caine threw a chin toward the door. "Go. Now. Into the car."

The merchant pulled his wife's arm and led her outside just two steps ahead of Caine.

Before he climbed into his four-door sedan, Caine tapped a brief message on his cell phone.

Khalifah, I am detained. Will be there soon. Don't start without me.

CHAPTER 74

Day 7: May 21, 0015 Hours, Daylight Saving Time
Sandy Creek—Sand Town—Rural Frederick County, Virginia

THE PUNCHES STRUCK with ruthless potency. My arms were bound behind me and my legs taped to a wooden chair. The beating had just begun and already the Iranian, Khaled I think, had scored serious points on my ribs. He started with a right hook to my jaw and then did a rumba on my chest and stomach. After five or six more tunes, he tired and called out in Iranian.

A tall, thin Persian stepped from the darkness and approached me. The man's arms were sinewy, and he flexed them as though preparing to continue my assault. His narrow face allowed a dangerous, dark smile through his tightly cropped, neatly trimmed beard.

"You are Jonathan Hunter?" the Persian said evenly. "I have heard so much about you from my friend Khalifah."

I shook myself to sit up straight. "Let me guess, you're Saeed Mansouri."

"I am." Saeed seemed happy I knew him as if he were a celebrity. "It is a shame we meet now, under these, ah, circumstances? I must leave you to Khaled. He will take proper care of you. I am so sorry. I would like to kill you myself. But it seems Khalifah wishes me to begin my next journey."

I was too late. "Care to share where you're going? Baltimore perhaps?"

Khaled grabbed my hair and yanked my head back so hard I thought it would snap off. "Shut up, pig."

Saeed nodded to the man to release me. "Baltimore? You know much. Too bad, Hunter. You know so much and can do nothing for it. Fear not, I will give Noor and Sameh your sorrowful good-byes."

They had Noor and Sam. They had me. *Damn.*

Saeed laughed, nodded to Khaled, and disappeared into the darkness. I heard him ascending steps deeper in the room, beyond where I could see. He spoke to someone before lighter feet descended the same steps and approached me.

A woman. She was a pretty Arab with black hair and dark features partially concealed beneath a *hajib*. She carried a plastic jug of water and a cup. She lifted the jug and poured a cup of water, extending it out toward me.

Khaled said something in Persian I didn't understand, grabbed the cup of water from her, and gulped it down.

She refilled the cup and waited for him to drink again.

While they exchanged water and cup, I took in my surroundings. The air was dank and stale. I tried to remember how I'd come to be there. Hours before, I'd awakened after the Taser attack at Noor's house. At last count, it had been five attacks. I was dazed and immediately strapped immobile to the chair in the dark. Sound was dulled and the room seemed small and walls near. There was cold, gritty concrete beneath my feet. Off and on during the hours, I'd been awakened and then tazed again. Somewhere along the trip, I'd lost hours. Khaled seemed to enjoy the ritual. In the moments I'd been lucid, I'd heard virtually nothing. I'd seen virtually nothing. I'd felt only the surge of pain from the Taser and felt the darkness come on.

The woman holding water to my lips was familiar. Oddly so. I remembered her. She was the woman from the café and Kevin's graveside. She was one of them.

Khaled knocked the water from her hands before I could take more than a mouthful. He grabbed the jug, threw it back toward the darkness and the stairs she'd emerged from, and shoved her hard onto the ground. He barked orders at her and she covered her face, preparing for his assault. Instead, he thrust a hand toward the darkness, ordering her from the room.

As she got to her feet, Khaled turned back to me and slid a long, thin knife from his belt. In broken, difficult English, he managed to explain to me what was about to happen.

"Now, pig, I will take your skin. One piece. Another. You will tell me who knows."

His eyes suddenly bulged. His body rocked upward onto tiptoes, and he tried to scream but the knife in his jugular didn't allow it.

The woman grabbed his sweaty, dirty hair and pulled him backward. She worked her knife deeper into his throat, backward and forward, until finally wrenching it out and allowing Khaled to drop to the floor.

What?

"Jon Hunter, are you to be okay?" The woman jumped forward and began cutting my bonds and freeing me from the chair. "They used electric gun on you many times. Then stick needle in your arm. But this has passed, I think. Can you stand?"

I grabbed her hand and pulled the knife from it. "Who are you?"

"I am Gianna Nazari." She stepped back beneath the single light that hung from the beamed ceiling. "It means, 'Allah is Merciful.' Kevin just called me 'G.'"

CHAPTER 75

Day 7: May 21, 0030 Hours, Daylight Saving Time
Sandy Creek—Sand Town—Rural Frederick County, Virginia

"Where is Saeed Mansouri?" Caine asked the mechanic standing on a ladder and inspecting the bus's engine. "Where is the other bus?"

"He left a while ago," the mechanic said. "He said he will meet you at the resting place. This bus would not start. I fix it now. You may go soon."

Caine looked around the garage at the bus. Seats had been ripped out and tossed about the garage. Three or four of Saeed's best mechanics worked feverishly outside the bus. Just walking off the bus were two men wearing gray, baggy biohazard suits complete with respirators. They moved sluggishly as they climbed down the stairs onto the garage floor. Sitting across the garage floor, eyeing Caine, were two of Saeed's men. Both held AK-74 assault rifles and lazily guarded the group of mechanics around the shop.

A young man, perhaps twenty, walked from a rear storage area carrying a heavy wooden crate that had the top open. Caine stopped him and glanced inside.

There were dull, grayish bricks wrapped in opaque plastic.

"Plastic explosives?" Caine asked the mechanic. "Where'd you get this?"

The man shrugged. "I do not know. Saeed had us place them inside the other bus. Now we must do the same to this one." He gestured to one of the biohazard-suited men to retrieve the box from him.

"Why was I not told about this?" Caine moved closer to the bus as the mechanic closed the bus hood and descended the ladder. "How long ago did Saeed leave?"

"Maybe an hour?" He wiped his hands on a rag from his pocket. "Is everything all right? I do what he say. Can I go home now? Will he release my wife?"

"I hope so." Caine threw a thumb over his shoulder. "Go now. All of you. Go to the old theatre building at the edge of town. Your families will be there. There are four dead men. Saeed Mansouri's men. Say nothing. All of you, stay in the theatre with your families until I come for you."

The mechanic's eyes got big and the other workers surrounded him. "What is this you tell us, Caine? Is this a trick?"

One of the armed guards spoke to his partner, and they both stood and approached Caine. The first guard said, "They stay. Their work is not done. Saeed ordered—"

Caine slid the silenced .22 from the small of his back and shot both guards where they stood. He turned to the group of garage workers and eyed them one at a time.

"Go. Saeed won't be back tonight. I'll come for you all in the morning. Go now. Stay there. No one will harm you or your families any longer."

* * *

Caine waited until the men were well down the road and gone into the darkness. He quickly inspected the mechanics' progress on the bus. They were all but finished. Only the explosives were left to be connected. The sarin cylinders had been connected to Doc's makeshift spray system beneath the bus and readied to be primed using the air tanks mounted inside the rear of the bus. With the plastic explosives in place, the bus would have been capable of killing thousands more.

He looked around to make sure he'd not missed any of Saeed's men on the streets. Satisfied he was still undetected, he carefully checked the cylinders inside the bus. He found the three notches he'd scrapped into the cylinders and breathed easier. Then he retreated from the bus.

Taking one last survey of the street outside the old garage, he tossed an M-67 fragmentation grenade into the open bus door and ran full flank for cover.

Five seconds later, the bus and garage erupted. The ball of flames lit the night sky like a ravenous thunderstorm and the explosion split the air with deafening percussion.

Operation Maya was nearly through.

CHAPTER 76

Day 7: May 21, 0030 Hours, Daylight Saving Time
Sandy Creek—Sand Town—Rural Frederick County, Virginia

"You're 'G'?" It had taken me a while to get my feet under me and shake off the beating and drugs Saeed Mansouri's men used to control me. But soon, I was able to move about. In a pile in the corner of the room were my running shoes, wallet, and even my .45 with my spare magazines. These guys were so confident I was done, they didn't bother to take them away. Unfortunately, they were cautious with my cell phone. They had smashed it to bits.

I checked my .45's chamber and slipped it into my jeans. "You worked for Kevin?"

"*Baleh.*" Gianna searched Khaled and pulled a .32 Derringer out of his pants. She tucked it deep into the front of her jeans. Then she pulled her dull blue work shirt out and hung it over the almost unnoticeable bulge from the handgun. "He pay me to tell him things about Saeed and Caine. Things he could not find himself."

"I understand. Did you send Ghali to meet me at the library?"

She nodded. "*Baleh.* I think maybe you help me after Kevin killed. But you did not stop Saeed's attack on the mall, so I was not sure. Ghali say he help me. Now, Ghali dead, too."

"I'm so sorry. It wasn't my fault."

She looked down, pulled her *hajib* off her head, and nodded. "*Nah*. It was *my* fault."

As I moved slowly around trying to get my muscles to fully awaken, I watched her. She watched me, too. Finally, I asked the million-dollar questions.

"Gianna, do you know who killed my brother?"

"*Baleh*." She looked down. "Kevin was a good man. At first, yes. Kevin ask my help and we make a deal. Later, he change very much. He demanded more and more until I tell him I no help him anymore. He was a different man."

Whatever happened to Kevin was more than I knew. "What happened? Do you know what changed him?"

"No." She looked away. "But he not the same man. Must be something very bad. Then I find out about Khalifah's plans from Saeed Mansouri's men. I tell Kevin. He very scared. He very angry. I try to find out more but then he killed."

"Why didn't you come to me sooner, Gianna?" I found my Mark 1 injection kit jammed into one of my running shoes as I slipped them on. "You could have talked to me at the café or the cemetery."

"No, but Ghali and I tried to reach you after." She watched me. "We did not do well."

I went to her and took her arm gently. "Gianna, who killed Kevin?"

"Khalifah." She turned and walked to the stairs leading up to wherever. "Now, we must go. You must stop the buses."

The buses? "What buses, Gianna?"

She looked toward the stairs. "Khalifah's big attack. Maya. Saeed make the town men fix two buses. They steal them from somewhere I do not know. The men put strange pipes and things on these buses. I hear one of Saeed's close men say the pipes will spray gas and germs. The town men very afraid to work there, but Saeed has the families. Early today, the buses are ready."

I'd seen the buses. I'd been within twenty feet of them just yesterday. Khalifah had the sarin and it was loaded on those very buses. Operation Maya was about to launch, and I'd been right there and failed to know it.

She inched to the stairs and stopped to listen. "We must hurry."

I moved beside her. "Where are we?"

"You call this place Sand Town."

Of course. "Have you seen others? Kevin's wife and son?"

"*Baleh,* Noor and Sameh. Khalifah, he bring them here. Now, I think they with Saeed. They are in much danger. We hurry."

"Where are they now?"

She shrugged. "I do not know. I think Saeed take them and leave."

"Let's go." I started up the stairs following my gunsights. "Do you know where Khalifah is going to attack next?"

"No, I do not. I am sorry. Saeed already left in one bus. The gas they put on the buses is very bad. I have seen gas used in my country. It is horrible. Khalifah will use it soon with two buses."

There were two attacks? "How many of Saeed's men are around here?"

"Maybe six." Gianna tried to smile but couldn't. Her face was stone and her eyes cold and intense. "You kill them or they kill us. Noor and Sam Mallory, too. You kill Saeed's men first. Kill them all."

I liked Gianna. I liked her plan even more.

CHAPTER 77

Day 7: May 21, 0100 Hours, Daylight Saving Time
Sandy Creek—Sand Town—Rural Frederick County, Virginia

GIANNA AND I emerged from the basement of an abandoned shop on the outskirts of Sand Town. Hiding behind some overgrown shrubs outside, we scanned the streets and surrounding homes looking for any sign of Saeed Mansouri's men.

Nothing.

No, that wasn't true. Behind the row of buildings, two blocks away, smoke and flames billowed a couple hundred feet above the rooftops.

Careful to stay in the shadows, we moved along the street to a side road and found our way toward the huge blazing structure.

"What's that, Gianna?"

"The town garage. It where Saeed's men were working on the buses. I think they make a mistake. This is bad for them."

"It's good for us," I said. "But we have to stay away from the smoke. There could be dangerous particles in it."

Oddly, there was no one around. No workmen, no mechanics, none of Saeed's men. For as far as we could see along the dark streets, Sand Town was abandoned.

The empty streets unnerved me.

Rule five of mortal combat—know where your enemy is. I did not.

As we got closer to the garage, we saw a school bus buried beneath the collapsing roof. The bus looked like it had exploded from within and caused the blaze. Perhaps an exploding gas tank or other mishap. Whatever the cause, the garage and bus were lost to the fire. That was a good thing. If Saeed had started his operation with two school buses, he was now down to only one.

One bus down. One to go.

Surveying the area, I saw something that made my heart stop. A half-block from the burning garage, parked beneath a broad oak tree along the sidewalk, was Kevin's custom trike motorcycle.

"Gianna, what's Kevin's motorcycle doing here?"

She was grim. "Maybe Saeed's men bring it here. But, Sameh, he come here sometimes, too. I do not know why. I never speak to him. He does not know me. I tell Kevin Sameh come here and Kevin got very upset. I think it was a bad thing for them both."

"Do you have any idea where Saeed took Sameh and Noor?"

"I not know where." She thought a moment while watching the garage finish collapsing onto the destroyed bus carcass. "Some of Saeed's men do buildings. Construction? They work near the big road—495?"

"Interstate 495 around DC? Do you think that's where they went?"

She thought and her face brightened. "*Baleh.* I hear Saeed Mansouri say to park between the houses. There is much construction where they go. Many buildings. I bring them once when their car break down. I do not know the address but I show you."

A large construction site was a great place to hide an army in the early morning hours. If it was near the Beltway, that made sense. From there, they could hit I-495 and be in Baltimore in forty-five minutes. A school bus making that trip wouldn't draw attention.

"Do you have a car?"

She shook her head and gestured to Kevin's custom trike. "If you can ride a motorcycle, that looks very fast."

CHAPTER 78

Day 7: May 21, 0355 Hours, Daylight Saving Time
Ellie's Wood Development, McLean, Virginia

I WOULDN'T HAVE found Saeed Mansouri's staging area without Gianna. It took us nearly two hours to reach the Beltway, and the ride was interesting. I'd ridden my share of motorcycles and mopeds over the years, but the custom trike was very different. Gianna loved it. While she knew we were heading into danger, she giggled a few times as we roared down the highway and over town roads. Her fun didn't last, though. The closer we got to the Capital Beltway, the less she enjoyed the ride.

Once we reached I-495, we had to explore several construction sites looking for the right one. We were west of the Capital Beltway, just a couple miles south of the Potomac River. After two false stops at the wrong sites, we found the right one, and Gianna pointed out the entrance. Then, without a cell phone of my own, I was forced to retreat to an all-night convenience store to call LaRue. He was groggy from the hour, and I had to explain things twice before he understood why I was briefing him from the convenience store counter. He was not impressed to say the least.

My last warning to him was simple. "I'm going in, Oscar. I have no idea if they're in there or not. If not, we're screwed. If they are and you're late to the party, I'm screwed."

He grumbled at me and hung up. I'm sure he meant to tell me to be very careful and not take any unnecessary chances. But he was just tired and forgot.

A few minutes later, we weaved our way back to the development and into a woods where the development's upscale homes were under construction. Upscale meaning seven thousand square feet and a couple million bucks.

I parked the trike off the development's access road and made ready. I had my .45 and three magazines of ammo. Gianna had the Derringer she'd taken off Khaled during our escape. I felt wholly under-armed given the firepower Saeed's men had used before.

Hopefully, Oscar would balance the books sooner rather than later.

"Gianna," I said, peering around the darkness. "Wait here for LaRue's people. They should be along soon."

She looked at me with a strange face. "Jon Hunter, I help. I know how to use a gun."

"I'm sure you do. But I'm going in alone." I reached over and touched her arm. "Wait for my people. I have to get in there before sunrise. You'll have to show them where I am."

She turned away. "As you say. But later, you wish I come."

* * *

By the time I crept through the woods to the site, the sun had begun to rise and the darkness had started to ebb.

The construction site had dozens of new home-skeletons all in different phases of completion. Unlike most constructions sites, though, there wasn't a home being built in this site that was under a couple million bucks. A few were nearly finished with shingled roofs and glassed windows. Others were just frames of wood and pallets of stone, brick, framing materials waiting nearby.

If there was a safe place to hide a small army and a bus laden with sarin nerve agent, this was it.

I'd made it to the south side of the site and began a careful house-to-house reconnoiter. After the first partially constructed street, I found Saeed's lair at the end of a cul-de-sac where five new homes were in various skeletal stages. The entrance was partially paved and the rest dirt and gravel with the enormous structures surrounding the cul-de-sac. Several backhoes, bull-dozers, and tool shacks were scattered around the site amidst pallets of redbrick and other building materials. To my benefit, the builder had taken care to leave as much of the surround-ing woods intact so it would give the area an immediate ma-ture-neighborhood feel once completed. It also gave me cover. I could move in close without being observed. *Hopefully* without being observed.

Four vehicles lined the cul-de-sac entrance on both sides. Be-hind them were an old pickup truck and a large cargo van. Backed in between two homes in the rear of the cul-de-sac was the school bus. St. Somebody's Bus 219.

The entrance was guarded by two sentries positioned on an un-finished veranda on the right side of the road. Both were asleep. There seemed to be no one else around, but there had to be more of Saeed's IRGC commandos somewhere. He wouldn't leave a major operation like this, nor his bus full of sarin, protected by only two men. Perhaps they were in the vehicles out of view, sleeping. Perhaps they were asleep inside the buildings. Perhaps they were lying in wait for me to step into the open so they could kill me in a hail of bullets.

Perhaps.

It took me a solid half hour to find them. They were asleep throughout the buildings and vehicles parked around the site.

Saeed wasn't among them. Neither were Noor and Sam, Caine, or anyone who might be Khalifah.

The sun began to chase the darkness away, and a faint morning glow filtered over the trees. Sometime soon, Khalifah would give the order, and Saeed would send Bus 219 to kill thousands in Baltimore.

Since only movie heroes and fools rush in, I slunk through the darkness to Bus 219.

CHAPTER 79

Day 7: May 21, 0415 Hours, Daylight Saving Time
Ellie's Wood Development, McLean, Virginia

NONE OF SAEED'S men were guarding Bus 219 close up. Either Saeed was confident that he'd escaped any detection, or he'd put too much faith into his men. Well, there was another option—it was a trap.

It didn't matter. I had to take out Bus 219. Trap or not, that bus wasn't leaving this site.

The two garages that flanked the bus gave me cover to move from the trees and up close to examine the bus's exterior. Having not been gunned down yet, I crawled underneath its chassis.

My heart stopped.

Tubular steel arteries, perhaps a half-inch in diameter, were fastened along the undercarriage. They led to several small spray nozzles crudely mounted on the bus's frame. The piping merged in the center of the bus and disappeared up inside the cabin. I crawled out and sneaked aboard, crawling on my hands and knees to continue my inspection.

Halfway down the aisle, I realized I might already be dead.

Six stainless-steel cylinders, two feet long and six inches in diameter, were mounted under the center three seats on each side. The cylinders looked like giant whipped cream cans. Strange comparison, I know, but I like whipped cream. Well, not anymore. Each cylinder had metal tubes that connected to some kind of control unit in the rear of the bus along with a larger cylinder marked "Compressed Air." The control unit and connecting tubes formed an octopus that fed the spray nozzles beneath the bus. The cylinders had strange markings in Arabic. While I didn't read much Arabic, I didn't have to. The international symbol for Armageddon was multilingual—a circle around a skull and crossbones.

Unless this was a pirate treasure, I'd found Oscar LaRue's sarin nerve gas.

The design was basic. The sarin was combined with compressed air to form a mist that would be sprayed silently beneath the bus as it moved along Baltimore's streets. The movement of the bus would swirl the gas outward and into other cars, pedestrians, or buildings close by.

Sarin wasn't the only problem. There were wires that connected ten opaquely wrapped plastic bricks concealed beneath the seats—homemade plastic explosives. The bricks were packed beside the cylinders and connected to a wire harness that ran to a square metal canister the size of a child's lunch box in the rear of the bus. There, the lunch box was connected to coax cable that disappeared out the roof. An antenna. An antenna for remote detonation.

What, no thermonuclear bomb? No tarantulas or lethal pit vipers? Just homemade plastic explosives and sarin gas?

Steady, Hunter. One, two, three. Oh crap . . . ninety-nine.

Part of Special Forces training is explosives. Over the years, I'd seen my share of IEDs and even diffused a few when the bomb techs weren't available. I'm no expert, but in a pinch, I can figure out the blue and red wire most of the time. "Most of the time" are the operant words here. There were three things wrong with this bomb design in front of me—I had no tools other than a pocketknife, the clock was ticking and I was surrounded by bad guys eager to kill me, and, the biggie, there was a gadget affixed to the tangle of wires that I was certain was a tamper switch.

Time was against me.

I left the explosives and sarin untouched. Besides, I didn't want to get into that old argument, "The blue wire. No the red wire. Oh, what about the pretty pink one?" Am I right?

Bus 219 was loaded and ready. Someone would drive to Baltimore's Inner Harbor and spray the sarin nerve agent everywhere. It might kill hundreds. Maybe thousands. When the sarin ran out, the explosives would be remotely detonated and kill even more. There were enough explosives for half a city block.

Nice plan. Well crafted. Evil. Maniacal, even.

Thus far, the IRGC had used young refugees—Arab faces carrying out violence—taken hostage and forced to carry out their attacks. It was a blue-ribbon trademark of the Taliban and ISIS to make the innocent kill the innocent. By midday, some Americans would be striking out in anger and hate at anyone who looked Middle Eastern. Even those who were not. The insane retribution would swell across our country like a rogue wave out of control.

Unrest. Anger. Demonstrations. Revenge.

Khalifah chose the refugee families very carefully. For some reason, he'd chosen Noor and Sam Mallory, too. Was it because of Kevin? Because of me?

Oh, my God. Noor was going to be driving the bus, and Sam would be with her.

CHAPTER 80

Day 7: May 21, 0440 Hours, Daylight Saving Time
Ellie's Wood Development, McLean, Virginia

I NEEDED A plan. A good plan. A damn good plan. Spectacular, even. Unfortunately, I didn't have one, just an outcome—that bus could not leave this site. Since there wasn't time, nor did I have the tools to disarm the explosives and sarin, there was only one choice left.

Disable the bus.

I eased off the bus to look for tools. I made it about three feet.

A bullet smacked into the driveway inches from me. I dove for cover beside the bus's front wheel. I tugged my .45 and twice tried to inch around the wheel to make a move for better cover. Bullets kept me pinned down.

The pickup truck's lights came on at the far side of the cul-de-sac and illuminated several figures. Kevin's custom trike drove out of the darkness and headed straight for me. Ahead of it, Noor was being pushed toward me by two figures. She was gagged with her hands behind her. Saeed held a pistol to her head. Two more *Pāsdārān,* heavily armed, moved with him.

"Hunter, do not move or she will die." Saeed pushed Noor forward until they stopped at the end of the barren driveway in front of me. "Put down your weapon."

"Saeed, let them go and you can leave alive." It was the lie from every shoot-'em-up movie I'd ever seen. "The FBI is on their way. They'll bring an army."

Apparently, he'd also seen those movies. "I do not think this is so. Put the gun down." He swung his gun around and fired near my head. "Now."

The shot whistled past and sent a shiver through me. I glanced at Noor, who straightened herself defiantly, refusing to give Saeed any satisfaction.

Saeed called, "Put it down or I kill you next."

Around the site, several *Pāsdārān*—a half dozen at least—emerged from houses and from behind pallets of bricks and masonry. His IRGC commandos were heavily armed and ready.

I dropped my pistol. "Have it your way."

"*Baleh.*" Saeed turned to someone out of view and threw his chin. "Let us all get friendly."

A *Pāsdār* appeared through the dark and dragged Gianna with him. He punched her behind the head and sent her down onto the gravel beside Noor. She instantly got to one knee and refused to buckle further.

"Jon Hunter." Gianna looked up at me with disappointed eyes. "I am very sorry."

Saeed spat on her and then looked to me. "You will die very badly. You know this now, yes? Then I kill Gianna for betraying me. Maybe I keep your woman." He leered at Noor and put his arm around her "Yes, for my men. For me, too."

"I'm gonna gut you like a fish," I said dryly. "You know this, yes?"

Saeed mumbled to his minions as he pushed Noor farther up the driveway ahead of him to within feet of me. He held her close but left Gianna behind him at the end of the drive as his men surrounded me.

"You are a strong man, Jon Hunter. It will be enjoyable to kill you."

"Are you done with the cheesy lines yet?" I looked at Noor. Her face was tear-streaked and her big, beautiful eyes were dark and struggling. The last of her strength escaped down her cheeks. But when I winked, she straightened again. Perhaps she thought I had a big trap that Saeed had inadvertently sprung. Perhaps it comforted her that we'd die together.

I tried another movie line. "Keep me, Saeed. I'll drive your damn bus and do whatever you want. Let Noor go."

"Ah, you now negotiate?" Saeed threw his head back and laughed. "You are a funny man, Hunter. You have no idea. Noor will drive the bus for me."

"You mean for Khalifah and Caine." I sidestepped toward the *Pāsdār* on my right. "You're a flunky, Saeed. Khalifah yells shit and Caine asks how high. You clean the mess."

Saeed swung his pistol up and shot me.

I half-spun away but gritted my teeth and took the pain. If Noor and Gianna could stay tough, so could I. My luck held, such as it was. The bullet passed through the fleshy part of my left arm, just below the shoulder. It missed the bone. Somehow, I stayed on my feet.

Saeed grabbed Noor by the hair and shook her until I thought he'd yank it out. She cried out, but he shook her harder. With a coarse laugh, he hurled her to the ground, strode up to me, and pistol-whipped me across the face.

I went down.

Blood gushed from my cheek. The world spun and darkness flashed on-off-on-off. It took me a few moments to struggle back up onto a knee. "Pretty tough with an army, Saeed." Yeah, I saw that movie, too.

"I kill you now. It is a shame you do not know Allah."

"Let me ask you something." I spat blood and a tooth. "Does Saeed mean camel dung or something else?"

Rule six of mortal combat—don't antagonize the winning side.

Saeed drove a booted foot into my midsection and sent me backward, breathless and in damning pain. I refused to cry out. I couldn't. I had no breath. I wanted to vomit and gasped for air, but I needed to be strong and arrogant. Show no fear. I struggled.

He kicked me a second time and raised his pistol at my head.

"*Nah! Nah!*" Gianna jumped to her feet, shoved Saeed aside, and came to me. She knelt and pulled my head up and held me half-sitting. She began padding my bullet wound with torn pieces of my shirt and tatters from her blouse. "*Khahesh meekomam nakoshesh!*" She begged for my life.

"Poor Jon Hunter," he scoffed. "Women must save you? What big-shot CIA agent are you now?"

I spit blood at his feet. "I'm a consultant, Saeed. What's so hard to understand about that?"

He laughed and grabbed Noor's hair again, yanked her backward, and shook her off-balance. "I have a special surprise for you. You will love this, Hunter. I promise you this thing."

Gianna helped me to one knee and froze. She fixed on someone approaching through the dawn light. Her hands quivered, and she went rigid.

Victoria Bacarro, armed with a handgun and wearing body armor, eased toward us in slow, measured steps. She pivoted her Sig among the henchmen around me. Twice, she shot a glance over her shoulder, and when she finally steadied her attention on us, she leveled her pistol dead-center on Saeed Mansouri's chest.

Gianna's fingers cut the circulation in my arm. "Khalifah is here."

CHAPTER 81

Day 7: May 21, 0455 Hours, Daylight Saving Time
Ellie's Wood Development, McLean, Virginia

Khalifah?

Saeed lowered his pistol and commanded his men to do the same. He turned to me and smiled a cold, deadly smile. "Now you will see."

Victoria stopped a dozen feet away and kept her weapon trained on Saeed and his men.

"No one move," Victoria ordered. She glanced at me. "What are you doing here?"

"They have Noor and Sam." Was she friend or foe? "Where's your backup?"

"A few minutes out," she said. "You're wounded."

Gianna nodded to Victoria. "The bleeding has stopped. He will be fine."

Maybe Saeed was wrong and the joke was on him.

No, it wasn't.

I turned to find Saeed, but he had stepped back away from his men.

A gunshot from out of the darkness made Victoria cry out and she went down hard. Blood instantly pooled around her where she lay motionless at my feet.

"Victoria!" I started to kneel, but a figure walked from the darkness where Victoria had emerged moments ago. His gun was aimed at my head. "You?"

Artie Polo's gunsight locked onto my forehead. "Nothing personal, Hunter."

"Ha. You see, big-shot CIA man." Saeed raised his gun again at me. "It all bad for you now."

One, two, three. Steady Hunter. Steady.

Victoria laid still, the pool of blood growing beneath her.

I looked at Artie and considered the odds I could snap his traitorous neck before someone killed me. "Khalifah?"

"What's in a name?" He prodded the air with his gun to back me away from Victoria. Then he grabbed Gianna by the arm, dragged her to Noor, and shoved her to the ground beside her. "*General-Polkovnik Fedorov* thought it clever. Make everyone think there was an Arab calling the shots. I've been Khalifah since before we met in Riyadh."

Riyadh? "So, when you and I—"

"I tried to kill you then and it went wrong." He laughed. "I had to make the Saudis think I was with you. If they didn't, they would have discovered me for sure."

Saeed grinned. "It is a good story, Hunter. Now it is better. Now it is over."

"Bastard." I spat at Artie.

Artie threw a chin at Saeed who stepped back and took a position to guard us. Then, Artie went to the bus and did an odd thing. He stripped off his coat, shirt, and slacks and donned a dirty, dark-blue mechanics coverall. He tossed his clothes into the bus and returned to Saeed's side.

He grinned at me. "I don't want to get my suit dirty, Hunter. You know, you helped establish my cover over there. If not for you, I'd have been caught in that trap. You stumbled into it and it all worked out for me."

"You're a traitor. A terrorist son of a bitch."

"Perhaps." His sarcastic grin bit. "But I'm a multimillionaire son of a bitch. These past years I've banked twenty million. There's a two million bonus just for today."

"You're going to kill thousands. You'll start another war."

He shrugged. "My villa has no extradition." Then he yanked Noor away from Saeed. He wrapped one arm around her and pressed his Sig to her throat. With his other hand, he produced a cell phone from his pocket.

"Saeed, check the bus." Artie waited for Saeed to walk off toward Bus 219 before waving the phone at me. "Recognize this, Hunter?"

I said nothing.

"It's the phone that called Kevin that night. It's mine, Hunter."

"You? You lured him to the river to kill him."

"Oh, no." Artie laughed again. "To pay him."

The words filtered slowly into my head. Each one clicking on a piece of the puzzle that I'd refused to see before. All the clues started to come together. Kevin's mood change, the cabin, the cash, and his disillusion with the task force. It was Kevin working with Artie Polo.

My brother sold out. My friend was a terrorist. *Jesus*. What an ass I was.

"You bought him?" I'd known for days but saying it now seared it into my brain.

"It wasn't all that hard, Hunter," Artie said dryly. "He was over his head in debt and wanted more and more and more. One of his own snitches found me out and came to me. Except I was ready. That secret file about the refugee who killed your folks was the push over the cliff. That and money. Sure, sure, chump change as they say. At first, anyway. Then he got greedy."

My gut knotted. "He'd never go along with all this."

"Kevin was one of us." Artie read my mind. "Until he wasn't."

"He changed his mind?"

"It was too late. I'd already provided him new passports and money to run if things got hot. Of course, I had to retrieve all that and deliver Ghali to your cabin."

My face got hot. "I'm going to kill you, Artie."

"Sure you are. Anyway, Kevin was all in." He forced a laugh and drilled his hateful eyes through me. "Then he realized we had sarin and the Russians behind us. He changed his mind."

Kevin tried to back out. Sanity returned to him and he tried to get out.

Artie must have read my mind. "Your brother came to the river to call it off. I guess selling secrets and hiding illegals was one thing. Blowing up shopping malls and schools was something else. The fool pulled a gun on me."

"You murdered him."

Artie lifted a chin. "Law of the jungle. Too bad, too. I liked him. But not as much as Victoria did."

I glanced at Noor struggling against Artie's grasp. She stilled when her eyes locked on me. Denial turned to sadness. Kevin Mallory—husband and father—was a dirty cop. Not the man she'd married. Not the man she'd hoped.

I motioned to Artie's cell phone. "You gonna order pizza or phone the WFO with your confession?"

"Speed Dial 1." He turned the phone to face me. "It blows that bus and twenty bricks of explosives. High-grade stuff, too. My recipe, I might add."

Twenty bricks? I'd missed ten.

He continued. "But not until Noor sightsees. It's a beautiful day. Should be thousands on the sidewalks by seven."

Saeed returned from the bus and nodded to Artie. "It is ready."

"Hear that, Noor?" Artie tightened his arm around her. It's all ready for you."

Noor struggled to pull free but couldn't. Her eyes raged and tears rained. She managed to work the gag free and cried out, but Artie jabbed his Sig into her throat harder.

She still managed, "I will never do such a thing."

"No?" Artie said into her ear. "If you don't do as I say, Saeed will fillet your kid."

Saeed grinned.

"No. Do not do this." She looked at him. "I beg you. He is a boy. Where is he? Where is Sam?"

Saeed poked the air with his pistol. "He is Sameh, bitch. Heritage is important."

"Please, do not ask me to do this," Noor begged. "I cannot."

"Ask?" Artie sidestepped toward Bus 219, easily dragging her along. "There'll be a beautiful Iranian behind the wheel for all the security cameras to record. Maybe if you're good, I'll let you run when the sarin is spent. Maybe you'll make it. Maybe not. I'm feeling magnanimous today."

I stepped forward. "Artie, don't do this. It's not too late. Stop."

"Not too late?" He laughed and shook Noor again. "By nightfall they'll be rounding up refugees and beating them in the streets. Every cabbie with dark skin will be fair game. Those the government doesn't intern, the people will crucify. It's already too late. Even if the President learns the truth, he'll have to strike the Middle East. He has no choice. The people won't accept anything less than revenge. And we all know he is more than willing to take revenge. He's a bully."

I turned to Saeed. "You're okay with Muslims taking the blame for all this? Getting more killed and another war?"

"*Baleh.*" He glared at me. "The more innocents you kill, the more Muslims will rise up against you. You will bring about your own end. Allah promises your defeat of your own making."

Artie stopped at the bus door and laughed. "I'll be sitting rich and watching."

"I'm going to kill you, Artie." I aimed a gun finger at him. "See you soon."

Noor struggled harder and nearly broke free, but Artie smashed his pistol against her cheek and stilled her.

She pleaded, "Jon, *please.*"

I don't know what shocked me more—Artie Polo as the infamous Khalifah, my brother as a traitor, or the gunshot that snapped Saeed's head forward and dropped him dead on the ground.

None of that. It was Gianna holding the .32 Derringer that took Saeed's life.

No one, especially Saeed Mansouri, saw that coming.

CHAPTER 82

Day 7: May 21, 0515 Hours, Daylight Saving Time
Ellie's Wood Development, McLean, Virginia

CHAOS WASN'T NEW to me. Of course, often, I cause it.

Nothing came close to the eruption around us when Saeed hit the ground. One of his men turned an AK-74 toward Gianna for the kill. At that instant, *his* head exploded and he death-spiraled to the ground. Another *Pāsdār* got off a couple rounds at me before the same fate was exacted—one headshot from somewhere out in the dawn light. Saeed's remaining crew scattered for cover and delivered a barrage of AK-74 fire blindly in every direction, reverberating the air with deafening chatter.

Salvation approached with the *thump-thump-thump-thump* of helicopter rotors. They grew louder as two choppers swooped over the ridge behind us. One dropped down outside the cul-de-sac. The other circled overhead, turning its flank for a door gunner's field of fire. The *Pāsdārān* gunfire shifted toward the hovering chopper a second too late as the mechanical growl of a 7.62 millimeter mini-gun roared. The gunner raked the ground and silenced the attack.

More shouts. More panic. More gunfire.

A loudspeaker commanded, "*Aslahato bendaz. Tasleem!*" Orders to lay down their guns and surrender.

The rifle fire stopped. The shouting silenced. Only the rotor-thumps overhead continued its search for *Pāsdārān* resistance.

Two of Saeed's men barricaded themselves behind a pallet of red bricks beside the house on my left. They reloaded their AKs and readied for the first chopper's eventual ground assault. Their faces blanched as they babbled in rambling, excited tones. One glanced over at Gianna and their chatter hardened.

A hostage play.

I grabbed Gianna, spun her around, and shoved her toward the rear of another house. "Go!"

I looked for Noor.

Artie had her on the bus behind the steering wheel now. He stood behind her with his Sig plainly visible and jammed into her head. He intentionally left the bus door open so there would be no doubt he could kill her in an instant.

Gianna began to move but stopped and pointed into the darkness. "Hunter, he is coming."

I turned.

Caine walked casually out of the house at the center of the cul-de-sac. He looked around and closed the distance to me, a silenced semiautomatic at his side. As he did, the two *Pāsdārān* behind the brick pile made a dash for Gianna.

Again, the world turned upside down.

Without breaking stride, Caine ended both men, each with a single shot.

"Stand down, Hunter." He moved toward the bus and fired two rounds into the window near Artie's head. Both missed. "It's over, Polo. Next one's in your head."

Artie wasn't so sure.

The bus started, lurched forward, and accelerated down the driveway.

From behind me, Victoria got to her feet and staggered forward. She grabbed her Sig from the ground and half-jogged, half-limped into the path of the bus. She fell more than jumped into the open bifold doors as it careened past.

A shot cracked from inside Bus 219. Another.

Victoria spasmed in the doorway, slumped, and crumbled onto the bus stairs. Her legs dragged on the ground as the bus smashed past the cargo van and tore the bus's mirrors and side fender off. The jolt shook her lifeless body loose and it skidded across the ground.

"No!" I yelled.

The bus, and Victoria, were gone.

Bile made me look away.

"Stand down," a loudspeaker commanded. "Hold your fire! Hold your fire!" The command was repeated, first in Arabic, then in Persian. Finally, in English.

I turned to Caine. "Who *are* you?"

He dumped the magazine from his pistol and reloaded a fresh one. "I'm you, Hunter."

"What?"

A train of feet shuffled toward us with clatter of battle gear. A cluster of shadows formed halfway across the street.

"Hold!" a voice commanded. "Hold your fire."

Ten commandos clad in black body armor and wielding submachine guns snaked around the stacks of brick and machinery. They formed a defensive perimeter around us and faced out. One by one they chanted their mantra, "Clear!"

"Secure the area," the voice commanded, and the commandos sprinted in all directions. A second team emerged from behind us and retook their positions on guard. "For Christ's sake, Hunter, what a mess."

Oscar LaRue made his entrance dressed casually in a light-colored windbreaker, tan slacks, and a golf shirt. He carried a radio and barked instructions as he approached me. He stopped at Saeed's body, and for an instant, regarded the dead IRGC commander. Then he looked back at Victoria lying twisted and dead fifty yards away. Finally, he walked to Caine and me.

"The President's trip to the Inner Harbor has been canceled. He's staying in DC. The Israeli delegation will convene with him there."

"How about the rest of the Inner Harbor?"

"We're already there and ready." He looked solemnly at me. "Teams are positioned on the Beltway to stop them before Baltimore in a safe ambush zone. You've got fifteen minutes."

"Before what, Oscar?" I said, but his face explained everything.

He turned to Caine. "Do what is necessary."

CHAPTER 83

Day 7: May 21, 0540 Hours, Daylight Saving Time
Ellie's Wood Development, McLean, Virginia

CAINE WAS ALREADY moving. He grabbed my .45 from the drive and tossed it to me. "On me."

On him? Oh, okay. I followed at a run.

He reached the motorcycles and jumped on Kevin's custom three-wheel trike. He thumbed the engine alive. "We're not taking Polo alive. No trials."

"I'm not big on courtrooms." I climbed on the trike behind him. "Artie will understand."

"Good." He toed the trike into gear and shot forward. "That bus doesn't reach Baltimore, Hunter. No matter what."

Noor.

"I'm sorry." Caine revved the throttle and we rocketed out of the cul-de-sac. He yelled, "We need a plan."

"Get close to the bus. I'll figure it out then."

"That's your plan?"

* * *

By the time we sighted Bus 219, it was on I-495. It should have continued north toward Baltimore, but it did a curious thing—it veered right onto the ramp for the George Washington Memorial Parkway ramp—a key route into DC. From there the DC Streets were less than ten miles.

Jesus. Allah. It wasn't Baltimore.

Maya was set for DC.

CHAPTER 84

Day 7: May 21, 0550 Hours, Daylight Saving Time
Ellie's Wood Development, McLean, Virginia

"Caine, they're headed for DC, not Baltimore," I yelled. "Polo played us."

He touched a radio bud in his left ear. "I'll warn LaRue, but it'll take time to shift his people. It's on us for now."

It was nearing six a.m. and traffic on the Parkway was already building. Traffic might stop him ahead of us and cause more danger. In doing so, unsuspecting commuters would be in harm's way.

Fewer dead. An option?

Sirens wailed in all directions. Oscar had the police responding and they raced to establish roadblocks. They would stop Artie no matter what. Perhaps killing Noor in the process. Perhaps killing everyone within miles. Perhaps saving DC.

Fewer dead. LaRue's plan.

The bus was more than a mile ahead of us and Caine scared me to death closing the distance. Three times I almost flew off the bike. As we made a turn around a bend, traffic was heavy and lumbering along southward. I regained my balance.

Beyond the bend, Bus 219 was only twenty cars ahead and speeding south.

Seven miles to DC.

There was carnage in Artie's wake. Several cars had been knocked off the road with the motorists still at the wheel. Artie had forced Noor's hand and used the bus as a battering ram to bully his way south.

"Got a better plan yet?" I yelled.

Caine shook his head and thumbed the air.

One of LaRue's helicopters flew just above the trees. It swooped past the bus and dropped into its path a quarter mile ahead. A black-clad sniper hung out the door, strapped in and rifle ready. The bus's brake lights flashed for a second, but it swerved and kept going. Another swerve—left, right—before it slammed into a taxi on its left and rear-ended a minivan to clear a path forward. The chopper bobbed and weaved but was forced to pull up before a collision. Another mile and the game of chicken repeated. The results were the same. The bus knocked cars off the road as it weaved and smashed its way southward. The chopper tried and failed to slow it.

Five miles to DC.

The bus swerved violently side-to-side, nearly ran off the road, straightened at the last minute, and braked hard before continuing.

Caine tapped his earpiece again, listened, and then shouted, "Noor's fighting Polo."

"Get closer."

The bus swerved and slowed, sped up, and swerved again.

Caine maneuvered cautiously alongside. Should the bus swerve into us, we'd die. If they made it across the Teddy Roosevelt Memorial Bridge, they'd be in DC. Thousands would die. Before they made that bridge, the helicopter sniper would take his shot. If he did, we would die.

The lives of the many outweigh the lives of the few.

Caine and I were dead either way. Noor, too, and so many cops and firemen and commuters would fill the body count.

The bus swerved again, braked, swerved and sped on southward. For more than a mile it repeated the dance. For an instant, it braked hard, and I thought Noor had won. She hadn't. They accelerated and continued down the Parkway.

Three miles to DC.

Several shots cracked from the bus. Polo was shooting at the chopper.

The helicopter pulled up and banked. Another gunshot sent it banking violently and climbing away over the Potomac.

"Noor's down." Caine touched his ear again. "Polo's at the wheel."

"Get me to the side emergency door!"

"They won't let you." Caine slowed the trike. "We're too close to DC. They're taking the shot."

"If they kill Polo, the bus crashes. Those cylinders will break. We'll all be dead. Let me try!"

Caine shook his head but tapped the earpiece nonetheless. "One chance, Hunter. *One.*"

Two miles to DC.

Caine accelerated and swerved right around the rear of the bus. The side emergency door was halfway down the bus. Without mirrors, Artie was blind to our approach. But the moment I opened that door, the warning buzzer would sound and he'd know my plan. My only hope was he'd be too busy dodging sniper fire to worry about me.

Caine touched his ear and threw a thumbs-up.

"You ready?"

I patted his shoulder. "Go!"

Ahead, the helicopter hovered above the Memorial Bridge— the line in the sand. The sniper balanced on the helicopter's skids.

The bus would not cross. Beneath them was a line of police cars that blocked the bridge ramp. Pointless. At this speed, Artie could easily breach the barricade and continue on. The only thing that might stop him was the sniper's bullet.

Or me.

CHAPTER 85

Day 7: May 21, 0557 Hours, Daylight Saving Time
Arlington, Virginia—Along the Potomac River

A mile and a half to DC.

Steady, Hunter. One, two, three.

"Now!" I climbed to my feet on the rear seat and held Caine's shoulder for balance. My wounded left arm screamed in pain. It was a struggle to stay below the bus windows so Artie couldn't see us and I wouldn't tumble to my death. Caine nosed the trike in close. A foot separated us from the emergency door. I teetered there, trying not to disturb the delicate equation of speed and balance. My left arm throbbed and warm ooze flowed down my arm, weakening my stability. If I unsettled the trike in any way, we were done. At this speed, death would be swift and violent.

A mile to DC.

Our front wheel passed the bus door and two shots shattered the window glass above my head.

Artie knew.

He fired again and jerked the bus to the right to kill us.

The helicopter hovered ahead.

The sniper readied.

The bus accelerated.

Caine tried twice more to position us at the bus door. Both times Artie countered and then swerved away. We closed on the bridge and in another few yards the sniper would end it—and us.

Caine yelled, "They've waived us off. They're taking him."

"No." I swung the .45 up and fired two rounds into the doorway to distract Artie.

The bus swerved left.

Caine reached the side door.

The sniper fired.

Glass shattered. The bus lurched left. Lurched right. Lurched left again and veered out of control.

Seconds to the police blockade.

I balanced myself and grabbed the emergency door handle and pulled it open. Even above the road noise, the warning buzzer screamed my approach. Without a second to spare, I propelled myself into the open door. My right hand caught the side of the door. My left failed to find a handhold. My legs hung off the bus, feet dragging the asphalt.

Caine hit the brakes and pulled back. The bus struck him. The trike twisted violently, churned, and shredded on the roadway behind me.

No. Focus, Hunter. One, two, three!

With every ounce of my strength, I hauled myself up. We lurched left and the movement propelled me farther aboard.

I was aboard.

Keeping low, I crawled forward just as two shots whistled down the aisle at chest height. Artie was shooting blind, twisting his arm backward to shoot at me and navigate at the same time. Even shooting blind he was coming too close.

Noor.

She lay in the aisle a few feet ahead of me and I crawled to her. I knew what I had to do. It was dangerous. One mistake would release the sarin. The atropine and 2-PAM injectors were in my hand before I knew it. One after the other I thrust them into her, praying it wasn't futile.

Another shot whistled over my head, but as it did, the crack of the sniper's high-powered rifle made the bus jerk violently.

I got onto one knee as Artie's form twisted in the driver's seat. He raised his hand. His cell phone lit up. His thumb hovered over the keypad.

He was going to blow the explosives and release the sarin.

I jumped up and shot him. Once, twice. My first shot hit his arm and the cell phone clattered to the floor. My second struck squarely in the back of his head. A mass of bone and brain matter spackled the windshield. He slumped facedown across the wheel, unmoving, lifeless. He was gone.

All my rage welled and I lunged forward. I shot him a third time in the head to remove the little that was left of his traitorous face. Then, I threw myself on him, grabbed the wheel, and fought for control.

Three quarters of a mile to DC.

I straightened the bus as we bore down on the barricade. He was seat-belted tight behind the wheel. Both of his feet were planted on the accelerator, wedged against the floorboard wall, jamming it firmly in place. Ahead, two dozen policemen braced themselves.

So many would die.

I tried but failed to kick Artie's feet off the accelerator. I couldn't loosen his death grip on the wheel or extract him from the seat. I straightened the wheel but had no control to stop us.

The lives of the many . . . Sorry, Noor, in another life, perhaps you and me.

Teeth clenched, I forced the gearshift into reverse, wrenched the wheel, and held tight.

The transmission shrieked. Tires screamed. The world slid, tilted, and hurtled toward the stone median wall. Down. My feet left the floor and my hands lost the wheel. Everything churned. Metal and pain pummeled me with the crush of deceleration.

Darkness.

CHAPTER 86

Day 7: May 21, 0845 Hours, Daylight Saving Time
Arlington, Virginia—Along the Potomac River

THE HISSING WOKE me.

Light invaded my darkness and an awkward tightness held my face. I opened my eyes as someone leaned over me and pulled the oxygen mask free. A blinding light crisscrossed my eyes and words reached me that I didn't quite hear. Hands flew over me. My body was freed of wires and tubes.

"LaRue!"

A medic tried first to stop me but then relented and helped me sit up over the edge of the gurney. A rush of nausea and vertigo slammed me backward. Twice more and I made it upright. Moments later, my senses settled and I looked around.

"Easy, Mr. Hunter," the medic said. "You've had it rough."

I was in the middle of the Parkway. A helicopter waited on the road nearby, and I was positioned to be loaded.

Beside me, Noor laid on another gurney as a medic stitched the side of her head and another tended an IV.

LaRue appeared from nowhere.

"She'll be okay," the medic said. "A bunch of stitches. Broken arm, two broken ribs, and a concussion. Still, she's going to be fine."

"Thank God." To LaRue, now beside me, I asked, "Caine?"

LaRue looked away. "There was no Caine."

The lie of lies. Plausible deniability.

Not today. "Oscar, *Caine*?"

He tried mind control but gave up after a few seconds. "Gone."

I swallowed hard. The last thing I remembered was the motorcycle ricocheting off the bus into a death roll down the highway.

Damn. I watched the controlled chaos around me. A hazmat van spewed astronauts in their bubble suits and gear. A decontamination tent was up near the bridge ramp and the scene looked like a bad sci-fi movie. All around, armed operatives hustled and patrolled.

"Oscar, did the sarin . . ."

"No, my boy." He touched my arm. "You did it. Perhaps with some supreme help, of course. You crashed through the stone divider and rolled off the Parkway toward the Potomac. None of the cylinders were compromised. A miracle. Thousands thank you. They just don't know it."

Nausea seized me and I lay back. Life was a gift today. A gift to all of us. All of us except Victoria and Caine. They gave us their gift.

Artie had fooled us. All of us. In the end, on the bus, it was a coin toss for the winner. Had the coin landed on the other side, I'd never have known.

"All this for nothing." I sat up again and saw Noor stir. "Kevin, I mean. He went bad and died for what, money?"

LaRue was thoughtful for a long time. Then, he laid it all to rest.

"Kevin tried to redeem himself in the end, Jon. We believed Khalifah was a Middle Easterner. Troubling failure. He operated with impunity. General Fedorov's mastery of the game was brilliantly played. No one suspected it was one of our own. No one, including me."

"A game?" I shook my head. "The SVR played brilliantly? Christ, Oscar, people are dead. Hundreds in the last week alone. How many thousands had Khalifah—Polo—been responsible for over the years?"

"Of course. It was not a game." LaRue raised his chin and held a finger up to continue his epilogue. "Fedorov used the SVR to conceive a plan to reignite our presence in the Middle East. He'd believed we'd be so consumed that we'd take our eyes off them— the Russians. They could proceed to expand back into Eastern Europe unchecked."

"It would have worked." I recalled what Saeed had said. "Saeed was okay with starting another Mid-East war. He thought the Arabs would rise up together and destroy us."

"Perhaps." LaRue contemplated that for a moment. "Quite possibly. Polo was their secret weapon. He had access to intelligence that allowed Fedorov to maneuver. What we didn't know was how many other cells were involved. We could not act on Saeed without that knowledge. Had we, and there were others, they might have surprised us and hurt us even worse."

I dropped my eyes. "Kevin died for that?"

"No, my boy." He took my shoulder. "He died redeeming himself. He must have learned Polo was Khalifah and about Operation Maya. He knew it wasn't the refugees and not the families forced into terror by Saeed's men. He passed you the clue."

Tears welled. "Kevin said that the night he died. 'Not them.' He meant it wasn't the refugees. He knew. He said he was sorry. He knew I'd find out what he'd become."

LaRue nodded in slow, melodramatic movements. "Forgiveness, Hunter. He wanted yours."

He never knew Noor called me home. "Caine?"

Oscar let a sly grin form before he washed it away with spy games. "We removed the real Caine in Damascus years ago. Our Caine—my Caine—assumed his identity. As long as no one appeared who knew him, the deception was workable. Mo Nassar handled Caine for me and provided cover for him with the task force. That is what forced Nassar to recruit and compromise David Bond."

"Nassar. What a prick."

"He played a vital role," LaRue said, grinning. "Hunter, we did not know Polo was Khalifah. Not at first. You have my word. Caine suspected a leak in the FBI after Fedorov sent him here to assist Khalifah. I needed Mo Nassar to monitor the task force for me to ensure Caine remained unmolested."

"Nassar's still a prick."

LaRue grinned. "He feels the same of you."

I glanced at Noor's still form. "Why not lock down DC and Baltimore and just take Saeed? You could have stopped all this."

"No. We considered Baltimore a viable target right up until the end. We worried that if we acted on Saeed or Fedorov before we learned the totality of their plan, we might unleash a larger, more devastating series of attacks. We had to know how many cells were out there. That was Caine's mission."

Caine. "Were there other cells?"

"Fedorov denied it. I am not so sure."

A dark SUV pulled through the maze of federal and state emergency vehicles until it was near the chopper. A man in an FBI windbreaker climbed out and opened the rear door.

Sam Mallory slid out wrapped in a blanket.

The armed agent led him to us.

"Are you LaRue?" the agent asked LaRue. When LaRue nodded, the agent added, "My orders were to escort Sameh Mallory directly here after the scene was secured. We've had him in protective custody since he was released to us. I think he's in shock. We can't even touch him. My orders were to bring him to you."

LaRue raised a hand. "Whose orders?"

The agent looked oddly at LaRue and then over his shoulder at Sam, who pulled the blanket tighter around his shoulders.

"Agent?" LaRue repeated. "Who had him in custody and who ordered you to bring him here now?"

"Special Agent in Charge Arthur Polo," the agent said. "A couple hours ago. Is there a problem?"

Oh yeah, there was.

A hot poker stabbed my spine and worked its way to my brain. What had Saeed said to me, "*Two special surprises*"?

Artie Polo was Khalifah. That was the first surprise.

I rolled onto my feet and faced Sameh Mallory as he dropped his blanket and walked toward us dressed in an oversized barn coat. A dozen feet away, I noticed something in his hand when he slid it from beneath the jacket. He held a thumb plunger—a remote detonating device the size of a roll of quarters—that had a wire that disappeared up his sleeve to what I knew was a bomb-laden suicide vest hidden beneath the coat.

Rule seven of mortal combat—just when you think it's over, guess again.

Khalifah and Saeed had one more surprise. Another terror cell. Sameh Mallory was it.

CHAPTER 87

Day 7: May 21, 0910 Hours, Daylight Saving Time
Arlington, Virginia—Along the Potomac River

"YOU KILLED KEVIN. You killed my father. You killed Bobby and all those people. You lied to us all." Sameh's eyes were tiny round bullets staring straight at me. "I don't know who you are, but you are nothing any longer. *Alhamdulillah.*"

Oh crap. I held up my hand at LaRue's men, who were inching toward us. "Everyone stand down! Everyone! I have this. Everyone just back off."

Sam slowly raised his hand and showed the detonator to everyone around us. With his other hand, he opened his coat and revealed an old fishing vest. Instead of lures and other tackle, a macramé of wires and bricks of gray plastic explosives were fastened.

If he thumbed the plunger's trigger down just a half-inch, the explosives he wore would kill us all. It might yet explode the sarin tanks being secured down the riverbank. Khalifah and Saeed could still win.

I held my hands in surrender. "Sam, don't."

"Sameh." His voice was empty. Cold. Raw.

"Yes, Sameh." I took an uneasy step forward. "I didn't do any of those things. I didn't kill Kevin or Bobby. Artie Polo told you all that, didn't he?"

His eyes hardened. "He said you would continue to lie. You treat me like I am nothing. You lie to Noor. You are trying to take her from me, too."

No. Before I could say another word, a meek voice, almost a whisper, came from beside me. Noor was there, leaning on me and stepping toward Sam.

"Sameh, stop this now. No one is taking me from you. I am here. I am your mother. Stop this."

He raised the plunger higher. "No. Polo told me. My life is over anyway. First, it was that schoolteacher. It wasn't my fault! Now this. I will die for these crimes so this is no loss to me."

Jesus. Kevin adopted Sam after investigating him as a suspect in a murder at the reform school for boys. Kevin thought him wrongly accused. But he was wrong. Sameh was a murderer, and he was proving that now. Worse, somehow, somewhere along the way, Sameh Mallory became more than a murderer. He became one of them—a radicalized terrorist.

Sameh aimed the plunger at me. "Saeed Mansouri is a leader. He taught me to be a *Pāsdār*—a good Muslim protecting our people from all of you."

Holy mind control. Is this what changed Kevin's mind? Did he find out that Sameh was involved? "Sameh, did Kevin find out about you?"

A strange look spread across his face. Half sadness and half relief. "Yes. He did not understand. How could he? He was not Muslim. He was not my father. Saeed showed me. He helped me. Kevin did not understand. Saeed was a great man."

"Saeed Mansouri was a terrorist," I said flatly. "He wasn't protecting anyone. He and Polo were trying to start another war in the Middle East. Polo and Saeed took families hostage. *Muslim* families. He forced the men to bomb the mall and Union Station. Even the school. Is that who you want to be?"

"More lies. They warned me." His words were sharp, but his eyes were showing a crack in his armor. "They fought for Islam. I do that now."

"No." Noor clutched my arm and pulled me along for balance. "These things Jon says are true, Sam. It is they who have lied."

LaRue moved around from behind me and waved his men into position on our flank.

I had to make Sam understand. "Sameh, Artie forced Noor to drive that bus. She was to drive into DC to kill thousands. She would have died, too. It was Polo and Saeed taking her from you. Just as they took the other families. All this killing was them."

He faltered for a moment and tried to think. "No. No. I have been to Sandy Creek. You call it Sand Town, more insults. How amusing for you all. So many people there volunteer to help Saeed in the fight. They are good Muslims ready to die."

"Volunteer?" Noor lunged forward and slapped Sameh hard across the face. She recoiled and slapped him again. "Saeed Mansouri took their families. He killed them. He was an evil man who distorts Allah for violence and hate. That is not you, Sameh. Please, say it is not you."

Sameh just stared at her. His face was reddened by her assault and his eyes blossomed with tears. He began to speak, but she slapped him again, hard, and then held his cheek in her hand with a mother's love.

"Sameh, Kevin believed you could be responsible for the teacher. He loved you anyway."

Sameh's face blanched and his eyes exploded with grief. "No. He did not."

"Yes, Sam." Noor held tight to his face and refused to look at the detonator he still held above his head. "He loved you. In the end, he learned what Polo and Saeed were doing and fought back.

He died trying to stop them. Be like Kevin. Be like your father. Fight back. Fight them. Do not do this thing."

He wavered more now, his thumb shaking above the plunger trigger. His eyes couldn't see through the tears, and his hand became heavy and awkward over his head. Slowly, it dropped to shoulder height. "Hunter, he killed him! He killed Kevin."

"No, Sameh," I said. "No."

"He did not do that thing," Noor added. "Polo killed my Kevin. Even Victoria Bacarro. You know I hated her, but she died trying to stop Polo. Trying to save me and you."

Sam's mouth screwed up and his eyes darted from Noor to me and back to Noor. "Died? Polo said . . ."

I stepped forward and took hold of the plunger, holding it firm within his hand. "Polo killed her, Sameh. He killed them all— Bobby and Ghali from the library. All those families, too. Don't become like him."

Noor leaned in and fell forward into Sam's body. He instinctively grabbed for her to hold her up and steady her balance. When he did, he released the plunger, and I took control of it.

"Now would be good, Oscar," I called over my shoulder.

"Move," he ordered.

Four black-clothed operatives descended on us. One took Sameh by the arms and held him. Another pulled Noor away and returned her to the gurney she'd been lying on. The third took the detonator from my hand and eased it to his control, while the forth slid Sameh's shirt off and began disarming the explosive vest.

Time stood still. Seconds to moments. Moments to . . . the suicide vest slid from Sameh's body.

"We're clear, sir," the bomb technician called. "It's over."

No, it wasn't over. Not for Noor. Not for Sameh. Not for me.

CHAPTER 88

Day 7: May 21, 0930 Hours, Daylight Saving Time
Arlington, Virginia—Along the Potomac River

NOOR LAY ON the gurney still holding Sameh's hand until LaRue's men bound his hands in flex cuffs and led him away. Tears streamed down her face and her body shook as he disappeared.

I stood next to her. "He'll be okay, Noor. Oscar will help all he can."

LaRue nodded. "Of course. But you must understand. It will take some time. Longer than you realize, perhaps."

"I understand," she said, squeezing my hand. "I cannot lose him, too. Please, Jon Hunter. Help us."

"I will."

A medic reaffixed her IV and turned a lever. A second later, her fingers relaxed in my hand and she slipped into a comfortable, peaceful sleep.

I turned to LaRue. "He was the last cell, Oscar. I didn't see that coming."

"Nor I, my boy." He shook his head. "It could have been worse."

"Yes." I looked over at the wreckage that was Bus 219. "You were gambling with the sarin."

"That's complicated, Hunter. Caine was in the process of replacing the sarin with a placebo. Unfortunately, it was discovered by Khalifah's—Polo's—chemist. We switched half of the sarin but could not replace the remainder in time. Polo moved the new shipment elsewhere and Caine lost control of it."

"The chemist?"

Oscar shook his head.

No more chemist. "Caine and Polo were both double agents. One on each side."

"Yes."

"Did Caine know Kevin had gone rogue?"

"No." LaRue turned and faced me, master to apprentice, eyes-to-eyes. "That evening, Saeed and Polo went to collect a shipment of sarin from Sokoloff—Fedorov's operative. By the time Caine learned of the transfer and arrived, Kevin was dead and a cylinder of sarin had ruptured. You arrived, and Caine tried to scare you off. He had to burn the truck and destroy any contaminants."

I looked down. "Still, Kevin went bad."

LaRue simply nodded.

"Why didn't you tell me about Caine?"

LaRue looked at me with an expectant grin.

I missed it. "You wanted me chasing him. The more I chased, the more believable his cover. Right? Saeed, Polo, even Fedorov would believe that he was the real Caine with me on his tail."

LaRue dismissed further questions with a flutter of his hand. "We have more work to do. The White House is working to calm the nation. It's complicated since it involves the Russians. We've convinced him to stand down the military."

No bombs. No troops. No war.

LaRue was nodding again. "For us—you and me—it is time to move on."

Move on? My brother was a rogue cop. One of my oldest friends was a turncoat terrorist. My nephew was a suicide bomber. Move on?

LaRue leaned in close so no one could hear him. "There is no money, Hunter. The hundred thousand was never there. It was SVR money, not ours. Perhaps Noor can put it to better use."

"You're covering it up?" I couldn't believe it. "You're going to hide Kevin's complicity? All the money?"

He said nothing.

Jesus, should I hate him or love him? "Bond?"

"Bond was a lovesick cop who picked the wrong girl with the wrong husband. He had no idea what was happening around him. When we learned Polo was making his move soon, I instructed Nassar to co-opt him."

"Steal the evidence at the task force to protect Caine's identity a little longer."

He grinned. "Yes."

A stray thought burned in my brain. "Perhaps if I'd come home sooner."

"We all share some responsibility," LaRue said, looking away. "Perhaps me more than anyone."

Deep down, I wondered how true that was. "What about me?"

A familiar face walked through the crowd of emergency personnel. Shepard. He carried a sniper rifle over his shoulder and walked toward us with a sarcastic grin.

"You owe me, Hunter. Again."

Shepard? "Aren't you dead?"

"Sure." He winked. "But if I were, those guys at the construction site would have ended you. Things got complicated."

"Complicated? You faked Caine. You sent me to chase a terrorist who wasn't one. You died but didn't. Was anything uncomplicated?"

"Precisely." LaRue squeezed my arm and hardened his voice. "Now, what am I to do with you?"

"I'm not ready to retire, Oscar."

A voice, barely above a whisper, spoke behind me. "No, Jon Hunter."

I looked down at Noor lying on the stretcher where she was smiling. "Jon, do not go. Please. I need you here." She took my hand in hers and pulled me down to whisper, "I am ashamed. But these past few days, you are the first thing I think of in the morning and the last thing I think of at night."

The last time someone told me that . . . was never. "Sleep, Noor. I'll be with you in the chopper. I'll be close. Always."

"Good." She found my eyes through her haze and her voice was meek. "But, if you must return for Sadie, I will understand."

"Sadie?" LaRue laughed for the first time I could remember. "My dear, Sadie is a camel."

"A camel?" She coughed, tried to smile, and closed her eyes. "Jon Hunter, you must stay home." She drifted back to sleep.

LaRue turned to me. "What now, Hunter? A small town doesn't need your skills, even as uncontrolled as they are."

"Maybe I'll write a book." I tapped my temple. "You know, about this handsome, daring ex-consultant on dangerous missions. He's always harangued by his old spymaster. You know the type. The younger one is the hero, of course. The crotchety old guy is a pain in the ass sidekick."

"Again, you disappoint me." He lifted a finger into the air so the world would know he was about to impart his wisdom. "Your perspective is crass and misguided. Precisely why I must keep you close. Imagine the damage you could do without my guidance."

"Whatever, Oscar. As long as I get my $879,928.66. Plus interest."

He smiled and removed his eyeglasses for a polishing. "In time, my boy. In time."

31901062796448